I0592061

Samuel Law Wilson

The theology of modern literature

Samuel Law Wilson

The theology of modern literature

ISBN/EAN: 9783337203313

Printed in Europe, USA, Canada, Australia, Japan

Cover: Foto ©Andreas Hilbeck / pixelio.de

More available books at **www.hansebooks.com**

" The period in which we live is one in which new ideas are struggling to get possession of the popular mind. To this end they must be popularised and put into intelligible and attractive forms; and this is done through literature. It stands as a medium through which the abstract and far-removed ideas of the few may be made intelligible to the many."

ANDREWS' "Christianity and Anti-Christianity."

THE THEOLOGY

OF

MODERN LITERATURE

BY

REV. S. LAW WILSON, M.A., D.D.

EDINBURGH
T. & T. CLARK, 38 GEORGE STREET
1899

PREFACE

—◆—

THIS volume, prepared under disadvantageous circumstances and the imperious limitations of ministerial life, might have been committed to "the enduringness of print" without having prefixed to it anything of the nature of an introduction. But the Cæsar of custom is inexorable, and must have its due. One is not sorry, however, that the usual tribute is exacted, inasmuch as it affords one an opportunity of making a few explanatory observations which may be considered advisable. The object of the book is so apparent, that it is scarcely necessary to indicate it in more definite terms. It has long been felt that the theology which has now the largest and most direct access to the popular mind, is that which finds expression in the polite literature of the day. The theology which has now the widest circulation, is that which in solution is diffused through the poetry, fiction, and journalism of the times. This theology of the litterateur and the belle-lettrist the writer has attempted to examine and review, bringing it into comparison with the theology of Church and Creed, and where the two are not *en rapport*, as very often happens, indicating as accurately as possible the precise angle of divergence. Some typical and representative authors of the Victorian era are singled out for special study. An effort is made to fix their religious whereabouts, and to discuss their ethical bearings and spiritual tendencies, in a manner which it is hoped will illustrate the truth of Carlyle's saying, "Great men taken up in any way are profitable company." It cannot but prove interesting to ponder what some of the great thinkers and writers, who " blaze in the illuminated track of genius," have to say on those great spiritual problems which torture the questioning mind of man, and haunt his existence.

The accomplished authoress of *Isabel Carnaby* very truly remarks, that " every writer is an evangelist of some sort." The gospel of which some of our outstanding writers of the present day are the evangelists, the truths or errors, as the case may be, of which they are the proclaimers and dispensers, are in these pages indicated and commented on.

The writer desires it to be understood that the word theology throughout this volume is used in an elastic and accommodating sense, embracing not only what is usually understood by theology proper, but also the elements of morality, and religious teaching in general.

In conclusion, the writer has only to express his sense of inadequacy and shortcoming in the execution of his design. He is as deeply sensible as the most exacting of his critics can be that his abilities have not always matched the magnitude and importance of his theme. His attempt has only been to say some things which others could have said far more ably, but which as yet they have refrained from saying. If he has failed, his failure may at least be attended with the compensation that it may perhaps bring others into the field who will succeed. If the book shall prove the precursor of something more satisfactory than itself, the author will not grudge the time and labour he has expended on it. But whatever its imperfections, and whatever reception may be accorded it, it is now sent forth in the service of Him who accepteth a man according to what he hath, and not according to what he hath not.

S. L. W.

CONTENTS

---+---

INTRODUCTION

Christian Theology constantly thrown into close mental relations with the developments of Literature—How the two have acted and reacted on each other—The relations between the two not always cordial—Reasons of this alienation and estrangement—Principal Shairp on Culture and Religion—Hostility of polite literature to religion in days of John Foster—In what respects we have advanced on the eighteenth century—Popular and pleasing productions of modern times still unfriendly to evangelical religion—Fine writers who rail at Christianity—Chilling aloofness of many authors—Professor Lange on worldly literature — Conditions on which this unhappy variance may be removed—How Literature suffers when divorced from Theology —How Theology suffers when Literature is out of sympathy with it—Influence of the novelist in the formation of theological opinion—Theology no longer banked up in cathedrals and universities—Amateurish "dining-out" theology now so fashionable—One specially hopeful symptom discernible in the present situation—Abundant supply of good and wholesome literature—Good books and what they do for us—Literature of the Lower Self—One deplorable feature brought into prominence—Tendency of many writers to impugn the moral order of the universe—Dr. John Watson on what he calls an "Underlying Theology"—Much of the literature of the last few decades deeply tinged with unbelief—Teaching on God—Miracle—Prayer—Zola's message to his age—Dr. Shedd on the conflict between religion and literature—Prevalence of a cultured Agnosticism—Henryk Sienkiewicz the Polish writer—Olive Schreiner's *African Farm*—The poet Swinburne—Arthur Hugh Clough—Attitude of Tennyson—Influenced by Sir Wm. Hamilton's philosophy—"Knowledge is of things we see"—Aversion of men of letters to belief in the supernatural—Lucas Malet quoted—Pusillanimous anxiety to avoid evangelical

CHAPTER I

THE THEOLOGY OF EMERSON

CHAPTER II

THE THEOLOGY OF THOMAS CARLYLE

CHAPTER III

THE THEOLOGY OF ROBERT BROWNING

CHAPTER IV

THE THEOLOGY OF GEORGE ELIOT

CHAPTER V

THE THEOLOGY OF GEORGE MACDONALD

CHAPTER VI

CHAPTER VII

THE THEOLOGY OF MRS. HUMPHRY WARD—"ROBERT ELSMERE"

Mrs. Ward early familiarised with religious doubt and difficulty— First appearance of *Robert Elsmere*—Strikes a responsive chord in public feeling—Combines the interest of a religious tragedy and a theological debate—The most transparent defects of the book—Its one-sidedness—Nothing permitted to be said in defence of the faith which Elsmere surrenders—Unfairness the uniform vice of controversial fiction—Mrs. Ward's contempt of the Christian believer—Christianity a religion which can no longer be believed—The Gospels fairy tales—St. Paul a fallible man of genius—Elsmere but slenderly qualified for conducting a controversy with the army of Christian apologists —Insult to the Christian's Lord—Belated character of Mrs. Ward's scholarship—The Tübingen theory no longer available —The chief contention of Mrs. Ward's book—The untrustworthiness of human testimony—Squire Wendover's views and their bearing on the question of Christian origins—Unreasonableness of the position that all testimony previous to the nineteenth century is comparatively untrustworthy—All testimony to be put on its trial—Marks of the spurious—The "likelihoods of truth"—How the great modern historians sift testimony—A similar policy to be pursued with the four Gospels —The sacred writers trustworthy—The Squire's stock argument considered—The age in which Jesus appeared not a credulous or uncritical age—The "science of what is credible" better understood in gospel times than Mrs. Ward would have us suppose—The age in which Jesus appeared not characterised by any special preconception in favour of miracle—Mrs. Ward perpetuates an ancient sophistry of David Hume—Unfairness

b

CHAPTER VIII

THE THEOLOGY OF THOMAS HARDY

CHAPTER IX

THE THEOLOGY OF GEORGE MEREDITH

Mr. Le Gallienne's wise caution—The Olympian style of criticism
to be avoided—What distinguishes Meredith most from other
living writers—Central qualities of his genius—His hatred of
shams and snobbery—His faculty of unfolding the inner drama
of thought and feeling and motive—Deals with life more
subjectively than other writers—His skill in psychic analysis
and portraiture—Works in "the clay of human thought"—
His claim to rank as a great philosophical novelist—His theory
on the amalgamation of philosophy and fiction—The "subtlest
assertor of the soul" in novelistic literature—His inwardness—
Every novel of his deals with some problem—The *Egoist*—The
anatomy of selfishness—Meredith the "Harvey of the ego"—Mr.
Le Gallienne on what it was to write the *Egoist*—Meredith the
true child of his time—Made his advent at a period specially
prepared to receive him—Difference between the era of Shakespeare and that of Browning and Meredith—The instrument
on which Meredith mainly relies—His power of analogy—
Specimens of his metaphors—His expertness in the manipulation of words and coining of phrases—Passage from *Diana of
the Crossways* quoted—Expressiveness of his language—His

THE THEOLOGY OF
MODERN LITERATURE

———•———

INTRODUCTION

It is historically interesting to observe how all along the centuries Providence has placed Christian Theology in close proximity and neighbourhood to all the great Intellectual movements, and the leading developments of Literature. Christian doctrine has lain alongside of, and been thrown into close mental relations with, Platonism and Neo-Platonism, with Greek and Roman classic literature, with Aristotle and the Arabs, with Descartes and Leibnitz, with the writers of the Renaissance, with Kant and Fichte, and all the great philosophical systems of modern times, with Goethe and Carlyle, with Wordsworth and Browning. It was doubtless the Divine intention that the two should act and react upon each other, conferring and receiving mutual benefit. We must not overlook the fact that the establishment of a contact of this kind could not but be attended with transient obscurations and errors, injuries to theology and the Christian Church, and sometimes serious spiritual

I

damage to society. Yet it cannot be doubted that in the final issue and outcome, Christian truth has reaped a marked and permanent advantage. Literature has rendered a signal service to theology in constantly inciting, and giving her the occasion for a full unfolding and display of all her treasures. It has afforded a splendid medium for the impregnation of the popular mind with the elements of morality and truth. It has contributed very largely to the improvement of our ecclesiastical language, the widening of our religious culture, and the securing for Christianity many conquests in poetry, the drama, and the novel. On the other hand, Christian theology has indubitably exerted a salutary and exhilarating influence on the literary habits and progress of mankind. It has nourished and stimulated the higher minds whose acceptance it has won. It has encouraged intellectual development, and provided most amply its instruments and incentives. It has presented the thinker and writer with themes the most vital and majestic which the mind of man can be confronted with —themes which must always give rise to incessant and eager discussion—" themes which soar into the immeasurable blue, and purport, at least, to open to thought celestial gates."

Yet while to this extent there has been age-long commerce and interchange between the two, we are constrained to acknowledge that the relations between theology and worldly literature have seldom been quite cordial or harmonious. There is much to impress one with the belief that they have not always understood each other, and there have been long intervals of time

when the two have suspected and disesteemed each
other. Partial explanation of their mutual alienation
and estrangement may be sought perhaps in the fact that
literature draws its inspiration so largely from the old
fountains of pagan culture, and finds its standards not
only of taste, but of character and feeling, in the productions of Grecian and Roman genius, thus running the
risk, which it has not always successfully avoided, of
acquiring a paganised tone. Literature frequents Mount
Parnassus; theology treads the more sacred slopes of
Calvary and Mount Zion. The atmosphere inhaled on
these two eminences is very different, the scenery is
different, the outlook is different. Literature goes back
for its culture and gifts to Athens; theology goes back
for her knowledge and graces to Jerusalem. Hence the
literary conception does not always coincide with the
Christian, and a certain cleavage and divergence will
often supervene between the spirit of the one and the
other. An hiatus more or less wide is almost unavoidable; the difference between the Biblical point of view
and that of ordinary literature is so marked; the aspect
that life wears, when we accept a religious interpretation
of the world, is so opposed to the aspect that it wears
when we accept only a secular interpretation of it.
Ideally considered, literature should culminate in
theology, while theology should animate and control
literature. But a very slender acquaintance with
history, and a very slight observation of the times we
live in, are all that is needed to convince us that it has
not been so in the past, that it is not so now. As
Principal Shairp says, "Goethe, the high priest of

culture, loathes Luther, the preacher of righteousness." [1]
In our own day the long-standing discord is perhaps
more accentuated than ever.   While large districts of
existing literature have been leavened with the Christian
spirit, and have come under the influence of Christian
conceptions, it is still to be feared that, in any special
dogmatic sense at least, there are few phases of our
literature which can be considered deeply or pro-
nouncedly religious.   We are yet very far from having
outgrown the state of things which John Foster had
occasion to deplore in his day, in his famous Essay on
" The Aversion of Men of Taste to Evangelical Religion."
His words may still be adopted as perfectly applicable to
the present situation :—

" I fear it is incontrovertible that what is denominated
polite literature, the grand school in which taste acquires
its laws and refined perceptions, and in which are formed,
much more than under any higher austerer discipline, the
moral sentiments, is, for the far greater part, hostile to the
religion of Christ; partly by introducing insensibly a
certain order of opinions unconsonant, or at least not
identical, with the principles of that religion; and still
more by training the feelings to a habit alien from its
spirit." [2]

Certainly we can register a clear advance from the
sceptical eighteenth century, with its Epicureanism, its
tame and narrow spirit, its cold classicism ; and we can
draw encouragement from the fact that Christianity, not
in the form of doctrinal propositions, but Christianity as
a life, has powerfully blended itself with every branch of

[1] *Culture and Religion*, p. 16.
[2] *Essays*, p. 201.

our literature, elevating its ideals, purifying its conceptions of life and duty, as well as imparting a greater
vigour, passion, and originality. And yet if we examine
the most popular and pleasing productions of modern
times, that have gone far, so to speak, to form and fix
the opinion of the average man on a large class of
questions,—whether our examination concern itself with
novelists, historians, essayists, or journalists,—we find
them nearly all in more or less direct antagonism to the
truths of a positive Christianity, strenuously and often
contemptuously opposed to every form of evangelical
religion. In the great army of our would-be fine writers
there is a wing composed of extreme spirits, who rail at
Christianity with a vocabulary floridly rich in contemptuous and abusive epithet. Some of them will no
longer even call it by its name, but refer to it as an
Asiatic superstition, a bundle of Hebrew old clothes, or a
constellation of old Jewish stars now no longer aflame.
They tell us scornfully that " he who has science and art
has no religion." Some of them are so advanced as to
have arrived within measurable distance of Diderot's
position in the well-known saying, " The best religion is
to have none at all." At all events, if the attitude is
not exactly one of open apostasy or declared hostility,
it is one at least of scornful indifference, or chilling
aloofness and estrangement. " What seems to us," says
the late Professor Lange of Bonn, " the great harm in
the worldly literature of the age, is its unnecessary variance
with living Christianity—both in practice and confession
—a variance which on the whole characterises even the
literature of the noble, and causes it, in too many

instances, to sympathise with the irregular and the law-less." [1]

This unfortunate variance cannot, in our judgment, be healed until, on the one side, literature shall be induced to give larger recognition to the moral nature and spiritual needs of man, and until, on the other, theology shall seek more adequately to express the sublime conceptions of its Founder, and to exhibit a more exact reflection of His spirit. The remedy must be sought in the emancipation of literature from the dominance of a culture which is one - sided and incomplete, and in a more thorough interpenetration of present-day religion with the thought and spirit of the Master. We cannot help thinking that in proportion as such efforts are earnestly put forth on both sides, the din of the long conflict will die away, and misunderstanding and jealousy give place to a deep and lasting reconciliation. Such an irenicon cannot be arrived at too soon, for, as matters now are, literature suffers grievously, and theology suffers even more. Literature suffers, for the standard and perennial products of literature must always be grounded in faith— no other soil can yield them. Divorced from Christian theology, literature succumbs to the influence of dilet-tantism. Deprived of those magisterial thoughts and majestic objects of contemplation which theology brings into view, literature must of necessity become shallow, earthbound, and frivolous. When culture becomes separated from the deep problems and truths of religion, and moves wholly in the æsthetic region of art and fashion, it is bound to become superficial, pretentious,

[1] Address on " Worldly Literature and Christianity."

and insincere. But theology suffers too, for it cannot but prove embarrassing and damaging to have the brightest intellects of the time out of sympathy with it, or openly arrayed against it. But that is not the only way in which injury accrues to it. We all know that the disposition on the part of the average member of society to take his theology in a docile spirit from Church Councils and Decretals, from theological text-books or Divinity-Hall prelections, is rapidly disappearing, and there has come in its place the tendency to go for his theology to novels, poems, essays, review articles, and even the odds and ends of a scrappy and ephemeral journalism. It may be safely affirmed that there is no divine of the present day, however famous, no preacher, however influential, who is contributing half so much to the formation of theological opinion in the public mind as some dozen or two of popular novelists, who might easily be named. There is no occupant of a professor's chair, trained expert though he be in his subject, who contributes half so much to construct and formulate religious thought, so far as "the man in the street" is concerned, as the occupant of some chair editorial, who has only a bowing acquaintance with the subject in question, such as may be picked up from some cheap cyclopedia of handy knowledge. There was a time when theology was banked up in cathedrals and universities, but that time has long gone by. Time was when men used to have their religious creed drawn up for them by Houses of Convocation, Synods of Dort, or Westminster Assemblies of Divines; but *nous avons changé tout cela.* A few religious writers, of the furiously popular style,

manage the business for us now.   In a few dashing
sentences these self-appointed creed-makers will draw up
for us our Thirty-nine Articles—forty, for that matter,
if we like.   They will take us into their confidence of
an evening, and in the course of a brief fireside *tête-à-tête*
they will initiate us into all that is necessary to be
believed for this life and for the life everlasting.   We
have only to dip into their pages, and pick up as many
stray religious ideas as will supply us with a sufficient
stock-in-trade to set up a full-rigged theological establishment of our own.   Thus it comes to pass that theology
in our day has been recoined in the mint of literature,
and reissued for circulation with the stamp of a brand-new
image and superscription.   Whether we may think the
new coinage any improvement on the old, we must at
least be prepared for this, that the new is having, and
will have, the advantage of an enormous circulation.
Our literature is now flooded in all directions with an
amateurish belle-lettrist theology—an elegant, agreeable,
smooth-tongued, "dining-out" theology, prepared on a
moment's notice, in a talk over the soup or the dessert,
to favour you with its ready-made reconstruction of the
universe, or, in a confidential whisper, to acquaint you in
your passage from dining-room to drawing-room, with the
secret of all philosophies.   The theology which the
circulating library now uses its vast network of agencies
to circulate is very largely a theology which empties the
Scriptures of their meaning, substitutes uninspired
materials for inspired in the evolution of belief, sets up
a defiant individualism against the historic consciousness
of Christendom, resolves the grace of God into a " sweet

reasonableness," and insists that Christianity shall commit suicide by renouncing everything Christian. The
influence this theology is exerting is decidedly mischievous, especially on that younger class of educated
reader who have not yet reached what Wordsworth
denominates " the years that bring the philosophic mind,"
and gradually Christianity is being emptied of its vital
force and meaning, while religion itself is degenerating
into spongy sentiment, or comfortless unbelief.

There is discernible in the situation, however, at least
one hopeful symptom which we must not overlook.
That present-day literature should be so intensely theological in its own way, is a fact which carries with it
an evidential value all its own of no inconsiderable consequence. It proves at least, does it not, that it is natural
for men to theologise, and that the imperial themes with
which the Christian scheme of thought brings us into
contact are possessed of an unfailing interest and undying
charm. What is more, it shows conclusively that man is
religious in spite of himself, that religion is a fact and a
factor in human life of such depth and dimension that it
cannot be ignored, and that even when a man has
divested himself of the last vestige of dogmatic belief,
there may yet survive, deep down in his consciousness, a
kind of sub-religion, out of which may be evolved in new
forms some of the very cardinal elements of the faith to
which he has said adieu.

In attempting something like a general survey of the
imaginative literature of our time, keeping a steady eye on
its ethical and religious bearings, one is more or less
bewildered by the largeness and complexity of the theme.

At what point to begin, and on what lines to pursue the subject to the greatest advantage, so as to make it remunerative to the reader, are questions of considerable perplexity. We cannot go far wrong, however, if we avail ourselves at the very outset of the opportunity afforded us of recognising with thankfulness the abundant supply of good and wholesome literature which in these days stocks our bookstalls and our circulating libraries. People are left without any pretext nowadays for feeding on literary carrion, for "angels' food" is to be had, and in no stinted supply.   There are savages who in their indiscriminate voraciousness devour earth, and there are readers who, with morbid wideness of taste, consume literary trash and garbage, but certainly they are not doomed to such ignoble pabulum by the absence of better fare.   Good books have been defined by some one as "the souls that make our souls wiser," and it were possible to construct a catalogue of such books lengthy enough to tax to the utmost the resources of our ink and stationery.   There are books which, as Emerson would say, "set us in a working mood," and any book which has that effect upon its reader confers an inestimable benefit. There are books that take us by the hand and lift us out of the slough of despond, or the bottomless pit of humiliation, and make us stand upon our feet in dignity and self-respect, thus earning for their author the beatitude which Mark Rutherford has ventured to add to the Beatitudes of the Gospel, "Blessed are they that heal us of our self-despisings."   There are books that inform our ignorance, enliven our dulness, fertilise our barrenness, that raise in us what is low, illumine in us what is dark, and sow our minds with the seeds of all good things. But there is a reverse side to the picture. There are other books—books silly and vulgar, books palpably irreligious, tainted books, infectious books, books that assume an attitude of rebellion against all order, and cleanliness, and decorum.

The literature of the lower self is much in vogue just now, but for the present we have no immediate concern with it more than this, that it brings into distressing prominence one deplorable feature, unfortunately all too noticeable in many of our modern writers. We refer to their habit, which with some of them has grown inveterate, of *impugning the moral order of the universe.* The older generation of Victorian writers, such as Thackeray and Dickens, whatever their attitude might be to dogmatic religion, had never any doubts as to the existence and validity of the moral order under which it is the solemn privilege of all men to live. Their literary successors, like George Eliot, and the one first-rate writer now left to us, George Meredith, have shared the same firm belief. Thomas Carlyle enunciated with all the emphasis of an oracle the momentous doctrine that a man shall have meted out to him the due reward of his deeds, that in the fields of destiny we shall reap as we have sown, though he erred in confining the operation of this law too exclusively to the limits of the life that now is. But of late years this doctrine of a moral order has been assailed on all sides, especially by the light literature of the day. Some have openly proclaimed a reversal of the Divine arrangement, which attaches reward to well-doing and penalty to vice. According to

the dismal gospel of Mr. Thomas Hardy, the battle always
goes against virtue; innocence is always doomed to a
persistent run of bad luck; and Providence, if there be
a Providence, so far from helping a man in his struggle
after right, does not care whether he ever makes such a
struggle, and is just as likely to thwart him in it as not.
Others, again, have risen in insurrection against the ethics
of Christianity altogether.   They have maintained that
the moral restrictions imposed by religion are arbitrary
and unnatural, and the sanctions which sustain them a
mere bugbear of sacerdotalism.   They have incited their
readers to fly in the face of the Decalogue, and assured
them that they would find their truest happiness in law-
lessness and irregularity.   These books are not openly
immoral,—they would be less dangerous if they were so,—
but they contain insidious principles which sap and undermine the whole edifice of morality, and which, if they
were allowed free play, would infallibly break out in an
eruption of evil behaviour.

In his lecture on Burns, Dr. John Watson assures us
that there is what he calls an "underlying theology"
which is likely to be much the same in all men.
Particularly "the theology of literature, if we take a
number of novelists and poets, can all be harmoniously
stated in a few pages, though individual writers may
sometimes break off at a tangent.   The essence of all
religion is contained in Burns' poems, wherein he emphasises the goodness of God, the strictness of the moral law,
the folly of playing with conscience, the certainty that
what a man soweth that shall he reap, and the hope that,
in full conformity with the action of the great moral

laws, every man shall receive not only justice, but mercy from the Eternal." Dr. Watson has here reduced for us to what we may regard as the most meagre pittance, the most beggarly minimum, the amount of theological truth which we may fairly look for in our literature. If this is all that is essential, one need not be a Christian, need only be a Theist, to hold it. If this is all the creed our literary men may be reasonably expected to adopt, then Christianity is for them super-fluous. Yet there are wide tracts of modern literature, and if we could discover in them the presence even of this small residuum of religious belief, we should be at once relieved and thankful. But the number of "particular writers who break off at a tangent" is very much larger than Dr. Watson supposes, and their ranks are being swollen by constant accessions. We have a tolerably wide acquaintance with contemporary fiction, and we venture to affirm that we could easily take up novel after novel in which every article of even this scanty and stinted theological creed, with which Dr. Watson credits our modern writers, is either deliberately expunged or systematically ignored. Even the moral order of the universe is no longer accepted.

Much of the polite literature of the last few decades has been deeply tinctured with unbelief and contemptuous rejection of Revelation. Many authors have set up a pulpit from which they have preached scepticism "in season and out of season," and laboured hard for the infidelisation of the whole world of letters. They have exiled God from His own universe, and set up upon the vacant Throne some phantom of their own—the Unknow-

able, the Absolute, the Eternal Something, the Infinite
Energy, or Humanity itself. Before Jehovah was these
gods were, and yet they are no more objects of worship
than "the ugliest idol in India before which a majority
of the Queen's subjects chop off the heads of little
goats."[1]   As for miracles, these writers have long since
decided that they do not happen; prayer is a useless
exercise—there is no One to pray to; the Bible records
are not to be trusted; and the whole Christian standpoint
is an antiquated and childish one.   Monsieur Zola, great
high priest and prophet of nineteenth-century Realism
and Materialism, in his last pronouncement, "Paris," thus
sums up *his* message to the age: Abolish Christianity!
Cease to believe in God! Neither desire nor expect
Immortality! Live! Work! Love! Nothing more
calamitous could well befall us than the pervasion of our
literature by this sceptical spirit. "Much has been said,"
says Dr. Shedd, "concerning the conflict between science
and religion, but the conflict between religion and literature is far more serious. The scientific class is a small
one, but the literary class is a large one. Where one
person is made sceptical by a materialising physics, a
hundred are made sceptical by an infidel belles-lettres."[2]

But oftener the unbelief takes the form not so much of
a blatant and loud-voiced Scepticism, as of a cultured and
well-bred Agnosticism, which does not deny, but only
maintains that we cannot and do not know. "Inscrut-
ability" is the last word of philosophy and religion. We
cannot read the secret of the universe. To the supreme

[1] Justice Stephen in *Nineteenth Century*, 1884.
[2] *Orthodoxy and Heterodoxy*, p. 13.

questions, What am I? Whence came I? and Whither am I going? no answer is to be sought or expected. God Himself is but "the Eternal Why to which no man has replied: the infinite Enigma which no sphinx has solved." We take up the well-known novel, for example, *Without Dogma*, by the Polish writer, Henryk Sienkiewicz, recently translated into English, and we have not read very far till we come upon the following :—

"Nowadays, only provincial philosophers cling to that worn-out creed of atheism. Philosophy of our times does not pronounce upon the matter; to all such questions it says, 'I do not know,' and that 'I do not know' sinks into and permeates the mind. When questioned upon the immortality of the soul, it says the same, 'I do not know'; and truly it does not know, and cannot know. And now it will be easier to describe the state of my mind. It all lies in these words: I do not know. In this, the acknowledged impotence of the human mind, lies the tragedy. Not to mention the fact that humanity has always asked, and always will ask, for an answer, they are truly questions of more importance than anything else in the world. If there be something on the other side, and that something an eternal life, then misfortunes and losses on this side are as nothing. 'I am content to die,' says Renan, 'but I should like to know whether death will be of any use to me.' And philosophy replies, 'I do not know.' And man beats against that blank wall, and, like the bed-ridden sufferer, fancies, if he could lie on this or on that side, he would feel easier."[1]

In Olive Schreiner's *African Farm*, when Waldo propounds to his girl friend Lyndall a speculative question as to the ultimate reality that lies behind visible Nature, she smiles an agnostic smile, and answers—

[1] *Without Dogma*, pp. 17, 18.

" So you are at your old work still. Why, why, why ?
What is the reason ? It is enough for me if I find out
what is beautiful and what is ugly, what is real and what
is not. Why it is there, and over the final cause of things
in general, I don't trouble myself ; there must be one, but
what is it to me ? If I howl to all eternity, I shall never
get hold of it ; and if I did, I might be no better off. But
you Germans are born with an aptitude for burrowing ;
you can't help yourselves. You must sniff after reasons
just as that dog does after a mole. He knows perfectly
well he will never catch it, but he's under the imperative
necessity of digging for it."

" But he *might* find it."

" *Might !* but he never has and never will."

When Lyndall dies, the brilliant South African
authoress thus moralises on the event :—

" Had she found what she sought for—something to
worship ? Had she ceased from being ? Who shall tell
us ? There is a veil of terrible mist over the face of the
Hereafter."

The poet Swinburne voices the same feeling of bafflement and blank misgiving in reference to the problem of
future destiny. It finds expression in his fine poem,
On the Verge :—

" Shadows, should we question darkness ? Ere our eyes and
      brows be fanned
  Round with airs of twilight, washed with dews from sleep's
      eternal stream,
  Would we know sleep's guarded secret ? Ere the fire consumes
      the brand,
  Would it know if all its ashes may requicken ? Yet we deem
  Surely man may know, or ever night unyoke her starry team,
  What the dawn shall be, or if the dawn shall be not ; yea, the
      scroll
  Would we read of death's dark scripture, pledge of peace, or
      doom of dole ?

Friend, who knows if death indeed have life, or life have
  death for goal ?
Day nor night can tell us, nor may seas declare nor skies unroll
What has been from everlasting, or if aught shall always be ;
Silence answering only strikes response reverberate on the soul
From the shore that hath no shore beyond it set in all the sea."

But there is, perhaps, no poet of the Victorian era in
whom the Agnostic spirit has found more distinct and
articulate utterance than in Arthur Hugh Clough. To
him, the very essence of all religion worth having consists in the firm, resolute, unswerving conviction that
nothing can be known of the Supreme. Providential
schemes, creeds, and certainties are all in his estimation
a profane pretence of knowledge, and are to be strenuously resisted, as so many temptations to Baalism and
idolatry. The only recipe he feels himself justified in
prescribing, and he is never weary of recommending it, is
" contentedness not to know " :—

> "O Thou, in that mysterious shrine
> Enthroned, as I must say, Divine !
> I will not frame one thought of what
> Thou mayest either be or not :
>   I will not prate of 'thus' and 'so,'
> And be profane with 'yes' and 'no';
> Enough that in our soul and heart
> Thou, whate'er Thou may'st be, art."

In one of his longer poems, he assails the spirit of
religious certainty, and bids it avaunt as the evil genius
of Humanity :—

" What with trusting myself, and seeking support from within me,
  Almost I could believe I had gained a religious assurance,
  Formed in my own poor soul a great moral basis to rest on.
  Ah ! but indeed I see, I feel it factitious entirely ;
  I refuse, reject, and put it utterly from me ;

2

I will look straight out, see things, not try to evade them ;
Fact shall be fact for me, and the Truth the Truth, as ever,
Flexible, changeable, vague, and multiform, and doubtful.
Off, and depart to the void, thou subtle fanatical Tempter ! "

Tennyson himself is by no means free from the same
spirit.   While a sound theistic belief is omnipresent in
his poetry, it is unfortunate that so many of his utterances about God are cast in a mould and expressed in a
language which are very largely borrowed from the
Agnostic school.   Perhaps this is not to be wondered at,
when we remember that so much of his poetry had its
origin in the years when Sir William Hamilton's philosophy, as expounded and applied by Mansell, was the
dominant intellectual force of the time.   It cannot but
tend to qualify and dilute our admiration of Tennyson,
that so often under his faith there is a vein of scepticism
constantly outcropping.   He has unhappily left himself
open to be quoted by the prophets of unbelief in approval
of their sentiments, almost as frequently as by the
prophets of faith.   Many an assault on Christian belief
can reinforce itself by an appeal to Tennyson, and bless
itself with a text from his writings.   The note of Agnosticism is of frequent recurrence.   In the introduction to
In Memoriam, we read :—

> " We have but faith : we cannot know,
>   For knowledge is of things we see ;
>   And yet we trust it comes from Thee,
> A beam in darkness : let it grow."

Here is an explicit denial that matters of religion can
be objects of knowledge, since " knowledge is of things
we see."   We can only know sensuous phenomena ;
things supersensible we can apprehend by faith, but such

faith has no claim to rank as knowledge at all. The poet adopts the vicious principle that Science has only to do with such objects as can be taken up in metallic tweezers, or weighed in bulk in a pair of Fairbank's scales, and that, consequently, there cannot be a science of Theology. But is not Faith itself a higher sort of knowledge? And may not the loving heart and upright will be organs of vision as well as the dull optics of the body? Do not the "pure in heart" see God? And does not "he that loveth" know God? Is Science doomed to be purely materialistic, and can it never ascertain anything except what scalpels, retorts, lenses, and tubes bring within its ken?

But the special aversion of many of our men of letters just now is belief in the supernatural, which they hold to be incompatible with intellectual seriousness. Says Lucas Malet in her novel, *The Carissima*, "Of course we all join in denying the existence of the supernatural, and relegating it to the at present somewhat overpopulated country of Exploded Ideas: or only in permitting its existence in the form of some derangement of nerve ganglia, or of the intestines. The pill, to put it concisely, has superseded the prayer—to the great advantage of the vendor of patent medicines." [1] If it is not altogether ruled out of court, the supernatural has never more conceded to it than a grudging and reluctant acknowledgment. Everywhere there is discernible the most pusillanimous anxiety to avoid the subject, lest the reader might perhaps think it too directly religious. There is everywhere an unworthy care not only to shun

[1] *The Carissima*, p. 46.

the introduction of evangelical topics, which, perhaps, in a work of art may be quite excusable, but to exclude the slightest tinge of Christian thought, or the most distant allusion to Christian themes.   The Creator is scarcely ever mentioned, even in an undertone.   So far as any passing allusion to the Book. of Books is concerned, one might almost suppose that many of our authors were denizens of some heathen land where a copy of the Bible had never been seen.   As for any doctrine of Providence, the impression is left on one's mind that to the writer's way of thinking the march of humanity is untroubled by any supernatural agent.   As for Jesus Christ, there is seldom so much as a glance of recognition in His direction, rarely are we permitted to catch a literary glimpse of His personality, and, for aught that our fine writers have to tell us, we might never even suspect the existence of such a Being. It is very exceptional when we can say of any of these authors, " Thy speech bewrayeth thee "—they speak with a Christian accent so seldom, and so rarely deviate into the language of Canaan.   They are especially chary of allusion to a future state.   When Thoreau lay dying, he silenced a young friend who began to speak seriously to him about the life to come, with a wave of the hand, and the cynical remark, " One world at a time, please." There are ample portions of our elegant literature in which that seems to be the predominant sentiment, so rigidly is attention confined to the limits of this time-scene, and so severely is thought pinned down to the little clay planet we at present inhabit, and the petty drama enacted upon it.   The words of John Foster in his famous Essay, though written many years ago, are still as applicable as if they had been written but yesterday, and the ink was not yet dry upon the paper, when, speaking of their defective acknowledgment of the life beyond the grave, he says, " Many writers seem to take as much care to guard against the inroad of ideas from that solemn quarter as the inhabitants of Holland do against the irruption of the sea ; and their writings do really form a kind of moral dyke against the invasion from the other world." [1]   This we cannot but regard as a most disastrous policy, considered not only from the theological but from the literary point of view itself. For if anything has been made clearer than another by the whole course of literature in all ages, and especially in the flowering times of its choicest productions, it is that if the exalting influence of the spheres supernatural and of our intrinsic relation to them be taken out of poetry and letters, they are deprived of their noblest source of inspiration, and they will become thin, shallow, poverty-stricken, and frivolous.   Cut off from the vast and unseen domains with which our earth is associated, thought will lose its upward look, man will be shorn of his dignity, the world will become to us only what his kennel is to the dog, and human life, evaporated of all the grander meanings that a Shakespeare saw in it, will not leave the poet anything to sing about, nor the artist anything noble enough to call forth the best efforts of his brush or chisel, nor even the novelist anything to lift him above the dreary flats of the commonplace.   " If the blue heavens be closed and unattainable, what else

[1] *Essays*, p. 226.

can the poor poet do but limp along the common earth, with trailing wings and wounded heart ?"[1]   One must try very hard before one can conceive of a Comtist Shakespeare, or an Agnostic Wordsworth.

It is nothing short of calamitous that large tracts of our literature, especially that portion of it represented by fiction, should have been inundated to such an extent by that tide of depraving Realism which, within the last few decades, has come in upon us like a flood.   It would seem as if the sentiment of John Keats in his immortal line, " A thing of beauty is a joy for ever," is rapidly undergoing a temporary reversal.   Now it is the thing of ugliness, of deformity, the thing of brutality and offensiveness, that is held up to admiration.   No longer do our writers vie with each other as to which of them shall furnish us with the most faithful portrayal of the noblenesses and dignities of human nature ; rather the rivalry would appear to be as to which shall take the deepest dive of exploration into its morbidities, its mean-nesses, its leprous vices, its festering sores, its unspeakable degradations.   The contention seems to be, who shall go to the greatest length in reporting the unreportable, who shall mention the unmentionable with the most shameless explicitness, who in the general attempt at being brutally frank, shall best succeed in being frankly brutal.   Not to the zenith of human life and experience are we now con-ducted by the favourite writers of romance, but to its nadir : not to the heights of existence do they lead us, but to its defiled depths ; we are taken on a tour of inspection to the morgue, the gaol, the dissecting-room,

[1] *Quest and Vision,* p. 92.

the museum of monstrosities. Too often the modern novel finds its scenes of action in the hospital, the madhouse, the tavern, the torture chamber, or the brothel.

In Lucas Malet's *Wages of Sin,* one of the most powerful and penetrating works of fiction which has appeared in recent years, we are treated to a long and elaborate defence of the principles of Realism as applied to Art. Colthurst, the leading character, is himself an artist, one of those who have " the gift of calling spades spades, rather than agricultural implements." He assures us that " truth is always sad, and that the fundamental facts are not only sad but almost hideous. That is why Nature tries to hide them under leaves and flowers, and glories of colour, and of light and shade." [1] In short, the correct artistic Credo is that the Creator has organised the universe upon a ground-plan of ugliness, and the business of the artist is to exhibit that ugliness in the ugliest possible way. Nature at least spares our feelings so far as to veil the hideousness under leaf and flower, and the glories of light and shade. Might it not be well if artists of the Colthurst type, whether pictorial or literary, who make a special boast of being true to Nature, would follow her example in this; but instead of doing so, they take a pleasure in drawing aside the mantle of concealment and exposing what is behind to the indiscriminate gaze of the passer-by. Later on in the book, Colthurst is made to say—

" I want to go to the East : I want to see countries where men still treat each other worse than we treat our beasts; I want to see the ultimate possibilities of human degrada-

[1] *Wages of Sin,* p. 112.

tion. . . . The inside of a Chinese prison might suit me, I think, or the slave market at Bagdad." [1]

Having exhausted the horrors of Western civilisation, this artistic soul is seized with a desire to visit the Orient, that he may amplify his stock-in-trade by adding those of the East. He will prosecute his investigations, if need be, in the inside of Chinese prisons, or in the slave markets of Bagdad—the more sickening and repellent the scene the better for his purpose, for it will all the more enrich his knowledge of "the ultimate possibilities of human degradation." What contributions may not be made to the treasures of our art galleries by a man who has taken a tour of inspection on a Cook's tourist ticket round the world by way of extending his acquaintance with the degradations of human life! A similar preparation is considered necessary nowadays in the literary realm, if a writer is to achieve success. He must ransack the globe with Colthurst in quest of degrading things, and then come home to dabble in the carnal, the morbid, the unsavoury, and the downright nasty, till we are almost led to believe that there is no sacredness in woman, nor nobleness in man, nor dignity in life, nor secret in nature. This style of literary art has been sometimes called "Greek," but to say so is almost a libel on the ancients; paganism itself is quite respectable in comparison. Tennyson in his "Palace of Art" calls upon his soul to

"Arise and fly
The reeling faun, the sensual feast:
Move upward, working out the beast,
And let the ape and tiger die." In mem CXVIII

---

[1] *Wages of Sin*, p. 113.

But it is precisely the "sensual feast" which the poet fled from that to the Realistic class of writer appears to constitute the chief attraction, and it is just on the "ape and tiger" side of human nature that they concentrate attention, as if it alone were the part of us perennially interesting, and most likely to remunerate our study. Mr. Swinburne actually prostitutes his noble gifts to the serious maintenance of the monstrous theory that the highest style of poetry is that which occupies itself in the prurient details of "fleshly fever" and "amorous malady." Nor have we forgotten how, in some of his earlier verse, he chanted the praises of "the raptures and roses of vice."

But the chief offenders in this direction are, of course, the Continental writers, headed by M. Zola, that great sensuous Coryphæus who appears to revel in the beastly. He has been well described as the Nero of modern fiction. Unhappily, his methods and ideals are now being followed by a herd of English writers, who are doing their best to naturalise him on English soil, so far as British taste and sense of decency will stand the strain of such an experiment. To the great detriment of his own art, and the injury of his own reputation, one of our chief masters of fiction, Thomas Hardy, has elected to cast in his lot with the new school of Zolaism. The novels of Mr. George Gissing furnish abundant evidence that their author has made a similar election. His rebellion against the traditional morality, his peeps into the abysses of the nether world, his elevation of the courtesan into a heroine, for whom he claims the fullest sympathy and admiration of his reader, his maxim that "Art nowadays must be the mouthpiece of misery, for misery is the keynote of modern life," his advocacy of the theory that "the ideal union between a man and woman may be one of freedom," his "suggestive" writing, his Frithlike portraiture of "things as they are"—all lead to the conclusion that he derives his inspiration and encouragement from Continental sources. George Moore is another writer who seems to have acquired a considerable part of his literary education and outfit in a French school. He, too, is branded with the stamp and signature of Zola. He has distinguished himself by exploiting, for the purposes of the novel, such themes as servant-girlism, the gambling fever, drink, slumdom, and life below stairs. His descriptions have all the nude frankness of realism. Like Gissing, he depicts with minutest accuracy things as they are, especially when the things happen to be of a squalid or revolting character, mistaking, as most writers of his class do, mere representation for true Art. But mere accurate description of what one sees is not Art; it is only photography. If to depict things as they are is the highest achievement of the artist, then let him discard brush and palette and betake himself to the ever faithful camera. It will reproduce the object true to life, never fear, and catch with snapshot fidelity the precise momentary attitude it may chance to occupy, however unlovely— jumping, dancing, laughing, leering, grimacing, or what not. No doubt true Art also deals with things as they are, but then it takes care to idealise and ennoble them. Is not ideality the very essence of all Art worthy of the name—that is, the modification and transformation of fact in the crucible of the mind? Without, however, presuming to enter into the eternal controversy, in whose mazy intricacies so many of the finest intellects have puzzled and perplexed themselves in vain, as to what is the true function and aim of Art, we shall content ourselves with raising our protest against this defiant contempt for the beautiful which is now the fashionable attitude of our latter-day artists, whether pictorial or literary. After all, is not the true mission of the artist to please, to interest, to charm, to elevate? Is it expecting too much that artistic representations, whether on canvas or the printed page, should never extort from the onlooker or the reader the cry which Joubert attributes to the soul when it sustains any moral damage, or is spiritually outraged, " You hurt me! You hurt me!" Have not we average mortals, immersed for the most part in the deadly utilitarianism of the daily round, in the dull prosaic drab of everyday practical life, a right to complain, if for a moment when we turn for relief to Art, to seek in it something that will give " noble ground for noble emotion," we are forced to contemplate a literal reproduction of that very hideousness from which we are endeavouring to escape, and perhaps get ourselves roundly lectured for not appreciating what is served up for our delectation, because, forsooth, it is so cleverly done, because the technique is so masterly, and the style so finished? " I shall never forget," says a modern authoress, " the profound solemnity with which the foremost poet and representative of the later Victorian era said to me one day, pausing as we strolled on the terrace of his beautiful Surrey home: " They talk of Art for Art's sake. There is something higher than Art for Art's sake—Art for *man's* sake." Yes, Art *for man's sake* is a very much higher thing than Art for Art's sake. The service we render to Art is too dearly bought, if it can only be rendered at the expense of degrading men. We never can consent to the monstrous principle that Art is to be emancipated from all moral considerations; that the artist is to have no ethical sympathies; that virtue and wickedness are to be no more to him than what the colours on his palette are to the painter, simply the means of producing a certain effect, and nothing more.

But, to return to the realistic novel, what commentary shall we pass on such books as Mr. Frankfort Moore's *I Forbid the Banns*, Mr. Bellamy's *An Experiment in Marriage*, Miss Mona Caird's *The Daughters of Danaus*, Grant Allen's *British Barbarians* and *The Woman Who Did*, and Sarah Grand's *Beth Book*? We have in these and kindred productions, as some one has said, the culmination of those negative and destructive aspects of the marriage controversy which have been gathering to a head in our literature for so long. To Mr. Grant Allen especially, " wedlock is Nehushtan," as Mr. Stead observed in his review of *The Woman Who Did* when it first appeared—and his mission in life is to break the idol in pieces as with an iron rod. We could almost have forgiven him for having metrically aired his infidelity in poetically vindicating the alleged ape original of the human race, if he had not catered so assiduously in his novels for the corrupt Londoner and the Parisian *roué*, who are about the only class of reader likely to have an appetite for such a *menu* as is here served up. It is not surprising that some booksellers at the time refused his *Woman Who Did* a place among their literary wares, and declined to make themselves accessory to the spread of a species of literature so poisonous. As for Sarah Grand's *Beth Book*, suffice it to say that through several hundred pages of writing, intolerably tedious, the authoress drags the reader through the inferno of domestic incompatibility, through the horrors of the Divorce Court, with an occasional digression, by way of variety, into the torturing operations of the vivisectionist. Talk of "supping on horrors," but readers of the *Beth Book* may make up their mind to breakfast and dine on them too. In the productions of writers like these, and not a few others who might be associated with them, the reader will generally find himself "grubbing on the floor of realism," with no ideals to set like heavens in the sky above him, and when he rises he would require the immediate application to his garments of the clothes-brush, for he will be plentifully bespattered with mud, and may consider himself fortunate if some of it does not stick. Is it any wonder that a writer like Marion Crawford should indignantly exclaim, "Zola's shadow seen through the veil of the English realistic novel is a monstrosity not to be tolerated."[1] We have no intention to stain the reader's mind with quotations from the realistic writers of the day, nor to advance a step farther into the morass of foul literature, from which arises such a strong scent of corruption. These hidden cloacæ had better be left closed so far as we are concerned. To open them would be to diffuse a pestilential atmosphere which would prove suffocating alike to culture and religion. Speaking of

[1] *The Novel: What Is It?* p. 39.

what is known as the "hill-top" species of novel, a writer
in the *Fortnightly* has affirmed that a whiff from the
atmosphere which usually pervades it would infect the
Delectable Mountains themselves.[1]   To parody a well-
known couplet—

"You may paint, you may perfume the scene if you will,
But the stench of the 'hill-top' will hang round it still."

Greater, we believe, than any material need of the age
is the need of insight to recognise and courage to confront
this perilous tendency in a large section of European
literature to repudiate obligation to the law of goodness,
and to afford to the community an unfortunate education in the degrading things of life.   It is time that the
meekest of us had learnt severity enough and the most
tolerant dogmatism enough to meet this modern Satan
with a Get thee behind me!   For, as a modern authoress
well observes, "it is only by the adoption of a resolute,
militant, and uncompromising attitude that there can be
hope for a generation which has in so many directions
strayed so far from the paths of sanity, a generation which
tolerates the Rougon-Macquart novels; which exonerates
Verlaine, which accepts Walt Whitman as a poet,
Maeterlinck as dramatist, and Nietzsche as philosopher."[2]
Miss Marie Corelli pours out the vials of her fury on
this decadent generation, and takes certain female writers
of the day severely to task for ministering to its depraved
taste by dealing very coarsely with the sexual problem.
Yet, while condemning the offence in others, she occasionally commits it herself in a form not less objectionable

[1] R. Yelverton Tyrrell.
[2] Elizabeth Chapman's *Marriage Questions in Modern Fiction.*

than it is met with in those whose works she has so savagely assailed. She has not scrupled to pen a passage like this—

"I soon found that Lucio did not intend to marry, and I concluded that he preferred to be the lover of many women, instead of the husband of one. I do not love him any the less for this; I only resolved that I would at least be one of those who were happy enough to share his passion. I married the man Tempest, feeling that, like many women I knew, I should, when safely wedded, have greater liberty of action. I was aware that most modern men prefer an amour with a married woman to a *liaison* of any other kind, and I thought Lucio would have readily yielded to the plan I had preconceived."

Passages of the same unsavoury description disfigure the writings of Olive Schreiner. It seems almost inexplicable that a pure and high-minded woman, who has given proof of extreme sensitiveness to every other part of the moral law, should fail to see any serious breach of propriety in such a deflection from the ordinary law of chastity as is implied in the following passage in the *African Farm*, where Lyndall says to the father of her child—

"I like to experience, I like to try. I cannot marry you, because I cannot be tied; but if you wish, you may take me away with you and take care of me, then when we do not love any more we can say good-bye."

When even our female writers are thus invading individual sanctity and the monogamic basis of home life and family relationship, it is high time to sound the tocsin of a reformation for the purging of our literature.

Then, again, much of the worldly literature of the day

is vitiated by *the vein of fatalistic teaching* which runs
through it.   The philosophy now most in favour with
many of our fine writers is one which resolves human life
into a play of fatalistic forces, destitute either of merit or
blame.   The notion is assiduously propagated that man
is the helpless victim of a blind inevitable necessity, the
slave of circumstance, the creature of destiny, or the
product and resultant of hereditary forces which were in
operation before ever he was born, and which he is powerless to cope with.   There was a time when our litterateurs subscribed to the sentiment of the poet—

> " The fault, dear Brutus, is not in our stars,
>   But in ourselves."

But now they have introduced a kind of astrology in
morals which attributes our faults to the influence of our
" evil star," or lays the blame of our misdeeds at the
door of Fate, Heredity, or Circumstance.   Man's moral
freedom is denied : he is not his own master ; he does not
form his own character, it is formed for him ; what is
generally known as responsibility does not exist, and the
idea of blameworthiness or punishment is inadmissible.
Guilt, obligation, crime, righteousness are, on this theory
of life, outworn words which jar upon the ear of true
science.   Thomas Hardy has embraced these fatalistic
doctrines, and preaches them with all the zeal of an
apostle.   Readers of his books will remember how constantly his heroes and heroines lay the blame of their
faults on " the universe,"—on " things in general," which
are always so horrible and cruel ; and how, in their efforts
at reform, they are constantly victimised, hoaxed, and
thwarted by some malevolent divinity in the background,

or by the evil genius of Circumstance. They will remember, too, how he continually appeals to Heredity,
which, as interpreted by him, seems to furnish a handy
explanation of everything. When any of his characters
is guilty of anything criminal, it is usually condoned on
the ground of some bad trait in the blood, mixed descent,
or some constitutional weakness, or some unfortunate
legacy which has filtered through the veins of a remote
ancestry. In short, according to his philosophy, man is
started on the voyage of life with rudder lashed, and
not with a responsible hand on a free helm, able to
steer a course which is truly *his*, and for the taking
of which he is justly held accountable. In Mr. Du
Maurier's novel of *Trilby*, traces of the same dismal
evangel make their appearance; and we are sorry to
detect its presence also in the manly and soul-stirring
work of *Mark Rutherford*. Writers like Lucas Malet
and George Gissing are also deeply tinged with it. The
former prefaces her novel, *The Carissima*, with these verses
from Omar Khayyam; the book, we presume, is meant
largely to embody and develop the fatalistic philosophy
they contain:—

I.

"We are no other than a moving row
Of Magic Shadow-shapes that come and go
Round with the Sun-illumined Lantern held
In Midnight by the Master of the Show;

II.

"But helpless Pieces of the Game He plays
Upon His Chequer-board of Nights and Days;
Hither and thither moves, and checks, and slays,
And one by one back in the Closet lays."

3

" We had all played," says Hammond, the leading character in the book, "and we had all lost.   Destiny had
swept our stakes into her lap, as is Destiny's usual habit;
and left us, each in our own several ways penniless." [1]
The same personage excuses himself for not praying for
his own futile self, and his dear friends Leversedge and
Charlotte, by the consideration that his prayers could
avail nothing :—

" Who was I that I should be heard?   What
my petitions, that they should prevail to change the
course of history?   What would be, would be.   My
pitiful wishes weighed as a feather against the push of
Fate." [2]

In *The Wages of Sin* by the same writer the following
passage is typical of much :—

" But though, to make use of his own rather pagan illustration, Colthurst might forget the great Cat Fate, she
had not forgotten him.   Who indeed does she ever forget,
if it comes to that?" [3]

In George Gissing's *The Unclassed*, Waymark, the hero,
is made to say—

" Well, there was no help.   Whatever would be, would
be.   It availed nothing to foresee, and scheme, and
resolve."

Even in a novel so unexceptionable in tone as *Alywin*,
the same teaching gleams out upon us occasionally from
among the pages :—

" I did not know then, as I do now," says the hero of
the book, " how weak is human will enmeshed in that web

[1] *The Carissima*, p. 284.   [2] Pp. 285-286.
[3] P. 402.

of circumstance that has been aweaving from the beginning of the world."[1]

We cannot conceive a more harmful philosophy than that to which writers like these would commit themselves and their readers. Nothing but mischief can come to individuals and to society by the inculcation of such doctrines. Should they ever become general, or filter down to the lowest strata of our population, they will be sure to eventuate in their natural fruitage in the shape of some terrible outbreak of diabolism and shame. They leave no room for morality ; they render all attempts at self-improvement useless ; they make the pursuit of virtue a futility, blot out the prospect of reform, and in the end reduce the world itself to a hopeless hell. Besides, it must always be a cowardly and craven policy to blame our circumstances, our stars, or our evil genius, when we ought only to blame ourselves. He is no longer a man, but only "a miserable male," who has not courage enough to take the responsibility of his own actions. These literary fatalists could not do better than ponder and lay to heart the bracing and manly sentiment with which George Meredith rebukes their effeminancy in one of his shorter poems :—

> "I take the hap
> Of all my deeds. The wind that fills my sails,
> Propels ; but I am helmsman. Am I wrecked ?
> I know the devil has sufficient weight
> To bear ; I lay it not on him, or fate.
> Besides, he's damned. That man I do suspect
> A coward, who would burden the poor deuce
> With what ensues from his own slipperiness."[2]

---

[1] P. 43.   [2] Meredith's Poems, vol. i. p. 22.

Fortunately it will not be easy to bring the world round to this necessitarian philosophy, it is so flatly at variance with the most elementary facts of human nature and experience. It directly traverses facts the most incontrovertible, and instincts the most deep-seated and significant. It is a fact that men are free, and know that they are free, to obey or disobey the grand imperative of conscience. It is a fact that when we disobey we blame ourselves for it, and experience a feeling of compunction and shame in consequence of disobedience. It is a fact that man has shown himself competent again and again to master his circumstances, instead of being mastered by them. It is a fact that all the noblest productions of literature —its epics, its tragedies, its great novels—proceed upon a theory of life which affirms the very principles that fatalists deny. It is a fact that the science of jurisprudence, with its constant insistence on guilt and responsibility, and its painstaking analysis of motive and intention as determining the character of action, finds its very basis in human freedom and accountability. It is a fact that the vicious stream of hereditary taint may be clarified, and made to change its course ; that by a single decisive choice a man may arrest the process of deterioration ; that neither bad birth nor bad blood can necessarily doom him to a certain hell. " In my opinion," says Dr. A. H. Bradford, " all that makes life worth living for half the world, and all that saves from the abyss of pessimism those who are possessed with the enthusiasm for Humanity, is the simple fact that heredity may be modified by environment, that there is always something in a human being which was not destroyed by the first or any subsequent fall, which can respond to education and religion, and which may be expected to respond to them when given a fair chance." [1]

There is nothing more characteristic of the spirit and temper of much of our present-day authorship than *its attenuated conception of sin.* Perhaps in this day of Hegelian revival, when moral evil and natural are confounded with each other, our literature has no direr need than to be invigorated and morally braced by a fresh breeze from Dante, or the old Hebrew prophets, with their faithful delineations of sin, and their vivid illustrations of its voluntariness and its damnableness. In dealing with the vices and follies of mankind, our literary moralists too often treat them as if they were accidental to human nature, and not indicative of any intrinsic or deep-seated malady of soul. They are at most but wild weeds grown on a virtuous soil. Human nature is still a noble and dignified thing, with strong tendencies toward what is excellent, and if at times it lapses and retrogresses, we must not be too severe upon it ; we must not insist on constantly bringing it to the test of an ideally perfect standard ; in short, we must be accommodating in our demands, and not expect angelic conduct from beings who have not yet reached the angel stage. It is quite exceptional to find among modern writers any adequate realisation of man's moral condition, or of the exceeding sinfulness of sin. The whole tendency is to make light of sin, to call it by mild names, to conceal its hideousness behind fig-leaf aprons of apology, to

[1] Article on "Heredity and Religion" in *Theological Quarterly*, October 1884.

extenuate or ignore its guilt. Sin, defined and contemplated as an offence against God, a violation of the moral order of the universe, an hostility to all that is holy and beautiful—sin viewed in its true light as " the anomaly of the universe, the blot upon the creation which God made very good, the disgrace of mankind "—is an idea which has never yet been properly domiciliated in the mind of the modern litterateur. There is no place in his philosophy for the gloomy but incontrovertible facts of New Testament hamartology. He never seems to have taken a deep look down into the interior of his own nature, nor to have made any serious attempt to acquaint himself with the secrets of the dark psychology of evil. Consequently, sin is seldom to him anything more serious than infirmity, a necessary incident of human growth, a transitory but inevitable stage of imperfection in the moral development of mankind, a " fall upwards " into progress, a necessary result of the physical and social conditions into which we are born, an indication of our finiteness rather than our guilt. In a leading novel of the day which counts its readers by thousands,[1] the hero makes the astounding admission to a lady friend who comes to him seeking comfort under a deep conviction of her own sinfulness : " Sin has been a word without significance to me. As a boy it was so ; it is so now that I am self-conscious." " This overpowering consciousness of sin is an anachronism in our day "; and again, " Sin, if anything, is weakness." Mallock represents " Mr. Stork " as saying, " Sin is a word that has helped to retard moral and social progress more than anything." With such super-

---

[1] George Gissing's *The Unclassed.*

ficial and immoral shifts does the elegant literature of our day seek to minister to the mind diseased; with such wretched anæsthetics does it seek to quiet the throbbing of a neuralgic conscience, and dull the ache of unforgiven sin. Here is a new and choice consolation for all convicted ones, who like the publican go up to the temple to cry for mercy. Penetrated through and through with a sense of personal unworthiness, their eyes piercing the dust, their prayer punctuated with sobs and tears, how it will comfort them to know that "sin is a word of no significance"! How relieved they will go back to their house when some man of letters lays his hand on their shoulder and says, "My dear sir, why all this ado? you are vexing yourself about nothing—this overpowering consciousness of sin is an anachronism in our day"! Do not let us be misled by any such silly and contemptible subterfuges. Sin is not an affair of dictionary makers, nor a passing phase of thought, making its presence felt in one age, but outgrown and left behind in the next.

We naturally turn for relief from such teaching to some of the great master-spirits of our modern literature, but our appeal to them is disappointing. We have recourse to Goethe, for example; but for the great German, sin was simply the mistake of ignorance, the stumbling of the child who thereby learns to walk. It is but the consequence of our finite limitation, and the idea of escaping from it is, as he expresses it, "like the idleness of wishing to jump off from one's own shadow." We open our Browning only to find ourselves confronted with the same view, or something dangerously approximating to it. According to the greatest poet of our age, evil is only good in the making.   It is the blundering of inexperience, the ignorance that puts its fingers in the fire, the thoughtlessness which acts impulsively :—

"The Evil is null, is nought, is silence implying sound ;
  What was good shall be good, with, for Evil, so much good
    more." [1]

It is the natural foil or set-off to virtue, and even in a certain sense the cause and producer of virtue, for

" Every growth of good
Springs consequent on Evil's neighbourhood." [2]

But it is not by such philosophisings as these that the mystery of unrighteousness is fathomed.   If evil be a necessary means of good, and a promoter of good, then it has already lost the character of evil.   On such an explanation the moral idea is manifestly fading into the background already, and will very soon be lost sight of. Sin, as interpreted by Browning, is not the kind of sin that the Bible describes, or the law of God legislates against, nor the sort that penitents weep over, or that Jesus died for on the tree.   It must have been sin of another kind which gave birth to David's penitential Psalms, or that wrung from Paul the bitter cry of soul-agony, " O wretched man that I am, who shall deliver me ? " or that forced from the Son of God Himself the pained ejaculation, " My soul is exceeding sorrowful, even unto death."   " Sin explained," says Dr. Robinson, " is sin defended"; and certainly sin explained by many of our modern writers is sin defended, or at least sin trans-figured, sin condoned, sin blurred into indistinctness, or

[1] " Abt Vogler."
[2] " Parleyings with Bernard de Mandeville."

evaporated into a phantom. Against all such refinements and philosophisings our moral nature rises in revolt. James Russell Lowell says truly—

> "In vain we call old notions fudge,
>   And bend our conscience to our dealing;
> The Ten Commandments will not budge,
>   And stealing will continue stealing."

A wide observation and experience have established the fact that when a slight and attenuated estimate of sin prevails, the estimate of Redemption is sure to partake of a corresponding character. The saying of Tholuck is a very true one, "Without the descent into self-recognition there can be no ascent to the recognition of God." Any real "descent into self-recognition" is conspicuously absent, as we have just seen, from many of the most fascinating productions of our modern literature, and that being so, we are quite prepared for the discovery that they contain no "ascent" to the just recognition of God, especially of God as the Reconciler of the world to Himself, or the Bestower of the "unspeakable gift."

It is scarcely necessary to say that the views of sin commonly held are not such as are calculated to make us do justice to the sublime expedient of the Cross, or endear to us "the only Name under heaven whereby we must be saved." The incarnation and lifework of Jesus have done more to alleviate the mystery and burden of this strange existence than anything else that has ever occurred in the history of our planet. Yet how seldom is there even the most distant allusion to it, even by our professedly religious writers, not to speak of those who are purely secular. If some allusion to Him is unavoid-

able, and His name or work must be mentioned in some
way, it is done, as John Foster says it was done in his
day, " as with a certain inaptitude to pronounce a foreign
appellative, or with a somewhat irksome feeling at having
to come into momentary contact with language so speci-
fically of the Christian school." [1]   Not by any means
that we would expect our writers to set up a pulpit and
preach, or to treat the public to something like a course
of Bible readings,—the formal introduction of evangelical topics is of course foreign to their purpose,—but what
we may reasonably expect is, that where the truth of the
Christian religion is admitted, and the writer finds himself in accord with its principles and in sympathy with
its spirit, there should be some little indication, direct
or indirect, to show that the writer is not insensible to
the sovereignty of its claims, and that in what he writes
there is a manifest effort and intention to avoid everything which would be unconsonant with its teachings and
precepts.   We have a right to expect at least as much
as John Foster expected in his day, namely, " the presence
of a certain Christian tinge and modification, rendered
perceptible by a plain recognition occasionally of some
great Christian truth, and partly by a solicitous, though
it were a tacit, conformity to every principle of the
Christian theory."   Indeed, nowadays, when it has
become the fashion so much to write on subjects which
touch the Christian system at so many points, and so
intimately,—subjects which cannot be handled without
frequent explicit reference to the great topics of Religion,
—we should be justified, perhaps, in expecting a great deal

[1] *Essays*, p. 250.

more. And yet how often are such subjects expatiated
on at great length by our modern authors with as little
allusion to Christ, or the Divine revelation of which He
was the accredited Messenger, as if what they wrote was
written B.C., instead of two thousand years after His
advent. How often do such writers deliver themselves
on problems of the deepest concern with as little regard
to Biblical sentiment as if God had never " spoken to us
by His Son"! How often, with glib fluency, do they
rattle off their own individual opinions in the most reckless and arbitrary manner, just as if the Son of God had
never given us a lesson, or the New Testament had never
been written! Robert Hall complained in his day of
Miss Edgeworth as " the most irreligious writer I ever
read," not because she *attacks* religion, but because she
omits it, and " presents a perfect virtue without it." As
a typical instance of this same policy of omission,
which is still a characteristic feature of so much of our
literature, take the conversation between Robert Allitsen
and Bernardine in Miss Beatrice Harraden's novel, *Ships
that Pass in the Night :—*

" What do you think about death? Have you any
theories about life and death and the bridge between
them? Could you say anything to help one?"
" Nothing," he answered. " Who could? and by what
means?"
" Has there been no value in Philosophy," she asked,
" and in the meditations of learned men?"
" Philosophy!" he sneered. "What has it done for us?
It has taught us some processes of the mind's working;
taught us a few wonderful things that interest the few;
but the centuries have come and gone, and the only thing
which the whole human race pants to know, remains

unknown: our beloved ones, shall we meet them, and
how ?—the great secret of the universe. We ask for
bread, and these philosophers give us a stone. What
help could come from them,—or from anyone ? Death is
simply one of the hard facts of life." "And the greatest
evil," she said. . . . "We shall go on building our bridge,"
she said, "between life and death, each one for himself.
When we see that it is not strong enough, we shall break
it down and build another. We shall watch other people
building their bridges. We shall imitate, or criticise, or
condemn. But as time goes on, we shall learn not to
interfere, we shall know that one bridge is probably as
good as another, and that the greatest value of them all
has been in the building of them. It does not matter
what we build, but build we must ; you and I, and everyone."

It is not the Agnostic attitude which the writer has
chosen to assume toward the whole question of an after
life which here calls for criticism, so much as the
significant silence she preserves where a reference to
Christianity might have been reasonably expected.
Here we have a dialogue between two cultured and
well-informed individuals on the momentous problem of
future destiny. From the turn which the conversation
takes, there is a fair opening presented for a natural
and unforced allusion to the contribution which Jesus of
Nazareth is believed to have made to the solving of that
problem, yet all such allusion is studiously avoided. The
contribution of Philosophy, though held in very slight
esteem, is at least acknowledged with an honourable
mention. Why is there no similar acknowledgment
of what Christianity professes to have done, when it
might have been so naturally introduced ? If there is to
be speculation about a future state at all, it must surely

be considered defective, even to the degree of absurdity, if it takes no account of that sacred Person who, in the belief of Christendom, first completely opened the prospect of Immortality.   To discuss the subject of human destiny with all reference to the Christ of the New Testament left out is very much the same thing as it would be to write a treatise on the law of gravitation with no reference to Sir Isaac Newton, or a treatise on astronomy without any mention of Kepler or Tycho Bragh.   Miss Beatrice Harraden talks volubly of the many bridges which have been constructed to span the awful chasm between life and death, but has not so much as a distant allusion to the bridge which the Christ of God constructed, when by His resurrection from the dead He broke in upon the stern order of decay and death, and gilded the dark shadows of mortality with the prospect of reunion in a world of renewed and improved intercourse beyond the grave, turning guesses and conjectures into a working and recognised certainty, which could stand the wear and tear of discussion, of trouble, of desolating bereavement, and of life itself, and planting our feet once for all upon the soil of certainty.   As Victor Hugo puts it, He has turned the grave from being a " blind alley " into a " thoroughfare "; yet Miss Harraden writes as if no hint of the existence of such a bridge as this had ever been heard among men, and as if we were each under the necessity of building a little bridge of our own, one being just as good as another, and none of them in the long run of the slightest use.   Writing in the heart of Christendom, the gifted authoress could not have been

ignorant of the fact that in the faith of millions, Jesus
Christ has spoken the great final conclusive word on
human destiny; that He has rolled away the stone from
the sepulchre, and turned the darkness of the grave into
a great sunrise; yet she writes as if, so far as these
things are concerned, she had been all this time an
inhabitant of Mars or Saturn. Shall we meet our
beloved ones, and how? that is the one thing the world
pants to know, yet, according to our authoress, it remains
unknown. We had thought that Jesus of Nazareth had
provided an answer to that question which no one
professing to treat of the subject of an after-life could
afford to pass over in silence; but, in the estimation of
Miss Harraden, it is, after all, it would seem, but a
neglible quantity unworthy of serious consideration.
Instead of openly attacking the great Christian truth
that Jesus Christ has brought life and immortality
to light, she contents herself with quietly suppressing
and omitting it; and exclusion of this kind is scarcely
calculated to inflict less deadly injury on the Christian
faith than open assassination. Miss Harraden's general
conception of religion is one which it is to be hoped will
make few disciples. To a dying invalid, coming daily
nearer the great transition, and anxiously seeking for
some light and comfort, she makes her heroine say, that
"prayer and the Bible and that sort of thing do not
matter. What does matter is to judge gently, and not
to come down like a sledge-hammer on other people's
failings." In other words, a little amiability and good-
nature is religion enough for any one. Kindly feeling,
and a disposition to make allowances, constitute a

sufficient moral and religious outfit for a man to front
eternity with. With this viaticum Miss Harraden
thinks him sufficiently fortified to set out upon the last
journey. Thus it has come to pass that to turn from
what our elegant writers have to say on the great
themes of religion to what prophets and apostles have to
say, is only to afflict ourselves with a painful sense of
" the antipathy between the inspirations of genius and
the inspirations of heaven." In the one, God's remedy
for sin is hardly ever mentioned ; in the other, hardly
anything else is mentioned. In the one class of writings
the Cross is not visible ; in the other, it is lifted high as
the brazen serpent. In the one, the sublime anticipation of immortality dominates everything, and imports
a certain nobleness into all the occupations of time ; in
the other, it is but vaguely hinted at, or dimly suggested,
in the manner of one who had conversed on the subject
with Seneca or Cicero in the days of pagan twilight.
Was not Elizabeth Barrett Browning right when she
wrote that " the great want of much of our modern
literature was to have Christ wave His bleeding hand
over it all " ?

Infinitely more deserving of censure than anything
we have yet adverted to, is the modern tendency of a
certain class of literature to adorn sin, and veil its
intrinsic hideousness, by surrounding it with all the
charms of literary romance. In all the dark catalogue
of trangression there is scarcely a vice that has not
been shorn by dramatic skill of its repulsiveness, and
rendered half excusable. Sedition, murder, immorality,
theft, gambling, lying, intemperance, have all been

presented in forms romantically adorned, and garnished with literary merit of the highest order. It would be difficult to mention a single form of guilt or crime that has not its literature; there is no species of disgraceful action that has not been painted and bedizened by literary hands till it has become invested with a kind of Jezebel attractiveness. Scoundrelism is elevated into a degree of semi-respectability. Too often the way of sin, if we are to accept the representations of it in modern literature, is fringed with flowers, instead of thorns and briers, and is made to end in bowers of ease, instead of the hot chambers of torture. The death's head of sinful pleasure is so wreathed with garlands that the reeking skull beneath is concealed from view. We are not by any means proceeding on the assumption that a book is necessarily immoral because it deals with immoral subjects, or paints immoral characters. It may do both, and yet its moral influence be unimpeachable. The morality or immorality of the work depends on the bias it is calculated to give to our sympathies. If that bias is evil, we may write down the book as evil. The writer who engages our sympathies on behalf of vice may be unhesitatingly marked dangerous. It will always be found that the literature which makes sin alluring and successful has generally for its operation and consequence that it creates sin, and spreads it like an epidemic. Fortunately, this class of literary product does not usually enjoy a long lease of life, but while it does continue in being, in the course of its brief fugitive existence it inflicts much injury, and corrupts many unsuspecting minds. "From hell and for hell is the sole worthy description," says the

late Professor Lange, of this style of production. And
still more to be reprobated is the literature which
indulges in inuendo, in words that look two ways, in
emphasis in which lurks a hint of unchastity. Give us
outspoken grossness rather than the finished lubricity
and brilliant licentiousness of some of our present-day
novelists. They are both reprehensible, but the latter is
the worse of the two, and will work incalculably more
mischief. It would give us less uneasiness to see a
young person reading Swift or Rabelais than with a copy
of some of our realistic fiction-writers in his hand. In
both cases he would be reading what is impure; but the
result would not be equally harmful. Writers like the
former are indecent because of their brutal frankness;
writers of the latter class are indecent too, but indecent
because of their reticence. The one say what they
mean with downright abominable coarseness; the other
have recourse to hints, *double entendres*, veiled inuendos,
and often print a dash or a row of asterisks, when it
would have been infinitely less suggestive if they had
plumped out with a coarse word and a laugh all that
was in their mind. The one may be compared to Satan
in his own native form, the other to Satan posing as an
angel of light; and will not many be led astray by the
angel who would have shrunk with abhorrence from the
advances of the fiend? The lengths to which some
writers of the realistic school have gone in what is
known as "suggestive writing" is enough to shock the
sensibilities of the least fastidious. The Viscomte de
Vogüe, in his criticism of Zola's work, *La Débâcle*, in the
Revue des Deux Mondes, compares the relief with which a

reader takes up another work after Zola, to the relief of
the tourist whose skin is burning with the "heavy,
mephitic, and corrosive liquid" after a bath in the Dead
Sea, as he plunges into the neighbouring waters of the
Jordan, which, say the Arab guides, is the only way to
free oneself from the irritation. After reading certain
books, it needs a bath in the Jordan of some pure
literature to wash off the effects. There are books, and
after perusing them, one would require to have some
disinfecting fluid poured over the mind to deodorise and
cleanse it. It must have been books like these that
made Sir Anthony Absolute in his day pronounce the
circulating library "an evergreen tree of diabolical
knowledge,"—books filled with the narrations of mis-
conduct, and spiced with the pungent flavours of evil, to
meet a vitiated taste. If this were the place, it would
be quite easy for us to reproduce passages which no
father would read aloud to his children if he were paid a
guinea a line for doing it. Why, in the name of all
decency and reverence, should we have things put in
print by our fine writers for ladies to read, which, if a
drunken cabman addressed them to any lady in the land,
would entail on him from some of her gentlemen friends
that form of punishment known as "condign." In the
cabman's case it would be interpreted as wanton rudeness
and insult. Why should it be construed as anything
else in the case of an author who thinks himself charged
with the twofold mission, first, to select the nastiest
possible subject, and, second, to write upon it in the
nastiest possible way?

Just exception may be taken to much of our popular

literature, on the ground that the ideals with which it presents us are, in numberless instances, so low and unworthy. There is no possibility of any of us living nobly unless we have set before us noble ideals. To supply these is one of the high vocations of Literature, one of the grandest missions it can fulfil. That it has in the main risen so nobly to the requirements of its high calling, is matter for profoundest thankfulness. In the book world, as Mrs. Browning many years ago affirmed, there is no lack of God's saints and kings. In the roads and byways of literature one meets with many a prophet who allures to higher things and leads the way. Many an inspiring personality do we fall in with who gives our life an upward bias, and lifts us an inch or two nearer the stars. But, alas! we meet not seldom also with those whose tendency is to lower our spiritual vitality, and to depress and flatten us by confronting us with low and unworthy ideals of what we ought to be and do. "The worst sign of an age," says Dr. Kerr, "is not evil living, but low standards"; and that the standards of living are being lowered in our day, no one can doubt who cares to study the ideal of life to which much of our literature gives its sanction. Take up some of our popular novels, and see how life is almost invariably contemplated in strict detachment from the grand objects and deepest interests of life itself. They seem to go upon the principle that, if you would "see life steadily and see it whole," you must look at it through the windows of a London club or a Paris saloon. The general impression left upon the mind is something like this, that life is a certain brief span of existence to be trifled away, or

sported away, or sinned away, as seems good to the liver
of it—an interval of a few passing years to be spent in
vivacious idling, or clever fooling.   Life—it is a frolic,
a jest, a pantomime, a picnic, or a pleasure-party.   Life
—it is but an affair of dressing and promenading, of
gossiping and tea-drinking, of tennis-playing and story-
telling, of cards and billiards, of tavern-frequenting and
theatre-going.   Or, if not a fribble, it is a moan, a yawn,
a fit of *ennui*; if not a tripping dance, it is a dead march.
Life—it is but an occasion given us for the compassing
of a little profitable wickedness, for cutting a figure in
society, or scraping together a little heap of lucre, or
achieving some little inch-high distinction.   If one were
to take that solemn question, " What is your life ? " and
go through the world with it, putting it to one and
another as he met them, what sorrowful answers he would
get, if men spake honestly ; but more saddening still
would be the answers, were he to take the same inquiry
into the realm of fiction, and put it to the heroes and
heroines that people that region.   In Hawley Smart's
novel, *Social Sinners*, the life of the hero is briefly
epitomised thus :—

" Having devoted the springtime of his life to revel and
extravagance, its early summer to shifts, expedients, and
practices not good to look back upon, he resolved to devote
its noontide to money - making and respectability.   To
turn water-drinker is certainly the greatest change an
habitual inebriate can arrive at.   I don't go so far as to
say that Sir Frederick intended to fly from the nadir
of vice to the zenith of austerity ; but he had come to the
determination to what our French neighbours call *rangé*
himself." [1]

[1] *Social Sinners*, ii. p. 260.

Suppose for a moment we raise the question, What are the constituent and vital principles of true happiness? it may be interesting to inquire what sort of replies we shall be likely to gather from the representations of modern light literature. We shall find an immense assemblage of fine sentiments on that subject among the accomplished writers of our time, but the ideal they have sketched for us is extremely unsatisfactory. How few of them have even grasped the elementary truth that happiness has its seat and centre within, and depends not for its birth or maintenance either on worldly condition or external circumstance; that what men need to make them happy is not a change of scene, or change of residence, or change of circumstances, but a change of mind, a change of interior disposition; that everything will be right when they are right themselves. Socrates declared he could not tell whether the king of Persia was a happy man or not, because he did not know his character. The modern novelist seems not yet to have discovered that the simple secret of happiness lies in contentment of mind and a conscience void of offence. He is too much inclined to go upon the theory that a man is happy because he is rich, because he lives in a fine house, because he is surrounded with all the adjuncts of a vulgar display, because he is ministered unto by a large retinue of servants who dance attendance upon him and do his slightest bidding; or he is happy because society has awarded him some small certificate of honour, or because he has vanquished some social rival, or because he has been returned to Parliament, or his yacht has won at the regatta, or his horse come in first at the Derby. This kind of teaching is constantly inculcated by Mr. George Gissing :—

" Happiness is the nurse of virtue," said Jasper.

" And independence the root of happiness," answered Amy.

" True, the glorious privilege of being independent."

" Yes, Burns understood the matter."

" Ha ! Isn't the world a glorious place ? "

" For rich people."

" Yes, for rich people. How I pity the poor devils."

So it is insinuated that condition makes the man. Virtue is the consequence of wealth. High character is only possible to the fortunate and well-to-do. Existence is only endurable with abundant leisure, easy circumstances, comfortable surroundings, plenty of attendants, and an uninterrupted round of social functions. It seems a needless assertion of a trite and commonplace truth, that it is not in the power of mere externalities like these to confer happiness, any more than a golden crown can cure the headache, or a silver slipper the gout. Outward things such as a passion for acquisitiveness may accumulate, have no more to do with a man's inner life or mental condition than the clothes he wears, or the odds and ends he carries in his pocket. Our writers of fiction know this as well as any moralist or preacher, yet they constantly treat it in their writings as if it were an ascertained illusion. They preach from the hackneyed text enunciated by Becky Sharp: " I think I could be a good woman if I had £5000 a year." They write precisely as if the old distinction between what a man *is* and what a man *has*, between the contents of his soul and the contents of his ledger, were no longer valid, or as

if the old words of world-wide import had never been
uttered by the Greatest of all instructors: "A man's
life consisteth not in the abundance of the things that
he possesseth." "A cottage," says James Hamilton,
"will not hold the bulky furniture and sumptuous
accommodation of a mansion; but if God be there, a
cottage will hold as much happiness as might stock a
palace."

Again, in our mental rambles through the wide fields
of modern popular literature, let us take with us the
inquiry, What ideals of heroes and heroism are held up
for our admiration? The inquiry is an important one,
in view of the fact that there is a strong tendency in
human nature to hero-worship, and in view also of that
other fact, which has so often been commented on, that
the minds of well-informed people are often more stored
with characters from fiction than with characters from
biography, or history, or even from real life around
them. We talk about these characters as if they were
real flesh and blood entities; we enter into their experience, adopt their principles, imitate their actions. What
sort of heroes and heroines, then, are our modern authors
sending on to the stage, and how far is the contemplation
of them calculated to inspire and improve us? Well,
let it be gladly acknowledged that in many instances
they are grand creations, which immediately evoke from
every reader that instinctive testimony to the heroic
which God has planted in the heart of humanity. Many
of them have been promoted to a permanent place among
the *Lares* and *Penates* of the mind. Like those of
Scott, Thackeray, and Dickens, they have come to be

"cathedrally enthroned" in our affections. Sometimes
in our enthusiasm we have been in danger of making
idols of them, and the angel voice has not been unneeded,
"See thou do it not," for we were coming perilously near
to Mr. Carlyle's hero-worship. But these instances are
sadly counterbalanced and discounted by a host of others,
which make it painfully evident that by many fashionable writers it is no longer considered necessary to construct your hero out of what is truly great or noble in
our nature. Meaning to hold up to the reader's admiration a great man, many modern authors have only succeeded in depicting a greedy one, a vengeful one, a clever
or a self-complacent one. In their way of thinking,
greatness is too often the equivalent for the possession of
a certain set of material advantages, for social elevation,
or bloated plutocracy, or unscrupulous success. What is
their so-called hero often but a selfist or a cynic, some
lounger about the world in yacht or railway carriage,
some money-king or knowing man of the world, some
good liver or good fellow, some prince of the turf or
expert in baccarat and loo, some "botanist in woman-
kind," some languid Agnostic, or some young Realist " who
hasn't an ideal at eighteen and is *blasé* at twenty, the
only thing that would interest him being perhaps a new
vice." [1] These creatures of fiction are seldom troubled
with any principles, and their ethical code is never inconveniently stringent. As a specimen of their elastic
and accommodating morality, we cannot do better than
reproduce a passage or two from the well-known novel,
Without Dogma. The hero's conscience is troubling him

[1] Rita's *A Gender in Satin*, p. 78.

for his cruel and treacherous treatment of Aniela, and this is how he moralises :—

" These are ridiculous scruples. I have broken ties far different from these without the slightest twinge of conscience. . . . One prick of conscience more or less, what does it matter? We do worse things continually to which the disappointment I caused Aniela is mere childishness. A conscience that can occupy itself with such peccadilloes must have nothing else to do. There is about the same proportion of such kinds of crime to real ones as our conversations on the terrace to real life." [1]

In one of these " conversations on the terrace," one day, about a divorce suit, Aniela says to him, " You can prove anything, and yet when one does wrong, conscience tells us ' It is wrong, it is wrong ! ' " Thinking this over afterwards, the hero finds the standard of morality thus suddenly uplifted far too lofty and unbending for him, and expresses himself accordingly :—

" In this ethical code of hers there are no extenuating circumstances. As, according to it, the wife belongs to her husband, she who gives herself to another does wrong. There are no discussions, or reflections, no considerations— there is the right hand for the righteous, and the left for sinners, God's mercy above all—but nothing between, no intermediate place." [2]

And scarcely less objectionable than this low-pitched morality is the kind of knowing man-of-the-worldism which the novelist puts into the mouth of hero and heroine, and which is often made to do duty for a moral philosophy, or even supplies the place of a religion. We cull an excellent specimen from Hawley Smart's novel,

[1] Henryk Sienkiewicz's *Without Dogma*, p. 81.

[2] *Ibid.*, p. 261

Social Sinners. To his young cousin, Arthur Riversley, Sir Frederick volunteers the following piece of paternal advice :—

"Still in the blind state of puppydom! Now, don't be riled, but listen to me. I, recollect, have been some fifteen years collecting this little budget of wisdom I am going to transmit to you in considerably less than as many minutes. Society, at its best, will entertain you if you amuse it, and will drop you, as a rule, upon the first suspicion of your wanting a twenty-pound note. Society saps your energy, saps your finance. Half a dozen good attorneys are fifty times more valuable acquaintances to you than half the peerage would be at present. You have a weakness for the great world? Good. Score off your own bat and it is the great world comes to you, and then—be somewhat exclusive and know those only who may be of use to you, who wield real power. Queens of beauty, if you will, if they sway men who hold power, or command the whim, toy, ribbon that you have set your heart on. Never overlook, yet never overrate the power of women in the game of life."[1]

Polonius' advice to Laertes comes far short of this! As a fine specimen of low prudence, of the shallow lore of life, of the set maxims which might be put down for the headlines in the copy-books of selfish getting-on-ism, this could not well be surpassed. But more deleterious than speech like this is the gospel which John Ruskin assures us "is now the loudest that is preached in our Saxon tongue," and none preach it more loudly than the modern novelist, the gospel which is for ever telling you that evil things are pardonable and you shall not die for them; and that good things are impossible and you need not live for them. This is, alas! too often the deadening

[1] Hawley Smart's *Social Sinners*, vol. ii. pp. 176–177.

and benumbing message which hangs like dripping icicles about the lips of hero and heroine. Altogether these fictitious personages are responsible for much of that lowering of tone, and letting down of standards, that debasing of the moral currency, and depreciation of the Ideal, which is now recognised by men who have understanding of the times, as one of the most disquieting symptoms of the age we live in. If we remember right, it is the author of *The Gentile Life* who declares that " were all the world composed of Byron's heroes—Laras, Conrads, Cains, Manfreds, Don Juans—it could not exist for half a century ; in ten years it would be a hell." It would be equally interesting to conceive the kind of world we should have were it exclusively populated with human beings bearing any close resemblance to those whose portraits have been hung for our benefit on the walls of Modern Fiction. Imagine the effect if a few of these heroes and heroines were congregated in the same village ! That village would be neither safe nor habitable. Who among us would have the courage to live in it ?

Our fiction, like our fabrics, is largely governed by fashion. The latest vogue in contemporary literature is the so-called " religious novel "—an evolution peculiar to the times we live in, which may be said to be the direct outcome of the deep and increasing interest taken in speculation directed toward the other life and the world to come. When we hear of a " religious " novel, there is something reassuring in the very name, and we turn to it with some degree of hopefulness, only, however, to be quickly disillusioned, for as a general rule it will be found that the " religious " novel is the most irreligious of all.

The inseparable adjuncts that usually accompany it have
been described by a writer in the *National Review* as
consisting chiefly in bits of "suggestive" writing; in
passages which can scarcely be called "doubtful," because,
unfortunately, there can be no possible doubt about their
meaning; strongly coloured descriptions of illicit love-
making; lengthy music-hall episodes, in which the sensuality is thinly veiled.   Under the pretence of attacking
vice, the writer commonly contrives to minister to vicious
appetite by dealing copiously in the pathology of evil,
and by a free indulgence in the frankness of French
Realism.   The religion usually comes in in the shape of
some discussion about miracle, or the inspiration of the
Bible, some disquisition about heredity, some bit of
specious philosophising about pantheism, spiritism, or
hypnotism, or some treatment of occult forces, of theosophy, or faith-healing, of dreams, or ghost-lore, or reincar-
nation.   Once the cry used to be, " Give us romance and
adventure "; then it changed to, " Give us the detective
story "; then it came to be, " Give us the sex-problem
story "; now it has changed again, and the cry at present
seems to be, " Give us the Agnostic who perverts the
curate in twenty minutes," or, " Give us the curate who
converts the Agnostic in the last chapter."   Indeed, in
versatile capability for receiving and voicing whatever in
contemporary thought or life may for the moment stir or
interest society, the novel has come to be not far behind
the newspaper.   Hence it is not to be wondered at that
in modern fiction so large a place should have been
assigned to Religion.   Time was when it was considered
sacred in this respect.   Novelists hard up for a subject

did not consider themselves justified in encroaching on
territory which was universally regarded as lying outside
their precinct.   Until recently no author of note had
ventured to offer the public a caricature of the Church,
or a parody of a Biblical narrative under the form of a
romance.   But now these old-fashioned notions of reverence have been set at defiance, and a new departure has
been made, under the leadership of such writers as Hall
Caine and Marie Correlli.   Mr. Hall Caine tells us that
his desire has been " to depict, however imperfectly, the
types of mind and character, of creed and culture, of
social effort and religious purpose, which he thinks he
sees in the life of the England and America of the close
of the nineteenth century."   How far has this " colossal "
undertaking of his, as he himself with incomparable
modesty takes leave to describe his own work, successfully
accomplished the object which is here delineated ?   In
the opinion of many who may be considered advan-
tageously situated for forming a judgment on such a
matter, what we have in *The Christian* is not a faithful
portrait of the current religion, social effort, and prevail-
ing culture of these closing years of the waning century,
but rather a grotesque and offensive caricature.   Supposing we had no other source of information but this book
from which to glean our knowledge of the interior life
and inner workings of the Church of England in the
present day, would it not betray us into the grossest
misunderstanding of the true state of things ?   Do such
beings as Mr. Hall's monks, canons, prophets, and mis-
sionaries live and move in any average parish in the
Church of England ?   Have such creatures any real

existence outside the author's brilliant and fascinating chapters? The very fact that the proof-sheets of *The Christian* were submitted to a committee of experts, who were able to supply first-hand knowledge on the subjects treated, would seem to imply that the author was distrustful of his own knowledge, and felt himself insufficiently informed on what he was writing about. At all events, for a man to write his book first, and appeal afterwards to a company of experts for the authentication of his facts, is not a procedure calculated to inspire confidence. It is an established tradition of literature, that an author should only commit his ideas to print on such themes as he has made himself thoroughly familiar with by long and personal study and acquaintance. And what species of Christian has Mr. Hall Caine given us in John Storm? In his type of Christianity there is a distant and indistinct resemblance, perhaps, to that of Charles Kingsley, but then Charles Kingsley was neither an imbecile, a visionary, nor a hair-brained fanatic, and John Storm was all three. His principles and programmes have all the changefulness and shifting variety of a mutoscope. His ideas are so fluid and unsettled you can scarce arrest or detain them long enough to get any clear understanding of what they are. He is everything by turns and nothing long. To-day he is a modern Elijah thundering away in his pulpit, hurling fiery philippics at pewfuls of luxurious and pleasure-loving hearers. To-morrow he has divested himself of gown and surplice and donned the dress of a friar, having entered the monastery of " the Holy Gethsemane." Now he is kneeling before the Father Superior, solemnly taking on the vows of monasticism, but at the

next turn of the story we find him kneeling at the
marriage altar, taking on him the more congenial vows
of matrimony. Now he has purchased a chapel at Soho,
and anon has rushed away to the theatre to feast his
eyes on the triumph of Glory Quayle, as she entrances
the crowd with her clever performance. What he builds
up one day he throws down the next, and no sooner does
he climb up to some platform of apparent stability than
he kicks away the ladder by which he ascended, and
precipitates himself once more into some new slough.
He runs through the entire gamut of religious craze and
faddism, while simultaneously with this he carries on a
romance with a red-haired, hoydenish, music-hall heroine,
whose every other word is slang,—with the result that
his original enthusiasm for mission work in London
gradually sinks into a quite secondary and subsidiary
affair, and at the end of his erratic career he has nothing
to show but a series of futile attempts, a long list of
failures. And Mr. Hall Caine's hundred thousand readers,
we presume, are left to infer, if they are innocent or undiscerning enough to do so, that this is the average type
of sainthood that prevails in England and America in the
closing years of the nineteenth century ! If we are asked
what practical contribution does *The Christian* make
toward a solution of those complex problems of social
science and philanthropy with which it professes to deal,
we can only answer that we can discover none. We
turn over the pages, and there is not even a suggestion.
So far as indicating any remedy for the social evils that
confront us in such acute and aggravated forms in our
modern city life, there is nothing to help us,—we know

no more now than we did before *The Christian* was written.

Miss Marie Corelli, in the extremity of her desire to "go one better" than any previous dealer in sensationalism, and as if to disabuse our minds once and for all of the antiquated notion that any subject could be considered too sacred for treatment by the novelist, has decided to select the most sacred of all, and exploit it for the purposes of romance, with a view to producing a cheap effect. In her own peculiar style—and her style has been described by an admiring critic as 'appallingly' fine—she has retold the story of the World's Tragedy, and become the authoress of a Fifth Gospel, in comparison with which, according to some of her reviewers, the other four are but tame and impotent. "What, then, is it inconceivable"—we quote from a eulogy the authoress with charming modesty has permitted to be printed in her volume, *Barabbas*—"that the powerful pen of a cultured woman of genius should write a more potent picture of the World's Tragedy than was written by the fishermen of Judea?" In other words, the Gospel according to Corelli quite throws into the shade the Gospel according to Luke and John, and she herself declines not to accept the honours of a Fifth Evangelist. In our judgment Miss Corelli's genius has taken a most unhappy direction when it has invaded the sanctities of the New Testament, and utilised the story of Redemption as an episode in a love story on modern lines, with Caiaphas for the hero. To any adoring disciple of the Master the procedure comes little short of sacrilege. It jars on one's feelings, and grates on one's sense of propriety as painfully as would the singing of a comic song in St. Paul's Cathedral, giving lessons in botany on a mother's grave, or defacing a lovely landscape with some unsightly advertisement of Pears' Soap or Colman's Mustard. It is a profanation to reduce the story of our Lord's Passion to the level of a stage play and use it for the purposes of " thrill." We are not aware that any Agnostic or freethinker has ever taken greater liberties with the most sacred of all themes, or dared to give it a more unspiritual handling. No German Rationalist has ever ventured on such a line of treatment. Even Renan himself, with all his morbid vagaries of æsthetic sensuality, has scarcely perpetrated any grosser irreverence. We are quite aware that multitudes of readers profess unbounded admiration for the manner in which Miss Corelli has executed a task which was certainly beset with enormous difficulty ; they speak in terms of glowing panegyric about the " reasonableness and realism " of *Barabbas*, how much more potent and striking it is than the simple story of the Four ; but when we consider how much out of harmony it is with the recorded facts of the Gospel, and how directly it contradicts its spirit, how full the book is of anachronisms and inaccuracies, it would be much truer to say of it, in the language of one of its most incisive reviewers, " It is the Gospel as an extremely ill-instructed apocryphal writer bent on sensation might have given it to us, if almost unacquainted with Eastern usages." What the authoress has really succeeded in giving to the world is a Passion play, and all the overpowering objections to that innately profane species of entertainment apply with peculiar force to books like *Barabbas*.

5

Emboldened by the success of her experiment, Marie Corelli sought for another religious theme, and speedily hit upon one which was admirably adapted to her purpose. From the days of the Paulicians and Hussites there have always been a class of minds who have looked leniently on the Evil One, and even regarded him sympathetically as a wronged and suffering spirit. But it was reserved for our authoress to do him the honour of making him the infernal hero of a nineteenth century novel, in which he is alternately apologised for and panegyrised. Having rehabilitated Barabbas and Judas Iscariot, it was but a step to the rehabilitation of Lucifer himself. In the *Sorrows of Satan* the traditional view is dismissed in favour of another, in which he is no longer the vulgar diabolic being he has so long been taken for, but one who does his work of devil reluctantly, and who stands to God in the attitude of servant rather than that of rebel or enemy. At a flourish or two of Miss Corelli's magical wand, Satan is transformed, not simply into an "angel of light," but into a spruce modern gentleman of most affable manners, who has all the marks of wealth upon him, has a coronet on his visiting card, calls the Prince of Wales his friend, keeps a French cook, lives at a London hotel, and engages a private bath of his own. Utterly unlike any other Mephistopheles that has ever cut a figure in literature; no liar or murderer from the beginning is he, though the old Book happens to say so; no ghostly adversary of souls going about seeking whom he may devour, but quite a genial and courteous spirit, who, instead of plotting your moral overthrow or compassing your destruction, will probably invite you to lunch, or get up a picnic for you! Talk of Milton and Marlowe's conception of Satan after this, they are not in it with that of Marie Corelli!

It is to the credit of our authoress that her motives are above suspicion, and that she appears to be animated with a sincere desire to take sides with orthodoxy, and champion the faith once delivered to the saints against its modern assailants. She seems to consider it her special providential mission to combat Materialism, never missing an opportunity of coming down in sledge-hammer style on unoffending atoms and molecules, towards which she appears to entertain, for some reason or other, a spiteful grudge. In her a new prophetess, a mother in Israel, has arisen, whose lifework it shall be to silence all unbelievers, to put to flight the armies of Tyndallism, and make a clean end of the Atomic Theory. But while Miss Corelli takes to herself the whole armour of God and poses as a defender of the faith, it must be confessed her line and methods of defence are decidedly peculiar, and give rise to evils infinitely more menacing than those from which they would protect us. Her apology for Christianity is calculated to bring it into as much disrepute as any Voltairian assault that has ever been made upon it. Protecting the Bible from infidel attack, she herself manages to destroy all reverence for it. In the process of saving it from the inroads of Materialism, she plays into the hands of the Materalists. Depriving them of some of their old weapons, she unwittingly provides them with a number of new ones, which will serve their purpose equally well. It is well to exterminate the evils of Agnosticism, Positivism, and

Materialism, but if in the process of doing so we call into
being a new set of evils every whit as formidable, in the
shape of obscurantism, hysteria, and irrationalism, are we
much better off than before ? It is well to refute
unbelief, but if the refutation itself has a strong
tendency to the manufacture of unbelief in other
directions, what advantage have we gained ? Miss
Corelli's apologetics are unfortunately attended with this
very serious drawback, which will become more apparent
as we proceed. Her writings strikingly exemplify this
observation of a writer in the *Quarterly* : " Great and
manifold as have been the mischiefs wrought by unbelief,
it may be questioned whether any have surpassed the
evils of the reaction it has called forth—a reaction
which despises logic, turns faith into mythology, canonises
the absurd, and distorts the Christian so as to make him
at once an imbecile, a visionary, and a murderous
fanatic." As a champion of orthodoxy and defender of
the faith, Miss Corelli places all her reliance on
Electricity. In the preface to her *Romance of Two
Worlds*, she magnifies her office by this oracular deliverance : " If ever there was a time for a new apostle to
arise and preach his grandly simple message anew, that
time is now." In the person of the gifted authoress
herself the new apostle has arisen, and the " grandly
simple " message is published and promulgated for us in the
celebrated " Electric Creed," which extends over twenty-
two pages. This creed of hers, she assures us, " has for its
foundation Christ alone," and " its tenets are completely
borne out by the New Testament." The sum and
substance of that creed may be reduced to this single

sentence : " Believe in the electric spirit within you, and cultivate its powers to the utmost." If the reader in his innocence inquires why " electric "? he is answered magisterially that "God is a shape of pure Electric Radiance "; and if you have any doubt about it, you are told to search the Scriptures, and you will find that all the visions and appearances of the Deity there chronicled are " electric " in character. Christ is Himself " the Source and Centre of the earth's electric currents," and the object of His coming into the world was to " establish electric communication between us and God." The most remarkable events in Old and New Testament are but striking instances of electrical phenomena. In this category we are to place the thunder and lightning of Sinai, the fire in the burning bush which burned but did not consume, Elijah's fiery chariot of ascension, the radiance of the mysterious Fourth One who trod the fiery furnace with the three youths of Babylon, the shining effulgence of the Transfiguration, the lightning countenance of the angel at the tomb, the tongues of fire at Pentecost, the celestial radiance that smote Paul with sunstroke on the road to Damascus—all these were electrical theophanies, special manifestations of the one ever-present fluid which in physics we call electricity ; but which in the unseen world is known as the Divine Spirit. The conception of the Divine Being to which the writer here commits herself is certainly an amazing one. In one sentence it is affirmed of the Deity that He is a pure spirit, and in the next that He is an emanation of electricity, with definite and measurable shape. Yet Miss Corelli expresses the greatest surprise that any reader should see in this anything approaching to either a contradiction or a blasphemy. Her electric creed seems to absolve the believer in it from all necessity of recognising any distinction between a current that runs along a wire, and intelligence and will that have nothing in common with these imponderable but purely physical agencies. The creed has this additional advantage to recommend it, according to its author, that it is very "simple and makes all marvels easy." How easy of acceptance it makes all the Bible miracles, we have just seen. Supernaturalism need occasion no difficulty to faith any more, for what we have been accustomed to regard as strictly supernatural occurrences are after all purely natural, they are perfectly explicable without going outside the order of nature itself, and instead of exclaiming with superstitious awe, "This is the finger of God," the correct exclamation to break silence with is, "This is the finger of electricity!" Thus Marie Corelli's defence of miracle consists in abolishing the miraculous by reducing it all to the level of pure Naturalism. There never was a more perfect example of what the Germans call "throwing out the child with the bath."

But the electric power can do more than "make marvels easy." The range of its operations is something prodigious. Arraying herself in the venerable garments of Theosophy, and lowering her voice to the oracular whisper of occult science, the writer hastens to assure us that sometimes it is a force and gives people a smart shock; anon it is "a germ of Divinity within them which is capable of the highest clairvoyance and spiritual ability"; it enables her in trance to perceive the Central Planet; shows her that "everything is circular"; makes angels and demons as palpable and familiar as everyday acquaintances; and conducts her heroes up from earth on a celestial excursion to Saturn, Jupiter, and the Centre. If the reader will only cherish the electric germs within him, the unseen spirits that float, like the saints in the pictures, about this terraqueous globe of ours, will all become visible to his clarified optics in Swedenborgian vision. Nay more, in the triumphant flight of ecstasy, and the determined exertion of that will-power which ascends to celestial heights far beyond the reach of astronomer's telescope, there is nothing to prevent his reaching the Central Planet, the abode of the Almighty Himself. Should he travel far enough to reach it, he will find the Almighty seated there, and "before His eyes every thought and word of every inhabitant of every world is reflected in lightning-language as easily as we receive telegrams." Where are your Atheists and Materialists now? Our authoress has given them a knockdown blow, from the effects of which they shall not easily recover. Who shall doubt the existence of a Heaven any longer? Has not the authoress of a *Romance of Two Worlds* been on a visit to the Central Planet, and got safely back again to tell us all about it? What mocking Sadducee but must be convinced of the existence of angel and spirit when, if he only consents to become an adept of Miss Corelli, he may see more of them with his naked eye than Jacob saw at Bethel or John in Patmos. If he insists on a more realistic demonstration still, let him peruse *Ardath* and have his doubts for ever silenced, for is it not one of the leading episodes in this strange book that a fair young angel

spirit reincarnates and visibilises herself, that she may
appear once more in the body and tabernacle among
men, that she may form for herself a desirable marriage
connection with some young flesh-and-blood aspirant for
matrimony.   She succeeds in the object of her mission,
and lived happily ever after with the man of her choice
in a quiet vale among the mountains.   We had thought
that spirits in the glory-land were done with all fleshly
ties, and neither married nor were given in marriage any
more, but were henceforth like the angels of God, as the
Bible gives us to understand ; but in Marie Corelli's Bible
it is not so written, for the prospect of marriage has still
such a fascination for these fair spirits in Paradise, that
they will actually forego the Heaven of cherubim and
seraphim and revisit this cold world of storm and trouble,
if they may taste once more for a few years on earth a
little connubial bliss.   Now, since angels reincarnate
themselves repeatedly in this manner, and revisit the
glimpses of the moon, he would surely be a prejudiced
and unreasonable Materialist who would still persist in
his disbelief of the reality of spiritual beings and a
spiritual world.   As to God Himself, who can deny His
existence any longer ?   Has not the " Electric Creed "
proclaimed it that He is to be found seated like some
magnified and non-natural man at the Central Office of
the Universe, if not like Levi at the receipt of custom,
yet like some Chief Operator at the receipt of telegrams ?
This is Marie Corelli's conception of Omniscience, and
yet she is never weary of expressing surprise that any
one should ever have smiled at the absurdity, or detected
a trace of blasphemy, in these her electrical beliefs !   If

this is her conception of Divinity, which of us would not infinitely prefer the Agnosticism which prostrates itself before the Great Unknowable in deep and sacred nescience, and hesitates so much as to name Him, to define His nature, or invest Him with a single attribute, to this irreverent Gnosticism which indulges in a coarse morphology, and attempts to penetrate Divine mysteries with Swedenborgian clairvoyance, and read the arcana of the universe by the light of Occultism and Eastern Theosophy. The marvel is that the British public should ever have taken this crude amalgam of pseudo-science, Neoplatonism, hysteria, and Blavatskyism seriously; but then, as a reviewer remarks, there have been people who took Lemuel Gulliver seriously. And could anything well be more ludicrous than the war which Marie Corelli wages against Materialism, with forces which are themselves as purely material as any that can be weighed in scales, or seen through the lens of a microscope. We should like to know what advantage the Electric Creed has over the Atomic Theory? Is electricity a Christian force, is there anything specially sacred about it, or anything that makes it the natural confederate of orthodoxy, any more than those atoms and molecules on which Miss Corelli pours such volleys of bitter scorn? The one is no more spiritual than the other; both are material, and to cast out Materialism by forces which are themselves Materialistic, is but another form of casting out Satan by Beelzebub. If a resort to electricity suffices to overthrow the Materialistic philosophy of the day, may we not expect some other philosophic novelist to arise who will pin his faith to phosphorus, seeing that the think-

ing power is so largely dependent on an adequate supply
of this substance to the brain ? and he in turn may be
superseded by some other prophet who will select carbon
as his element, and proceed to construe the universe in
terms of carbon, and celebrate its virtues as the only
true counteractive to Materialism, inasmuch as it is
proved to be an indispensable constituent without which
organic life cannot exist.   If you can fight Materialism
with magnetism and electric batteries and torpedo
shocks, you can certainly fight it just as effectively with
agencies which you can buy at the drug-store, or take
from the shelf of a chemist's laboratory.   There is no
reason why we should discard Mr. Huxley's pail of
protoplasm in favour of Marie Corelli's leyden jar.
" But in sober earnest," as one of her reviewers declares,
in a recent article contributed to the *London Quarterly*,
" Miss Corelli does not know what is meant by Materialism ; and as regards her Christianity, it is a debased
offspring of the Neoplatonic school, daubed with the
colours of a hundred superstitions.   It has not come out
of the New Testament.   Its origin and history may be
traced through heresies without number ; and the faith
which it involves or demands is, in spite of her protesta-
tions, the result of an hysteria so hollow and earthborn
that it does not add one syllable to our knowledge of
things divine." [1]   Woe betide you, however, if you refuse to
homologate and countersign those peculiar views of Miss
Corelli.   If you would be saved—saved at least from
the vituperation and abuse of which our authoress has
such unlimited command—it is necessary above all things

[1] Article on " Religious Novels" in *Quarterly Review*, October 1898.

that you should believe the "Electric Creed." If you have the hardihood to continue unbelieving, you shall be pelted with abusive epithets, and have all kinds of depreciatory adjectives hurled at your defenceless head. The clergy, for some reason or other, have incurred Miss Corelli's displeasure, and, in consequence, have had the misfortune to get a very bad mark opposite their name, and to be written down in her immortal page as " the morbidities and microbes of national disease." For what precise offence they have merited this delicate and truly feminine bacteriological allusion, does not exactly transpire, unless it be that, like the intractable and unresponsive children in the market-place, they have not danced when she piped to them, neither mourned when she has lamented. If we might hazard a conjecture, it would be that the clerical world has not perhaps been so ready as some other worlds to welcome the advent of a fifth Evangelist; they have not entered as sympathetically as they might into the sorrows of Satan; they have been slow of heart to believe in the " Electric Creed "; they have not duly exhorted their hearers to cultivate the electric germs within them; they have not seen their way to organise aërial trips to the Central Planet, nor to resolve all things into magnetism, as the old Greek philosophers resolved them into fire or water, nor to adopt a lightning-rod as an appropriate coat of arms for their Christianity. Do you, good reader, take care that you sympathise not with this unreasoning clerical heterodoxy, lest you also should find yourself classed some of these days with " the morbidities and microbes of national disease." But the clergy may well be reconciled to the scant courtesy meted out to them by Miss Corelli, when they can console themselves with the remembrance that even Apostles have failed to command her respect. In *Barabbas* she has travestied the character of St. Peter, and done him the terrible injustice of making him an accomplice of Judas on the dark betrayal night. St. Paul has fared even worse, for, according to Marie Corelli, Paul had no valid claim to any calling or election as an Apostle, and she brings against him the railing accusation that he was the person chiefly responsible for "upsetting the pristine simplicity and beauty of the whole Christian faith." " Nothing," it has been said, " is sacred to a sapper," or, we might add, to a latter-day nineteenth century religious novelist. There is scant respect even for the chief of Apostles. Pauline claims are derided, and Pauline inspiration dismissed as a superstition. It is not the first time Paul has had his apostleship challenged. The Judaisers of his own day called it in question, and were vigorously retorted on in the Epistle to the Galatians, to which Miss Corelli might still be referred as the very best rejoinder to her insinuation. One sometimes wishes Paul were alive again to reply to some of his modern assailants. As to his upsetting the primitive simplicity and beauty of the early Christian faith, this view has attracted so much attention in recent times that it may be worth while to devote a word to it in passing. We must get back from the Pauline Epistles, we are told, to Christ Himself. Pauline meddling and interference with the truth which was originally transmitted to us by the Master Himself, has only warped and spoiled it. In an unlucky hour he seized upon it and made it technical, ran it into the moulds of logic and intellectualism, and turned into a theology what was originally given to us by Jesus as a religion. Hence the cry has become popular, "Back to Christ." And, indeed, there can be no mistake about it, that for those who want rid of the doctrines of the Trinity, the Atonement, Regeneration, Justification by Faith, Union to God, Predestination, and the Last Judgment, they can get quit of these much more easily if St. Paul is out of the way. Paul is the great obstructionist to the carrying out of their designs, and if only his teaching can be shelved, an immense subtraction will have been made from the materials which destructive criticism has to deal with. The policy, "Back to Christ," is supposed to insure simplicity, and it is also claimed for it that it does honour to Jesus. Simplicity, however, may be bought too dear, and it is a very questionable kind of honour to do to Jesus to slight Him in the person of those whom He has ordained as His commissioned messengers and custodians of the truth, and of whom He declared so solemnly when He sent them forth, " He that receiveth you receiveth Me, and he that despiseth you despiseth Him that sent you." Moreover, we fail to see where the honour comes in, if we deliberately ignore or set aside His own words—words spoken by Him on that day when He no longer spake in parables, but told them all things plainly. On that occasion He explicitly acknowledged the incompleteness of His own teaching, and declared that very much was still held in reserve which He had wished to communicate, had their capacity been equal to its reception : " I have yet many things to

say to you, but ye cannot bear them now." In the
same discourse He plainly indicated how His teaching
would be completed. The Spirit of truth would come,
who would teach them all things, bring His words to
their remembrance, and guide them into all truth. If
in the Epistles we have not a supplement and expansion
of His own teaching, had these promises ever a fulfilment?
In these promises we have the guarantee for the inspiration and authority of the apostolic form of Christianity.
If the Apostles were led into *all* truth under the direct
tutelage and tuition of the Spirit of God, are we not
under obligation to receive the truth into which these
Spirit-led men were guided? It is therefore a poor
way of glorifying Christ to reject the Epistles in order
to do honour to the Gospels, for the Gospels themselves
proclaim their own incompleteness, and refer us for the
fuller knowledge of the truth of God to a subsequent
Teacher. Back to Christ by all means, but when we do
get back to Him, He sends us on to the Apostles. This
policy of cutting our New Testament in two, running a
line of cleavage through the midst of it, the one half
having a supreme authority, and the other no authority
at all, is one which goes clean in the face of the teaching of Jesus, and one, therefore, which should have no
countenance from any disciple of His.

Though something like the germ of the modern religious
novel may be said to have had a pre-existence in earlier
works, to Mr. Mallock perhaps belongs the credit of being
its pioneer in recent times; but it was not till Mrs. Ward
had given to the world *Robert Elsmere* that an appetite
was developed for this particular form of literature.

That *Robert Elsmere* is a clever and brilliant book, goes without saying. It is impossible not to be impressed with the subtle skilfulness of its workmanship, with the ardour that inspires it, with the ability, strenuousness, and erudition which the writer has brought to bear upon her task. All that talent and pains and polish, and wide reading and fine writing can do to make the book effective, has been done, and yet all these in combination cannot atone for that fatal absence of insight which is the chief limitation on Mrs. Ward's genius. In her attitude to Christianity she has always impressed us as one who has only an extern acquaintance of it; one who takes her observations and forms her judgment of the Great Temple from outside, surveying its exterior with an eye that misses nothing, advancing perhaps as far as its portico or outer court of the Gentiles, but never once penetrating into its sunlit interior, nor ever catching a glimpse of the glorious Shekinah that dwells within the veil in its Holy of Holies. "With all her study," says a writer in the *British Weekly*, "she is always on the outside, on the outside of the human heart, on the outside of every religion but her own ghostly creed. She is, and promises to remain, the most conclusive demonstration of the fact that labour and calculation can never stand for sight." Only an outsider of this description, having no deep interior acquaintance with Christianity, could picture Robert Elsmere, otherwise described as a man of large information and wide intellectual culture, as yielding up all his faith in supernatural religion because he had come to have some doubts about the authenticity of the Book of Daniel. Suppose he had, what was there in that to disturb his personal relation to Jesus Christ, or lead him voluntarily to deprive himself of the spiritual benefactions and boons of grace which that Christ brings to man's weary and heavy-laden spirit ?   The faith of a Christian does not stand or fall with questions of Biblical Criticism. It seems strange, too, that so thoughtful a writer as Mrs. Ward should have pictured Elsmere as surrendering the citadel of his faith under the infidel assaults of Roger Wendover, without ever arguing back or striking a blow in his own defence.   There is no argumentative dialogue, for the representative of the Christian side of things has not a word to say for himself, makes out no case, and helplessly yields up all the treasures of his faith the moment the squire points at him a few dogmatic denials, and calls on him to stand and deliver.   The book speaks of " the long wrestle " between the two men, but of this wrestle there is no sign or trace.   All the wrestling there is is done by one of the combatants, for the other makes no show of resistance.   The squire has it all his own way, and wins an easy victory.   As Mr. Gladstone happily phrases it, " it is a fictitious battle between the two on the subject of religion, where the one side is a pæan and the other a blank.   A great creed with eighteen centuries of testimony behind it cannot find an articulate word to say in its defence."   Is it possible that Mrs. Ward purposely declined to argue the question at stake, because she secretly felt her inability to demolish Christianity that way ?   It looks so like it, that if anyone chooses to infer as much, he does her no injustice, for she has certainly left herself open to that insinuation.   Any arguments which are advanced in the book scarcely deserve the name, for they amount to nothing more than a series of dogmatic assertions and sneering allusions about the disinclination of the theological mind to examine evidence, about the value of testimony, about miracles being the invention of superstitious ages, rendered credible only by the universal preconception in their favour. If our religious beliefs are so tottering and insecure that they can really be shaken by a book like *Robert Elsmere*, we shall find it difficult to retain any respect for them, and to be bereft of them altogether cannot any longer be considered a very serious deprivation. They are not worth keeping, if they can be upset by the shallow sophisms and plausibilities of Squire Wendover. Mr. S. B. M'Kinney's remark about *Robert Elsmere*, and the altogether disproportionate opposition it called forth when the book first made its appearance, is very pertinent: " The citadel that shakes when a drunken man falls against it ought at once to be demolished; and the ship that hoists signals of distress for fear of collision with a jelly-fish cannot be destroyed too soon."

The influence of so strenuous a writer as Mrs. Humphry Ward, as might have been expected, has made itself felt on not a few other novelists belonging to the same order. In *Sheba*, by the well-known authoress " Rita," we have a mild imitation, a feeble echo of *Robert Elsmere*. Sheba, the heroine of the book, has a polemical cast of mind, and holds long theological dialogues with her brother Hex. Her difficulties are with the Old Testament, in which she finds many stumbling-blocks to faith. She makes capital out of the hardening of Pharaoh's heart, which to her mind affords the clearest

6

evidence that the Jehovah of the old Hebrew Scriptures
is both cruel and unjust.   Her sympathy for the unhappy
Egyptian monarch is quite effusive.   She talks of him as
"poor Pharaoh," as though he had been harshly used
and terribly wronged by the Almighty.   But any Sabbath-
school teacher could have told her, that while the Bible
attributes the hardening of Pharaoh's heart to God, it
takes care to attribute it also in the very same passage
to Pharaoh himself; and the obvious explanation is that
Pharaoh was finally confirmed in his obstinacy by the
free exercise of his own proud self-will, the only part
God had in it being this, that He refrained from inter-
fering with that prerogative of freedom, and left the
wicked king to fall under the depraving influence of his
own self-made character.   When in scriptural phrase
God is said to harden the heart, it cannot be intended
that He exerts a positive malign influence upon men to
make them worse.   At most He can only be the negative
cause of the hardening by withholding from the sinner
the restraints of His Spirit, and leaving him to the
unrestrained tendencies of his own heart, and the un-
counteracted influences of his evil environment.   The
Divine Being does not impel or entice men to evil, but
He abandons those who abandon Him, and suffers them
to continue in their unsanctified obduracy till they become
derelict.   We have seen the matter illustrated in this
way.   Suppose a farmer to sow his field with thistle
seed.   In due time the crop appears, and it is covered
with thistles.   Who did it?   The Bible says, and the
best science says also, that God did it, for He it is who
endows the seed with vitality, causes it to germinate and

grow, and He alone supplies these skyey influences of air, moisture, and sunshine, without which growth of any kind would be impossible. But it would be an equally correct answer were we to say that the farmer himself did it, for undoubtedly he sowed the seed, without which there could have been no such deplorable harvest. If he had sown wheat or corn, he would have been rewarded with a crop of the same. So it is as between God and Pharaoh. Pharaoh sowed the seeds of obstinacy and rebellion, and God still maintained in operation His wise and beneficent law that all seed shall germinate, and that the nature of the seed shall determine the nature of the harvest. The farmer, and he alone, would be responsible for his harvest of thistles. Pharaoh, and he alone, was responsible for the hardness of his heart.

Then, again, to the questioning mind of Sheba a fresh difficulty presents itself in the story of Cain and Abel's offering. What harm did Cain do that his sacrifice should be rejected? Was it not better to bring to the altar a bloodless gift, in the shape of the fruits of the earth, than to kill lambs, and come before the Most High with hands sanguinary from the slaughter of unoffending creatures? Now, when we turn to the eleventh chapter of the Epistle to the Hebrews, we find it there expressly affirmed that "by faith Abel offered unto God a more excellent sacrifice than Cain, by which he obtained witness that he was righteous, God testifying of his gifts: and by it he being dead yet speaketh." Wherein lay the superiority of Abel's offering we are at no loss to discover. Not only was it presented in faith, and in the lowly spirit of obedience, but it proceeded on an entirely different view of sacrifice from that which commended itself to the mind of Cain. In the whole transaction the one brother represented the spiritual view, the other the carnal and the secular. Cain considered it enough to render the returns of gratitude for the fruits of the earth and such blessings as contributed to the comfort and enjoyment of life, but did not recognise the necessity of coming before God as a guilty sinner, needing a forgiveness which could only come to him through an oblatory sacrifice. Abel, on the other hand, whilst just as grateful as Cain for his temporal mercies, felt his need of pardon, cordially acquiesced in and consented to God's method of salvation by vicarious sacrifice, and proceeded throughout upon the principle that without shedding of blood there is no remission. He was not content therefore to bring to the altar an unbloody sacrifice, but singled out one of the firstlings of his flock, that by the shedding of its blood as an atonement for sin, he might solemnly express his faith in the great God-provided Victim for a world's offences, who would appear once in the end of the world to put away sin by the sacrifice of Himself. Cain thought a thank-offering sufficient; Abel took a deeper, truer view, and felt the necessity for a sin-offering, and " by it he being dead yet speaketh." That sacrifice of Abel's has a voice. It is vocal with a solemn message. It speaks, and what it says to all ages and lands is this: In coming to God you must approach Him through the medium of sacrifice. You must come depending on an atonement, seeking redemption through God's slain Lamb, even the forgiveness of sins. It is upon these grounds that the Apostle affirms the superior excellence of Abel's offering.

Now all this Biblical information was just as accessible to the authoress of *Sheba* as it is to us, but she did not care to avail herself of it, because her object simply was to wage a species of guerilla war against the Old Testament Scriptures.

Enough has been said to show, and in the body of the work it will become still more apparent, that in recent times there is a widespread tendency to look upon theology as a sort of open common or recreation-ground, where light minds may disport themselves, and give free play to all kinds of speculative vagary and extravaganza. The ancient and noble science of Theology has come in our day to be a special field for amateurs in which to try their apprentice hand and ventilate their crude and ill-considered opinions, a " feminine pastime," as Lord Lytton says in *Kenelm Chillingly*. Why it has been reduced to such a pass it would be curious to inquire. It certainly cannot be that it is any more easily mastered than other competing sciences, that it calls for less sustained or strenuous intellectual effort than other studies, or that its great ideas admit of more facile and rapid conquest than those of other departments of learning. But it lies close to human life, and touches at many points multiplied social interests. New ideas are constantly emerging, and those who share them think themselves competent to understand and refute the old. It seems to be commonly assumed that men of genius, simply because they are men of genius, have a perfect acquaintance of any subject on which they may choose to issue dogmata or make pronouncements; especially must they be presumed, as a matter of course, to have a perfect under-

standing of a subject so much upon men's tongues, and
so familiar to their ears from their cradles, as religion.
But men of genius can claim no exemption from the law,
any more than other men, that they must remain ignorant
of any subject, if they will not bestow upon it painstaking study, and give it earnest attention and candid
consideration. For this reason it often happens that men
of high intellectual culture live in religious communities,
and in the full blaze of religious enlightenment, and yet
display a profound ignorance of religion. They have
never made a study of it, never concentrated upon it any
prolonged or persevering regard, never candidly examined
its credentials, nor honestly investigated its claims to
their intellectual homage and assent. They live in a
little literary world, or a little art world, or a little
culture world of their own, and anything lying outside
its confines they do not think worthy of any serious
thought or attention; just as commercial men will sometimes live in their little money-world, and spend a lifetime of such complete absorption in the service of
mammon, that they have not so much as a side glance
or a passing notice for learning, religion, social recreation,
or anything else that is not governed by cash considerations, or that cannot be converted into money. They can
take a long drive through a beautiful region of country,
and take no notice of scenes entrancing enough in their
loveliness to set a poet crazy, and perceive not the flowers
that fringe their pathway with brightest colour, and hear
not the birds that make the woods vocal with their song,
because all the while their thoughts have been pre-
occupied with monetary considerations, with financial

plans and schemings, with processes of mental arithmetic, and sundry secular interests which constitute a moral obstruction to all higher vision. And in the same way a fragmentary and one-sided culture which leads a man to treat religion with neglect and contempt, which sets beauty above truth and goodness, makes art the supreme end of education, and schools and disciplines itself into a profound indifference to the great spiritual problems of life, cannot but narrow and belittle the man, cannot but contract his views, obscure his vision, and dwarf the true dimensions of his spiritual stature. In instances well-nigh innumerable the sneers of men of genius at religion prove and imply, not that these men, having given the subject their careful and candid attention, have felt constrained, after deliberate and painstaking investigation, to throw the weight of their great intellects against it, but only that they have neglected to think of it, that they have not taken pains to inform themselves about it, or to satisfy either their minds or their moral judgment of the justness and validity of its claims. In the first Christian century there were thoughtful and cultivated Romans to whom Christianity was a mere foreign superstition. Tacitus characterised it as "destructive"; Suetonius called it "new and noxious"; while Pliny the younger described it still more emphatically as "perverse and extravagant." Why did they designate it by these spiteful and contemptuous epithets? The only possible answer is that they passed a sweeping and hasty condemnation on what they did not comprehend, nor even thought it worth while to take the trouble to comprehend. Their pronouncement was not sustained by any adequate background of knowledge. They had not taken pains to inform themselves of the facts that contributed to the truth and establishment of the new religion which had entered so silently into history ; they had neither examined its vouchers, nor gauged its forces, nor measured its latent potencies, nor given its advocates a hearing. Eighteen centuries have come and gone, and there are men of letters to-day, thoughtful and cultivated too, whose disdain and contempt for Christianity is susceptible of the very same explanation. Like Tacitus, Suetonius, and Pliny, only far less excusable than they, they have denounced the Bible only because they have not read it, and condemned religion only because they were ignorant of what it was. The Christian religion has never suffered a grosser or more palpable injustice than has been inflicted upon it by the great and, in other respects, cultivated intellects, who have brought in a verdict against it without weighing the evidence, or hearing what it had to say for itself.

In these circumstances, it is not surprising that the trained and educated theologian should hold in slight estimation those literary divines who condemn religion without knowing what they condemn, and make war on the Bible, yet can scarce quote a text from it correctly, and show no further acquaintance with its contents than that which is implied in familiarity with certain scraps of Scripture which occur in the Prayer Book, or are heard in after - dinner conversation. Has not a very distinguished literary celebrity gravely referred his readers before now to Paul's *Second* Epistle to the Ephesians ? But while the professional theologian may be disposed to

smile superciliously at the flimsiness of what passes for
religious teaching, or does duty for religious argument, in
much of our popular literature, he forgets the literary
charm by which it is recommended, and makes far too
little allowance for the fact that, flimsy as it is, it has
found articulate expression in literature, that it will
circulate among thousands of readers, utterly unprovided,
as a rule, with any material to furnish a single refutation, and will come to them endorsed with the signature
of great names, and with the imposing recommendations
of genius.   Instead of taking no notice, or treating it
with silent contempt, the defender of Christianity will
be better advised if he proceeds at once to expose the
real character of what may be so destructively fascinating,
because it comes to the reader backed by the name of
some distinguished man of letters, who converts the
reputation he has earned in other departments of thought
into an instrument of unfair and injurious assault upon
religion.   "Good Heavens! has this narrow-minded tom-
foolery its literature?" is the exclamation which escapes
the lips of the hero in Mr. Watts-Dunton's novel, *Aylwin*,
when some story-books were appealed to as an authority
for a theory which he strongly disapproved of.   We have
often been tempted to break silence with some similar
ejaculation when we have found ourselves perusing some
piece of more than usually shallow scepticism, some
puerile assault on revelation, some contemptuous rejection of miracle, some irreverent pleasantry at the expense
of the Church or churchgoers, some old outworn heresy
dressed up in modern habiliments, its wrinkles smoothed
out with the paste of some literary bravery, some mani-

festo of Agnosticism, making a god of its own indifference
and a Bible of its own " Perhaps," some incoherent chatter
about Occult Science and Eastern Mysticism, or some
plausible attempt to trace our human genealogy to
ancestral apes or patriarchal pollywogs.   Good Heavens !
we have been inclined to exclaim, has this ·sort of thing
also been dignified with a literature ?   Yes, each and all
of these have their literature, and just because they have,
it is imperative on all those who would resist the errors of
the times and defend the Truth which was revealed from
Heaven eighteen centuries ago, to administer a counteractive, and expose their real character.

And, in further indication of the correct attitude for
the theologian to assume in the peculiar combination of
circumstances he is now confronted with, we would like
also to add that he should resolutely decline to surrender
his independence.   In matters of literary criticism and
adjudication he will of course always endeavour to exhibit
a becoming deference to the professional litterateur.   In
the domain of letters he will bow to the judgment of the
man of letters as presumably more just and accurate
than his own.   But when the literary class overstep the
frontier of their own province, and contemplate the
annexation of territory which is distinctively theological,
therein to set up a suzerainty of their own, the
theologian cannot but resist the encroachment.   It is his
bounden duty to preserve his independence of the secular
spirit, and popular literary opinion, in the interpretation
of Scripture, in the framing of his message, and the construction of his creed.   He is not going to humiliate
himself, or the science which he represents, by knocking

at the study doors of a few literary and scientific hiero-
phants, asking them kindly to come forth and tell him
the meaning of the Bible. He is not going to call in the
aid of physicist or belle-lettrist to frame for him the
articles of his belief. For him the one supreme
consideration is, what is the mind of God in revelation?
not what are the opinions of men in poetry, fiction, or
philosophy? He is more solicitous that his sails should
be filled with the breath of a Divine inspiration than
with the fitful gust of the *Zeitgeist*. He is prepared to
say with the sainted Leighton, "While so many other
voices are speaking for the times, let one poor wight
speak for Eternity." He refuses to belong to that
vacillating fraternity whose faith rises and falls with the
monthly issue of some leading review, with the periodic
pronouncements of some literary expert, or the latest
manifesto of some religious novelist. When irrespons-
ible scribblers would have him to exchange a sincere and
fruitful attachment to doctrines which he has tested and
proved by long study and acquaintance, for a universal
flirtation with all views in general that happen to come
in his way, he refuses to lend himself to such a proposal.
When the votaries of human culture would alter the
very contents of Christianity by claiming the right of
injecting their views into it, by way of liberalising it, and
getting rid of anything in it that collides with their
sentiments or offends their taste, he will disallow
the claim. When newspaper editors, journalists, and
novelists adjure him in the name of a pseudo-culture, and
on pain of losing caste with so-called educated people,
instantly to cremate all his wonted beliefs, he will

decline to gratify them by any conflagration of that kind. When these literary divines modestly insist on rewriting our Bible for us, on recasting the historic creed of Christendom, on flouting all authority and cutting themselves loose from all traditional influence, on teaching the Christian Church what she is to believe and what policy she is to adopt, the Christian Church should turn a deaf ear to such arrogant assumption. When an amateurish theology sneers at the confession of sin, draws the crimson thread of atonement out of the Life and Gospel of Christ, raises the old cry which once reverberated on Calvary, "Let Him come down from the Cross, and we will believe Him," insists on the wholesale eviction of the supernatural, and, while thus emptying Christianity of all that is distinctively Christian, claims a monopoly of all intellectuality, the Christian theologian may well be excused if he treats such arrogance with silent disdain. He is not to be brow-beaten or concussed by what has after all no pretension to rank as anything higher than the merest theological dilettantism. The passing opinions of a few oscillating litterateurs, with the dead leaves of which every autumn is strewn, ought no more to disturb or displace the stable and standard theology of the Church, as it has been formulated for her by some of her own Spirit-filled and Spirit-led souls, who have devoted to the work the consecrated labours of a lifetime, than the perturbations in the orbit of Mars should disturb the truth of Kepler's law. It is needful that Christian Theology should in these days claim for itself a distinct place as an independent science in the domain of thought. To borrow the expressive phrase of John

Howe, Theology must "keep state," relying solely upon its own God-given credentials and resources. As it should never consent to become the slave of philosophy, so neither should it allow itself to be made the vassal or the tool of literature. It is time that it stood upon its dignity as an independent and self-sustaining science, finding its materials in the Christian consciousness, not in the secular; going for its testimonials to the Church, and not to the world: neither reflecting the world's spirit, nor echoing its sentiment. It was one of the merits of Schleiermacher, amid all his limitations and defects, that he maintained so strenuously that Theology should stand alone. We need another Schleiermacher in these days to draw up for Theology a new Declaration of Independence, to reassert its dignity, to recover for it the royalties and prerogatives it was once possessed of, to bring it back from dethronement and exile, to give it recoronation, and make it once more what it used to be among the other sciences, the queen in the midst of her retinue, the Sabbath among the days of the week.

I
THE THEOLOGY OF EMERSON

I

THE THEOLOGY OF EMERSON

Mr. HAMERTON prefaces a volume of his Essays with a
choicely-worded introduction expressive of his indebtedness to Emerson.   Mr. Hamerton is not the only one
who might put on record his obligations to the Sage of
Concord.   Who is not his debtor who has ever held
converse with that virile and inspiring personality ?
Who has not gathered from his page mental booty and
intellectual enrichment such as he has derived from few
other masters ?   A profound and original thinker himself, he has set up many other thinkers.   A seer, he has
taught many others to see.   Rich with a Californian
wealth of thought and illustration, which he has dealt
out with spendthrift profusion, he has supplied intellectual capital sufficient to endow a whole crowd of
mediocrities.   What Emerson said of Carlyle may with
equal propriety be applied to himself—" he has spoken
to us with an emphasis that deprives us of sleep."   This
man and his message, then, not only challenge our
attention, but, we are persuaded, will richly reward it.
Fortunately, his leading traits and characteristics stand
out in such bold relief, that we have no difficulty in

7

arriving at a knowledge of what they are.   We are at
once impressed with his mysticism, his transcendentalism,
his gay and tonic optimism, his philosophic equanimity,
his distrust of logic, and his reliance on intuition, as the
only divining rod for the discovery of truth.   And then
there is that amazing style of his, a veritable cloth of
gold spangled with the sheen of diamonds, every sentence
glittering like stars on a frosty night.   We cannot but
be responsive to the charm of a writer that Professor
Tyndall tells us got him out of bed at five o'clock in the
morning through three long dreary German winters.
Himself the most unscientific of men, Emerson exerted a
marked influence on the most brilliant exponent of the
exact sciences our century has seen.   Tyndall quotes no
writer so frequently, and gives not a few indications that
Emerson's views of religion and theories of the universe
were not a little congenial to him.

When we are face to face with an athletic and original
thinker, it is natural to institute some inquiry into his
cardinal principles, and inform ourselves as to his methods
of investigation.   Emerson's fundamental maxim would
seem to be that man is himself the source and the
measure of all truth.   In our quest for truth, we are to
call no man master ; we are to take nothing on authority ;
the one fountain of truth is our own individual and
immediate perception of its reality.   Only that is true
for us which is authenticated by the inner witness in our
own breast.   Of course this general principle has its
limitations, which Emerson is ready enough to see and to
admit.   We are free to consult the past ; we are welcome
to ransack the archives of ancient wisdom ; let us glean

from literature and history what lessons we can ; yet, in
the final issue, the mind of the inquirer himself is the
seat and fontal origin of all knowledge. "Seek not
beyond thyself" is the Emersonian watchword ; consult
no authority, whether of books, men, or theories ; but
what you want to know excavate it out of the quarry of
your own intuitive perceptions. "Great is the soul and
plain," says he; "it is no follower. It never appeals
from itself. It believes in itself." [1] Philosophers, poets,
prophets, apostles, even Christ Himself, are only to be
deferred to in so far as they give evidence of possessing a
broader vision and an ampler wisdom than you yourself
can boast of. But then you can really boast of so much,
that there is no necessity for an outside appeal at all.
According to Emerson, the common inheritance of every
man may be catalogued in this modest inventory—

> "I am the owner of the sphere,
> Of the seven stars and the solar year;
> Of Cæsar's hand, and Plato's brain,
> Of Lord Christ's heart, and Shakespeare's strain."

Such lordly proprietors as this makes us out to be, need
not travel beyond their own private domain in quest of
anything. We are too rich to go begging. All this is
very flattering to human vanity, but it is a dangerous
and deceptive view. Man, on this theory, becomes a
self-contained, self-sufficing thing—an intellectual all in
all. He is his own revelation, his own Bible, his own
Christ. Human nature is raised to a pitch of exaltation
so idolatrous, that few men living, except, perhaps, the
present Emperor of Germany, will take it to themselves.

[1] "The Oversoul."

Yet these are the tests by which Emerson proposes to try everything—Creeds and Churches, the Bible and Christ, Christianity, Judaism, and Mahomedanism, and all the rest. With merciless rigour he applies them all round; there is nothing so sacred, so venerable, so awful, as not to be coolly subjected to. this terrible scrutiny. The experiment is an interesting one, and we are curious to watch its outworking, and to tabulate its results. One immediate consequence of the experiment is, of course, that all possibility of Divine revelation in the strict sense is at once ruled out of court as inadmissible. We must look for no help from the Bible; and as if to reduce us to more utter helplessness still, the next step is that we must not look for any assistance either to our logical faculties. One of the singular peculiarities of Emerson is his distrust of logic—his repudiation of the whole science of inference. He never proves nor argues. He announces, but does not reason. He never reaches truth by a process of inference. He sees it by intuition, which is his only guide, and what his intuitions reveal to him is self-evident. In 1838 Emerson delivered an address in the Divinity School of Harvard, which produced, as one of his biographers tells us, a gusty shower of articles, sermons, and pamphlets, and he became the object for the time being of quite a theological onset. He held aloof from the controversy. " There is no scholar," he wrote to a friend, " less able or less willing to be a polemic. I could not give account of myself if challenged. I delight in telling what I think, but if you ask me how I dare say so, or why it is so, I am the most helpless of men." We have no sympathy

with this haughty superiority to logic, which so many
smaller men now delight to indulge in, having caught
the cue from Emerson. What is this offending science
of logic but the laws of correct thinking in relation to
the True; and surely, no matter in what department a
man may be conducting his investigations, he will conduct
them all the better if he does it with a logical mind, and
the results arrived at will be all the better for the fact
that they can be shown to rest on a sound logical basis.
We quite agree with a recent criticism of Bishop
Huntington's, when he declares that "to a great extent
Mr. Emerson's aberrations in religious thought are due to
his inaptitude for thinking consecutively and logically on
any abstract subject." It certainly does impress us as
a singular weakness on the part of any thinker, more
especially in such a giant as Emerson, that, having taken
up a definite position on any serious subject, he should,
when called upon to vindicate himself, be only able to
feebly whimper, "I cannot give account of myself if
challenged." What would any of those great thinkers,
with allusions to which his pages are so plentifully
besprinkled, and who to Emerson almost rank as
divinities — what would they say of such a man?
Above all, what would Spinoza say, who stood to
Emerson in the relation of a spiritual progenitor, and to
whom Emerson was largely indebted for his whole system?
Spinoza was nothing if not logical. Pantheism in his
pages is unfolded with almost mathematical precision,
and is recumbent on the methods of pure and simple
deduction.

Dismissing Divine revelation as chimerical, and haughtily declining the aids of logic, Emerson both narrowed the sources of information, and rigidly confined himself to intuition as his only working instrument. When he approaches the momentous question of God's existence, he denies the validity of all the customary arguments, such as are usually formulated in theological text-books, on the ground that they all share the fatal defect of being based on logical processes. He substitutes a shorter and more expeditious method of reaching the same great conclusion. While others are climbing with slow and toilsome effort Nature's ladder up to Nature's God, or the equally tedious ladder of syllogism, Emerson sees God by immediate perception, knows Him by direct cognition. By an agile mental leap, he vaults at a single bound into a knowledge of the Divine existence, using as his only spring-board the native intuitions of his own soul. What others reach only after long and laborious courses of reasoning, he reaches by a flash of intelligence. While others are groping after this light and the other, the daystar has arisen in his heart. His mind is flooded with the Divine presence. Instead of going round by the long spiral staircase, which only long-lived experts have time to climb, of Ontological argument and Cosmological, and all the others, he cuts short the road, and *takes the elevator*. This patent home-made elevator of his, however, though exceedingly con-venient, affording swifter access to the stars than even Jacob's ladder, is considerably discounted by the fact that its foot does not rest on any substratum of solid philosophical support. For God is not known by intui-tion. Consult the philosophers and see. All that are worth quoting sharply antagonise Emerson on this very point. They all combine to tell us that our cognition of God is neither necessary, nor self-evident, nor universal; and as these, all the world over, are the tests of intuitive truth, our knowledge of God cannot be intuitive. The best thinkers of Emerson's own time taught this, and Emerson made no effort to demonstrate the contrary. We believe of a surety that our knowledge of God is evident, but we cannot assert that it is self-evident, as our conceptions of space and time, or any other of our necessary ideas. Clear as any axiom it certainly is, but still it is not axiomatic. The Divine existence requires only one step of reasoning to reach it, but that one step must be taken; and the very fact that it needs to be taken puts the Divine existence into the category of derivative truth, and out of the category of primitive. We are quite aware that some students of Emerson's philosophy have professed to see in his claim for intuition only "a fresh and healthful assertion of spiritual independence," and when freed from its extravagancies it may perhaps be susceptible of that construction, but as a means of gaining the exalted vision of the Eternal it is certainly unsatisfying. Lindsay in his *Essays Literary and Philosophical* puts it strongly, but not, I think, too strongly, when he says, "I for my part grant much to the power of intuition, but I should almost as soon expect the sea to blossom into beds of roses as expect pure and simple intuition to yield a God as complete as the incomplete Deity of Emerson." [1]

But suppose on this point that we give this prince

[1] *Essays*, p. 130.

of intuitionalists his own way, other contradictions soon
set in, and fresh difficulties await him.   The multitude
of ordinary mortals at once retort upon him, "We too
have all the instincts common to the race, and we do
not discover in ourselves this 'God-consciousness' of
which you make so much." Emerson saw what was
coming, and in his own way prepares for it. He is
compelled to declare that this knowledge of the Absolute
and Eternal is no everyday affair.   It is a rare privilege,
reserved, in the very nature of the case, for rare and
select spirits.   The vision only becomes accessible after
we have qualified ourselves for beholding it by a process
of special preparation.   We must go into retreat, as it
were, forsake our usual haunts, take refuge in seclusion
from the distractions of society, break away from experience, custom, and example; above all, the passions must
be subdued, and all that is bad in us must go under.
Having wound ourselves up to this state of exaltation,
we may expect the incoming of the grand intuition.   It
discloses itself to the soul in a sort of fourfold revelation.
We first "behold identity and eternal causation"; then
comes "the intuition or preception of truth and right";
this is followed by the comforting intuition "that all
things go well"; and to finish with, we get the intuition
of "the resolution of all into the Ever-blessed One."   A
keen and competent critic of Emerson takes leave to
doubt whether the Sage himself really complied with
some of the conditions which he postulates as essential
for these mystic raptures.   He is specially dubious about
Emerson getting away from men for the better beholding of his vision.   He has a strong suspicion that the

Sage was not just in Patmos solitude when he enjoyed that Apocalypse of his, that men somehow followed this Moses up the slopes of his Mount Sinai—that is to say, the thinkers, the logicians, the philosophers, the moralists were not so far off as Emerson thought they were. Plato, and Socrates, and Kant, and Schelling, and Spinoza were all there, jogging his mind, and making their suggestions; and this critic is even unkind enough to say that from that Mount of Vision the towers of Harvard College were dimly visible in the distance. Emerson's own words certainly lend countenance to the surmise. In moments of simple insight and pure intuition a man does not employ the scholastic terms and philosophic distinctions that Emerson does. The Seer may have got away from "the man in the street," but he certainly could not have got away from Schelling when he talks of "identity," nor from the Pantheists when he talks of "the resolution of all into the Ever-blessed One." Evidently the Seer brought down with him from his Watch-tower of Contemplation very little that he did not take up with him. But be that as it may, if the knowledge of God is to be attained only by the formal and elaborate preparation which Emerson stipulates for as essential, obviously it must continue inaccessible to all but the upper circles of humanity, the children of culture, the select few. Conditions which our philosopher himself found it difficult, if not impossible, to comply with, will prove insuperable to the average mortal. Hence the system must continue a purely esoteric one. If to gain the prizes of intuitionalism, we must go into retreat, break up the ordinary usages of life, liberate ourselves

from the trammels of custom, and get away where the
voices and the footsteps of our fellows will only be
heard as the distant murmur of the sea is heard in
some inland valley, it is not too much to say that the
candidates will be few, for the conditions are practically
prohibitive of any general competition on the part of the
multitude.

Many of us can look back to a time when there were
warm disputes as to what was Emerson's real view on
the subject of God and God's relation to the world.
There are single expressions and occasional passages
which, on the mind of a careless or casual reader, might
easily leave the impression that Emerson occupied the
Christian point of view. But a closer acquaintance with
the general drift of his writings by no means confirms
that impression, but rather leads to the opinion that the
general quality of his views was decidedly pantheistic.
At least, if we are doing our thinker any injustice in
saying so, we can only plead that he has not been just
to himself, and has certainly taken no precautions to
prevent a pantheistic construction being put upon his
creed. If he did not intend to denominate himself a
Pantheist, his language is singularly unfortunate. Only
a disciple of Spinoza could speak of " the resolution of
all into the Ever-blessed One," or apostrophise the world
as he does in his poem " The Adirondacs," and then add
the reflection, " So like the soul of me, what if it were
me ? "   Only an adherent of the pantheistic view of the
universe could employ such language as he makes use of
in his essay on "The Oversoul": " Ineffable is the union of
God and man in every act of the soul.   The simplest

person who in his integrity worships God is God"; or
again, in the same essay, when speaking of the contemplation of the Eternal Spirit in Nature, he affirms
that "the act of seeing and the thing seen, the seer and
the spectacle, the subject and the object, are one." If it
be Pantheism to destroy the distinction between the
Creator and the creature, to merge God in the universe,
and allow ourselves to be absorbed in Him as the dew-
drop is absorbed by the sun, swamping our individuality
in the ocean of life universal, then surely the teaching of
these passages, and many others that might be adduced,
must be interpreted as pantheistic. We have no wish
but to avoid doing our philosopher an injustice; we are
not unmindful of the wise dictum, "It is always hazardous to state a man's beliefs for him"; but that we are
justified in putting a pantheistic construction on his
views will be all the more apparent if we consider for a
moment a certain Emersonian peculiarity which no
reader of any intelligence can help observing. I refer to
the strange solicitude he everywhere exhibits to avoid
any outspoken recognition of a personal Creator, and
even to expurgate the name of God from his vocabulary.
The diplomatic evasions he has recourse to rather than
commit himself to anything that has a colour of theism,
would be amusing were it not that they are offensive.
Of course he must say something to indicate the Unseen
Power which no earnest thinker can quite get rid of.
Why, then, must he beat about the bush and say
"Nature," "Law," "Fate," "The Stars," the "All," the
"Absolute," "The Oversoul," "Jupiter," "Woden,"
"Thor"—anything but *God*? If Emerson be a theist,

why hem and haw and hesitate so much about using the
language of theism ?   Why such reserve in mentioning
the Name to theists dear ?   And when he does break his
philosophic reticence, and the Divine Name does manage
to force itself into his speech, why does he blush for it,
as if he had been guilty of an indiscretion ?   If Emerson
had only asserted the Divine immanence in Nature and
in man, as unsuspecting readers might at first sight
suppose him to have done, he would have asserted a
great Christian truth, which is taught with emphasis
both in Old Testament and in New, and which has
received expression and endorsement in modern literature, notably in Tennyson and Wordsworth.   But
Emerson has gone further, and blended the human and
Divine in mystic confusion, swamped his own life in
what he calls the All-Life, and sacrificed to God, not
simply heart and soul, a sacrifice which God requires,
but his very personality as well, a sacrifice which God
never requires of any man.   For God respects our individuality, and never treats us as mere drops to be
absorbed in the ocean of His own existence.   Tennyson
and Wordsworth were, in this respect, wiser than the
Sage of Concord.   While they did go in for what we
may call a Christian Pantheism, they were careful never
to carry it so far as to divest themselves of personality,
or deprive the Divine Being of His.   In this they
showed a true Christian philosophy.   For we need
scarcely say that if we are not persons ourselves, and
the God to whom we pay homage is not a person, we
thereby destroy at a single stroke all possibility of
worship and religion.   Only between persons can there

be that free interchange of love and fellowship which
is the essence of all religion, and the basis of all virtue.

It will be remembered that on the occasion of Emerson's visit to Carlyle the two Sages held solemn converse, as they rambled together through Wordsworth's
beautiful country, on the Immortality of the Soul.
The question is of such paramount interest to all men,
that one wishes he could really know what Emerson's
convictions on the subject were.   We consult his
writings with a view to ascertain them, but we come
away with an unsatisfied feeling.   Sometimes the arguments for the larger destinies of man are so sharply stated,
that for the moment we can scarcely help believing that
the author himself was convinced by them.   But then,
in the very next paragraph, perhaps, we have the recur-
ring note of scepticism, or a black bar of doubt is drawn
across the fair face of belief.   In one sentence some
strong evidence is cited, but in the next it is sure to be
traversed by some conflicting piece of evidence.   He
gives us guesses, hints, glimpses, doubts, omens, presages.
He never gets beyond a questioning attitude.   He always
falters in his testimony.   As one says, " his reserve is
tremendous, his hold neither firm nor convincing." [1]   Take
as an instance of that reserve the closing words of his
essay on " Heroism " : " And yet the love that will be
annihilated sooner than treacherous has already made
death impossible, and affirms itself no mortal but a
native of the deeps of absolute and inextinguishable
Being."   Here is certainly no hint of the soul's personal
survival after death, but, if anything, a clear implication

[1] Lindsay, *Essays*, p. 154.

to the contrary. In a passage in his essay on "The
Oversoul," he snubs our curiosity about the future state as
something low and vulgar, tells us God has no response
for it, and that any verbal answer that might be given
would be no answer. In still another passage we find
the following : " Men ask concerning the immortality of
the soul. They even dream that Jesus left replies to
these interrogatories." And is it only a dream, then, that
Jesus left any answer to the momentous inquiry, " Am I
to live for ever " ? We dare affirm, even in the face of
Emerson, that Jesus did leave replies to precisely that
interrogation—replies which have been deemed satisfactory by intellects as capable as Emerson's. Does no
reply come from those immortal words which have been
sobbed by so many deathbeds and recited over so many
graves—" In My Father's house are many mansions : if
it were not so, I would have told you. I go to prepare a
place for you " ? Does the little churchyard at Bethany,
with the voice of a Great and a Mighty One reverberating
through its solitudes, " I am the Resurrection and the
Life," furnish no reply ? Above all, do the first Easter
morning and the shattered masonry of yon broken tomb
in Joseph's garden give no reply ? If it be a fact that
Jesus rose from the dead on the third day—and there is
no better authenticated fact in all the annals of the race
—there must be an hereafter, for Jesus has been in it and
returned. There must be " some transcendent life reserved by God to follow this," for the living Christ has
visibly ascended into it in the presence of His disciples.
There must be a Paradise of future bliss, for Jesus went
to it and came back to tell us of it. We often hear

quoted certain lines about "that undiscovered country from whose bourne no traveller returns." But it is not so. One traveller at least has explored that undiscovered country and returned from His pilgrimage. He said that on the third day He would be back again, and He was true to His word ; so that now among the green hillocks of the churchyard we can chant the doxology : " Blessed be the God and Father of our Lord Jesus Christ, who hath begotten us again unto a lively hope by the resurrection of Jesus Christ from the dead, to an inheritance incorruptible and undefiled, and that fadeth not away." At all events one thing is clear, that if Jesus has left no replies to our wistful inquiries about the future, we shall get no replies from Emerson that will do much to reassure or comfort us. If no light breaks on this question from Olivet and Galilee, assuredly we need not look for any from the shapeless metaphysical fogs that overhang Concord.

So lately as 1870, Emerson delivered a lecture in Boston on the subject of "Immortality." In that lecture he reminds us of· nothing so much as a certain statesman, whom Lord Macaulay describes as "a man who saw so many sides to a question that he never could take any." It was throughout an elaborate, and more or less successful, attempt to be on both sides of the house at the same time—as perfect a specimen, we should say, as one can imagine of the *pro* and *con* style of advocacy, a swinging to and fro between conflicting opinions, a kind of mental see-saw which is positively irritating. One who was present on the occasion has told us that, as the throng moved slowly out of the hall, a religious Radical

was heard to say, " Well, he don't believe in immortality,"
and a perplexed Christian answered, " Perhaps he does."
It seems to me these two conflicting opinions voice for
us pretty accurately the general impression which
Emerson leaves on the mind in regard to this great
subject of immortality.   Like ourselves, Emerson had his
broken friendships, his crushed affections, his sore bereave-
ments, but so far as we can gather from his letters and
the outpourings of his heart on these sorrowful visitations,
he would seem to have extracted from all this painful
discipline no lesson of personal survival after death.
When he lost a beautiful child, the grief-stricken father
poured forth his feelings in an exquisite threnody which
critics   have   not   hesitated   to   rank   with   Milton's
" Lycidas," Shelley's " Adonais," and Cowper's soliloquy
on " The Receipt of his Mother's Picture," but it is an
essentially pantheistic effusion.   Here are some of its
lines :—

> "The deep Heart answered, 'Weepest thou'?
> Worthier cause for sorrow wild
> If I had not taken the child . . .
> My servant Death, with solving rite,
> Pours finite into infinite . . .
> *What is excellent*
> *As God lives, is permanent;*
> *Hearts are dust, hearts' loves remain,*
> *Heart's love will meet thee again . . .*
> House and tenant go to ground,
> Lost in God, in Godhead found."

In these lines the deep Heart corresponds to what he
elsewhere calls " The Oversoul."   This " Deep Heart "
consoles him with the assurance that " Death pours finite
into infinite," *i.e.* Death resolves the individual existence

into the life of the Eternal Spirit that pervades all things. We are absorbed into "the deeps of absolute and inextinguishable Being." The lines that follow are usually interpreted as if they implied Emerson's belief in the personal survival of the child, in its continued affection for himself, and in the prospect of a renewal of love and fellowship beyond the grave; but that can only be regarded as a Christian construction put upon lines which in themselves are not Christian. The question is not what thoughts we read into the words, but what thoughts Emerson put into them when he penned the verses. It is "the excellent," you observe, which survives, and the excellent is the "heart's love," and not the heart itself in which it once found a home. "Heart's love" will meet us again; not, however, in the actual face to face meeting of the friends we have lost in the bright world beyond, but in the new friends we shall afterwards meet with on earth, who will encompass us with the same old human love that beats in the breasts of all, a common and universal inheritance. "House and tenant go to the ground"—that is, body and soul, the jewel and the casket that contains it, alike return to dust; "lost in God, in Godhead found"—that is, we are swept away in the floods of Pantheism, and, all reckoning of individuality lost, we mingle with the universe. Representations like these, from whatever cause, have just now a peculiar and fatal fascination for a large class of minds in our day. Strange that it should be so, for any doctrine of immortality that denies the *personal* existence of the soul—what better is it than annihilation? It is a virtual denial of immortality altogether. If I myself

8

am annihilated, or spirited away into some common fund
of being, it is a very imperfect satisfaction to me to be
told that my example, my thought, my love, my fame,
my memory will survive.   What matters it, if *the man
himself* has perished ?

In forming a judgment of any system, the estimate it
puts on sin must be taken into account as an element of
preponderating importance.   "Without the descent into
self-recognition," says Tholuck, "there can be no ascent
into the recognition of God."   It is incumbent on us,
therefore, to inquire into Emerson's view of sin—the
burden and impediment of the soul.   The moral outcome
of the pantheistic tincture in his teaching is here painfully in evidence.   In his explanations of moral evil
he has a tendency to fall back on nature, treating evil as
a natural product or development, our necessary and
unavoidable inheritance.   "Nature," says he, "is no
saint; if we will be strong with her strength, we must
not harbour such disconsolate consciences."   In "Self-
Reliance," he says, "no law can be sacred to me but that
of my own nature : good and bad are but names readily
transferable to that or this."   It is a dangerous experiment for a man to follow the law of his own nature,
unless his nature has been assimilated to something higher
than itself ; and when we imbibe the idea that right and
wrong are only shifting distinctions, movable as passing
scenes in a diorama, mere labels with which our actions
may be ticketed indifferently, with no scrupulous reference to their moral quality, we have surely entered on
a perilous incline.   According to Emerson, sin is but
natural imperfection, a consequence of our finiteness and

limitation. It is our misfortune rather than our crime, our weakness rather than our guilt. Moral evil is but the inevitable shadow that accompanies moral good, a necessary stage of development on our way to ultimate perfection. It is time to hoist the danger signal when we meet with views like these. The moment sin is represented as something inevitable, it ceases to be sin. The one refutation of all such theories of the origin of evil is, that they are at once disowned and rejected by the conscience itself, which will admit no explanation of sin that omits its guilt and turpitude. Emerson would have arrived at juster conceptions in this part of his philosophy, if he had seen things through the eyes of Dante, or some of the old Hebrew prophets. As it is, he has no adequate idea of the exceeding sinfulness of sin. No one would ever infer from his pages that sin was "the anomaly of the universe, the blot upon the creation which God made very good, the disgrace of mankind."[1] Accordingly, we are not surprised to find that in the Emersonian scheme of things there is no provision for dealing with the problem of sin's removal and forgiveness. No method is indicated whereby a sinful soul may be harmonised with its own past record, and may attain peace with conscience, and peace with the eternal verities, before it passes hence. Emerson knows nothing of God's remedy for sin. The Cross is not visible from Concord. But though propounding such an attenuated philosophy of sin, sin itself he repressed and avoided in his own life as few men except the very saintliest have done; and as for his writings, the

[1] Stearns' *Present-Day Theology.*

supremacy of conscience has never found a sturdier advocate, and no reader of his has ever risen from his page without having derived from it a moral tonic that has braced and strengthened him.

The same easy-going and indulgent temper which betrayed Emerson into such lenient treatment of sin, will account also for his having so little to say about the more sombre aspects of human life in general. The darker problems of existence do not trouble him; he makes no attempt to solve them, does not even notice them. The misery, the suffering, the injustices, the social inequalities, the tragedies which supply the pessimist with materials for his gloomy philosophisings, give neither headache nor heartache to Emerson, whose blue-sky optimism shines on persistently, refusing to be overcast by such passing cloudlets as these. Our philosopher is always gay and happy, content to take "the potluck" of things just as they are, takes life just as he finds it, and solaces himself with the cheery conviction that "man, though in brothels, and gaols, and on gibbets, is on his way to all that is good and true." As Mr. Morley puts it, "he will see no monster if he can help it." Precisely so; if any monstrosity comes his way, the Sage of Concord will take to the other side of the road, and give it as complete a go-by as priest and Levite gave the wounded traveller in the parable. There is just one and only one radical tragedy in life which Emerson feels and admits — "the distinction of More and Less." If I am poor in faculty or shut out from opportunity, that is indeed a tragedy. "But see the facts closely," says he, "and these inequalities vanish. Love reduces them as the sun melts the iceberg. The heart and soul of all men being one, this bitterness of His and Mine ceases. His is Mine. I am my brother, and my brother is me." Mr. Morley's criticism on this is so just and trenchant, that it renders all other comment superfluous. " Surely words ! words ! What can be more idle than when one of the world's bitter puzzles is pressed on the teacher, that he should betake himself to an altitude whence it is not visible, and then assure us it is not only invisible but non-existent."[1] This imperturbable optimism, maintaining its light-heartedness by sealing its eyes to the gruesome and disagreeable, may perhaps to some extent be accounted for by the fact that Emerson was the denizen of a New World, where wrongs and injustices were fewer and less inveterate than in the Old. In North America, social and secular life did not wear so bleak an aspect as it did in Europe ; it was not defaced by inequalities so glaring, had not so many desperate problems on hand, and had not inherited from the past so many unfortunate legacies.

By this time the reader will be asking what does Emerson think of Christ ? Well, not to the Sage of Concord need we go for a satisfactory study of the Son of Man. His attempts to revise the belief of Christians and of Christendom concerning Jesus of Nazareth form very painful reading. True, there are many passages which show that the character of Jesus had impressed him in no ordinary degree. He speaks of " the unique impression which Jesus has made upon mankind," and says that " His name is not so much written as ploughed

[1] *Miscellanies.*

into the history of the world." " Jesus always speaks
from within," he declares, " and in a degree that transcends all others." But while the Son of Man is
patronised with many passing compliments of this kind,
and hailed with many salaams of respectful salutation, the
fact very soon discloses itself that between his Christ
and ours there is a great gulf of difference, an unbridg-
able chasm of separation. Emerson's utterances on this
grave subject are sufficiently explicit. When the creed
of Christendom surrounds the head that once wore the
thorn-crown with the halo of divinity, Emerson protests
against the procedure as " a noxious exaggeration." He
will not concede to Christ any position of unshared
eminence. " Do not degrade the life and dialogues of
Christ," he says, " by insulation and peculiarity." To
the American philosopher Jesus in no way transcends
human nature, and His character and work are quite
susceptible of explanation on purely natural principles.
He constantly perpetrates on Christ the gross indignity
of classifying Him with human notabilities. In a manner
which sends a shudder of resentment and recoil through
every adoring disciple of the Master, he invariably
mentions Him in the same breath with earthly com-
petitors. Jesus is no more than many others whom he
can name. Cæsar's hand and Plato's brain, Shakespeare's
strain and Lord Christ's heart, are all slumped together
in vicious equalisation, as if they had all precisely the
same claim on the recognition and homage of mankind.
Two special passages may be quoted which will serve to
show how utterly Emerson has misconceived the quality
of Jesus. The first is from the essay on " Experience " !

" 'Tis the same with our idolatries. People forget that it is the eye which makes the horizon, and the rounding of the mind's eye makes this or that man a type or representative of humanity, with the name of hero or saint. Jesus 'the providential man' is a good man, on whom many people are agreed that these laws of optical delusion shall take effect."

These sentences are very painful reading, and their bearing is not to be mistaken. The reverence which men have been according to Jesus ever since the first disciples worshipped Him, is pure idolatry. He has been promoted to the rank of Divinity only as the result of an optical illusion of the mind which many people agree shall take effect on Him; and if that same illusion happened to take effect on other specimens of the race, they too would appear to have the same qualities as Jesus, and might serve our purpose equally well. The second passage is from his "Address" to divinity students: "He (Christ) said in that jubilee of sublime emotion, I am Divine; through Me God acts, through Me speaks. Would you see God, see Me: or rather, see thee, when thou also thinkest as I now think." Christ, therefore, if we are to believe Mr. Emerson, believed in His own Divinity in a fit of fanatical emotion, while we have come to believe in it in a fit of mental illusion: nay, if we can only bring ourselves to think as Christ thought, we may become Christs ourselves. For these wild and reckless speculations, not an iota of justification is advanced. We have nothing for them but Mr. Emerson's word. Is it not enough that he has said it? The issue is a very plain and simple one. It is the old question of what rank in the hierarchy of being we shall assign to Jesus, and it just comes to this—if the Churches are right, then Mr. Emerson is hopelessly and egregiously wrong. If Mr. Emerson is right, we are all idolators, and the sooner we cease paying any exceptional deference to Jesus the better. There is in the four Gospels a formidable series of adamantine facts which cannot be squeezed into the moulds of the Concord philosophy. Running through the fourfold story the Evangelists have left us, there is an argument for the superhuman quality of Jesus which peremptorily and for ever sets aside the assertions of Emerson. One thing stands out with special clearness from the pages of the New Testament—Jesus with tremendous self-assertion claimed the honours of Divinity. That claim cannot be evaded. Whether we admit or disallow it, it must at least be disposed of. To that question Emerson never once seriously addressed himself. To say that that claim of Jesus originated in a paroxysm of fanatical emotion is only to trifle with a great subject, and to impute to Jesus, moreover, a fanatical weakness of which He exhibits not a trace in the four Gospels, and which must be regarded as entirely alien to a judgment so well balanced as His, and a nature so serenely poised.

As Emerson only gave Jesus a niche in his temple of divinities along with Plato, Confucius, Socrates, and Marcus Aurelius, so also he reduced the Bible to the level of human literature. The inspiration of prophets and apostles did not materially differ from the inspiration of Shakespeare, Newton, or Goethe. " The Bible," says Emerson, " is the most original book in the world. This old collection of the ejaculations of love and dread, of the

supreme desires and contritions of men, proceeding out
of the region of the grand and eternal, by whatsoever
mouths spoken, seems, especially if you add to its Canon
the kindred sacred writings of the Hindus, Persians, and
Greeks, the alphabet of the nations." There is no im-
propriety, then, in Emerson's way of thinking, in adding
to the Canon of Holy Scripture other scriptures of a
kindred order. In recent years the Oxford Press has
issued no fewer than thirty-six volumes of the Sacred
Books of the East ; Mr. Emerson would place the Bible
on the same shelf with these, and treat them all together
as the natural expression of the religious sentiment in
man—so many interesting products of religious evolution.
This view has now a great fascination for a certain class
of thinkers, who, in these days of universal toleration,
try to win a cheap reputation for width of vision by
holding out to us the Bible in the one hand and the
Koran in the other. The Bible will not brook such
treatment. It asserts its own supremacy. It will not
do obeisance to other sacred writings. It will not live
in peace with any other book that is allowed to compete
with it for the faith of mankind. It will tolerate no
additions to its Canon, for the Book closes with the significant assurance that its Canon is closed, and threatens
with all the plagues written in it the man who dares to
reopen it. Against the mistaken liberality that would
level down the Bible in this way, we cannot do better
than adduce the testimony of Sir Monier Williams, himself a lifelong student of the doctrine of evolution in
connection with religion, when in memorable words he
declares : " Place the sacred writings of non-Christian

systems on the left side of your study table, but place
your own holy Bible on the right side—all by itself, all
alone—with a wide gap between."

It will be evident from what has been said that in the
Emersonian philosophy there is no room for miracle.   In
any pantheistic view of the universe such as that to
which Emerson commits himself, where God so dwells in
nature as to become a part of it, all that savours of
miraculous interference is of course excluded.   To the
Sage of Concord the very idea of miracle is " a profanation
of the soul."   " The word miracle," he once told his
hearers, " as pronounced by Christian Churches, gives a
false impression, it is a Monster.   It is not one with the
blowing clover and the falling rain."   Any event, therefore, that is not as purely natural and as easily accounted
for as the field of clover, or the shower of rain, is to be
rejected as a monstrosity.   If in the presence of such a
devastating principle we can manage to retain our Christianity at all, it must be a Christianity shorn of the
miraculous.   The turning of water into wine, the walking
on the sea, the raising of the dead, not being on a par
with " the blowing clover or the falling rain," must be
dismissed as unworthy of credence.   The Incarnation
itself shrivels into a superstition, and the resurrection of
Jesus Christ from the dead sinks to the level of a nursery
legend.   Mr. Emerson seeks to comfort us for the loss of
the miracles with the tranquillising assurance that we
may be well content to lose them, " for no person capable
of perceiving the force of spiritual truth but must see
that the doctrines of the teacher lose no more by this
than the law of gravity would lose if certain facts alleged

to have taken place did not take place"; that is to
say, if it should transpire that Jesus Christ never rose
from the dead at all, Christianity would lose as little by
this as the law of gravitation would lose, if some fact connected with it should turn out never to have happened.
It is amazing that so keen a thinker as Emerson should
ever have penned such a statement as this, indicating as
it does such a woful inability to comprehend the real
issues at stake, or the evidential value of the great
foundation fact of the Gospel by which those issues must
be determined.   Jesus Christ staked the whole truth of
the Christian religion on the fact of His own resurrection.   He appealed beforehand to this very certificate as
the most powerful of his credentials—that which was to
give the Divine signature to His mission and His claims.
The one sign which He gave to an unbelieving generation was· that in three days He would build again the
ruined temple of His body; and our supreme reason for
believing in Him to-day is that He has been as good as
His word, that He has redeemed His pledge.   Again and
again the Apostle Paul argues that the resurrection of
Christ is so bound up with the religion that bears His
name, that you cannot deny the one and yet retain faith
in the other.   Part with your belief in the resurrection,
and you have not merely parted with an important incident in the Gospel history, you have parted with Christianity as a whole.   "If Christ be not risen, your faith is
vain."   "If Christ be not risen, ye are yet in your sins."
And are we to be told in the presence of facts like these,
which lie on the very surface of the New Testament, that
it really does not signify to Christianity whether its

Founder rose from the dead or not ?   Nay, it signifies so vitally, that if Christ is still unresurrected and "the Syrian stars look down upon His grave," Christianity collapses, as certainly as does the arch when its keystone is removed.   There is surely a lesson here which should not be lost upon those who seek to commend. Christianity to a doubting and reluctant age by first of all reducing it to a non-miraculous scheme of religion.   The thing cannot be done.   If the Biblical conception of God and of God's relation to the world be true, then it would be the greatest of all possible miracles that miracles cannot happen.   A Christianity without miracle would be a Christianity without God.   Mr. Matthew Arnold is pleased to acknowledge that the Christian religion is the greatest and happiest stroke ever yet made for the perfection of humanity.   But let us not fail to understand that that stroke never could have been made if there had been no miracle of Incarnation at Bethlehem, and no miracle of Resurrection at the garden tomb of Jesus.

We are now in a position to appreciate the justness of the appellation which has sometimes been applied to Emerson—"the religious revolutionist of America."   His thinking was revolutionary in the extreme.   He succeeded in unsettling everything in Boston.   His constructive power was small, but he had a genius for upsetting.   The predominant feature of his intellect and the keynote of his teaching was undoubtedly his scepticism—a scepticism which respects nothing sacred, interrogates all accepted beliefs, revolts against all authority, contemplates all creeds, and takes leave to doubt all.   Comparing Emerson and Carlyle, Mr. Lowell says : " Both represented the old

battle against Philistinism. It was again as in the times
of Erasmus, Lessing, and Wordsworth, a struggle for fresh
air, in which, if the windows could not be opened, there
was danger that panes would be broken, though painted
with the effigies of saints and martyrs." [1] Emerson was
certainly not the man to die of suffocation, and in the
process of letting in the fresh air he wielded the hammer
of iconoclasm with a will; he is responsible for many a
broken pane, and was never deterred in the congenial
work of demolition by any thought of the panes being
painted with sacred and venerable figures. That the
breach between him and the religious sentiment of New
England was not wider than it was, is perhaps due to the
peculiarly insinuating attitude he assumed toward it.
While Channing would have abandoned it, and Theodore
Parker was ready to wage a war of extermination,
Emerson professed to find in it a new and beautiful
significance. Why destroy these old beliefs? These
also are products of nature, and as religious naturalists
let us not refuse them a place in our cabinet of specimens: these also are "penetrable to the spirit"; let us
refill the old bottles with the wine of a new meaning;
let us discover for them a set of correspondences in our
own philosophy; let us transfigure and transmute them.
And so, while in reality Emerson was vaporising the old
Puritan beliefs and spiriting them away, he only seemed
to be transfiguring them, appeared to be innocently
engaged in giving them a new and improved restatement,
and even posed as a prophet who had come not to destroy,
but to fulfil. When Dean Stanley returned from America

[1] *My Study Windows.*

in 1879, it was to report that "religion had there passed through its evolution from Edwards to Emerson, and that the genial atmosphere which Emerson had done so much to promote is shared by all the Churches equally."[1]   To a Broad Churchman like Stanley such "evolution" would doubtless be a gratifying phenomenon, but we suspect the good Dean has rather exaggerated the extent of it.   New England is yet very far from having cut the moorings that have anchored it to the Edwardian Theology.   From the grasp of that giant intellect it has not yet succeeded in effecting its escape.   Edwards may not indeed have possessed the poetic insight of Emerson, his wide culture, his superb imagination, or his literary craftsmanship, but in all that constitutes a *thinker* we are persuaded the palm must be accorded to Edwards.   In grasp and range of intellect, in closeness and subtlety of reasoning, in metaphysical acuteness and precision of thought, Edwards is as much the superior of the Sage of Concord as the Sage of Concord, in some other directions, is his superior. As to the "genial atmosphere" which, according to Dean Stanley, Emerson did so much to promote, if the Dean had used the word sceptical instead of "genial" he would have been nearer the truth.   Emerson's theology was undeniably a "genial" one—so genial that it confounded Christianity with Pantheism, dispensed with the Gospel miracles, denied uniqueness to Jesus, put the Bible on the same shelf with the Koran, made little of sin, saw no necessity for a disconsolate conscience, took no account of the bleak and wintry aspects of life, and blotted out the prospect of personal existence beyond the grave.   And

[1] *Macmillan's Magazine,* June 1879.

this is what Dean Stanley understands by the diffusion of a "genial atmosphere" among the Churches! This is the evolution from Edwards to Emerson!

After this, it will be a small surprise to us to hear that the holding of such views had a very disturbing effect on Emerson's Church relations and on his religious life in general. He believes the Church to be an effete and worn-out institution; thinks meeting-houses would be put to a better use if turned into schools and hospitals; he grudges the dollar he sometimes gives to Missions as a mean compliance with opinion, and hopes some day to be virtuous enough to refuse it; he thinks the Sunday-school a piece of pious boredom, and looks on temperance and other popular reforms as so many vain nostrums for the regeneration of Society. In 1832, Emerson resigned his pulpit, the immediate occasion for the step being his adoption of views in relation to the Sacrament of the Lord's Supper which were in conflict with those held by his congregation. At a later date he separated from the Church altogether, and in the end abandoned the ministry. While our admiration for Emerson must be an admiration with many reserves, still, after every deduction has been made, there is much in the man himself and in his writings which it cannot but delight and fortify us to remember. His life was gracious and dignified. From Father Taylor, the Boston missionary, he won the singular encomium, " Mr. Emerson may think this or that, but he is more like Jesus Christ than anyone I have ever known. I have seen him when his religion was tested, and it bore the test." This is indeed a noble certificate of character, and serves to furnish one other instance of the fact, which we have so often had occasion to observe, that, wide as a man's aberrations from the faith may be, he may nevertheless continue unswervingly loyal to all goodness and virtue. Matthew Arnold's brief and exquisite character of him is that, perhaps, which best summarises the merits of Emerson, and will linger longest in our memories: "He was the friend and the aider of those who would live in the spirit."

II

THE THEOLOGY OF THOMAS CARLYLE

THE THEOLOGY OF THOMAS CARLYLE

FROM the Sage of Concord we naturally turn our attention to his illustrious contemporary, the prophet of Chelsea —another of those intellectual sovereigns who still rule us with undisputed sway. Commenting on the influence which Carlyle has exerted on English sentiment, Martineau characterised it many years ago as "a power revolutionary and pentecostal," which, however, he adds, "is perhaps nearly spent, and will descend from the high level of faith to the tranquil honours of literature." Those "tranquil honours" have come. Carlyle belongs to literature. He is one of the fixed stars in the heaven of history. He has taken his place in the immortal ranks of those whom the poet Shelley designates "the enduring dead." The niche assigned him in the Valhalla of the world's great spirits is beyond all reach of alteration or disturbance from booksellers, reviewers, or critics. Nothing that may be said or written of him now can subtract a ray from his glory, or crumple a single leaf of his laurels. Among all the prophets who have ever been burdened with a message to their nation, and who have been straitened till it was delivered, a greater hath

not arisen than this Annandale peasant, who shot down
upon us from among the Dumfriesshire hills like a son of
thunder, and struck us with the force of a battering-ram,
his look a judgment, his words like the trump of doom.
He was the John Baptist of his age.   A vehement preacher
of repentance, a fiery apostle of reform, he has been among
us in the spirit and power of Elias.   He laid the axe to
the root of many a corrupt tree that cast its upas shadow
and dripped its poison-drops upon our national life.   His
fan was in his hand, and he has throughly purged our
floor, making much chaff to fly.   With an iron flail he
laid about him most vigorously, smashing all sorts of
shams and make-believes and hypocrisies without mercy,
the sworn enemy of all things magnificated and insincere.
This man was emphatically the preacher of the age—a
preacher who knew his text and kept to it, who never
left his pulpit, and always made himself audible.   No
smooth-tongued, velvet-mouthed orator was he, but a
rough alarmist who succeeded in waking a slumbering
generation from what, but for him, might have been its
death-sleep.   Many a much-needed but unpalatable truth
has he driven into the brain and heart of England, with
as much precision of aim and deliberateness of stroke as
Jael when she sent home the nail into sleeping Sisera's
temple.   He has preached up the duty and the dignity of
work till men have felt ashamed of their idleness, and
blushed for their good-for-nothingness.   He has taught
us that in lowly attention to the humblest tasks of life
there lies the secret of our true worth and felicity here
below.   "Blessed is the man who has found his work,"
says he, "let him ask no other blessedness."   He has

glorified toil, and beautified it, putting a smile on the
face which was once forbidding, and girding it with
angel robes till men have grown enamoured of it.   He
has inspired us with a contempt for unproductiveness,
and led us to brand as a crime the life of selfish ease.
He has asserted the victoriousness of simple goodness,
and the indestructibility of right.   He has revived our
faith in ourselves and our individuality, infusing into us
some of his own self-reliance, and letting us see what
one brave heart and one stout arm can accomplish.
George Dawson calls attention to it as one of his
sublimest services, that he has for ever put to flight the
diseased and enfeebling notion that "men are but frac-
tional units, and that you must put some twenty thousand
of them together before it is believed to be safe to move."
Carlyle cured us of that folly, by personally conducting
us down the corridors of history, and showing us single
men, and what they have done single-handed.   One
other lesson, too, of incomparable value he has graven
on the tablets of our hearts—that all true reformation
must proceed from within ; that everything will be right
when we are right ourselves.   He had no faith in men
mending society, mending the laws, mending the Parliament, without ever making any personal attempt to
mend themselves.   Rectify a man's spirit, he contended,
and you have rectified everything.   Get his interior
disposition right, and his speech will be right, and
his behaviour will be right, and very soon his whole
environment will be right too.   But it would be
impossible to recount all the fruit-bearing ideas which
have dropped upon us from that great thought-tree

Carlyle has planted in our midst, and whose shadow still falls so gratefully upon our national life and institutions. We really have no calculus which would enable us to aggregate the number of winged seed-thoughts which have emanated from this prolific thinker, the movements he set vibrating, the tendencies he initiated, or accelerated. When we think of all he was and did, the dying witness of John Sterling is the only adequate expression of our reverential gratitude: " Towards England no man has been and done like you ! "

It does not fall within the scope of our present purpose to dilate on Carlyle's literary services, which in themselves constitute such an immense claim on our regard, else with what pleasure we might have reminded ourselves and our readers of what we owe to him as the most vivid of our historians, and the most penetrating of our critics. We might proceed to claim for him that he " first taught England to appreciate Goethe "; that he was the literary Columbus who first discovered for us the genius and resources of German literature, hitherto almost a *terra incognita* ; that his splendid drama of the French Revolution has " done more to bring before our slow-moving and unimaginative public the portentous meaning of that tremendous cataclysm than all the other writings on the subject in the English language put together ";[1] that he first gave resurrection to the reputation of Cromwell, and cleared his memory from the age-long vilifications which had been industriously heaped upon it, once and for all exploding the theory that the life and character of this " uncrowned king " are only

[1] Morley, *Miscellanies.*

rightly construed on the assumption of his being either a
cheat, knave, or hypocrite; that in his *Life of Frederick
the Second* he gave us a vivid narration of facts
previously inaccessible, as remarkable for its painstaking
mastery of dry-as-dust details as for the coruscations of
genius that scintillate in its pages; that he first reversed
the accepted and registered judgments on such men as
Burns, Johnson, and Boswell, teaching us to see in the
one something more than a tipsy poetiser, in the next
something more than a literary dogmatist or a fossil
Tory, and in the third something more than a booby
or a sycophant; and, finally, that he first supplied us
with the proper tests and standards by which to arrive
at a just estimate of men so persistently misunderstood
as Voltaire, Mirabeau, Diderot, and other continental
heroes, of whom we had no human or lifelike portraits
till Carlyle supplied the want.   Here are abundant
materials for the literary critic, but we must resist the
temptation to linger on them, not because we are not
interested, but only because we are supposed to occupy
ourselves with other aspects of the man and his message.

For similar reasons we do not feel it incumbent on us
to attempt any but the very briefest adjudication on
Carlyle's services as a social reformer or practical philosopher.   If his labours in this department are to be
estimated by their practical outcome or nett results, they
will be found on the whole disappointing.   The social
and political problems to which a complicated and corrupt
civilisation has given rise, the national crisis through the
throes of which the country has been passing, were
certainly visible to his eye as they were to no other;

and if others did not see them as vividly as he, it was through no fault of his. He realised the urgency of the case, and made his somnolent contemporaries realise it; he felt the gravity of the situation, and insisted that the whole nation should feel it too. The policy of drift and *laissez-faire* had no countenance from him. He loudly inveighed against the infatuation of staggering blindly onwards toward social disintegration and anarchy. The "Condition of the People" question, the relations of Capital and Labour, Master and Servant, Landlord and Tenant, Governing and Governed—all this was a never-ending theme with Carlyle. According to Mr. Morley, it was Carlyle's chief merit and distinction that, for the space of forty years, he kept these things constantly and conspicuously before his own mind and the mind of his generation. His own attention was never for a moment diverted from them in all that time, and he took care that the nation's attention should not waver any more than his own. But when this much has been said, we have perhaps accorded to Carlyle as liberal a measure of recognition as may be justly awarded him. In practical suggestion he is weak. His solutions are extremely inefficient. For desperate maladies he has nothing to offer by way of remedy but a few palliatives in the shape of increased education, and a systematised emigration scheme. "Over practical politics," says Mr. R. H. Hutton, "it is needless to say that he wielded no direct power,—indeed, would have despised himself if he had wielded power. The deep scorn which he poured on the whole machinery of modern politics, the loathing with which he looked upon the great national Palaver, the contempt which he felt for the modern conception of liberty as a barricade against most needful and necessary government—all prevented him from offering any but the wildest and most impracticable suggestions to practical statesmen." [1] The man was a prophet; and whilst we recognise in the prophet the true king of men, nevertheless it is not exactly to that high functionary we turn for help when in want of practical solutions of pressing everyday problems.   But, be this as it may, the fact remains that Carlyle does not materially assist us, unless it be by getting into a temper with us, savagely rapping us on the knuckles as dull boys who will not get our lessons, and continually scolding us for our unreason, our blunders, and our crimes.   Now it goes without saying that mere vituperation never settles anything, that ravings and thumps and warrings furnish no solutions, and that a constant indulgence in growls and shriekings, in apostolic exhortation and dehortation, does not further us a single step towards the discovery of any practical outlet from our embarrassments.   Sterling had the courage to tell Carlyle as much in a very outspoken way in his criticism on Teufelsdröckh.   " Wanting peace himself," said Sterling, " his fierce dissatisfaction fixes on all that is weak, corrupt, and imperfect around him; and instead of a calm and steady co-operation with all those who are endeavouring to apply the highest ideas as remedies for the worst evils, he holds himself in savage isolation." He devotes, for instance, a whole volume to the discussion of Chartism, and at the end of the book, looking back on all he has written, he can only say: " What a

[1] *Modern Guides of English Thought*, p. 8.

black, godless, waste-struggling world in this once merry
England do such things betoken!" There is not much
in such pessimistic wailings calculated to achieve anything in the way of helping that once merry England to
recover her vanished merriment and be happy yet again
as of yore. Similarly the problem of Ireland was brought
under his notice by some patriots sincerely interested in
her welfare, in the hope that the great prophet of
Chelsea might have something helpful to say on such a
subject, and perhaps devise some ameliorative measures
for that distressful country. He crossed the Irish Sea
on a tour of inspection, saw the patient for himself, went
into a minute diagnosis of the disease, gave a lurid
description of the symptoms, and finally came to the
conclusion that nothing he could say or write on the
subject would be of the slightest use. "It is a huge
suppuration," said he, "and there is nothing to be done
but let it go on festering till it breaks!" The services
of an expert in social science and political specialist are
requisitioned, and all he does is to drench us with this
cold drizzle of despair! We have only to imagine our
statesmen, reformers, and philanthropists, when face to
face with the ailments of humanity and the festering
sores of the world, acting on this hopeless recommendation—a doctrine worthy of a Schopenhauer—and what
a lazar-house and Aceldama of a place this earth would
soon become! It is all very well for Carlyle to come
to the bedside of the sick man and tell him how sick
unto death he is, to deliver long-drawn clinical lectures
on the virulence of the complaint, to berate all the other
physicians as a set of doltish incapables, and throw their

medicine out of the window as a trashy Morrison's pill;
but when he brings forth his own sovereign cure-all, is
it not after all but another Morrison's pill, with this
difference only, as Mr. Lowell suggests, that it contains
a larger amount of aloes, and comes to us recommended
by the superior advertising powers of a genius.

In further illustration of Carlyle's ineffectiveness in
practical suggestion, and the general impracticability of
his political philosophy, we may advert for a moment to
that favourite doctrine of his that men everywhere should
bow down to their superiors, wherever they find them,
and allow themselves to be ruled by a real aristocracy,
" a corporation of the best and the bravest." This is the
famous hero-cure which, if we do not consent to have
administered to us, we are past hope of recovery. The
hero is to mount the driver's seat, and the multitude are
to get between the shafts and consent to be driven by
him whithersoever he listeth. But when our hero is
not forthcoming, when the " real aristocracy " are not to
the fore, or when they abdicate their functions and will
not lead, what are the people to do ? According to
Carlyle himself, heroes are a scarce commodity. One
or two of them may be born in a century, in his way
of thinking. Frederick the Second was about the last of
them that made his appearance among us. We have no
control over the very precarious supply of these heroic
spirits which from time to time step on board of our
planet, and in the dreary interludes which are unmarked
by any such arrivals, in the long stretches of barren
commonplace and characterless mediocrity that occur
between the exodus of one great man and the coming of

another, we cannot help asking what is poor Demos to
do ?   Nothing, according to Carlyle, but sit down there
in helpless passivity, like a group of exiled Jews under
the willow-trees by the Babylonian canals, and anxiously
wait the advent of some demi-god—nothing but lie on
their mattress of despair by Bethesda's pool, waiting till
some hero makes a ripple on the stagnant waters ; and
if they find the time rather heavy on their hands, they
can repent of their sins, and grumble at things in general,
and otherwise treat themselves to a little comfortable
misery.   But supposing the long suspense at an end, and
the conquering hero actually to have stepped on to the
stage with world-shaking tread, what then ?   The mass
of mankind are not just so many sheep which will
tamely submit to be shepherdised by him, and coerced
into the way chalked out for their feet by the free
application to their backs of a rod and staff which,
unlike those in the Psalm, are *not* comforting.   Men
are creatures of will, and sometimes even of wilfulness ;
they are endowed with freedom and rationality, and they
will never for long submit to be treated as so many
puppets and marionettes in the great world-show, manipu-
lated by a few forceful and ambitious spirits.   No one
attaches more importance to the free play of will-power
in individual biography than Carlyle, yet, singular to say,
as a practical philosopher he makes little or no allowance
for its operation in the multitude.   Altogether his social
and political teaching is extremely disappointing.   Purely
negative in its character, it leaves things very much as
it found them.   He does not count for much as an
emancipator who only takes his stand outside our dungeon

gates to tell us how unfortunate is our lot, how dark is our prison, how fettering are our manacles, and how impossible it is to get out.   Or, to vary the figure, if our national and social affairs are in a state of impending shipwreck, we poor wrestlers with the troubled sea will be glad of any hand of rescue reached out to us from the shore; but if our would-be deliverer, instead of bringing on the scene some life-saving apparatus, can only bring a Diogenes lantern from which to flash a lurid light upon the tragic spectacle, or a camera, it may be, with which to take snap-shot views of it, or pencil and paper with which to take notes for a thrilling and picturesque description of it, we must be excused if we fail to see that such a one has wrought any real deliverance on the earth. All this and much more might be urged, yet it still allows us to feel grateful for the vigour and perspicacity with which Carlyle pressed on the world's attention the urgency of the social problem, for his awakening of thought on the subject, and for recalling the banished Angel of Consideration to the nation's council-board.

We have ventured on this digression, even at the risk of incurring the charge of irrelevancy, because we feel that Carlyle is not to be rightly interpreted if in approaching him there be no considerations present to the mind but theological ones.   We have now to consider his attitude to Christianity, and the answers he has left behind him to the old yet perennially interesting questions which the human soul must ask in its moments of heightened consciousness and reflection.   The task before us is one beset with difficulty.   Perhaps no writer was ever a cause of greater perplexity to that type of mind which will insist on classifying than Carlyle. He does not lend himself easily to any such process. He has not taken sides on any of the great theological issues or debates which have agitated and divided the modern mind. He has not ranged himself under any particular flag, nor shouted any of the usual religious shibboleths or war-cries. You can identify him with no *ism* or *ology*. He is too universal for you to label or ticket him, or assign him a place in your cabinet of specimens. He stubbornly refuses to fit into any of those little pigeon-holes into which classifying minds find it so exceedingly convenient to thrust all sorts of men and things. We defy you to distil his essence and bottle it up, and put it on the shelf, duly catalogued, marked, and numbered. He is too massive to be classed, too vast to be tabulated. To add to our embarrassment, his writings by no means abound in theological landmarks, or other indications of his religious whereabouts. Rather are they pervaded by an air of hazy and mystical religiousness, which, to put it as mildly as George Dawson, " is perhaps not quite what we would have." " He is unwilling," the same writer continues, " to supply us with too much, to give a cut and dried formula to save us from thinking." But if that be all the exception which can reasonably be taken to Carlyle as a religious thinker, we might shut up our critical apparatus altogether and keep silent. To hint, as Dawson and some other of his critics have done, that he erred chiefly by a defective recognition of the higher doctrines of Christianity, is to take a very lenient view of his theological shortcomings. To affirm with Mr. Morley that Carlyle has maintained on matters of religious belief a wise and politic reserve " more full of meaning than his most pregnant speech," that he has " preserved unbroken silence as to the modern validity and truth of religious creeds," is to state what is at variance with the facts, as we shall presently see, and to attribute, moreover, a policy of stratagem to one who, whatever other virtues he may have lacked, certainly never failed to exhibit courage and outspokenness. Neither do we derive much assistance from Sir Henry Taylor's designation of him as " a Calvinist who had lost his creed." It is a nice question how much of the Calvinist survives after the Calvinistic creed has been dropped, as it would be how much is a man still a Platonist after he has read the burial service over his Platonism, or how far is a man still a Darwinian after he has washed his hands of Evolution ? All that could possibly have remained for Carlyle was the Calvinistic temper of mind, its mode of regarding the universe, and its way of looking at things in general. This much at least may be allowed to have survived the evisceration of his creed of all dogmatic contents, and this much he may be said to have retained to the very last in spite of all mental vicissitudes. To say with others that Carlyle was an instance of a man " who had a very large capital of faith not yet invested," is a way of putting it which can only be accepted with modifications. We know some things which he did invest faith in, and the investment did not turn out so favourably that we can afford to congratulate him on the result. On the other hand, we know certain other things in which he did not invest a farthing's worth of faith, which are usually regarded as affording a safe output for intellectual capital. Faith " not yet invested " can only mean a latent faculty or disposition to believe which has never yet found anything worthy of being believed. That, in Carlyle's case, there was no investment of faith in what is commonly known as organised Christianity, is a fact that emerges at once from the slightest acquaintance with his writings and private correspondence. The various helps and traditions which the Church has to offer, he wrathfully looked upon as so many " miserable spy-glasses " through which to survey the universe—" Puseyite, Presbyterian, Free Kirk, Old Greek, Middle Age, Italian—imperfect, not to say distorted, semi-opaque, wholly opaque, and altogether melancholy and rejectable spy-glasses, if one has *eyes* left. On me the pressure of these things falls very heavy. . . . I confess that Exeter Hall, with its froth-oceans, benevolence, etc. etc., seems to me amongst the most degraded platitudes this world ever saw : a more brutal idolatry, perhaps,—for they are white men, and their century is the nineteenth,—than that of Mumbo Jumbo itself." This breach with ecclesiasticism, however, is a fault for which the temper of the age will readily forgive him. But he must be held to have committed a much graver offence when he refused to invest any faith either in pure New Testament Christianity as it existed before man's organising genius had set to work on it at all, before the meddling fingers of ecclesiasticism had yet begun to manipulate it, and while yet its pure historic stream had not been muddied by the subsequent admixtures of defiling sediment which it contracted in its onward course through the centuries. According to

Carlyle, the Christian religion has no foundation of historical reality. He did not believe that the facts recapitulated in the Apostles' Creed had ever really happened. The miraculous birth at Bethlehem was to him an occurrence on the same level with the incarnations of heathen mythology, and could only have been credited in an age when it was an article of universal belief that the gods came down to earth and appeared in the likeness of men. And as there was no room in his view of Christ for the incarnation, so neither did it admit of any place being found for the fact of His resurrection. He never actually rose from the dead at all. He was only *believed* to have risen by men who made no sharp distinction between legend and history ; the story of His rising again gained credence in an age destitute of the spirit of historical reflection or critical inquiry, and is now only of any value or significance in so far as it is the symbol of a spiritual truth. As Christ rose from the dead, so are we to rise from moral torpor and the death of sin into the new life of righteousness. The whole story of Jesus of Nazareth is but the beautiful product of mythical times, when belief in miracle presented no difficulty, and creature and Creator were supposed to be in constant communication ; and for all times the *soul* of it is essentially true, but it has been unfortunately associated with a body of dogma which, being mortal, is doomed to perish. The soul or essence of this Christian myth is what Carlyle designates " the Worship of Sorrow," " which, assign what origin we may to it," says he, " has been originated and is here."

10

" Knowest thou that Worship of Sorrow ?   The Temple
thereof, founded some eighteen centuries ago, now lies in
ruins, overgrown with jungle, the habitation of doleful
creatures ; nevertheless, venture forward ; in a low crypt,
arched out of falling fragments, thou findest the Altar
still there, and its sacred Lamp perennially burning." [1]

So the Temple of Christianity, it would seem, is now
fallen into a sad state of dilapidation ; the Altar, indeed,
is still standing, but is now ministered to by a fraternity
of sham priests ; a frippery of conventional adornments
hides it from the eyes of men ; while Religion has meanwhile withdrawn, " and in unnoticed nooks is weaving for
herself new vestures wherewith to reappear, and bless us
or our grandsons." [2]   We need another Luther and a new
Reformation.

On this symbolical representation of Christianity we
venture a few passing observations.   In the first place,
before we enter this Temple of Sorrow and prostrate
ourselves in silent worship before its Altar, we must take
leave to differ with Carlyle in treating the question of
the origin of that Temple, and the genesis of that
Worship, as a matter of pure indifference.   " Assign to it
what origin we please," says he, " has it not been
originated," and is it not enough for us to know that
it is here ?   True, but when we come to assign origins
at all for an event so stupendous as the establishment
of the Christian religion   and its world-regenerating
effects, we must surely be careful to assign only such
origin as is capable of originating a phenomenon so
immense and enduring.   It is here, but in our attempted

[1] *Sartor,* bk. II. ch. ix. p. 133.
[2] *Ibid.* bk. III. ch. ii.

explanations of how it came to be here, we must seek to postulate some cause adequate to its production. To allege, as Carlyle does, that it all originated in myth, is to do violence to all the laws of historical possibility, and disregard even the simple canon that there must always be some proportion between instrument and effect. Until men bore Mount Cenis tunnels with drills of opaline glass, or construct Pyramids out of the floating sands of the desert, it cannot be accepted as a rational explanation of the genesis of the Christian Church, that it was conceived and cradled in Myth. The regeneration of the world has not been accomplished by a few fancy pictures. The revolution Christianity has effected, and the moral triumphs which have marked its victorious march across the centuries, must have been begotten of some parentage more creative than a bundle of pious fables, a collection of Jewish folk-lore, or a few mythological dreams. "*A myth*," says Professor Christlieb, "*cannot form*, cannot produce; it is itself only a product, a reflection of the popular mind, and that in prehistoric times; it cannot, therefore, have begotten the Christian Church; nay, it cannot even have helped to beget it. The establishment of the Church, this immense achievement, demands a *personal* will, a creative power of the greatest energy; it cannot be accounted for by the empty pictures of imagination." [1]

According to Carlyle, the preternatural facts recorded in the Gospels are not real occurrences, but only poetic beauties, or symbolic representations of spiritual truths. At the central point of all history, what we come upon

---

[1] *Modern Doubt and Christian Belief*, p. 423.

is not a divine-human Personality, but a number of ideas
or intellectual conceptions expressed by certain external
events which did not actually happen, but were *believed*
to have happened by excited and enthusiastic disciples.
The whole development of Christianity, on this hypothesis,
is made to rest, not on the objective demonstrable fact of
Christ's resurrection, but on the subjective belief of His
followers in it; not on Christ Himself, but on the
disciples; not on a Divine and supernatural *occurrence*, but
on a certain *inexplicable impression* left upon the minds
of men. But who does not see the ambiguity? The
real question at issue is, on this theory, studiously evaded
—Was the resurrection of Christ an outward, historical,
ascertainable event, or was it due only to the subjective
belief of the disciples?—in other words, has Christ indeed
risen, or are we to be satisfied with knowing that He
was believed to have risen, and have we in this latter
knowledge a sufficient cornerstone on which to rest the
superstructure of the Church and of Christendom?
"The faith of the disciples," says Beyschlag, "in the
resurrection of Jesus, which no one denies, cannot have
originated, and cannot be explained otherwise, than
through the *fact* of the resurrection, through the fact in
its full, objective, supernatural sense, as hitherto understood." A distinguished theologian of the present day
propounds as a test of the adequacy of the view of Christ
taken by any writer or school of thought, whether it is
able to take in the resurrection of Christ as a constitutive
part of it. Tried by that test, the Carlylean view must be
pronounced a failure. The attempt to set faith and historical evidence in opposition to each other must always fail.

Returning to the "Worship of Sorrow," the idea, like a good many other items in Carlyle's mental furniture, came from Germany. It was borrowed from his great master, Goethe, who had such a singular fascination for his English disciple, and to whom he always considered himself under profound obligation. Indeed, not the least perplexing thing about Carlyle is his overweening estimate of this German poet, and how he ever came to commit himself to the pilotage of such a man as his guide, philosopher, and friend. We can understand his being dazzled with the witchery of Goethe's intellectual brilliance, and his falling under the spell of his consummate genius, but we confess to not a little difficulty in accounting for his choice of this man as a patron saint and spiritual adviser. John Sterling always refused to see him as Carlyle saw him, and persistently maintained that the proper theory of the man was that of a great intellect in unison with a depraved heart. Sterling was right. Goethe was an intellectual Pagan, and morally his life was one long violation of social decency and the ordinary sanctities of life. He may have been, as his critics are never weary of telling us, "the most splendid specimen of cultivated intellect ever manifested to the world," but he was also as perfect a specimen of the literary free-liver as either Swift, Sterne, or Rabelais. His path through life was strewn with the wreck of woman's happiness, and the blighting of woman's hopes. His fugitive attachments follow each other with startling rapidity, recalling the Frenchman's excuse for inconstancy, "Je change l'objet, mais la passion reste." But passion would be a misapplied term—there was so little heart in the matter. "What

he wanted was a *beau ideal* to excite his fancy and
stimulate his creative faculty." [1]   Read the long chapter
of his infidelities, his amours, his flirtations, his *liaisons*;
ponder the fact that he is known to have deliberately
trifled with the affections of women, in order to make a
cold-blooded psychological study of their feelings for
literary purposes; or the other fact, like unto it, that he
dug almost every drama he ever composed out of some
woman's broken heart; remember that he suffered
eighteen years to pass away before he formally and
legally made Christine Vulpine his wife, and you will
perhaps share our wonder that a man reared as Carlyle
was on the ideals of Scottish Puritanism could ever—we
will not say have done obeisance to the German poet's
genius, for that is quite intelligible—but could ever have
kissed the toe of this man as a spiritual father in God,
or hailed him as a moral deliverer, a second Mr. Great-
heart to conduct him on his soul-pilgrimage, the apostle
of a new religion, and that the only religion which it was
worth while for a thinking man to adopt!   In a letter
to John Sterling he says—

"As to Goethe, no other man whatever, as I say always,
has yet ascertained what Christianity is to us, and what
Paganity is, and all manner of other *anities*, and been
alive at all points in his own year of grace with the life
appropriate to that. . . . The sight of such a man was to
me a Gospel of Gospels, and did literally, I believe, save
me from destruction outward and inward."

If, therefore, we would hear the Gospel of Gospels,
and see a man who will "tell us all things," not to Paul
or Luther, but to Goethe we must go.   If we would

[1] Hayward.

ascertain what Christianity really is, to whom shall we go but to one who showed scant allegiance to its most elementary precepts ?   He is the only Bible exegete and expositor worth listening to.   Let us make him our Gamaliel, and he will pour revealing sunshine on all the mysteries of this perplexing universe.   Again, we cannot help remarking on the strangeness of this procedure on the part of Carlyle.   No man can frame a religion for us who is not himself religious.   A depraved man is a poor expositor of the holy secrets of Christ's pure evangel, and can conduct us but a little way into the realm of spiritual truth.   If only the pure in heart can see God, we must gravely question the clarity of Goethe's vision in Divine things.   But as he happens to be, in the opinion of the Chelsea philosopher, the only man capable of ascertaining for us the real meaning of Christianity, we had better hear what he has to say.

We get it all in the philosophic views which in brief compass he has propounded in *Wilhelm Meister*.   He there outlines for us what he is pleased to call the *Religion of Reverence*.   Naturally, the mass of men are destitute of the feeling of reverence, though they have enough of that fear which trembles, and which is the mother of torment.   This latter must be banished from the mind, and be replaced by the true reverential spirit in which the essence of all real religion consists.   The reverence which Goethe inculcates assumes three forms or phases.   There is first of all the reverence which leads us to venerate that which is above us.   Then comes the reverence for self, of which Christ was at once the Teacher and the most illustrious Exemplar.   Jesus had such reverence for self that He thought it not robbery to be equal with God, put Himself on a level with the Godhead, and even declared that He was God. This, according to the poet-theologian of Germany, is the Philosophical Religion which Christ came to introduce, and it justifies man in taking himself at his very highest value, and putting on his nature and performances a superlative estimate. Then comes the third and last stage—reverence for that which is beneath us, viz. afflictions, persecutions, pain, death, etc. Here also Christ is the chief Instructor and most conspicuous example, but specially in His sufferings and passion. We here enter the " Sanctuary of Sorrow," and become fellow-worshippers at that sacred shrine with Christ Himself, who has taught us to see the Divine side of these things, and to recognise their purifying and ennobling influence on character.

Such, in brief outline, is Goethe's Scheme of Philosophical Religion, of which, in its leading features at least, Carlyle became so enamoured that it tinctured and flavoured all his subsequent religious views. The dire omission, the fatal flaw of the scheme, is its ignoring of guilt, its failure to provide a remedy for sin, or even to recognise the havoc which sin has wrought in human nature, and the disturbing effects it has had on the relations between man and God. We are conscious of having sinned, and in consequence we fear to meet our Maker, or to come face to face with the unescapeable record of our own past. Goethe and the philosopher of Chelsea tell us to dismiss our fear, because reverence, and not fear, is the proper feeling, and the only one which the true religion permits us to entertain.   But our fears are too well founded to be waved aside with any fairy wand of the kind, for no son of man but must fear, so long as he has not attained "harmony with an undivorceable conscience, harmony with an unescapeable God, and harmony with an ineraseable past"; and for proof of that affirmation we need not appeal to the Bible at all, it will be enough to appeal to our Lady Macbeth with her little bloodstained hand, to our Byron just after he has written "Manfred," or to our Tennyson just after he has written his "Palace of Art." The reader will remember how, in that last-mentioned poem, Tennyson pictures Culture as passing through five stages, and shows how only in the fifth and last, when she awakes to some proper conception of the necessity of pardon and holiness, does she attain to peace.   In the four preceding stages she runs through a series of experiments like Solomon in the Book of Ecclesiastes, trying one after another all the regalements of history, literature, and art, all the manifold resources of that self-culture which Goethe worshipped, and in which our age is still seeking satisfaction for its deepest wants, but the long experiment ends in most mournful failure.   Not till she builds a cottage in the vale where she may "pray" and be "purged of her guilt," does she attain to peace, the supreme necessity, and not till then does she begin to pass into the attitude of Christian thought. Now Goethe and his English disciple have never got further than the mood of Culture in which so many literary and scientific coteries of the present day seem satisfied to linger, and we have the authority of Tennyson for regarding that stage of development as a crude and

juvenile attitude of soul which every serious thinker
must outgrow and leave behind by " time's unresting sea,"
as the nautilus the shell for which it has become too
large.   On our celestial pilgrimage there is no skipping
or passing by that " cottage in the vale," to which the
soul must . retire to pray for forgiveness with strong
crying and tears, and to have her guilt purged away ;
and it is precisely the fault we have to find with such
men as Goethe and Carlyle, that they never repair to
that cottage, nor so much as see any necessity for repair-
ing to it ; in their spiritual geography it is not marked on
the map at all ; with them it is not a station, or a port of
call, at which the pilgrim must touch on his way heavenward.   Have you any fears on account of a violated law
and an outraged conscience ? Dismiss them, says Goethe,
for fear is not the best form of religion, and begin to
cultivate reverence.   Altogether reverence with Goethe is
a sovereign balm for every ill, and works wonders.   Is God
offended with you ? Reverence Him, and He will lay
aside His displeasure.   Are you afflicted ?   Reverence
your afflictions, and they will lose their power to trouble
you.   Are you sin-stained and defiled ?   Reverence
yourself even when there is nothing in you to command
reverence, nothing deserving of self-respect, not to speak
of veneration, and there will soon be an improvement in
your condition.   If this self-reverence be a cure for sin,
sin is not after all such a deadly thing as we had supposed
it to be ; the Bible takes it quite too seriously, and the
gospel specific for its removal is needlessly drastic, and .
costly even to the point of wastefulness.   It is all very
well for a German poet attired in the robes of culture to

stand by and minister to a mind diseased by simply saying dismiss your fears, but there is only one spot in all this universe where sinful men can afford to dismiss their fears, or where they have any ground for dismissing them, and that is a place called Calvary, where through the crucified body of God's Son a new and living way of forgiveness and reconciliation has been opened up for a guilty and commandment-breaking race. But this aspect of the truth receives no recognition from the poet-theologian of Germany or his English follower, neither of whom even admits that Christ came into the world in the capacity of a Saviour at all, but only as a Teacher to give mankind a course of instruction in the Religion of Reverence. He came not to make expiation, but to give information; He came not to die for us, but to instruct us. So little did the idea of offering an atonement enter into His programme at all, that His object was rather to imbue us with the idea that the gulf between God and us was by no means so hard to bridge as we had imagined, and to give us lessons in the art of bringing God down to our own level, that we might have all the better pretext for reverencing ourselves. It is easy to see that here we have the germ of that "Hero-Worship," the new cultus, of which Carlyle was afterwards to be the Apostle and High Priest.

Such, in brief, was the specious version of Christianity to which Goethe gave the high endorsement of his genius, and which he made poetical. Carlyle was at perfect liberty to adopt it, and domesticate it in the English mind if he could, but when he insists on identifying it with New Testament Christianity we demur

to any such procedure.   Let it be clearly understood
that this is the Gospel according to Goethe, and let it
take its chance of winning converts accordingly; but there
must be no attempt to make it do duty for the Gospel
according to Matthew or Mark, Luke, or John.   It is a
Gospel "made in Germany," not in Judæa, which must,
therefore, stand or fall on its own merits ; but we offer a
resolute opposition to the tactics which would foist or
father it on Jesus Christ, or seek to throw over it the
ægis of Biblical sanction and protection.

This new and improved Christianity Carlyle seeks
further to fortify and secure by resolving it into a form
of natural religion.   In his essay on Voltaire, he sets
himself to establish its virtual independence of miracle
and all historical documents.   The essence of it is
written in ineffaceable characters on man's own heart,
lies embedded in the very constitution of human nature.
The truth of it becomes discernible through the primary
instincts of the soul.   To evoke and interpret these was
the pre-eminent service which Jesus rendered to the
race, and in virtue of which He has taken rank as the
world's greatest Religious Philosopher.   Finding not only
the evidences but the contents of our Christianity, not
in a book but in our own bosom, where Divine fingers
had already traced it in mysterious hieroglyphic, Carlyle
thought he could afford to treat with indifference
Voltaire's attempts at the overthrow of miracles and the
invalidation of the scriptural records.   Even should the
French infidel be successful in demolishing all these, and
should storm one after another the external fortifica-
tions by which theologians have sought to buttress the

Christian position, Christianity, secure in its inner citadel, would still survive, being certified by the witness from within.

"That the Christian religion," says he, "could have any deeper foundation than books, could possibly be written in the nature of man in mysterious, ineffaceable characters to which books and all revelations and authentic traditions were but a subsidiary matter, were but as the light by which that Divine writing was to be read—nothing of this seems to have, even in the faintest manner, occurred to him.   Yet herein, as we believe that the whole world has now begun to discover, lies the real essence of the question. . . . Christianity, the 'Worship of Sorrow,' has been recognised as Divine on far other grounds than Miracles, and by considerations infinitely deeper than would avail in any mere 'trial by jury.' Religion is not of sense but of faith—not of understanding but of reason; and he who has failed to unfold the reason in himself can have no knowledge of the Christian religion!"[1]

Carlyle goes further, and even considers the French sceptic to have rendered good service in demonstrating that the confidence which men reposed in the external evidences of Christianity was a mistaken one. Voltaire has the good wishes and the blessing of Carlyle in his destructive assaults on miracle, and on the Bible—the explanation of which may perhaps be found in the fact that the Bible goes dead against Carlyle's particular form of Christianity.   At all events, as Mr. George M'Crie shrewdly remarks, "it is an ugly symptom of the Christianity he has adopted that it claims to be benefited by the great apostle of infidelity!"[2]   This tendency to revert to a purely natural religion is becoming a very noticeable

<hr>

[1] *Essays*, vol. ii. p. 172.
[2] M'Crie, *Religion of our Lit.*, p. 43.

feature in some of the recent attempts at theological reconstruction with which we are being favoured in these days. Not a few of our modern guides are depreciating revelation, and turning in ever increasing measure to Nature as the true source of all reliable knowledge of Divine things. Our Christianity is being rapidly de-christianised, and our Christian theology is being natural-ised. We are expected to rest satisfied with whatever handfuls of information we can glean from the works of creation without, and our own nature within. And, of course, if we first of all take care, as Carlyle does, to empty our Christianity of everything distinctively Christian, if we denude it of its Christian traits, and erase from its table of contents such doctrines as the Trinity, the Person of Christ, the Atonement, and the work of Supernatural Redemption, it is a very simple process to reduce what is left of it to the level of a pure naturalism. But this means nothing short of the obliteration of Christianity altogether. " For all the Christianity of theology on the one hand, and all the Christianity in religion on the other," as Professor Warfield well puts it in a recent article, " comes from the Bible. Apart from the revela-tion of God, deposited for us in the Scriptures, there is no Christianity. Obliterate this revelation—theology may remain, but it is no longer a Christian theology ; religion may remain, but it is no longer the Christian religion."

But it is to *Sartor Resartus* we must turn for the fullest disclosure of Carlyle's religious history and beliefs. In that book, written among the solitudes of Craiggen-puttock, we have a revelation of his own interior life, though to some extent veiled and symbolical. Herr Teufelsdröckh is the spiritual counterpart of Carlyle himself, and the work partakes of the nature of an autobiography. Through its pages we get a vivid insight into the mental struggles, heart-sorrows, and soul-conflicts of an earnest and thoughtful man, groping his way through the thick darkness of scepticism out into the daylight of faith and liberty. Autobiographies are a species of literature in whose favour we are not much prepossessed, they are so often stilted and artificial, and so manifestly got up for effect. But no such suspicions can possibly attach to *Sartor*, which is undoubtedly the product of a sincere and unaffected soul, and enjoys the reputation of being " one of the truest self-revelations ever penned." It is one of those books with which, as George Dawson says, we may retreat and find in it " an interpreter of the inner life, a guide into the land of light." The storm-tossed thinker describes his own early conflict with the demon of religious doubt. He is stumbling in the Serbonian bog of his own scepticism, a veritable " Slough of Despond," where solid footing there is none. He comes at last to that peculiar position which he describes as the " Everlasting No," which is the negation of all his early beliefs, the loss of faith, the triumph of doubt, with the orphanhood and desolation of spirit consequent on such a distressful state of mind. From this wild waste of all-devouring scepticism he ultimately emerges, the chaos is reduced to something like a cosmos, through the operation of two or three simple primary principles, which, amid the universal wreckage, still survived, and now came to his rescue ; chief among which was the idea of his own individuality as a something different and other from the world without.   This feeling of self, of freedom, of will, of power, able at any moment to assert itself and put an end to this state of scepticism by an act of suicide —this became the turning-point in his salvation.   It also contributed not a little to his deliverance, that all through this intellectual ferment he never.lost the sense of duty.   Call in question what he might, one thing admitted of no question, that it was always right to be sincere, and faithful, and truth-loving, and valiant ; that one was always under perennial obligation to follow the admonitions of the monitor within.

" Thus, in spite of all motive-grinders and mechanical profit-and-loss philosophers with the sick ophthalmia and hallucination they had brought on, was the infinite nature of duty still present to me; living without God in the world, of God's light I was not utterly bereft; if my sealed eyes could not see Him, nevertheless in my heart was He present, and His heaven-written law still stood legible and sacred there." [1]

Acting up to the full measure of what light he had, living out all the duty he knew—this was one of the keys of Promise with which Carlyle unlocked the doors of Doubting Castle, and let himself out into open air and liberty.   Those who have read the biographies of Horace Bushnell and F. W. Robertson will remember how they too availed themselves of that same key, how it wrought magically for them also, and became the instrument of their spiritual emancipation.   In the case of Carlyle, as in that of many other inquirers, the central thing in his experience, and that which proved to be the clue which led him out of the winding catacombs of mental bewilderment and unrest,

[1] *Sartor Resurtus,* p. 113.

and brought him to what he calls "sunlit slopes," was self-surrender to the best he knew, a full and affectionate yielding to the best light he had. This capitulation to conscience, this faithful following of what he knew to be duty, was the very pillar of fire that led him into the Promised Land. By means of this he obtained a solid foothold for his faith, and from this vantage ground he battled so successfully with the spectres of the mind, that ultimately he fought his way to belief in a personal and omnipresent God. "It was his adoption of theism," says Joseph Cook, "which first untied the knot which choked him."

"How thou fermentest and elaboratest in thy great fermenting-vat and laboratory of an atmosphere of a world, O Nature!—Or what is Nature? Ha! why do I not name thee *God*? Art thou not the 'Living garment of God'? O Heavens, is it in very deed *He* then that ever speaks through thee; that lives and loves in thee, that lives and loves in me?"[1]

Having attained to a clear, unquestioning faith in a personal Creator, we do not say that all his doubts were dissipated at a moment's notice. By no means; but if they lingered on for a while, they were "like the mighty pines on the mountain-tops after the lightning has smitten them. They did not fall, but they ceased to grow. They are no longer trees: they are timber." One point of vantage gained, he went on to gain another and another, till at length all mental tumult subsided, and a great calm fell on his exasperated spirit.

"Foreshadows, call them rather foresplendours, of that Truth, and beginning of Truths, fell mysteriously over my

[1] *Sartor Resartus*, p. 130.

I I

soul. Sweeter than day-spring to the shipwrecked in
Nova Zembla; ah! like the mother's voice to her little
child that strays bewildered, weeping, in unknown
tumults; like soft streamings of celestial music to my
exasperated heart came that Evangel. The Universe is
not dead and demoniacal, a charnel-house with spectres,
but God-like, and my Father's!"[1]

The "Everlasting No," with all its dismal negations,
now lies behind him for ever; the problems of life are
understood, doubts are laid, and after long conflict he
has come at last to the "Everlasting Yes," by which we
are to understand firm and assured belief, duty discerned,
equilibrium of mind, and the felt influence of eternity on
human life. The autobiography closes with this supreme
psalm of triumph :—

"I see a glimpse of it. There is in man a higher than
love of Happiness: he can do without Happiness, and
instead thereof find Blessedness! By benignant fever-
paroxysms is Life rooting out the deep-seated chronic
Disease and triumphs over Death. On the roaring billows
of Time thou art not engulphed, but borne aloft into the
azure of Eternity. Love not Pleasure: *Love God.* This is
the *Everlasting Yea,* wherein all contradiction is solved;
wherein whoso walks and works, it is well with him."[2]

Passages like these, which might easily be multiplied,
are Carlyle's best vindication from the charges of
Pantheism which have sometimes been levelled at him.
In saying so we are not unmindful that his friend
Sterling had some complaints to make when the Clothes
Philosophy first made its appearance, and could not rid
himself of the painful impression that Teufelsdröckh had

[1] *Sartor Resartus,* p. 130.
[2] *Ibid.,* pp. 132, 133.

struck a very uncertain note on the subject of the
Divine Personality. He went so far as to embody his
feelings in a letter to Carlyle, which drew from the Sage
the following characteristic rejoinder. It seems to us a
conclusive settlement of the point in dispute, and if no
other evidence were forthcoming, might in itself suffice to
show the groundlessness of Sterling's suspicions :—

"You say finally, as the key to the whole mystery, that
Teufelsdröckh does not believe in a 'personal God.' It is
frankly said, with a friendly honesty for which I love you.
A grave charge, nevertheless,—an awful charge,—to which,
if I mistake not, the Professor, laying his hand on his
heart, will reply with some gesture expressing the
solemnest *denial.* . . . And now may I beg one thing :
that whenever in my thoughts or in your own you fall on
any dogma that tends to estrange you from me, pray
believe *that* to be *false*, false as Beelzebub, till you get
clearer evidence."

"This is an explicit statement," is Mr. Froude's
comment on this pronouncement, "and no one who knew
Carlyle, or has read his books, can doubt the sincerity of
it." For ourselves we have never seen any reason to
doubt that belief in a personal God was a foremost article
in Carlyle's creed, and one which he held with no feeble
or relaxing grasp. To him, as to all of us, it was "flatly
and for ever inconceivable that intellect and moral
emotion could have been put into him by an entity
which had none of its own." The gifts and faculties he
was endowed with, all that he admired in himself or
others of wisdom and goodness and right—who or what
could by any possibility have given them to him, but
One who first *had* them to give? This was his favourite
argument, his short and easy method of reaching the

great theistic conclusion, the only way, to his thinking, that the matter was construable. " This," he would say, " is not logic. This is axiom. Logic, to-and-fro, beats against this like idle wind on an adamantine rock." Indeed, not the least of Carlyle's claims upon our gratitude lies in the vigorous protests with which his writings are studded against the mechanical view of Nature and Man with which the French thinkers, in their desire to abolish the supernatural, had leavened the thought of the age. The world was reduced to a vast chemical laboratory, and man himself to a bundle of nervous processes, a physiological dust-heap to be dispersed again by the same blind forces by which it was swept together. To this dismal philosophy Carlyle dealt many a staggering blow, from which it has not yet recovered. He emphasised the spiritual conception of the universe. Man was something other and more to him than a temporary embodiment of material particles, and in Nature's vast chemical laboratory he detected the presence of a great Chemist presiding over her processes. He was severe on men like Humboldt, because they saw nothing in the universe but " an old marine-store shop collection of things putrifying and rotting under certain forces and laws." Theirs was a soulless view, robbing nature of its poetry, stunting admiration, and leaving no room for wonder. Carlyle characterised it as " a most melancholy picture of things " !

Yet it must be admitted that the God whom Thomas Carlyle came to believe in and in his own way to worship, is not wholly satisfactory. The mystery and incomprehensibleness of the Divine Being, which we all feel and acknowledge, would seem to have so oppressed him, that in his case they came to mean the same thing as vagueness and blankness.   His Deity is nothing better than some great Unknowable and Unnameable, surrounded by an impenetrable haze.   There is a great First Cause, but to profess to know anything of its perfections or attributes is to be guilty of a presumption or a profanation.   We must never forget that it *is*, but from all shapings of it, or namings of it, we must reverently refrain.   " The Highest *cannot* be spoken of in words "— so he writes to John Sterling.   Our only proper attitude in presence of the Supreme Reality is silence, awe, speechless prostration.   We are to say with Faust, " Who dare name Him ? "   There is truth in what some-one has said, that Carlyle talks of the Divine Being very much as if he had been living in some desert island of the ocean unvisited by the Gospel.   While most people are rejoicing in some definite acquaintance with God, derived from the revelation He has given us, he lapses into pantheistic maunderings about " the primeval Un-speakable," and studs his pages with mystic allusions to " the stars," " the Everlasting Silences," the " Immen-sities," and " the Eternities."   Of these latter Mr. John Morley is very distrustful, and declines to take them seriously, choosing rather to regard them as " a kind of awful background " thrown in for the purposes of stage - effect.   According to him, too much has been made of this spirituality of Carlyle, and its place in his writings has been entirely misstated.   We cannot share that view.   To Mr. Morley's secularism, of course, the " eternities " and " immensities " are but the veriest piece

of cloudland, and he no doubt finds it difficult to conceive that these unspeakable presences have any more
substance or reality for others than they have for himself.
But Carlyle was no Secularist, and it is most unfair to
him to suggest that the constant appeal to the invisible
realm and its unseen laws and forces which runs through
his writings, amounts to nothing more than a little bit
of stage-machinery.   The Secularist Philosophy jealously
guards this life from any inroad of ideas from the world
to come, and considers it is best lived when it is confined
within the circumstances of the present state and the
considerations of duty that proceed therefrom, without
any regard to what John Foster calls "the final
references."   But Carlyle took a very different view.   If
there was one thought which, more than another, had
imbued the mind of Carlyle, and under the conscious
influence of which he lived and worked, it was that this
life opens into the life to come, that Time is the seed-
field of Eternity, and that this brief span of earthly
existence is the hinge on which swings the great door of
our eternal state.   To men imbued with secularistic
ideas, this habitual regard to the "final references" may
be but the merest moonshine of otherworldliness, and
many a modern belle-lettrist has introduced it for the
purely artistic purpose of supplying his pages with a
sublime and impressive background; but to Carlyle it had
all the intensity of a profound and solemnising conviction.   It was the root-idea of his religion.   It prompted
and inspired his worship.

But that worship of Carlyle's is itself a rather singular
phenomenon, and may well detain us for a moment.   As

he himself said, " it was chiefly of the silent sort," which, being interpreted, is but another way of saying that it contained no specific acknowledgment of Father, Son, and Holy Ghost ; it proceeded on no definite recognition of the tenets of Christendom, and was practically independent of any belief in the distinguishing doctrines of the Gospel. It was but a species of inarticulate religiousness wholly disconnected from any settled convictions concerning either the character of God or man, concerning either sin or salvation. One bright Sunday morning Carlyle received a letter bringing the sorrowful intelligence of the death of John Sterling. " If on that day," said he, " I did not worship in the great Cathedral of Immensity, surely the fault was my own." Analyse the worship he offered on that sad occasion under the open sky, and it resolves itself into a vague, speechless awe under an oppressive sense of the mystery of life and death, a gush of pathetic emotion, a mixed and tumultuous feeling surging through the soul, and investing man and the universe with deep solemnity. But we search in vain for any evidence that his worship had any relation to the Trinity, that it was offered through the medium of the God-man Mediator, or that it involved the confession of sin, or the remission of it, through the great atonement made. Clearly in that Cathedral of Immensity there was not that Throne of Grace to which the ordinary Christian makes his approaches. Calvary's Cross was not uplifted there ; on its lectern there was no copy of the Gospel ; the worshipper made known no specific requests to a God whom he really believed to be listening to him ; and the way into the Holiest of All

was not the blood-besprinkled one which Jesus trod, and
through which He has given us access to the Father.
Many of our literary men are suffering under the same
woful delusion, that a true worship may be rendered
without a true Biblical Creed being believed. But mere
religiousness is not religion, the Cathedral of Immensity,
grand and awe-inspiring as it is, can never be a substitute for the Church of the Living God, with Jesus in
the midst, and a vague feeling of mystery under the blue
dome of heaven is a poor equivalent for petition and
penitence, confession, and thanksgiving, and love. We
are convinced a truer and more acceptable worship arises
from simple praying souls in the smokey cottages of the
poor, than from awestruck philosophers in their moonlit
rambles under the vault of night, burdened with the
mysteries of this strange universe, and maundering about
" latent pieties " and " deep wells of reverence " within
the hidden part.

Carlyle's references to the problem of guilt and its
removal are few and far between, but when he does
touch upon it it is interesting to observe how he proposes
to deal with it. He was seldom visited, it would seem,
with a sense of sin. When, however, on rare occasions
he did experience the perturbations of conscience, he had
recourse to a very singular quietus for assuaging the
fears of guilt.

" Shall I be saved ? Shall I not be damned ? What
is this at bottom but a new phase of egoism, stretched
out into the infinite ? Brother, endeavour to rise above
all that. Thou art like to be damned ; consider that as a
fact ; reconcile thyself even to that if thou be a man : then
first is the devouring universe subdued under thee, and

from the black mirk of midnight, dawn of an everlasting morning shall spring. . . . Thy future fate, while thou makest it the chief question, seems to me extremely questionable. Norse-Odin, immemorial centuries ago, did not he, though a poor heathen, in the dawn of time teach us that for the dastard there was and could be no good fate ? . . . A greater than Odin has been here, and has taught us not a greater dastardism, I hope. My brother, thou must pray for a soul ; struggle to get back thy soul. Know that religion is no Morrison's pill from without, but a reawakening of thy own self from within." [1]

This, then, is the manner in which Carlyle disposes of the question of guilt, this is his recipe for an uneasy conscience. The person to whom he is here tendering advice, on the most momentous of all concerns, is supposed to be in a state of anxiety and alarm about his future destiny. He is supposed to be making this the chief question. Whether he is right in doing so we need not dispute with Carlyle ; if it is only a matter of precedence or priority over other and competing questions, there is little to be said. But he is counselled not to make it a question at all, and is dissuaded not from entertaining an undue amount of fear, but from entertaining any. He is advised, not simply to moderate his fears, but to defy them. He is told that such fears are an evidence of cowardice, and to yield to them is to be guilty of dastardism. He is not told that they are groundless ; on the contrary, he is informed that there is good cause for all his anxiety, that his damnation is likely enough, and the only course open to him is to " reconcile himself even to that," manfully to face it, and brave it out. Let him screw up his courage, shake his

[1] *Past and Present*, p. 101.

fist defiantly in the face of his fears, and display a little
of the Norse-Odin " consecrated valour," and they will
vanish like ghosts at break of day.   This fear of God
and retribution, this fear of death and what comes after
death, is but a species of contemptible cowardice.
" Brother, rise above all that."   Do but try the efficacy
of a little grim-eyed defiance and Norse-Odin bravery,
and your fears will " fold their tents like the Arabs and
as silently steal away."   A recommendation so impious
and audacious is worthy only of a Napoleon " taking
God into his own hands," or a Byron silencing the
regrets that sat like harpies on his death-pillow with a
" Let me be a man to the last "!   Surely never has
poorer prescription for a mind diseased made its appearance in print since the day when men began to seek out
many inventions!   A man must have poisoned himself
with some befooling drug before he can seriously propound a philosophy of defiance to a soul sensible of its
guilt and anticipating the judgment to come!

The policy is so stupid and senseless, that we have
some difficulty in persuading ourselves that Carlyle
meant seriously to recommend it.   Perhaps his notion
may have been that sin is not really penal, and did not
entail on the transgressor any retributive consequences in
the world beyond.   In that case our guilty fears, of
course, are groundless, and the recommendation is a very
proper one, that they should be dismissed as cowardly.
But the very question to be determined is—are they
groundless?   Shakespeare did not think so ; Dante did
not think so, nor Socrates.   The consciences innumerable,
which in all ages have been inflamed and sore with the

ache of unforgiven sin, might, on this theory, have been saved a vast amount of distress, and thousands of disconsolate souls might have dispensed with their sighs and bottled up their tears, if they could only have been of the same happy turn of mind as the Chelsea philosopher. But to them their fears were terribly real, driving them to the borders of despair, and nothing gave them a safe and holy quietus but the Cross and Sacrifice of Christ, through whom alone we have peace with God, and therefore peace with ourselves.   When face to face with " a conscience which is a thousand swords, and a God who is a thousand consciences," valour, defiance, and Norse-Odin bravery are idle and impossible expedients.   Nothing will prove of any avail but the blood-drops of the great Propitiation.   " Let it be argued, as it easily may, very learnedly," says Isaac Taylor, " on grounds metaphysical and on grounds ethical, that the Christian doctrine of Propitiation for sin is ' absurd,' and that it is ' impossible,' and that it is ' immoral,' and that it is everything that ought to be reprobated—let all such things be said, and they will be said to the world's end—it will to the world's end also be true that each human spirit, when awakened toward God as to his moral attributes, finds rest in that same doctrine of the vicarious sufferings of the Divine Person, and finds no rest until it is *there* found." [1]

Yet this glorious Gospel expedient for the removal of sin Carlyle designates in contemptuous accents " a Morrison's pill from without "; for the atonement, being an external remedy, he must have meant to include it in

[1] *Restoration of Belief*, p. 320.

the reference.   But, not to speak of the irreverence and offensiveness of the allusion, the truth is that, while pouring the vials of his scorn on Morrison and his patent nostrums, Carlyle could dabble a little in Morrison drugs himself.   Heaven knows, some of his own prescriptions are Morrisonian enough, and certainly none more so than when he counsels a distressed and distracted soul to seek its comfort in self-assertion and defiance, and "consecrated valour."   Altogether, we have no hesitation in characterising the religion of Carlyle, in so far as it bears upon the problem of guilt, as wanting in intellectual and moral seriousness, and unsatisfactory in the extreme.   It was not satisfactory to himself.   After he had undergone what he regarded as equivalent to what is known among Christian people as "conversion," he emerged, he tells us, into "a higher atmosphere, and gained a constant inward happiness that was quite royal and supreme, in which all temporal evil was transient and insignificant."   But this "royal and supreme happiness" of his, as Mr. Leslie Stephen suggests, must be taken a little on trust.   It was not of long duration. In after years it suffered frequent eclipse.   The gleams of this happier mood were fitful, and were soon shrouded in murky gloom.   If peace of mind were his, it certainly never appeared in his life.   The poetic optimism of *Sartor* died away into a chronic pessimism, and at last, in his old age, he exclaimed, with wailing pathos, that God does nothing.

We must now advert for a little to the peculiar doctrines Carlyle has propounded on the subject of Heroes and Hero-Worship.   We would not be insensible to the eminent service he has rendered in holding aloft for public admiration the inspiring examples of great men. It was a service for which his sympathetic insight, his power of vivid portrayal, and picturesque description pre-eminently qualified him.   Few authors have done more than he to regulate our admiration for the great spirits of the past, making it wise and discriminating, and helping us to fix it on such objects as alone are worthy of it.   It is of the highest importance that we should have our heroes wisely chosen for us, and our reverence centred only on such as have something in them to command and deserve it.   The heroes whom the world has perched upon its pedestals, and on whom its pæans and panegyrics have been lavished, have not always been worthy of the canonisation conferred on them, and Carlyle is entitled to our gratitude, if for nothing else than this, that he has helped to uncrown the worthless and enshrine the noble in their place.   If he had stopped there no word of exception would have been called for.   But he has gone further.   He in-culcates " Hero-Worship " as part of Goethe's Religion of Reverence, and even presumes to identify it with the religion of Jesus Christ.   But whatever may be thought of this new cult, which for the space of thirty years Carlyle did little else but advocate, one thing is tolerably clear, that by no possibility can it be incorporated with Christianity.   As we understand it, the purpose of Chris-tianity was not to exalt and glorify human nature ; it did not come to preach the dignity of man and inflate him with an overweening sense of his own importance. Its aim was not to make demi-gods of men, but to con-

vince them of sin, to humble them, to show them how
lost and ruined they were, and to reveal a way of salvation.   No doubt the religion of Jesus does not fail to
accentuate the native dignity that belongs to man as a
rational and immortal being, but at the same time it is
careful to administer a check to all tendency to pride
and presumption, by constantly . reminding him of his
creaturehood, his finiteness, and his subjection to God.
It does not forget that he wears the image of the
heavenly, though defaced and disfigured by the Fall, but
it dwells much on his littleness, his frailty, and his
limitations.   It is matter of history that wherever the
Bible has come, man-worship has disappeared, and only
as Christianity has relapsed toward heathenism has it
fallen into the adoration of canonised mortals.   Nor does
the Christian religion ever propose to ameliorate and
reform the world by setting up for its admiration examples of moral excellence.   As a moral specific, reverence
for the heroic in human nature counts for very little.
It is not so that depravity is overcome, vice restrained,
or men turned to righteousness.

Heroes, then, are not demi-gods to be worshipped, and
still less are they to be regarded as an inspired race
of which Christ was one.   If we are to believe Carlyle,
all his heroes are seers, prophets, Divine messengers, each
bringing a revelation from God.   So we are bound to
believe that their diverse and contradictory messages are
all true : Christianity true, for at the head of it stands
the Hero of the Manger and the Cross ; but Judaism true
also, for Moses was a hero ; Paganism true, for it, too,
had its heroes ; and Mahommedanism not less true, for

Mahommed was a hero. The message which the hero brings may be one whose morality is doubtful, and in some cases may even minister incentives to vice, yet all the while it is inspired, and we are bound to receive it as a direct communication from the skies. But the most objectionable feature of all is the introduction into this hero family of the man Christ Jesus—the first and foremost member of it, no doubt, but still only one among others. Here we are treading on ground of much solemnity. We are willing to recognise greatness wherever we see it. We are prepared to do honour to it in its degree. But there is something in the example of Jesus of Nazareth which is not to be mentioned on the same day or in the same breath with the examples of great men. In that peerless life which the four Evangelists present for our homage and love, so immaculate in its purity, so unapproximated in its conjunction of benignity and lordliness, we feel instinctively that we are no longer in presence of the human, that we are moving in an altogether different region from that of your Mahommeds, your Napoleons, and your Luthers. To twist the laurels of Hero-Worship around the spotless brow that once wore the crown of thorns, is a degradation and an insult, which the Christian conscience must always indignantly repel. " Honour superiority, pay tribute to eminence," says William Arthur, " but bring not Jesus to the level of great men. Say that Britannia is one of the Hebrides, that America is one of the West India Isles, that the Sun is one of the planets ; but say not that He who was ' holy, harmless, undefiled, and separate from sinners ' was one of the better born of the hero race."

Carlyle did much damage to the religious life of the age by the encouragement he gave to that species of naturalism, now making itself heard both in literature and science, which denies the uniqueness of Jesus and the exclusiveness of Christ's Gospel, and adopts as its liturgy Pope's Universal Prayer.   To concede its demands would be the extinction of Christianity.   The early Christians might have purchased themselves immunity from persecution and the privilege of unmolested worship in the days of Pagan Rome, had they only consented to place a bust of Jesus Christ in the same Pantheon with Jupiter and Apollo, and to put Christianity among the *religiones licitæ*, the allowable religions. The same demand is being made of the Christian Church to-day.   It must be determinedly repelled.   To yield to it would be to be guilty of a great betrayal.   It would be a denial of the Lord that bought us.   Popular writers and modern belle-lettrists must have entered but a little way into the feelings of Christian disciples, and have but scant understanding of the attitude of the Christian mind, when they imagine that at their mandate Christendom is going to receive religious instruction from Buddha, or get Divine illumination from the " Light of Asia."

We have no desire to exaggerate Carlyle's departures from orthodoxy, or to represent his angle of divergence from Church beliefs as wider than it really was.   At the same time his errors are too grave to be extenuated. We confess our inability to think so lightly of them as critics like Mr. Leslie Stephen have done, whose verdict seems to us to err from excessive leniency.

" The difference between Carlyle and his Scottish fore-
fathers," says he, " was one rather of particular beliefs
than of essential sentiment. He had changed rather the
data on which his convictions were based, than the convictions themselves. He revered what his fathers revered,
but he revered the same principles in other manifestations,
and to them this would naturally appear as a profanation,
whilst from his point of view it was but a legitimate extension of their fundamental beliefs." [1]

When a man suffers to drop away from him piece by
piece the " particular beliefs " of his early creed, it
requires a very delicate perception to see how " the
essential sentiment " of it is still retained. To us it is
all too painfully manifest that not merely " the data "
on which his convictions rested, but in many instances
the " convictions " themselves underwent a saddening
change under the crumbling touch of scepticism. Not
merely did the " principles his fathers revered " receive
at his hands new " manifestations "; there is too much
ground for believing that the " principles " themselves
gave way under the solvents of modern thought. To
represent his various theological errantries—his rejection
of Inspiration, his denial of historical Christianity, his
letting go the supernatural, his reduction of Jesus Christ
to the level of human heroics, his defence of Idolatry,
and his vindication of Popery—to represent these as
" legitimate extensions of fundamental beliefs " is, to say
the least, a very mild and euphemistic way of putting it.
His Scottish co-religionists, Mr. Stephen indicates, have
been led to view these deviations of a great mind more
seriously, owing, it may be, to their stupidity, or their

---

[1] *Hours in a Library*, vol. iii. pp. 273, 274.

want of that critical insight with which Mr. Stephen himself is so liberally endowed; but one thing at least may, with confidence, be affirmed of these same co-religionists, that they know their own creed well enough to perceive when it has been tampered with, that they are capable of recognising a change of front in a man's religious attitude when it takes place, and when he parts company with the Evangelical Theology they know what he has done.   Still, when all needful reserves and deductions have been made, and the writings of Carlyle have been winnowed from the theological hay and stubble which have mingled with them, there yet remains a residuum of pure gold so immense, an accumulation of precious stones so vast, as to justify the verdict of the Victorian era, which has promoted him to exalted rank in the hierarchy of our great prophets and teachers.   Two generations have now elapsed since he described for us, as he only could, the Hero as man of letters.   "That rare dignity," as a number of admiring friends once assured him, on his eightieth birthday, "he sustained, during a spacious fulness of years, in all its possible splendour and completeness."

III

THE THEOLOGY OF ROBERT BROWNING

III

THE THEOLOGY OF ROBERT BROWNING

" When a strong, brave man," says Dr. Berdoe, " has proclaimed his message to the world for six and fifty years, it is worth while to listen to him, especially when we know that he has lived up to his own professions, and carried out faithfully in his own long life the precepts and maxims he has propounded to the world at large." In the opinion of many, no such message as that of Browning has sounded in the ears of any generation since the days of Shakespeare himself. Like many another message, however, of sage and prophet, it did not meet with an immediate response. It fell at first upon a dull and unappreciative audience, and recognition was long of coming. It is depressing to remember, and almost makes one despair of literary criticism, that reviewers should have had nothing better to say of a poem like " Paracelsus," on its first appearance, than what they could condense into the one word " *rubbish*," and that even of " Pauline " some indolent and incapable scribe should have written the astounding comment—" A piece of pure bewilderment." Jeffrey's famous criticism of Wordsworth—" This will never do "—is about the only

parallel we can think of to the stupid and undiscerning
verdict passed upon Browning's earlier productions.   But
this period of temporary disregard soon reached its limits,
and in its place there came intelligent sympathy, which
in its turn was speedily to pass into general favour and
acclaim.   The poet gradually emerged from the cold
shade of neglect and disparagement, established for himself an assured place in the true poetical hierarchy, and
is now, to use his own happy phrase, " pedestalled in
triumph."   There are many reasons why the message
which such a man as Browning brings us should be
devoutly listened to, as though our whole body were an
ear, and why we should strain every faculty to understand and appraise it.

For one thing, it is above and beyond all else a purely
modern message.   Robert Browning is the one great
rhythmic spokesman of the age we live in.   No other
writer has so thoroughly reflected and interpreted the
ideas, hopes, aims, and aspirations of the nineteenth
century.   No other has shown himself so conversant
with the modern spirit, or addressed his reader with such
a distinctively modern accent.   Every man, as Lowell
says, is " the prisoner of his date," but to none of the
elect spirits of literature, the controlling powers in the
world of mind, is the remark more profoundly applicable
than to Robert Browning.   He lives in the present,
confines himself to the immediate here and now.   He
is a denizen of his own times, a native of his own generation.   He lives in it, and for it; thinks its thoughts, asks
its questions, faces its problems, uses its light.   Browning
has become a leader of men because he knows so well

what men are thinking, and can put into words thoughts which in other minds are vainly struggling for articulation. He can put himself inside their mental clothes, as it were, and wear them in a mode that dignifies them. He can take their dim ideals, heart-longings, and twilight gropings after truth, and give them back to them again, only transmuted and glorified by the transfiguring touch of genius. Browning has absorbed and assimilated the very science of the age to an extent which perhaps only the trained student of science itself can perceive and appreciate. Many of his poems are quite undecipherable unless we know something of optics, chemistry, physiology, botany, and music. He has achieved what many might consider the impossible feat of wedding science to poetry, and making even the scientific temper itself poetical.

There is supposed to be a certain contradiction between the poet and the man of science. The two are thought to deal in commodities diametrically opposed, and high authorities might be quoted in favour of the contention that as science advances poetry declines. The world in which the poet revels is a world of wonder, mystery, and enchantment. Science is the enemy of these : ever pushing on along the path of discovery, ever encroaching on the unknowable, and wringing one other secret from "Nature's cold reserve." Science "strips illusion of her veil," explains the inexplicable, dissipates much that was considered supernatural, and thus narrows the regions of Poetry, and restricts the flight of Imagination. To analyse the rainbow is one thing, to write an ode on it is another. It is one thing to "vivisect" the nightingale and probe the secret of its note, but a very different thing to make the little feathered songster the subject of poetical treatment. The man of science pulls the rose to pieces, botanises upon it, and indexes it as one of a class : the poet chants its beauty. The two appear thus to occupy adverse and contradictory attitudes ; yet Robert Browning has shown us how possible it is to reconcile them. It is just because Browning's scientific information gives him such an accurate insight into the mysteries of Nature, and enables him to depict her processes and phenomena so exactly in all their varying moods, that he is so well qualified to be the instructor of an age which claims to be in scientific advance of every other, and whose intellect can only be successfully approached along scientific avenues. " I know no thinker on religious subjects," says an admiring critic, " so worthy of confidence as he, because he is so well abreast of all the scientific thought of the age."

But concerning Browning's message we would like still further to say, that it is pre-eminently the message of a *thinker*. " No one ever reads him," it has been said, " without seeing not only his great ability but his great *mind*." [1] His writings are everywhere pervaded by a profound philosophy—in fact, if one were disposed to be critical, the preponderance of the philosophy over the poetry might even be construed into a defect. The poet deals with some of the most recondite and abstruse subjects that can engage the mind of man, while his treatment of them is always as deep as the subjects themselves, frequently verging on an obscurity for which in some quarters he has been severely condemned. But,

[1] Walter Bagshot.

grappling as he does with the great problems of life and destiny, threading his way through the intricacies of this complex nature of ours, depicting soul-struggles and the birth of great thoughts, we cannot expect to find in him the simplicity of an Oliver Goldsmith, or the transparency of a Cowper. No author demands such strenuous intellectual effort on the part of his reader to arrive at an understanding of his meaning, while, on the other hand, it is also true to say that no author more amply rewards it. It has been said that no other modern writer compels us to work so hard for our intellectual living, but then from no other do we derive such a good living, or draw such large mental dividends. He himself assures us, it is true, that he never consciously tries to puzzle his reader—yet what reader has he not puzzled ? There are passages which we may consider ourselves fortunate if we can fathom their meaning after repeated dippings —some have baffled us altogether. All this, however, proves not so much that Browning is obscure, as that we do not know enough to follow him ; we have not the necessary mental preparation for comprehending him. Browning, as one has said, " has become to us the seer and the sayer of the abysmal things of life." The reader who takes up a poem of Browning as something to while away an idle afternoon with, will very soon lay him down again. " I never intended," says the poet himself, " to offer such literature as should be a substitute for a cigar or a game at dominoes to an idle man—so perhaps on the whole I get my deserts and something over—not the crowd but a few I value more." Who would . not aspire to belong to that select minority ! but if we would, we must assuredly gird up the loins of our mind, and brace ourselves for some psychological gymnastics. He is one of those writers who, like the ocean, do not roll out their choicest things upon the shore; his pearls have to be dived for. His excellences do not lie upon the surface to be picked up by any passing straggler; it will be necessary to sink a shaft and commence mining operations; but as certainly as we do this, we shall be enriched by many a glittering find. We do not wonder that Browning Societies have been started, or that Browning primers and handbooks are so much in vogue, or that we have a Browning bibliography so copious as to amount almost to a literature in itself—it takes all such helps and auxiliaries to unfold the merits of Browning and initiate us into some adequate acquaintance with that mass of robust and virile thought which is now embalmed in the seventeen volumes which comprise his works, and which may be said to embrace almost every department of human knowledge.

Furthermore, Browning's message is that of a sincere and ardent *believer*. In a dubious age, like that in which our lot is cast, when Science with her questionings is continually at our elbow, and infidel breath is seeking to blow out the tapers that have lighted us on our way for nigh two thousand years, it is positively refreshing to meet with a thinker who has managed to keep his faith alive and vigorous, and who speaks on all the great essential verities with something like an accent of certainty. True, Browning does not write as a man whose faith has never known disturbance, or who thinks it sinful to doubt. On the contrary, he is one of those who hold that doubt has a distinct mission to fulfil in the development of the soul.   With him it is a sort of purgatory, through which the thinker must pass, and without which it is not possible to form the highest type of intellect.   Thus he makes Rabbi Ben Ezra say—

> " Rather I prize the doubt,
> Low kinds exist without,
> Finished and finite clods, untroubled by a spark."

With Browning, as with every right constituted mind, the point to be careful about is—

> " How can we guard our unbelief ?
> Make it bear fruit to us ? "

The doubt which now so commonly affects the nine-teenth-century mind does not reach a dangerous or deadly stage till it comes to the point where it is prepared not only to part with what we believe, but to part with the very disposition to believe, and has for its aim, not the ultimate reception of the truth, but doubts for the sake of doubting.   Scepticism is not merely the disbelief of some propositions, it is " the habit and pre-ference of disbelieving." [1]   From scepticism such as this we may well pray to be delivered, for it cannot but be blighting and ruinous.   Much of the scepticism prevalent in our day is unfortunately of this class : much of it arises from mental trifling ; much of it has at the bottom of it mental perversity or intellectual conceit, and, in cases not a few, even moral obliquity ; there is every-where the disposition to find out something which does not need to be believed rather than to find out something which does need to be believed.   For this species of unbelief

[1] Phillips Brooks.

Browning has but scant respect, but for the honest
doubter he at all times evinces the warm sympathy of
one who has himself " faced the spectres of the mind and
laid them." We can well understand, therefore, how the
poet has become to many a veritable Moses, conducting
them through the wilderness of speculative doubt, to a
land of promise where Faith can plant her feet firmly.
Browning has the merit of never having succumbed to
the pernicious sentiment that it does not signify whether
a man believes or not, and that *what* he believes is of
very trifling consequence. On the contrary, he stoutly
maintains that—

> " Belief or unbelief
> Bears upon life, determines its whole course."[1]

In his very first published poem, " Pauline," he declares—

> " That he will give all earth's reward
> But to believe and humbly teach the faith."

If there be any truth in Phillips Brooks' saying, that
" the way in which a man begins to think influences all
his subsequent thinking to the end of his life," we are
prepared to find in Robert Browning through all his
after course the strenuous believer. Nor did he ever
belie that promise of his early prime. He is always the
man of faith, " planting a sure foot upon the sunroad,"[2]
and helping others along the same shining path of
ascension. Nor did his faith consist merely in the
absence of doubt. It was something better than Bishop
Blougram's, which meant only " perpetual unbelief kept
quiet." The mere suppression of unbelief, or smothering
of doubt, did not suffice for Browning. His faith was

[1] " Bishop Blougram's Apology."   [2] " Paracelsus."

something positive and aggressive, and seemed ever engaged in studying how much it could believe, and not how little. To any doubt-tormented soul, anxious to escape from its own scepticism, and to be " no longer faithless but believing," we could prescribe nothing better than a course of Browning. In the preface to a recent work of his, Dr. Berdoe tells us how by a careful perusal of Browning's works he was rescued from the Agnosticism in which he floundered so helplessly ; how the poet solved his doubts, and " put him right on a hundred points which had troubled his mind for many years, and which had ultimately caused him to abandon the Christian religion." To those who may be sceptically inclined, Dr. Berdoe proceeds to recommend the poet as a guide, philosopher, and friend. In the body of the work I find this passage, which may be profitably pondered by those who have succeeded in divesting themselves of the old faith. " My heart goes out towards such poor naked souls," says he, " and I long to introduce them to my spiritual clothier. If Robert Browning cannot cover their mental nakedness, I fear they are like the casuals in our workhouses who tear up the clothes given them by the guardians, out of sheer determination to be different to other people, and go about *in puris naturalibus.* Browning has no desire to dress them in any particular uniform. All he desires is that no reasonable soul should be without a reasonable garment of faith, and that, I make bold to declare, he will bestow on any patient and serious student." [1]

[1] *Browning and the Christian Faith*, pp. 160, 161.

There are young men of contracted and fragmentary culture, who, because by dint of hard cramming they have taken a degree at the University, think themselves entitled to take on the airs of scepticism, and say adieu to their parents' faith, who sport their doubts very much as a dandy sports a new suit of clothes, to whom we would be rendering an inestimable service by presenting them with a set of Browning; and there are young ladies fresh from the boarding-school, with a smattering of knowledge, and a thin lacquering of accomplishment, who think it interesting to pose and attitudinise as disciples of Agnosticism, to whom a similar presentation might be made with incalculable advantage.   They would not be in the poet's hands very long till they would begin to feel their intellectual littleness : he would convince them of their ignorance : he would humble them into juster estimates : and, after these needful preliminaries, he would supply them with something like a reasonable faith, a working creed. Browning is one of those who, as Walter Bagshot puts it, "has battered his brains against his creed till he believes it," [1] and just because he has, he is so pre-eminently qualified to make believers of other people.

One other feature of Browning's message we should like to notice is, its *deeply religious* character.   Browning is undeniably a Christian poet, not perhaps in the narrow or technical sense of the word, but in the sense that his intellectual attitude is Christian, his culture is Christian, his sympathes are Christian, his aims are Christian, the

[1] *Literary Studies*, vol. ii. p. 376.

influence he exerts is Christian, the atmosphere he generates is Christian.   The religion to which he introduces us
may not, indeed, command in every point and particular the
assent of those who have been accustomed to insist on
scholastic definitions for every article of their faith, and who
have hedged round their thought with the wire-fences of
rigid theological demarcation, to overstep which is to go
upon a perilous excursion and incur a deadly risk.   In
Browning's religion there is nought for the sectist, the
theological partisan, or the man in quest of a professional
formula.   He takes sides with none of us.   He shouts
no party watchwords, unfurls no rival flags for us to
rally to, and supplies no uniforms.   We cannot ticket
him as belonging to any school.   His dimensions are so
vast that he will not fit into any of our little denomi-
national cabinets.   Because the poet is so universal,
because his sympathies are so wide, and his thoughts so
large that cramped and tight-laced natures cannot encircle
him within their narrow boundaries, they will even
challenge his title to rank as a Christian poet at all.
They are looking to Browning for something which it is
not in his line to supply—for the religion of the dogmatist, the Churchman, or the professional theologian;
whereas what we really find in Browning is "just the
reasonable belief of a great English nineteenth century
thinker, who is in sympathy with the science, progress,
mental activity, and inquiry of our day." [1]   It is in this
direction that Browning helps and benefits us most.   He
seems to us to have rendered a distinct service to Religion
in making manifest, as no other thinker has, its perfect

[1] Berdoe.

reasonableness, and putting it on such a basis that intelligent and thinking people can accept it consistently with all their light and culture.   More than any other writer we know of, he has recaptured for Religion science and philosophy, won them to her side in an age when they seemed to be slipping away from her, and established between all three a Triple Alliance which shall prove more than a match for all the forces which unbelief can bring into the field.   Not only has he brought Science and Religion to understand each other, and live on happier terms, but we may even go so far as one of his most advanced critics, and claim for him that " he has made scientific religion an accomplished fact." [1]   He has cleared away obstacles to faith ; he has demonstrated on what philosophical foundations the great Christian verities are resting ; he has restated those verities in a manner so captivating and ingenious, as to win acceptance for them even with many who have turned their backs on Church and altar.   If the scepticism of our age shows signs of abating ; if the wave of rationalism which, after submerging Germany, passed over these countries, has spent itself, and already begins to break in harmless foam along the shore ; if our journals and magazine literature are more respectful to religion than they once were ; if everywhere the conviction is gaining ground that, whether as a nation or as individuals, we cannot get on without religion,—the one man who, of all others, has done most to bring about these happy omens is undoubtedly Robert Browning.

We enter on more debatable territory when we

_____
[1] Berdoe's *Browning and the Christian Faith*, p. xvii.

attempt to determine the extent to which Browning's Christianity conforms to the Christianity of the Churches and creeds. How much he holds in common with ordinary theists, and with the average Christian believer, is a point on which opinion seems to be exceedingly diversified. Mr. William Sharp, one of his biographers, considers his attitude as a religious teacher unimpressive, because it amounts to nothing more than "acquiescence with codified morality."[1] Mrs. Sutherland Orr is quite convinced of Browning's heterodoxy. The Rev. John Rickaby, in a paper contributed to the *Month*, is strongly of opinion that Browning falls short of orthodoxy, that he is an anti-dogmatist, that his writings are hostile to anything like a settled faith, and considers it time that a warning voice was raised to counteract the assertion that Browning is one of our greatest religious teachers. On the other hand, such students of the poet as Thomson, Lyttleton, and Kirkman are just as strongly convinced of his sympathetic attitude to Christianity. The latter writes, in an essay on Browning: "I must claim for the poet the distinction of being pre-eminently the greatest Christian poet we have ever had. Not in a narrow, dogmatic sense, but as the teacher who is thrilled through and through with Christian sympathies, as with artistic or musical."

Dr. Berdoe has no hesitation in denominating him as "something more than a Theist—he is a Christian."

This diversity of opinion arises very largely, no doubt, from the dramatic form into which most of his poetry is cast, and the consequent difficulty of determining when

[1] *Life of Browning*, p. 200.

13

we are listening to the poet's own individual beliefs, and when only to those which he puts into the mouth of his *dramatis personæ*, to whom he stands in no deeper relation than one of literary sympathy. In reply, however, to the allegation that when using Christian arguments Browning is only speaking dramatically, most of us will be satisfied with this rejoinder from one who has devoted many years of patient study to the poet's works: "Candidly, I must say that I do not believe Browning was enough of a dramatist to escape from himself in any of his poems; and, as every one of his characters talks Browning, it follows that a good many Browning thoughts find expression in his works."[1]

For our own part, we fail to see how any candid reader of the Browning literature can come to any other conclusion than that the poet was not only a Theist, but a true Christian believer. We would be disposed to deduce this conclusion, however, not so much from a citation of passages from the poet's writings, a long array of quotations in which he testifies to this particular doctrine or to that. By the very same process it would be easy to make out that Browning was an Atheist, an Agnostic, or a Deist. It would be a somewhat barren and unremunerative exercise to resolve the poet's writings into a huge dictionary of proof-texts, or construct out of them something bearing a near resemblance to a theological manual. Behold we show unto you a more excellent way. Better any day than a proof-text is a *proof-trend*, and it is by an appeal to what we may call *proof-trends* that we would be disposed to settle this question. We should be inclined

---

[1] Browning's *Message to his Time*, p. 4.

to call attention to the vast space which Christianity occupies in the poet's writings; to the enormous extent to which it has leavened the poet's thinking; to the profound reverence with which he everywhere treats it; to the perennial interest it has for him as a philosopher, a psychologist, and student of human nature; to the constant readiness he evinces to take sides with it against its adversaries, and to the fact that he constantly represents it as a manifestation of the Divine, and as the high-water mark of all man's spiritual attainment.

It is hardly possible even to turn over the pages of Browning without seeing what a staunch believer he is in the existence and reality of the Supreme Being. He begins his religious experience at a point where most men end theirs—he is "very sure of God." He never dispenses with the Divine Being, nor leaves Him out of His own universe. The very first article of the poet's creed is that God is the Creator of all things, and that His presence is immanent in all His works.

> "I find first
> Writ down for every A B C of fact,
> In the beginning God made heaven and earth."[1]

Materialism and Pantheism, with all that even leans in their direction, are at once for Browning ruled out of court as inadmissible. "God, Thou art Mind," says Paracelsus, thus repudiating the idea that He is merely a "force," or a "stream of tendency," or a "working hypothesis" by which to construe the universe, or a convenient "name for the sum-total of things." To Browning, as to Carlyle, it was flatly inconceivable that reason, intelligence, and

[1] "The Ring and the Book."

conscience should have been put into us by an entity that had none of its own.

> "Behind me is my cause—that's styled
> God ; after in due course succeeds the rest." [1]

The human mind itself, rightly interrogated and interviewed, implies the existence of a Mind outside it, Eternal and Supreme. Of that Mind all Nature was, in Browning's system, the manifestation and disclosure. Matter is not to him " the dead thing of the laboratory," but a " crystallisation of the thought of God." " What fools call Nature," says the poet, " I call God." [2]

> "God dwells in all,
> From life's minute beginnings, up at last
> To man—the consummation of this scheme
> Of being, the completion of this sphere of life." [3]

It is not only among stars and planetary systems the poet looks for God, not alone among the Immensities and Eternities that he perceives the trail of His garment, or hears the sound of His footfall. He detects the thought of the Divine mind in a speck of March dust blown in the wind, in the starfish that " crawls in a wash of weed," in the simplest sacs and most rudimentary of infusoria, in the perpetual dance of those atoms and molecules of whose wondrous potency present-day science, supplementing the vision of the eye with the vision of the microscope, has given us such surprising revelations that the infinitely little has become to us the awful and the incomprehensible ; " the Name," says our poet—

> "comes close
> Behind a stomach cyst, the smallest of creations"; [4]

---

[1] " Parleyings with Furini."   [2] " The Ring and the Book."
[3] " Paracelsus."   [4] " Mr. Sludge, the Medium."

alluding to the fact that the gulf which separates the living from the not-living can never be bridged over but by the forth-putting of creative power on the part of Him who is the Life.   Browning is as much a believer in the enduements and affinities, the attractions and repulsions of atoms, as " the Abraham of scientific men " himself, and allows as limitless a play to molecular action as even Professor Tyndall could desire.   But behind all, and antecedent to all, for Browning, is " the Name."   If atoms are possessed of the mysterious potencies ascribed to them, they have them only because the Creator invested them therewith ; if molecules can evolve such wonders, it is only in virtue of properties which are delegated and derived from a creative source. The heavens declare the glory of God, and not merely the glory of molecular action ; the firmament showeth *His* handiwork, and not the handiwork only of, monads.

> "We find great things are made of little things;
> And little things go lessening, till at last
> Comes God behind them." [1]

While the poet acquiesces in the usual arguments for the Divine existence, such as are commonly advanced in sermons, lectures, and theological text-books, he would seem to have a preference for swifter and more immediate methods of reaching the same great conclusion.   That God exists, is not so much for him an inference deduced from a long and complicated chain of reasoning, consisting of many links, and not at the best stronger than the weakest of them, as an experience ; not so much the result of a demonstration, constructed on philosophical

[1] " Mr. Sludge, the Medium."

principles, as an intuitive perception, an immediate knowledge. We have the sanction of a great modern
theologian[1] for saying that there are certain truths
so necessary to the life of man that they do not
need proofs : they may indeed be confirmed by inquiry,
but they do not rest upon it—the truth, for example,
that we are morally free, and the truth that we are
under obligation to do right. Browning is of the very
same opinion, and evidently recognises the truth of the
Divine existence as belonging to this category—

"Call this God, then, call that—soul, and both—the only facts
    for me.
Prove them facts? that they o'erpass my power of proving,
Proves them such."

Instead, therefore, of reaching the truth that God is as
the last rung on a long ladder of toilsome syllogism, he
prefers to take the elevator and mount up to the Divine
existence by experience and immediate discovery, believing as he does with Paul, that "the eternal power and
divinity" of the Godhead may be "*clearly seen*" in the
things that are made, and that direct contact of the soul
with God is possible through trust and love and heart-
union. In Browning's philosophy the heart is far more
the organ of faith than the head, and the attainments of
intellectualism are always rated at a much lower value
than those of love—

"Love gains Him by first leap."

"So let us say,—not 'since we know we love,'
But rather 'since we love we know enough.'"[2]

---

[1] Dr. Dale.

[2] "Ferishtah's Fancies : A Pillar at Sebzevah."

And is not the poet right? When we analyse our own belief that God is, and trace its genesis, and the process generally by which, in the last issue, it was eventually lodged in our mind, do we not find that it rests far less on ontological or teleological considerations than on the direct sense and feeling of His august presence and power, when, "in some high hour of visitation from the living God," we have felt as the poet Wordsworth did—

"A presence that disturbed us with the joy
Of elevated thoughts ; a sense sublime
Of something far more deeply interfused,
Whose dwelling is the light of setting suns
And the round ocean, and the living air,
And the blue sky, and in the mind of man."

The mind of the Creator, impinging on our mind, and acting upon it as the mind of the poet acts upon us through his written verses, the contact of the Eternal Spirit with our spirit, to which it is originally so related as to admit the possibility of that contact—our belief in God is never so well grounded as when it rests on an experimental basis like this. If we walk with God as Enoch did, if we talk with Him as Moses did, if we commune with Him as David did, and hear the whisper of His still small voice with the inner ear—what need we any further witness? We shall indeed thankfully avail ourselves of all the reasons for our belief with which philosophers and theologians can furnish us: we shall gladly seize on every confirmation of our belief which may come within our reach, but still we shall recognise that our faith is not dependent on these accessories, for we have got past them to some-

thing better, we have outsoared them, and can say
with Job, "Now mine eye seeth Thee." So at any rate
it is with Browning, who attains to his belief in God's
existence and reality, not as the last result of an
illative process, but rather as a secret communicated
from above.

"God has a few of us whom He whispers in the ear,
    The rest may reason and welcome : 'tis we musicians know." [1]

The argument, as far as we can see, has only one
drawback. While perfectly valid for himself, it is not
convincing to others. It is possible for others to turn
upon the poet and say that it is all an illusion, that
he is only mistaking his own dream for a sober reality ;
and if they choose to do so, we know not that
there is anything left for the poet to answer, except
that his proof is satisfying to himself, and has
proved satisfying to the world's best and noblest spirits,
of all ages and nationalities, for nigh two thousand
years.

Sure of God, Browning is equally sure of the future
life. He is emphatically the poet of immortality. He
is deeply convinced of the Divine origin and larger
destiny of man. To him the soul is something more
than a bundle of nerves, a physical function, or a physiological dust-heap swept together by the action of law and
dispersed again by the approach of death. He knows
nothing of that coarse materialism which proceeds upon
the principle that "as a man eateth so is he," and thus
resolves every spiritual and ethical consideration, on the
last analysis, into a bill of fare. With Browning, man's

[1] "Abt Vogler."

nature is ethereal, capable of allying him with God, and holding converse with the infinite.

"Mind is not matter, nor from matter, but above."[1]

He makes Guido say—

"Christ's maxim is—One soul outweighs the world."[2]

From no other of our bards have the arguments for Immortality received so strenuous an affirmation. The rational and philosophical grounds for belief in a future life are so convincingly set forth, that they almost take from the face of death its terror, and turn the grave into a great sunrise. A favourite argument with Browning is that derived from the inherent grandeur and immense possibilities of human nature. By his very build and make, it is manifest that man is constituted for some ampler destiny than he ever reaches here. In the human soul are germs betokening a far more majestic tree than they ever develop into on earth. Foundations are laid in it so broad and deep, as to suggest a nobler edifice than is ever erected in Time. As Emerson says, "we do not build magnificently for mice." If this life is all, we are built on too large a scale, and too heavily freighted with faculty. It is like building a man-of-war to sail across an inland lake. Such splendid powers and capacities have not room or verge enough for their complete development within the narrow limits of an earthly lifetime. Says the poet—

"I know the earth is not my sphere,
For I cannot so narrow me but that I still exceed it."[3]

---

[1] "The Ring and the Book."
[2] *Ibid.*   [3] "Pauline."

And again—

"Earth is no goal, but starting-point of man."[1]

Moreover, to Browning's way of thinking, the lack, the shortcoming, the incompleteness of this present life are such as fairly to imply and necessitate another life to follow. We are intended to accomplish great things, yet we achieve but little. We finish nothing. We reach to no finality. We have to be content with fragments. "All here is halved, not whole." From the eager pursuit of our grandest enterprises, we are suddenly beckoned unawares. Our life music is rudely broken in upon, often in the very midst of its choicest bar. In the prosecution of our noblest projects we are abruptly interrupted with cruel stoppage and closure. Just when, by dint of long training and education of many years, we have got ourselves equipped for the doing of something worthy of us, we are shot down before death's fatal archery. No sooner have we acquired the mastery of our piece and stepped upon the stage to act well our part, and receive the plaudits of the audience, than the curtain drops and the lights go out. To all this fragmentariness, lack, and failure, Browning's poetic soul is keenly sensitive. His fine-strung nature is as a nerve over which all this creeps till it is felt acutely, and his feelings find vent in the cry of the dying and disappointed Paracelsus, "There needs another life to come"! "My foot," says he, "is on the threshold of a boundless life." "Leave Now," says the Grammarian, "for dogs and apes! Man has For Ever."[2]

[1] "The Ring and the Book."
[2] "The Grammarian's Funeral."

In those exquisite lines addressed to his wife in " One Word More," he complains that in the years at his disposal here he can paint no pictures, carve no statues, make no music " which would all-express me "; verse alone is all this life allows him, but he looks forward to a career of limitless expansion and possibility beyond the grave—

> "Other heights in other lives, God willing." [1]

Let us not forget either the famous passage in which he compares life to a rehearsal, which does not always go off smoothly, but which nevertheless tests and prepares for the after performance—

> " All's for an hour of essaying
> Who's fit and whose unfit for playing
> His part in the after-construction
> —Heaven's piece, whereof Earth's the Induction." [2]

Another aspect of the question on which Browning is fond of dwelling, is that connected with the sense of justice so deeply implanted in the breasts of all men. We have the profound and invincible feeling, of which nothing can rid us, that goodness ought to be followed by reward and happiness, and sin by suffering and punishment. But in the moral order which at present prevails, this law of retribution is not maintained. It is constantly disregarded in a way which shakes the faith of multitudes, for daily observation forces on our attention the dismal fact that reward and penalty are distributed most unequally, and without any scrupulous regard to moral character; so that, while for virtue there is often no guerdon but tears and heartbreak, for successful scoundrelism there are all the prizes of life. Punish-

[1] " Men and Women."   [2] " Pacchiarotto."

ment often lights on the innocent, while the real offender
escapes the Nemesis which should overtake him for his
crimes. If we take this world only into view, justice is
not done. The Maker would seem to have organised
our life upon a ground-plan of fundamental unfairness
and inequality. Shelley thought this was "a wrong
world," and many have been driven to think the same.
Hence the necessity for postulating, as Browning does,
another world to supplement this wrong world and set
it right. "This first life," says the poet, "claims a
second."

> "If this be all—(I must tell Festus that)
> And other life awaits us not—for one,
> I say 'tis a poor cheat, a stupid bungle,
> A wretched failure. I, for one, protest
> Against it, and I hurl it back with scorn." [1]

Browning lays great stress, too, on those intimations of
immortality derivable from the depths of our own nature,
when it is not biassed or sophisticated by some counter
philosophy.   Immortality has been designated the "great
prophecy of reason."   We cannot look into ourselves
without finding it; it is part of the outfit and the very
contents of our being.   About our whole nature there is
an upward look, a forward leaning, an onward gesture.
We are "yonder-sided" beings; we pant after God; we
grope and aspire after a fuller and diviner form of being.
It is infinitely reassuring to lesser minds to find a genius
like Browning, one "crowned with prose and verse," and
"wielding Learning's rod," putting his endorsement on
all this, and cherishing the invincible hope that "deathly

[1] "Paracelsus."

mists cannot quench us"; that, piercing the final gloom,
" we shall emerge one day." [1]

> "In man's self arise
> August anticipations, symbols, types,
> Of a dim splendour ever on before
> In that eternal circle run by life."

In his treatment of the problem of moral evil Browning is not nearly so satisfactory. On the dark things that trouble and perplex our existence—sin, and pain, and death—he does indeed succeed in flashing many a brilliant sidelight, which if it does not wholly dissipate the darkness, at least lights it up with a momentary gleam of unusual brightness. Or, to vary the figure, if his philosophy does not quite bridge over this great gulf of mystery, it must be confessed it at least shoots out into it a far-reaching promontory. The poet is quite successful in combating the contention of J. S. Mill, that God must be either a malignant or a limited Being, else He would not permit under His moral government so much imperfection, misery, and evil. Browning is not seriously embarrassed by this view. He is impatient of it, and almost seems to think it unworthy of being seriously advanced by any responsible thinker. He has little difficulty in showing that sin and suffering, and all the lowering shadows and difficulties which constitute what Horace Bushnell calls " the night-side of creation," are quite reconcilable with the existence of an All-loving and All-powerful Creator. These disturbances and complications of the moral order are permitted because they are necessary for the proper development of the soul, for

[1] " Paracelsus."

stimulating the growth of the good, for the right forming
of character, for conveying moral benefit, and working
out our moral perfection, which can only be secured by
a lifelong war with the forces of Evil that set themselves
in array against us, and dispute every inch of our progress, as we go on to the goal. Browning's philosophy is
thus, it would seem, possessed of two features at least
which should strongly recommend it to favour—first, that
with him there is no inclination, as there is unfortunately with so many other philosophic writers of the day,
to disallow the existence of final causes, or treat them
with disrespect, as the fond and foolish conceits of minds
accustomed to look at everything religiously; and, second,
that he recognises the great truth that "moral and not
physical uses are the last ends of God in everything."[1]
Clinging to this twofold conviction, Browning is enabled
to take a comparatively optimistic view of those dark
troubles which infest our existence, because he sees that,
however perplexing and baffling they may be, they may,
nevertheless, become tributary to the ends of moral
government, and the high uses of life.   It is only by
struggling with opposition, and overcoming hindrances,
that we can really develop and progress—is not this the
unvarying note of all Darwinian teaching?   Wisdom can
only come after long contest with ignorance, virtue after
long wrestling with the obstacles that antagonise and try
it; character is but the ripened fruit of many years of
toil, discipline, and vigilance.   "We are upborne," as the
poet puts it, "by what we beat against."   "A world,"
says Dr. Martineau, "without a contingency or an agony

[1] Bushnell.

could have had no hero and no saint." Results corresponding to these are evolved by Pain; it, too, has its uses. It imparts seriousness and solemnity to life. It is our "pungent educator" in many gifts and graces which are among the choicest of our moral endowments. It generates the heroism of the sickroom and the martyr's stake. It evokes pity, and creates sympathy.

> "Put pain from out the world, what room were left
> For thanks to God, or love to man?"[1]

Moreover, if there was no pain there could be no pleasure; for had we not a nervous system capable of writhing in agony, neither could we ever know what it is to thrill with ecstasy.

> "Pain's shade enhanced the shine
> Of pleasure, else no pleasure."[2]

Had the poet gone no further than these philosophisings there would have been nothing to condemn; but unhappily, in the process of developing them, he has broached a theory of evil, a doctrine of sin, which is erroneous, and would land us in a virtual denial of the moral turpitude, and even the very existence of sin. It is not a new theory, for it coincides with that of Leibnitz, and has evidently been inspired by the Hegelian theology. It is to the effect that the existence of sin is only relative. Browning cautions us repeatedly against looking upon evil as a real thing. We are to regard it only as the inevitable shadow that must accompany the Good, the dark background that acts as a foil for virtue, helping to set it off by the force of a transient contrast, having

[1] "Ferishtah's Fancies."   [2] *Ibid.*

but the same relation to it as night to day, or shade to shine.

> "Fair and good are products
> Of foul and evil: one must bring to pass the other,
> Just as poisons grow drugs." [1]

We are exhorted to "concede a use to evil," [2] because it is—

> "The scheme by which through ignorance
> Good labours to exist." [3]

Good and evil grow together: what know we—

> "But proof were gained that every growth of good
> Sprang consequent on evil's neighbourhood?" [4]

In the famous passage from "Abt Vogler" we have the same thought enunciated still more explicitly—

> "The evil is null, is nought, is silence implying sound;
> What was good shall be good, with for evil, so much
> good more."

Now we do not hesitate to characterise such definitions of evil as not only incautious and misleading, but practically subversive of the real nature of sin. If moral evil discharges the functions and effects the purposes which it is here credited with, it has already lost the character of evil, and is transmuted into a positive good. To treat Good and Evil as correlatives, as Browning does, to regard them as implying and necessitating each other, as standing in no deeper relation to each other than that of contrast, implies the most serious misconception of

---

[1] "Pietro of Abano."
[2] "Parleyings with Bernard de Mandeville."
[3] "Sordello."
[4] "Parleyings with Bernard de Mandeville."

their true nature. It is a frivolous and insufficient treatment of a momentous subject, to set down evil as only a contrast to good, its foil, its shade, its background: it is something very much more, and very much worse—it is positive hostility to good, a something arrayed against it in direct and clenched antagonism, combating it at every point, and bent on nothing less than its extermination. Still more objectionable is it to represent evil as actually promoting the good, assisting it, "bringing it to pass," and actually adding to the good "so much more" good, and making it in the end "a better good" than it would otherwise have been. What sort of evil is it, we would like to ask, whose office or function it is to be promotive of the good? And what sort of good is it that accepts of the offices of evil, is "brought to pass" by evil, is ministered to by evil, nursed into special excellence by evil, and, in the last issue, owes its perfection to evil? Certainly not the kind of evil which God resents and legislates against, and not the kind to which our own consciousness testifies when it brings its indictment against our own life; not the kind that the Bible thunders against on its every page with all the awfulness of Divine intonation, nor the kind that Conscience agonises over, or that Penitence bathes with her tears; and certainly not the kind of good that the Scriptures describe, that Conscience accepts, that God approves, or that Heaven rewards. "If good," says Julius Müller, "seeks to produce or supplement itself by evil, it thereby ceases to be good"; and, similarly, if evil is conducive to good, and accessory to it, it thereby ceases to be evil. We do not deny that there is a sense in which the two are correlat-

14

ive.   Our knowledge of evil may often eventually lead
to a deeper acquaintance and a heightened consciousness
of good.   If it were not possible for man to sin, it would
not be possible to predicate goodness of his acts.   There
is a sense in which sin may become tributary to high
moral ends and uses, but this happy result, it must be
borne in mind, always flows from the interposition of
redeeming grace, restraining sin, ordering it, subjugating
it, and otherwise powerfully bounding it : sin itself has
no inherent tendency to produce these results, but is
always and only positive hostility to good.   " What
Divine grace is able to bring out of evil, supposing it to
be already present, and the salvation which it is able to
work out from a state of arbitrariness and perversion by
overcoming evil, cannot certainly be referred to as a
proof of the necessity of evil.   Christian poetry may
have ventured to adopt the expression in reference to the
introduction of sin by the Fall, ' O felix culpa ! ' but the
calm and deliberate reflection of Science can never venture
to adopt such language." [1]   So writes Julius Müller, than
whom no more eminent authority can be appealed to on
the problem of evil.   In handling that problem, we shall
be in much safer custody if we commit ourselves to his
lead than if we follow the poetic imaginings of Browning.
In attributing the origin of evil to God, the poet comes
perilously near to consecrating every abnormal impulse of
human nature.

When we propose to catechise a man upon his spiritual
beliefs, we cannot do better than begin, not with this
peculiarity of his creed or that, but at once propound

[1] *Doctrine of Sin,* vol. i. p. 386.

this crucial and momentous inquiry—What does he think of Christ ? If he is wrong here he is likely to be wrong everywhere. If he is right on this central point, he is likely to be right to the very circumference of his thinking on all other articles of vital belief. If he thinks little of Christ, he will think little of sin. If he has low thoughts of the Mediator, he will have low thoughts of the Godhead. If he has an erroneous conception of the God-man, he will have an erroneous conception of himself and his own spiritual state. What, then, does Robert Browning think of Christ ? What has he to say of that Holy Being who once walked the fields of Palestine, lived the incomparable life recorded in the Gospels, and from that day to this has attracted to Himself the permanent admiration of the race ? What answer does he return to that momentous question which for nineteen centuries has " riveted the eye of thinking and adoring Christendom "—" Whom do men say that I, the Son of Man, am ? "

If we note down the many references to the Divine Man with which the poet's writings are so plentifully interspersed, and make a careful examination of them, we cannot come to any other conclusion than that Browning was a pronounced believer in the ascendency and divinity of Jesus Christ. On the whole subject of Christology the poet moves in an intellectual atmosphere identical with that of the believing and adoring Church. There is something nourishing to faith and hope in the fact that, while in these days the face of the God-man may have become less real than it was, because we have been forced to behold it through the murky atmosphere of unbelief,

and has faded more or less into indistinctness because
wreathed in the mists of speculation or clouded with the
smoke of criticism, so masculine a thinker as Browning
is so deeply convinced of the Divine Personality and
superhuman character of the Christ.   In his estimation,
that face of Jesus, so far from vanishing, "rather grows,
or decomposes but to recompose."[1]   Christ is to him no
fabulous or legendary hero, no shadow that once flitted
across the stage of history, no religious Genius deified by
the fervid and uncritical enthusiasm of his followers, no
product of Oriental imagination, no "dead fact stranded
on the shore of the oblivious years."   "He saw in Christ,"
says Dr. Augustus Strong, "the most effective revelation
of God.   When he seeks stimulus for sustained effort,
and inspiration for enduring virtue, he finds them in
Jesus Christ."[2]   Nay more, Christ is to Browning the
medium through which he does all his thinking about
God, and Man, and human society : every subject is
looked at through Him, as the stars can only be looked at
through the enfolding atmosphere.   He is the key for
the deciphering of every problem.   In His light we see
light clearly.

> "I say the acknowledgment of God in Christ
> Accepted by the reason, solves for thee
> All questions in the earth and out of it."[3]

The poet's allusions to Christ, which are many and
various, are invariably characterised by the profoundest
reverence, manifestly the utterances of one who lives

[1] Epilogue to "*Dramatis Personæ.*"
[2] *Theology of the Great Poets.*
[3] "Death in the Desert."

under His empire, and has felt the spell of His presence. In his beautiful poem, " Christmas Eve," in which occurs a description of the Midnight Mass at St. Peter's, Christ is referred to as

> " He who trod,
> Very man and very God,
> This earth in meekness, shame, and pain."

Very touching, too, in the same poem is his prayer for the Göttingen Professor, for whom Christ was but a mythological dream—

> "May Christ do for him what no mere man shall,
> And stand confessed as the God of salvation."

In " Saul," that wondrous oratorio, which many have considered the noblest of all Browning's religious utterances, we have the magnificent tribute—

> "O Saul, it shall be
> A face like my face that receives thee : a Man like to me,
> Thou shalt love and be loved by for ever ; a Hand like this
> hand
> Shall throw open the gates of new life to thee ! See the Christ
> stand ! "

The sympathetic student will have little difficulty in convincing himself that Browning accepted also the great cardinal fact of Atonement. His explanation of it, however, must be considered defective. In his philosophy of the Cross his weakness as a theologian betrays itself. The poet's scheme of salvation differs very materially from that which has commended itself to the historic Christian consciousness in all ages, and what is of more consequence, it is at variance with that which is unfolded in the Scriptures. With Browning the great central constructive principle round which everything revolves is

that God loves humanity ; not, however, in the sense
that He has provided for us, in the person of His Son, a
propitiation for our sins, or devised a glorious expedient
by which there might be a righteous exercise of His
mercy, and a free outflow of His Divine benevolence to a
guilty race without any sacrifice of principle.   According
to Browning, God is love in a sense which excludes the
other and complemental truth that God is law, God is
inflexible justice, God is immutable righteousness.   To
invest Him with these attributes is an entire mistake,
and arises from deluding ourselves with the idea that
God has less love in His composition than we ourselves
have.   We would go any lengths to save a man, but
unfortunately we credit God with an unwillingness to do
the same.   Hence the necessity for some convincing
demonstration that God is not different from ourselves in
this respect.   To afford that demonstration, to assure us
that God is animated by views and feelings akin to our
own, that there is originally resident in the Godhead a
true humanity—this is the object of the Incarnation,
this the end Christ had in view when He went up to the
Cross, and down to the grave.   That Cross with its
bleeding burden has been lifted up that the world might
have the brightest possible manifestation of the truth
that God is animated towards sinning mortals by feelings
and judgments not materially different from our own ;
that, to use a phrase of Browning's own, " He is human
at the redripe of the heart.".   That we have correctly
interpreted the poet's sentiments, the reader may satisfy
himself by a reference to his poem " Saul." David is
represented as having a passionate longing to save Saul

everlastingly, but checks himself in the indulgence of that longing by the reflection that he has really no warrant for entertaining it.   Then he despises himself for harbouring so dark a thought, or allowing it to have any weight with him, and indignantly spurns the idea that God does not love as much as he does, that his human affection for Saul outsoars and surpasses the affection of Saul's Creator.

> " Behold ! I could love if I durst,
> But I sink the pretension in fearing a man may o'ertake
> God's own speed in the one way of love !
> Do I find love so full in my nature, God's ultimate gift,
> That I doubt His own love can compete with it ?   Here the
>   parts shift ?
> Here the creature surpass the Creator ?   The end what began ? "

David, having an intense desire to save Saul, argues in the style of a modern rationalist that God must have a like desire, only with the Creator it exists on a scale of infinity ; and on the strength of this reasoning he proceeds to predict for Saul, and all other sinning, suffering mortals, the advent of God's Son into the world to bleed and die——but with this object only, to disabuse our minds of the mistaken notion that there is anything in the Divine character but sympathy and love, or, as he expresses it further on in the same poem, to convince us that " God's love is almighty," to reassure us by discovering to us " the flesh in the Godhead."   Lest it might be thought that Browning is here speaking dramatically, that these sentiments are only put into the mouth of one of his characters, and are not really the poet's own individual opinions, it may be advisable to reproduce here a conversation which Mrs. Sutherland Orr once had with the poet on this very subject, and which, fortunately, she has preserved for us. Assigning a reason why, in his judgment, humanity required Christ, the poet said—

" The evidence of Divine power is everywhere about us; not so the evidence of Divine love. That love could only reveal itself to the human heart by some supreme act of *human* tenderness and devotion : the fact of Christ's Cross and Passion could alone supply such a revelation."

Exception may be taken to this scheme of Atonement on the following grounds. In the first place, it proceeds upon an incomplete and onesided view of God, thus resting on a partialism, and not on a full-orbed conception. There are other attributes in God besides love. There are other aspects of the Divine nature besides those of gentleness, benignity, complaisance, and readiness to pardon. There is unflinching rectitude and immaculate holiness. There is an unbending truthfulness, which will fulfil its threatenings as unerringly as its promises. There is an authority which must be upheld at all costs, and a moral order guarded by all the severities of truth, and all the firmness of empire. " There is a steadfastness of principle running through the Divine administration, from which the august Being who presides over it was never once known to recede or falter." [1]   After a survey of all creation, Browning comes back to hand in the report " All's love." Surely if his survey had been a little more inclusive, and had he looked a little deeper, he might have seen that there was another side to things besides that represented

[1] Dr. Chalmers.

by sheer benevolence. When the Apostle Paul took a similar survey, with eyes more wide open than Browning's, he saw "the goodness *and the severity* of God." He saw in Him the authority as well as the fondness of a Father. He saw the smile of an indulgent Deity, but he saw also the frown of an indignant Deity. He saw a Great White Throne which will tolerate no tampering with those principles of inviolable sanctity which are the very pillars that support it, and a Lawgiver seated thereon who cannot look upon sin but with abhorrence. Browning chooses to blink or ignore all this, or he covers it over with an ingenious gloss. "Any scheme," says the late Principal Cairns, "which does not recognise and proceed upon the moral order of the universe, upon the moral character and government of God, and the righteous sentence of law binding over the transgressor to penalty, is not, in any proper sense, atonement, but only displacement of law."[1]

We take further exception to this scheme, on the ground that it makes God altogether such a one as ourselves. It credits Him with no judgments and feelings in regard to sin and salvation but those which are human and terrestrial. It must always be a fatal and egregious mistake to make our defaced and defective morality the measure of God's faultless morality, our derived morality the metewand by which to gauge the stature of a morality original and radiant. We look with benign tolerance on things which God by His very nature must look upon with abhorrence. We smile complaisance on offences on which God must frown dis-

[1] Paper read at Pan Council on "The Vicarious Sacrifice of Christ."

pleasure. Infirmities of conduct, which in our coarse and blunted estimate are quite venial, are in God's estimate deeply criminal. Dr. Chalmers, for instance, in one of his sermons, points out that we should never think of making an acquaintance an object of indignation merely because he was a stranger to prayer and destitute of piety. No man would ever think of vehemently denouncing his neighbour merely because he was alienated from God in the spirit of his mind, and lived in a state of practical unconcern about the affairs of eternity. Yet in God's eyes this alienation and forgetfulness amounts to a capital offence, sufficient in itself to bring upon him Heaven's anathema, a high crime and misdemeanour which will be rigorously dealt with, and visited with condign punishment. "It is a dangerous delusion," the great preacher goes on to say, "that we estimate God by ourselves—His antipathy to sin by our own slight and careless imagination of it—the strength of His displeasure against much evil only by the languid and nearly extinct moral sensibilities of our own heart." Into this very delusion not only the poet Browning but many of our popular writers have fallen, to the moral injury of themselves and their readers.

A third objection to this scheme of Atonement lies in the fact that it entirely fails to account for the production of the moral impression on the hearts of men which it is its very purpose to effect. The design of Christ's sufferings and death, according to Browning, was to afford the world, by means of a sublime act of devotion and tenderness, such a radiant and impressive display of the Divine love as to convince us of God's sympathy and compassionate interest, and thus soften and subjugate the alienated hearts of men. But on this theory of it one is utterly at a loss to see what there was in the death of Christ calculated to produce the effect which Browning declares was its sole design. If His death had no vicarious significance or expiatory value, as the poet maintains, it was to all appearance but a needless and gratuitous expenditure of blood and agony which cannot be specially impressive to anyone. If no great external benefits accrued to us from our Lord's dying, it was apparently but the infliction of needless suffering on a Being who was liable neither for His own nor for others' sins, and who in equity, therefore, ought rather to have been exempted from all suffering ; and what special proof of love is there in this, or what special evidence does such a scene afford of a kindly and conciliatory disposition on the part of the Father in heaven towards His children on earth ? If the Father dealt thus severely with His own holy and immaculate Son, might we not take it as a display of cruelty rather than of love, and might not the effect of it be to alienate rather than to conciliate, to repel rather than to draw us ? For if the sufferings of Christ were not for a great and important end which could not otherwise be reached, what are we to think of God, by whom they were not only permitted but appointed ? To inflict dire pains and penalties on the most perfectly holy Being who ever lived on earth, and whose devotion to God was such that it was His meat and His drink to do God's will, and to inflict them for no adequate end—what is there in this to afford us an unparalleled manifestation of God's parental affection, or what special inducement is there in such a tragedy to yield ourselves to God in obedience and piety ?   Is not such a painful and tragic exhibition calculated rather to harden us in our rebellion than to subjugate or soften, to drive us from God rather than to draw us to Him ? For, as has been justly remarked by Henry Rogers, " His sufferings have a double aspect: they affect our apprehensions of Him who appointed them no less than of Him who endured them, and give us but little encouragement to trust in the equity and benignity of the Divine administration which thus visits perfect innocence with deeper woes than the foulest guilt in this world was ever subjected to." [1]   But if, on the other hand, our Lord's sufferings and death saved us from penalties which must otherwise have fallen on us, or secured for us substantial benefits which otherwise we must have forfeited—if, in one word, they had a vicarious character and a propitiatory design—we can readily understand how they evidence and commend God's love to us, as the sacred writers say they do, and how they furnish us with a firmer ground of assurance that God is willing to be at peace with us than we had before.   Moreover, it is a conceivable hypothesis that God could have made the requisite moral impression on the human heart by the direct action of the Holy Spirit on the soul, who can surely convince us of God's love as easily as He can of our own sinfulness.   If, then, the objective exhibition of love on Calvary's Cross could have been dispensed with, and God could have attained His end in another and less costly way, it follows that the

[1] *Greyson's Letters.*

display of God's infinite love is less luminous on the
theory which supposes that the necessity of our Lord's
dying might have been obviated by the adoption of
another alternative, than · on the theory which supposes
that there were deep reasons within the Godhead itself
and within the Divine administration, rendering it absolutely necessary that Christ should suffer these things,
and enter into His glory.   Not only so, any student of
human nature and its susceptibilities knows that as a
rule the scene which fails to impress is the scene which
has been intentionally and expressly got up for the sake
of making an impression.   If our Lord's suffering was
incurred, as we believe it was, because it was incidentally
necessary to the prosecution of His great redemptive
work, because it had to be faced if He was to accomplish His Father's business and fulfil His mission, then
indeed we can conceive of nothing more grandly impressive to the onlooker.   But if, on the other hand, His
sufferings were studied, prearranged, and specially gotten
up with the object of making a pathetic appeal to our
sympathies, they must for that very reason largely defeat
their own end, and become just the reverse of impressive.
The appearance of contrivance spoils the spectacle, and
it degenerates into a stilted, stagey, theatrical display,
deprived of all effect and impressiveness by its own
affectation.   " If the sole design of the redemptive work
of Christ," says the great Princeton theologian, " is to
produce a moral effect upon the sinner, as some men
insist, the glorious transactions of Gethsemane and
Calvary, which the Church has always regarded as
infinitely real, intense with Divine attributes in action,

are reduced to the poor level of scenes deliberately contrived for effect, finding their sole end in their effect as scenes."[1]   And just in proportion as they study effect do they fail to be effective.   It is a notorious fact that the Moral Impression theory of the Atonement is of all theories the one that has proved least influential in producing impression.   Its failure to impress is admitted by Horace Bushnell himself, who, in the closing pages of a treatise written in its elucidation and defence, is forced to acknowledge that his only hope of rectifying this peculiar weakness which attaches to the theory, is by assimilating it to the commonly received theory of a sin-expiating and God-propitiating sacrifice.

Browning's views of the Incarnation and Atonement react injuriously on his views of Divine revelation.   If God has incarnated His Son to show that the sentiments of humanity are not different from His own, then, upon the whole, we cannot go far wrong in following the sentiments of humanity ; in these we really have a safer guide and a surer standard than the Bible itself.   Not a little of Browning's poetry is written with the object of glorifying the dictates of nature and the instincts of humanity as preferable to any rule whatsoever, God's Word not excepted.   There is discernible in many of his productions an undue exaltation of the individual consciousness above Scripture as a source of inspiration, and a test of certainty in regard to religious truth.   Man is, in fact, the repository of the Divine on earth, and is therefore in himself the source and standard of all truth. The human mind is " a convex mirror, wherein are gathered

[1] Hodge, *On the Atonement.*

all the scattered points picked out of the immensity of the sky to reunite there";[1] so it need not excite surprise, if this be a correct description, that the Mind itself is to be regarded as the final court of appeal. When the poet lapses into these rationalistic moods, it is quite useless for us to appeal against his conclusions to Scripture, for we are told in reply that man is his own Scripture. The Bible is but "a tale in the world's mouth," which the poet condescends to believe to be credible, but which he accepts only so far as it may be indorsed and authenticated by his own reason. If there is any conflict between the two, Browning invariably decides in favour of the individual consciousness. It is not enough for the establishment of any Christian doctrine that it should be countenanced by Scripture, it must also be countersigned and sanctioned by human judgment and feeling. Many of his characters, indeed, are held up to our admiration just because, "steady in their superb prerogative," they have turned a deaf ear to the pronouncements of the written Word, and dared to listen in preference to the dictates of their own nature, the whisperings of the oracle within.

> "There is besides the works, a Tale of thee
> In the world's mouth, which I find credible,
> I love it with my heart; unsatisfied,
> I try it with my reason, nor discept
> From any point I probe, and pronounce sound."[2]

In all this there is a strong tincture of Rationalism. It is precisely at this point that Browning, according to

[1] "The Ring and the Book : The Pope."
[2] "The Ring and the Book."

our judgment, opens a wide door for a flood of mystical, obscure, erratic, and often mischievous speculations. We know of scarcely any theological vagary so wild, or any heresy so audacious, that it does not find shelter and hospitality from this amazingly convenient theory. To affirm that because my individual feelings and preferences are not satisfied with any particular doctrine which is clearly revealed, I may therefore reject it as uninspired, is to arrogate an authority for the human spirit far beyond anything to which it is lawfully entitled. It is a proud rationalistic conceit, a piece of latitudinarian mysticism, highly convenient, as we have said, for any thinker who wishes to get rid of unpalatable truths and lead a life of theological adventure. It is no longer what the Holy Spirit, speaking in the written Word, communicates that we are to believe, but what we ourselves deem to be Christlike and worthy of God. The Scriptures are no longer to decide what is worthy of God and what is not ; each man is to decide for himself what is worthy of God from the data supplied him by his own individual conceptions. It is no longer what the Bible teaches we are to believe, but what we think the Bible ought to teach us. Our conception of what ought to be is henceforth to govern in everything our conception of what Omnipotence and Omniscience ought to do in the creation and government of the world. Because we consider it not worthy of God that there should be anything in Him to fear, therefore we are justified in concluding that there is nothing in Him to fear. Because we deem it unworthy of God that there should be any element in His nature which requires an atonement for human sin, therefore there is no such element in His nature. Because, in our way of looking at things, it is not Godlike that any soul should be capable of so sinning as to be lost, therefore we must become champions of Universalism; and if the Bible declines to favour Universalism, it must either be browbeaten, or twisted by some process of strained and violent exegesis into lending it some shadow of sanction, or else it must be quietly shelved as having no authority on the subject. Because, according to our feelings and judgments, it would not be Christlike that any lost soul should be continued in being by God, we must instantly conclude, either that the lost are given over to annihilation, or have extended to them a second probation, and a gospel of second chances. "It is thus," as some one observes, "that liberalistic mysticism agrees with liberalistic Rationalism in demanding a religion more Christian than Christianity, and more Christlike than Christ." This individualism in theology, whether it be regenerate individualism or unregenerate, unless when it is kept in strict and constant subordination to the written Word, is a most wayward and vacillating guide, and the history of all religious speculation from age to age proves it to be so. It lands us in the swamps of an infinite subjectivism. It leads to mysticism, obscurity, arbitrariness, and individualistic extravagance. Putting the oracle within above the "more sure word of prophecy," it becomes arrogant and tyrannical, setting up something of the nature of a little Popedom within the human breast. It offers a fatal facility for theological recklessness. It makes room in the domain of religion, not only for the importation of every species of neology, but for the

15

indulgence of fancy, caprice, and even individual whim. It is regrettable that a theory which has proved the fatal and fascinating source of so much error should have been so extensively advocated by our men of letters, and that it should have found in Robert Browning its poetical apostle.

IV

THE THEOLOGY OF GEORGE ELIOT

IV

THE THEOLOGY OF GEORGE ELIOT

As far back as the fifties, George Eliot wrote an article, in which she laboured to show that among female writers only the women of France had exhibited original genius, and they only had attained to the permanent distinctions of literature. Like many another brilliant generalisation, this would seem to have been too hastily arrived at, and to have been based on insufficient data. The names of not a few English women will at once suggest themselves to the reader which might fairly be cited as exceptions to the rule, while George Eliot herself lived long enough to furnish a conspicuous refutation of her own theory. Since she passed from among us, her reputation, like that of many another as great as she, has had its vicissitudes. The chorus of hyperbolic eulogy which followed immediately on her demise, has given place to systematic attempts at depreciation, in which even such a friend and admirer as Mr. Frederic Harrison has not scrupled to join. Admiration for George Eliot has of late gone out of fashion, and her fame has suffered a certain decline, which in her case, as in that of Dickens, Carlyle, and Kingsley, was perhaps inevitable. Men who aspire to

be thought clever and penetrating have taken upon them
to revise the popular verdict, reviewers have "shouted
with the shouting crew," and a coterie of small critics
have addressed themselves to what Tennyson used to call
"the ripping up process." They have flung their
depreciatory adjectives at her pedagogic style, her
incessant moralisation, her pompous sententiousness, her
didacticism, her novel with a purpose. But fortunately
reputation is not fixed by the passing cries of a shrieking
criticism, nor by the fickle taste of the moment. This
process of attempted belittlement will not lower the
pedestal of George Eliot's fame a single inch, nor even
seriously modify the general verdict already registered in
her favour, by which she has been accorded a place
among the select few in our day to whom the epithet
"great" can be conceded with a perfect sense of justice.
"Racine will go out of fashion like coffee," wrote Madame
de Sevigné; but the prediction has remained an unfulfilled
prophecy. Racine held the field, and so did the coffee
for that matter. The "bubble reputation" is, of course,
at all times a fragile and uncertain thing; it takes
more or less the varying colours which the passing
moment reflects upon it, and is liable to puncture and
collapse; but in George Eliot's case we are persuaded
the bubble will retain its perfect globularity in spite of
the stabs of critics' pens, and will continue to shine with
ever-increasing lustre as the generations come and go.
George Eliot wrote for eternity, and has therefore put a
great gulf of difference between herself and those "jerry-
builders of literature," as they have been not inaptly
described, "who produce showy glittering novels as

rapidly as a row of villas are run up in a London suburb."

To the theologian George Eliot offers, for a variety of reasons, a most fascinating study. The bent of her mind was distinctively theological, and underlying all she wrote there was a theological conception of life and of the universe. Dr. Selby thinks that "Nature meant her for a great theologian"; and undoubtedly, had her life chanced to develop in that direction, the high constructive genius of which she was possessed would have enabled her to reap immortal distinction. Be that, however, as it may, there is such a strong infusion of theology in her writings that those interested in that neglected science will be richly rewarded by their perusal—indeed, they will find her books a vast theological storehouse. Moreover, for the theologian she has this additional attraction, that in her alone among our novelists we have the outcome and expression of the modern spirit of Positivism; that she alone has heralded in the pages of imaginative literature the new Religion of Humanity, by far the most popular substitute for the Gospel which has yet been offered to our age; and that she alone has voiced in artistic form and won an audience in the novel-reading community for some of the leading ideas of Comte, Mazzini, and Darwin. And her interest in this respect is still further enhanced by the vast amount of religious and ethical teaching which has been compacted into her works. There is a larger body of positive truth in her pages than in those of Carlyle, while her ethical code is much more definite than his. The lessons which she inculcates are unmistakable. She has taught us the

divineness of duty, the deep value of that renunciation
with which, according to Carlyle, all true life begins, the
inexorable connection in their moral outworking of
cause and effect, the incalculable effects of hereditary
transmission with the terrible responsibilities it involves,
the value and pathos of commonplace lives, the irreparable consequences of human error, the privilege of living
for others in the humble offices of everyday life, the
responsibility of men to satisfy the claims of every social
and domestic bond, and to pursue unflaggingly that life
which will be most beneficial to the community, and to
which she herself aspired in the famous prayer—

> " Oh may I join the choir invisible
> Of those immortal dead who live again
> In lives made better by their presence.
> .   .   .   .   .   .   May I reach
> That purest heaven, and be to other souls
> The cup of strength in some great agony,
> Enkindle generous ardour, feed pure love,
> Beget the smiles that have no cruelty,
> Be the sweet presence of a good diffused,
> And in diffusion ever more intense ;
> So shall I join the choir invisible
> Whose music is the gladness of the world."

Singular to say, the very feature in George Eliot's
works which imparts to them a supreme interest for the
student of religion and theology, is that to which special
exception has been taken by the critics. On all sides
we hear it reiterated, even to weariness, that George
Eliot as a novelist violated the canons of true and correct
art. She brought to the task of fiction, it is said, too
serious a turn of mind. She evinced too eager a disposition to preach and instruct. Not satisfied, as she should

have been, with simply depicting human life, she insisted on furnishing the reader with a philosophical analysis of it as she went along.   She spoiled her story-telling by needlessly obtruding her own personality on the reader's notice, by interweaving it with too many ideas, and by a too frequent introduction of her own convictions, with the object of making converts for them at the point of the pen.   In the end she succumbed to her own pedantry, and degenerated into a kind of pompous schoolmistress with an irritating tendency to explain things, and for ever pointing a moral when she should only have adorned a tale.   In one word, she was guilty of what is nowadays considered the unpardonable offence of writing novels with a purpose.   The "purpose novel," as it is called, is the very *bête noir* of the critics, with whom it seems to be a sort of Eleventh Commandment : "Thou shalt not take upon thee any other function but that of amusing —thou shalt not be guilty of didacticism."   This raises the vexed question over which literary circles of late have lashed themselves into a state of tempest—What is the novel, and what are the legitimate ends at which alone it may aim ?   The final adjustment of this ticklish point may well be left over as one of the adjourned problems which the nineteenth century passes on as part of its legacy to the twentieth ; but for our part we have long ago arrived at a settlement of it which, to ourselves at least, is quite satisfactory.   Why should purposeful writing be interdicted to the novelist alone as a forbidden fruit which he must neither touch, taste, nor handle ?   What earthly reason is there why a writer of fiction should not combine instruction with amusement, provided he keeps the former within due bounds, and in its proper place ?   Why should it be stigmatised as a fault for a novelist occasionally to take his reader into his confidence, and explain to him the meaning of life as it is being enacted before him in the various characters which the author has called into being ?   Why should it be an illegitimate procedure for an author to have ideas of his own, to ventilate them in his pages, and seek to infect the reader with them if possible ?   Is there any great harm in making a story-book the medium for propounding some far-reaching principle, or conveying some useful moral, or advocating some needed reform ?   This, and only this, is the head and front of George Eliot's offending ; and it is precisely because she defied these so-called canons of a pseudo-artistic taste, and brushed aside these technical regulations of a redtape criticism, that her writings are possessed of a religious interest and ethical value so rarely to be found in fiction.   The great sin of which she has been convicted by the critics is the sin of having ideas—a sin so rarely committed by the modern fiction writer that for once it may well be forgiven.   She had the impertinence to allow subjects in which she was deeply interested to engage her powers as an author ; she had the audacity occasionally to introduce for the benefit of her reader a little bit of philosophy, and now and then to preach a little sermon to him such as he never hears in church, but never in such a clumsy or inartistic way as to interfere in the slightest degree with the free movement of her characters, or the absorbing interest of the story.   And what sensible or right thinking reader objects ?   Who will not heartily concur in Mr. Leslie

Stephen's remark, that much as he likes to read about Tom Jones and Colonel Newcome, he is also very glad when Fielding or Thackeray puts aside his puppets for the moment, and talks to him in his own person. We are persuaded that a vast multitude of at least the more thoughtful novel-readers of the day do greatly like a writer to take them occasionally into his confidence, to exchange opinions with them, and, as a pleasing variation of his programme, to follow amusement and diversion with spells of occasional seriousness and instruction. Mr. Marion Crawford, in his little book on *The Novel*, has branded it as one of the worst faults of which a novelist can be guilty, from an artistic point of view, to abolish every now and then the stage on which his *dramatis personæ* are acting, and set up a pulpit in its place, from which he proceeds to deliver a lecture to his reader just when he is expecting to be amused. This is substantially the very thing that George Eliot has done, and it is just because she has done it that multitudes of readers like her so much, and recur to her pages with an interest that never flags. It is precisely because the stage sometimes disappears, and she sets up her pulpit instead, that she commands a hearing, and will continue to command it, from such a vast audience of thinking and reflective people. Apply Mr. Crawford's test to George Eliot's work, and you will have to draw your pen through some of her very finest passages,—passages which will live as long as the English language,—and you will obliterate touches which have lent a charm and a perfection to all she has written. Apply it to Thackeray, and you will denude his writings of nearly all that is quotable and memorable—all that we have copied into our notebooks, and learnt by heart, as the very choicest specimens of his workmanship.

The book of life opens for George Eliot with a chapter of happy childhood in a Warwickshire village, followed by a chapter of thoughtful and earnest girlhood, in which we find her a sincere disciple of the Crucified, prostrate before the Cross, seeking the truth in Jesus, and striving for the conversion of her soul with penitential cries and outpourings. There was nothing in the girl's general deportment which jarred in the slightest on the feelings even of her good Wesleyan aunt, though that lady's ideals of life were a little rigid, and her discipline somewhat tinged with austerity. Marian Evans was the most pious member of the family to which she belonged, and, from a religious point of view, by far the most promising. She was at this time strongly imbued with the simple faith of a Christian believer, and aglow with the holy fervours of Evangelicism. As she herself declares, she was " eagerly bent on shaping this anomalous English Christian life of ours into some consistency with the spirit and verbal tenour of the New Testament." If we would draw aside the curtain and get a glimpse into her inner life at this time, we have only to read the portrayal of Maggie Tulliver's spiritual experiences, for it is all faithfully mirrored there. Nothing outward or unreal could satisfy the soul of Marian Evans. She was utterly sincere, and what she appears to have pursued at this time, with the ardour of one in quest of the Holy Grail itself, was the discovery of " something to live for beyond the mere satisfaction of self, something which

would be to the moral life what the addition of a great
central ganglion is to the animal life." Evangelicism
meanwhile supplied her with this, as well as with many
other requisites of a true spiritual life. The Christian
religion had found in her an attached and enthusiastic
disciple, and she threw all her powers into its service
with a zeal that bordered on asceticism. And what
malign influence or evil agency was it which nipped as
with an untimely frost the opening blossom of her early
piety ? What withering sirocco blighted as with brim-
stone breath the promise of her prime ? How came it
to pass that ominous shadows so soon began to darken
the face of this fair picture ? Darkened it very soon
was, for the young evangelical enthusiast, from whom the
Church was expecting great things, passed by a very
rapid transition into what she herself described as " a
crude state of freethinking." Just at the time when the
spirit of thoughtfulness and inquiry had awakened
within her, she was unfortunately thrown into the
deadening society of a group of Coventry Socinians. In
an unlucky hour she was favoured with an introduction
to the Brays and the Hennells, two influential Warwickshire families who had been smitten with the
fashionable Rationalism of the day. The period of from
twenty to thirty, as has been often observed, is frequently
a very critical and decisive one in the lives of illustrious
men and women, and just at this formative and momentous juncture Marian Evans was thrown into the intimate
society of friends who had imbibed unorthodox views,
who indulged in reckless speculation and rationalistic
talk, and suggested doubts which it was easier to raise

than allay, until gradually the leaven of an insinuating scepticism began to ferment her thoughts. In their pretentious philosophisings the young English maiden found, or thought she found, if not a new creed, at least a new "religious synthesis." At this time she abandoned the practice of attending Church, much to her father's grief, though afterwards, at his urgent solicitation, it was resumed for a time. "No human being," says Mathilde Blind, "can be fully understood without some knowledge of the companions which at one time or other, but specially during the period of development, have been intimately associated with his or her life." The observation is very mournfully exemplified in the history of George Eliot. We cannot fully understand her till we know that companionship with the Coventry Socinians was the first influence that made havoc of her life.

About this time she was unfortunately prevailed upon, through the intervention of one of her Hennell friends, to undertake for the publishers a translation from the German of Strauss' *Life of Jesus*, which had not hitherto appeared in an English dress. The specious but one-sided arguments of the German philosopher exactly harmonised with the direction in which George Eliot's mind was already moving, and so the seeds of his desolating criticism fell upon soil prepared to receive them. For a young girl with the training and tastes of Marian Evans, this could not but have been a repulsive bit of work, and we do not wonder that her better feelings winced in the execution of it, or that it wrung from her more than once expressions of distress and pain. She fairly broke down at the story of the Crucifixion and the Resurrection. She describes herself as "Strauss-sick," and it almost made her ill dissecting the story of the Cross in the heartless, cold-blooded style of the German critic. Yet in this ghastly employment she occupied herself for more than two years; and perhaps the most singular circumstance connected with it is, that she kept Thorwaldsen's famous sculpture of the Christ before her continually, and was wont to gaze upon it for inspiration and comfort. Gazing on the image of Jesus all the while for inspiration, forsooth, in helping a German Rationalist to undermine His sovereignty and evaporate His historical reality into a mythological dream!—inspiration to shatter the household gods of her own family as with an iron rod, and convict her own sainted ancestry of a lifelong idolatry!

But if the work of Strauss confirmed her in her unbelief, it was undoubtedly her friend Hennell's book which had originated it. This book, which had such a deleterious influence on her religious development, was entitled *An Inquiry into the Origin of Christianity*, in which the author sought to establish the conclusion that the Christian religion was but the product of purely natural causes. It is difficult to realise that this work should have had such an unsettling and devastating influence on the faith of Marian Evans, for it is essentially a weak book, and, judged by the best advanced criticism of subsequent times or of the present day, it would be considered as little better than the production of a tyro. Men like Baur, Renan, Schenkel, and Keim would have regarded it as the amateurish performance of an apprentice hand; and we know that Strauss himself, in introducing it to German readers, felt it necessary to apologise for some of its crude and ill-considered positions. Its chief weapon is irony, and irony it was which proved the most effective instrument for the undermining of George Eliot's faith. Yet irony, as Mr. Hutton has said, can be used by a mind of any capacity, and used effectively, against almost any convictions or any doubts; so that irony, as such, should weigh little or nothing in the scales of a wise judgment. The substance of the book may best be gathered from a synopsis of it supplied to the publishers by George Eliot herself, in which, in her anxiety to advertise the work, she brings out its salient features, and emphasises the views which had made such a deep impression on her own mind. The fundamental position which it seeks to establish is that the long array of wonderful facts connected with the history of Jesus, unique and unparalleled as they are, do not demand a supernatural explanation, but may be easily accounted for on principles of the purest naturalism. According to Hennell, "an impartial study of the sayings of Jesus produces the conviction that He was an enthusiast and a revolutionist no less than a reformer and a religious teacher, and there was scarcely anything absolutely unique in the teaching of Jesus." Much of what He taught is explained by the fact that He belonged to the sect of the Essenes, and was brought up in their school of philosophy.

"With the elevated belief and purity of life which belonged to this sect, He united the ardent, patriotic ideas which had previously animated Judas of Galilee. . . . The profound consciousness of genius, a religious fervour which made the idea of the Divine ever present to Him, patriotic zeal and a spirit of moral reform, together with a participation in the enthusiastic belief of His countrymen, that the long-predicted exaltation of Israel was at hand, combined to produce in the mind of Jesus the gradual conviction that He was Himself the Messiah."

As to our Lord's miracles, the book ascribes them to exaggeration, the excited feelings of the disciples, and the predisposition on the part of the people to believe what they wished to believe, or what it might be in their interest to believe.

But the supernatural element in the Gospel narrative is not so easily eliminated. If it were, why had men like Strauss, Baur, and Renan to strain their ingenuity and tax their inventive resources to the very utmost in order to devise some feasible scheme whereby to extract the thread of miracle from the web of Gospel history? Manifestly Hennell's short and easy methods of accounting for the presence of supernatural events in historical and biographical narratives did not commend themselves to the great masters of destructive criticism. Difficulties which Hennell could overleap with easy agility, they had to overcome by circuitous and elaborate tactics. According to the Hennell-Eliot criticism, Jesus traded very largely on the popular Messianic expectation which was so widely diffused among the Jewish nation before His advent. He threw Himself into the current of national hopes, and thus was drifted along into that conquest over the minds of men which He ultimately attained. " He determined," says Hennell, " to imitate Moses and fulfil the prophets by assuming the character of the Messiah, or the Prophet-King of Israel." But if

16

Moses was distinguished for anything it was for the working of miracles; and if there was one power more than another which the expected Messiah was to wield, it was the power of doing mighty works, such as would far surpass those wrought by any Old Testament prophet. Well, Jesus of Nazareth comes upon the scene; according to George Eliot, He has no more supernatural power than any other enthusiast, yet He claims to be the Messiah; and though the one distinguishing mark, the one shining credential of Messiahship, is wanting, He succeeds in getting His claim acknowledged and His Messiahship accepted by the populace.   The objection is fatal to the theory.   The long-expected Prophet-King of Israel was a well-known and well-defined personage; the marks and lineaments which should lead to His recognition when He appeared, were all most minutely depicted in the prophetic literature of the Jews: can it be supposed that Jesus persuaded a large body of Jewish followers that He was that personage, in spite of the fact that the leading credential by which He was to be attested was wanting?   Besides, the notion that Christ made capital out of the Messianic expectations which were rife in His day, and pressed them into His service, is discountenanced by the plainest representations of the Gospels themselves.   So far from studying any correspondence to the popular idea of Messiahship in many of its essential particulars, He crossed and contravened it. Again and again He offended the people by correcting and combating their conception of what the Messiah was to be.

As little worthy of respect is Hennell's contention,

that the life and teaching of Jesus are but the natural outcome of the age in which He lived. That the mind of George Eliot should have succumbed to such a theory cannot but strike us as passing strange. What the age was in which He made His appearance we know, and what type of mental and moral character it was capable of generating we know also. Its spirit visibilised and exemplified itself in priests, rabbis, scribes, literalists, wrangling controversialists, zealous upholders of national privilege, sticklers for orthodoxy, petrified formalists, pompous ecclesiastics, casuistical moralists—men who were the very contradiction and antithesis of Jesus Christ, and whom in the course of His ministry He had had occasion more than once to wither with the blast of His denunciation. The temper and the aim of Jewry were not the temper and the aim of Jesus. The moral and intellectual drift of the age in which He lived was not with Him but against Him. Its currents of thought, its movements, its moral ideas, its aspirations, were not such as would naturally ally themselves with the teaching of Jesus, or coalesce with the programme of Jesus. Was the age of the Zealots, of Theudas, of Judas the Gaulonite, likely to contribute much to the development of a character and cause like those of Christ, or would it likely furnish Him with any effective assistance in the establishment of a spiritual empire? The age was one of formalism, but Jesus was deeply spiritual; the age was scholastic—Jesus belonged to no school; the age was burdened with traditionalism and dead Leviticism— Jesus was absolutely untinged by either the one or the other; the age was bigoted and exclusive—Jesus overflowed the boundaries of caste and sectism, and about all He did and said there was the note of universality, and never the accent of provincialism.   He deemed Himself related to the whole human race.   He declined every field for His operations narrower than the world.   In the words of Channing, we cannot but feel that a new type of Being, a new order of mind, is taking part in human affairs.

But the point on which the Hennell-Eliot criticism is most halting and confused is the resurrection of our Lord.   There is an attempt to show that the apostles never affirmed anything more than a spiritual resurrection, and nothing more than this really took place.   A good deal of capital is made out of the words of Peter, " Christ was put to death in the flesh, but quickened *in the spirit* "; and it is argued that when the apostles claimed to have been witnesses of the resurrection, the language does not necessarily mean eye-witnesses, but only that they were witnesses of a spiritual rising from the dead. This attempt to get quit of the inconvenient fact of the resurrection is so puerile and childish as scarcely to deserve serious refutation.   It is nothing short of the merest trifling to take the word resurrection and use it in a non-Biblical and unnatural sense.   As used by the apostles, no one can doubt that the word is free from all ambiguity, and it is an intolerable liberty for any school of criticism to play fast and loose with this word for its own ends, and to violate its consecrated usage. It does not appear from Hennell's book, or George Eliot's synopsis of it, what precise meaning is attached to the phrase " spiritual resurrection."   In one passage it is represented as nothing more than the immortality of the soul. But it is surely a shallow and uninformed philosophy which identifies resurrection from the dead with the immortality of the soul. The exigencies of the situation must indeed be desperate when men are driven to fall back on such a *dernière ressort* as this. But possibly the term " spiritual resurrection " may be intended to signify that only the spirit of Christ ascended into heaven and was glorified. If that be the sense in which we are to understand it, we might just as well speak of the resurrection of the penitent thief when that day he entered Paradise, or the resurrection of Stephen, when, kneeling amid the shower of stones, he cried, " Lord Jesus, receive my spirit." David has risen from the dead in the same sense ; so have all the saints who lie in the myriad graves of old, and Paul was entirely mistaken when he spoke of Christ as " the first-fruits of them that sleep." It is open to any Rationalist to call in question the story of the resurrection, but one thing that admits of no question is that Peter and Paul meant to affirm and teach and illustrate a literal bodily reappearance of the Christ who died and was buried. From beginning to end of their speeches and writings, there is nothing to suggest that the modern idea of a " spiritual resurrection " had so much as dawned on their minds. On the theory of a spiritual resurrection what becomes of Paul's argument in the fifteenth chapter of First Corinthians, or of his famous sermon on Mars Hill ? If, when discoursing to the philosophers of Athens, Paul meant only to assert their own favourite doctrine of the immortality of the soul, or had selected a word which implied nothing

more than the ascension to heaven of the human spirit
at death, he would have saved his faith from a volley
of scorn, and secured for his message a polite and
deferential hearing.   But Paul meant a great deal more
by the word "resurrection," and we may therefore
properly insist that the word shall be understood in its
Pauline sense.   The theory is irreconcilable, moreover,
with the contents of the Gospel narrative itself.   At
first in their bewilderment the disciples were disposed
to think as the upholders of a "spiritual resurrection"
now do.   We are informed that on the first appearance of
Jesus before their astonished vision "they were affrighted,
and supposed they had seen a spirit."   With the express
purpose of correcting that mistaken impression, and dis-
abusing their minds for ever of all ghostly and spiritual-
istic notions, Jesus submitted His hands and side to a
physical inspection, saying, "Handle Me, and see; for a
spirit hath not flesh and blood, as ye see Me have"; and
as an additional corrective still, He "took a piece of
a broiled fish, and of an honey-comb, and did eat it
before them."   Passages like this entangle the theory
in hopeless difficulties, which can only be obviated by
the violent expedient of an arbitrary and wholesale rejection of the Gospel histories.

We have deviated into this cursory examination of
Charles Hennell's book for the purpose of showing that
the forces before which George Eliot succumbed, and to
which she made the great surrender, so far from being
overwhelming in their cogency, as one might have expected, were not even formidable.   The foremost sceptics
of subsequent times have pronounced them inadequate,

and unbelievers in our day of any standing would be ashamed to bring them into the field. The book which had such a devastating and destructive effect on George Eliot's faith was in reality a crude and ill-jointed production. On the strength of reasonings destitute of any really convincing or commanding quality, and of arguments susceptible of easy rejoinder, she flung from her as a superstition that early faith of hers, of whose power to satisfy our deepest personal needs, to ally us to God, and inspire tranquillity of mind and fortitude of spirit in presence of the ills of life and the terrors of death, she herself had seen, even in her own circle, so many interesting and striking proofs. To Hennell's assaults on her Christianity she offered no resistance, nor even show of resistance. " Nothing strikes me more in her biography," says Mr. R. H. Hutton, " than the absence of the least trace of struggle against the rationalistic schools of thought through which George Eliot's mind passed." [1]

We have thus detailed the circumstances which led to the eclipse of faith in the greatest female writer of the century. It is profoundly affecting to think that before George Eliot sat down to the composition of her first novel she had ceased to be a Christian believer. Though she could not but have felt the painfulness of the wrench it cost her to part with so much that was dear, and though she did show some concern at the grief she caused her friends, yet she quailed not before consequences, nor ever once exhibited any vacillation of judgment, nor any sign of recantation or retreat. She never appears to have faltered in her unbelief, never seems to have doubted the

[1] *Modern Guides of English Thought*, p. 270.

rectitude of the change which had come over her. Speaking at this time of the *cooled* glances which in certain circles had been cast at her, and the remonstrances which had been addressed to her, she declares they were only to her as a shower of hailstones, which made her draw more closely around her than ever the mantle of determinate purpose. There was much, however, that survived the shipwreck. Her heart never wholly concurred in the denials of her intellect, and she was never quite satisfied with the rôle which her own unbelief condemned her to play. Many admirable things which she had learned in the early days of her quiet girl-life at Griff stayed with her and found their way into her writings. There still hovered about her a lingering aroma of religion which perfumed all she wrote; not a few of the ideas and principles of that very Christianity whose historical credibility she had thought fit to repudiate, still clung to her, and received splendid inculcation from her pen. Dr. Selby is fully justified in the statement that " in her own soul there was a subtle residuum of theology which nothing could volatilise or destroy." We can well believe Mr. Cross when he testifies that she was a woman of strong religious tendencies; and strong they must have been, when they were not utterly benumbed and frozen to death under the ice-cold dripping shadow of George Henry Lewes' chilling and barren negations. She never wholly discontinued the reading of her Bible, and the *Imitatio* was her constant companion; when she died, a well-worn copy of it lay near her lifeless hand, a pathetic memorial of the past. On one occasion she was even known to express to a young lady friend of hers who shared her views, her regret that they were deprived of the comfort that attended on the observance of the old practice of family prayer.   One thing cannot but command our respect.   She never sought to make other feet travel the same road that she herself had chosen.   She never set herself to rob another of his faith.   She never stooped to that last and lowest employment of the mind, the manufacture of infidels.   In a letter of 1862 occur these words :—

"Pray don't ask me ever again not to rob a man of his religious belief, as if you thought my mind tended to such robbery.   I have too profound a conviction of the efficacy that lies in all sincere faith, and the spiritual blight that comes with no faith, to have any negative propagandism in me.   In fact, I have very little sympathy with free-thinkers as a class, and have lost all interest in mere antagonism to religious doctrines."

Her example in this respect is one which may well be commended to the imitation of all those whose own religious beliefs have become fluid or unsettled.

> "Leave thou thy sister when she prays,
> Her early Heaven her happy views ;
> Nor thou with shadowed hint confuse
> A life that leads melodious days."

We have now been led up to an event which completely changed the flavour and complexion of George Eliot's life, viz. her connection with George Henry Lewes.   Herself writing to Mrs. Bray in September 1855, fourteen months after this step had been taken, she says, " If there is any action or relation of my life which is and always has been profoundly serious, it is my relation with Mr. Lewes."   That relation, as everybody knows, was one of unmarried companionship.   Marriage in the ordinary

sense of the term was out of the question, Lewes' wife
being still alive; but they decided to live together, and in
the summer of 1853 they took upon them the position
and responsibilities of a married couple. This was the
"governing incident" of her career—rather might we
describe it as the "*misgoverning*" incident, for it undoubtedly exercised a most sinister influence on her whole
future.   It was the beginning of an independent and
irregular life from which it had been infinitely better to
have refrained her foot.   It was a revolt against the
acknowledged canons of Christian morality, a violation
of the traditional sanctities of life, a trifling with an
institution sacramental in its sacredness, an infringement
of social order, and a lending of her influence to the
weakening of bonds and the relaxation of restrictions
which women of all others should most jealously guard.
Henceforth her life presents a very painful spectacle—
"the spectacle of an industriously regulated career cloven
in two by a sudden and striking breach with a moral
law which the great majority of men hold to be of the
very essence of social purity."[1]   She and Mr. Lewes
had always an abundance of sophistical language at
their command with which to justify their action, and
some of their admirers have tried hard to cover up
its ugliness under a veil of poetic sentiment; but no
amount of special pleading or casuistical attorneyism
can procure any sanction for the illegal union, which
must ever be regarded as "the disgrace of her life and
the condemnation of her philosophy."   It was a step
which she had the very least excuse for taking: she did

[1] Hutton, *Guides of English Thought*, p. 274.

not take it in ignorance ; she had come to years of dis-
cretion ; she was not betrayed into it by the stress of
temptation, nor driven to it by the pressure of poverty :
and it was a step, we may add, which she never would
have taken had she not first of all parted with her evangelical faith.   That faith would have steadied her ; the
grace of Christ would have given her strength to fling
from her the very thought of a *mesalliance*, as Paul shook
the viper from his hand : it would have saved a noble
woman from the sacrifice of nobility, and she would have
come down to us with example untarnished, and moral
influence unimpaired.   " Moreover, I very much doubt,"
says Mr. R. H. Hutton, " whether, if George Eliot had
continued to believe in the spiritual Judge of all men,
she would have found it so easy to absolve herself from
the provisions of the moral law of marriage as she did
find it.   To a very proud and self-reliant intellect like
hers, it must certainly be easier to take a final resolve,
which sets social traditions at defiance, if it disbelieves
in any true spiritual censorship, than it can be when it
regards its own decisions as liable to be scrutinised and
reversed by a perfect and omniscient Judge.   The mere
belief in the existence of a court of moral appeal is a
great security for care and humility in most natures." [1]
But George Eliot became a freethinker, and, as very often
happens, freethinking prepared the way for freeliving.
Her scepticism confused her views, weakened her moral
sense, lowered the fine tone of her being, and thus made
possible the scandal of her life.   Lewes himself was
sceptical of everything, and we can readily imagine

[1] *Guides of English Thought*, p. 292.

how well adapted was George Eliot's companionship
with such a man to confirm and complete the work
which the Coventry Rationalists had begun.   To sit
day by day under the cold drip of George Lewes' cheerless scepticism was a terribly deteriorating process for
anyone.   " She was half hypnotised," as Dr. Selby says,
" by his cold and dreary negations."   Moreover, this
unfortunate alliance had the effect of bringing her
into swift and sharp collision with the religious world,
which, of course, could not but condemn her action, and
thus she was forced into an attitude more or less hostile
to religion itself, which otherwise she might not have
assumed.   Naturally enough she resented the action of
those who ostracised her, and in consequence became
spiteful towards the Christian faith itself.   It was this
that prompted many of the sharp thrusts and stinging
sarcasms which she afterwards levelled at Evangelicism.
There is one aspect, indeed, of this painful interlude in her
history which has a pathetic interest all its own.   It is
a fact that in dealing with the marriage problem in her
books, George Eliot never assumed the attitude of the
" revolted " woman of the present day.   Revolt in that
sense she never preached ; it was always abhorrent to
her nature.   It is paradoxical, but the paradox tells in her
favour, that " she who had herself taken such a defiantly
independent course should so often inculcate the very
opposite teaching in her works — should inculcate an
almost slavish adherence to whatever surroundings, beliefs, domestic ties, and family bonds a human being may
be born to." [1]   True, but one cannot help feeling how

[1] Mathilde Blind.

terribly all such teaching is discounted by the force of her own example! The finest chapters in the *Mill on the Floss* are those in which George Eliot argues against herself, and demonstrates with all the force of genius and conscience that true happiness lies in the pursuance of a course the very reverse of that which she herself had followed. Everyone will at once recall the passage where Maggie Tulliver is entrapped into an elopement with Stephen Guest. In Maggie's passionate contention that she can never consent to snatch happiness for herself by the betrayal of others, and in the lecture she reads Stephen on our duty to Society, Mr. Dawson, reading between the lines, thinks he can detect the confession of George Eliot's own soul. " It has the effect," says he, " of a personal recantation. Her ultimate conscience speaks, as Balaam did, and it blesses that which she might have wished to curse." It is well to be charitable, and Mr. Dawson may be right, but it does strike one as an unfortunate circumstance, to say the least, that this " ultimate conscience " did not assert itself a little sooner. One's pleasure in reading these very passages referred to is unpleasantly disturbed by the haunting thought of Lewes' wronged wife in the background, who always will make herself felt. There is that spectral face of hers always at the window looking in upon us; and even should we succeed in banishing her, we cannot banish the tragic fact that all this superfine philosophy of disinterestedness, of living for others, and never snatching at a happiness for ourselves which involved the betrayal of a fellow-mortal, was powerless to restrain the writer herself from exalting a lawless fancy over the plainest of duties and the most sacred of obligations. Though George Eliot protests that she never repented the step she had taken, or experienced any secret condemnation on account of it, yet we think there is abundant evidence to show that she felt she had made a mistake, and that she was supremely anxious to expiate that mistake, and, if possible, correct and counterbalance it, by her subsequent work as an authoress. To a critic of such insight and penetration as Mr. Hutton, it is quite clear that, on the whole, she intended her literary work ever afterwards to atone for the evil effect of her example, and exhibited a constant anxiety that men should be guided rather by the moral teaching of her writings than by the practice of her life.

George Eliot had been for years a diligent student of Auguste Comte, and in the course of time she became deeply imbued with the Positivist philosophy. Mr. Morley thinks she stopped short of complete adhesion to Comte's scheme; but she was never tired of protesting that he was a really great thinker, and for many years, up to the time of her death, she was a subscriber to the Comtist Fund, though she never directly associated herself with the Positivist religion. Be this as it may, her writings are extensively leavened with the godless principles of the Positivist philosophy. Not by any means that she gives them explicit advocacy or enunciation, but rather that they subtly underlie the presentation of human life as limned in her pages, and silently operate in many of her characters as the real motive and inspiration of their daily conduct—as, in fact, their working creed, though they themselves are not always conscious of it. Her characters are generally good Christian people, who are presumably influenced by the love of God and the fear of an hereafter; but while reckoning themselves disciples of the religion of Christ, in all the critical situations and deeper passages of life they are really thinking and acting as disciples of the Religion of Humanity, for the supernatural element in their beliefs is represented as having no practical effect on them. Their conduct is not any longer influenced by the thought that it has reference to a Being above themselves, to whose will they are subject, and for whose sake they are to keep themselves dutiful and pure; rather is it inspired by the consideration that they are living for humanity. Collective humanity — this is the new Divinity to which their duty and allegiance have been transferred, "the real author," as Comte calls it, "of the benefits for which thanks were formerly given to God." The service and sacrifice formerly rendered to their Father in heaven is now rendered to their fellow-men on earth. So far as morality is concerned, they have shifted the centre of gravity from a theological to a purely sociological basis. "My books," says our authoress in one of her letters, "have for their main bearing a conclusion without which I could not have cared to write any representations of human life—namely, that the fellowship between man and man, which has been the principle of development, social and moral, is not dependent on conceptions of what is not man; and that the idea of God, so far as it has been a high spiritual influence, is the ideal of a goodness entirely

human (*i.e.* an exaltation of the human)." And as men
may lead a life of high endeavour, pure morality, and
noble enthusiasm, without any help from the thought of
God; so also, if we are to accept the representations of
George Eliot, they may live that life without any
assistance derived from the anticipation of the life to
come. The life that now is suffices them; this brief
span of earthly existence affords them scope enough
for all their consecrated energies without making any
drafts on an ampler life beyond; men are quite equal
to the duty of loving virtue for its own sake and
hating vice for its inherent hideousness, and not because
their inner eye has always a squint towards reward
and punishment looming in the distance; they are
just and honest in this world, not because they expect
to live in another, but because they shrink from
inflicting injustices on their neighbour which they
would not like to have inflicted on themselves;
morality is strictly confined within the limitations
of the here and now. We can no longer exhort the
individual—

> "Choose well, your choice is
> Brief, but yet endless."

We can only say that the choice is brief, but it has no
moral connection with any other world than that in
which we are now living. Accordingly much of what
George Eliot has written is vitiated by the subtle
presence of a philosophy which rails off this life from
any encroachments from the life to come, and roofs it in
from the downpour of those celestial influences that are
rained upon us from the realm of the invisible. It is on

these grounds that Mr. Mallock has adjudged her, and it is impossible to quarrel with the classification, "the first great godless writer of fiction that has appeared in England," or, as he elsewhere expresses it, "the first legitimate fruit of our modern atheistic fiction."[1] Not atheistic in the vulgar sense of a violent and undisguised attempt at the abolition of God, but in the sense of quietly dispensing with God, and showing, as by a long series of diagrams and object-lessons, in the characters she has delineated for our benefit, that human life can be lived, and lived nobly and successfully, without any reference to, or help from, the thought of God. She does not deny God, she only silently and skilfully shelves Him; He is a superfluity. Life can be carried on without Him. Professor Tyndall informs us that, though he had rejected the religion of his earlier years, yet, granting him proper health of body, "there is no spiritual experience such as he then knew, no resolve of duty, no work of mercy, no act of self-renouncement, no joy in the aspects of life and nature, that could not still be his." The very same is the implicit teaching of all George Eliot's novels. The great twin thoughts of God and Immortality are laid on the shelf as a part of our moral outfit no longer needed. The manner in which this feat is accomplished is remarkable, and Mr. Mallock cites as the most striking instances of it the character of Mr. Lyon in *Janet's Repentance*, and that of Savonarola as he looks out upon us from the pages of *Romola*. Rufus Lyon is a clergyman of very average gifts, but passionately devoted to his sacred calling, and exhibiting many

[1] *Atheism and the Value of Life.*

17

interesting qualities calculated to elicit our sympathy and admiration; and yet, as Mr. Mallock says, the writer contrives to exhibit all that she wishes us to admire in him as resting on a basis with which his religious beliefs have nothing at all to do. The creed to which he has given his intellectual acceptance, especially the supernatural elements in it, exerts no really regulative or controlling influence. The true dynamic of his life lies elsewhere. We see the same thing in Savonarola. When the famous reformer seeks to convert Romola to the precepts of Christ, there is scarcely any appeal in all the arguments he plies her with to the Divine or supernatural side of Christianity. "Savonarola is the spokesman of Humanity made Divine, not of Deity made human." At his instigation Romola's devotion and self-sacrifice are transferred from God to a new Divinity which is henceforth to intercept and appropriate the girl's life-service—collective Humanity, mankind in general. "Make your marriage vows," says Savonarola to her, "an offering too, my daughter: an offering *to the great work* by which sin and sorrow are to be made to cease." It is this atheistic pietism, this severing of life and morality from their roots in God, this resolving of our brief span of earthly existence into a little outlying islet cut off from the mainland of Eternity by unnavigable seas, that constitute the chief danger and seductiveness of George Eliot, at least for unsuspecting readers.

It is a painful feature of George Eliot's history, that she discarded all belief in the precious doctrine of personal immortality. In this eclipse of faith she died. The only form of survival after death to which she per-

mitted herself to aspire, may be gathered from that
impassioned prayer of hers already quoted—

> "Oh may I join the choir invisible
> Of those immortal dead who live again
> In lives made better by their presence."

She only hoped to be perpetuated in so far as she
lived in the hearts of others, in so far as her transmitted
influence might continue to leaven human thought, in so
far as her life had made any lasting contribution to the
common fund of human progress, or to the social good.
At the most she might hope to pass into the heaven of
literature, and join the select aristocracy of those whom
posterity raises to the rank of celebrities, and crowns with
the rewards of fame.   But meanwhile the woman's own
personal self, with its enduring consciousness, with its
own history of thought and love and action, its own
struggles and ideals, victories and defeats, has faded into
extinction ; her whole inner life, to use her own words—

> "Is gathered like a scroll within the tomb,
> Unread for ever."

What is this but a virtual denial of immortality
altogether ?   Deck it out with all the fine phrases you
may, and cover up its dismalness with poetic euphemisms,
wherein does it differ from the eternal sleep to which the
Buddhist consigns himself when he sinks into Nirvana ?
Such a devitalised and diluted version of immortality
cannot meet the needs of the individual heart, nor satisfy
its deep cravings for an inextinguishable life, nor take
the place in its estimation of the Christian's heaven.
Such a theory is of no assistance in solving the enigmas
of existence ; it does not help us in the adjustment

of the old problem suggested by the injustices and
inequalities of our present state of being; it gives no
impulse to our upward tendencies, supplies no leverage
for action, brings no reinforcement to a failing will, no
joy to unrequited labour, no victory to lonely suffering.
Nothing can be more delusive than the notion that you
can subtract from this life belief in a life to come, and
still have left you some satisfying remainder.   You deplete
and impoverish this life, and deprive it of all true per-
spective, if you insist on confining it within the horizon
of the visible.   Separate man from the God who loves
him, and from the eternity to which he is moving in
solemn march heavenward, and you have only a thriving earthworm, or at the most an intellectual animal.
There is nothing left to give dignity to his existence, or
grandeur to the beatings of his heart—

> "He toils and is clothed with derision;
> He sows and he may not reap;
> His life is a watch and a vision,
> Betwixt a sleep and a sleep."

Man needs an ampler field of action for the full play
of his energies than that which is afforded him by the
handful of years allotted to him here, and if you crib
and cabin him within the narrow limits of mortality, it is
like expecting a musician to render an elaborate piece of
music on an instrument whose keyboard is too short to
provide him with a full range of notes.   Pin a man's
thoughts to earth, narrow his experience within time-
limits, tear down the veil which thinly divides him, as
he thinks, from another state of being, and tell him there
is nothing behind it but an infinite blank, and, in spite of

all George Eliot's fine Comtist talk, you have deprived that man of the one great secret of the right use and management of life. We never act our part in this world so well as when we keep the other world steadily in view, and realise the thousand moral ligatures that connect the two. We never get the mastery of earth till we see its littleness domed by heaven's greatness, and its tumult brooded over by heaven's peace. The transient is best handled by those who have a firm hold on the eternal. That is a wise word of Samuel Taylor Coleridge, where he warns us against the folly of making terrestrial charts without taking celestial observations. Time will be best spent by those who see in its scant round but the field for sowing the seeds of further destiny, and talents are likely to be well employed by men who feel themselves working, as it were, on the outskirts of infinitude, who are heirs of immortality, and not the mere toilers of a day in the perishing vineyard of earth! The thought of something overhead, immense and unsearchable, of which this onlooking spirit of ours prophesies, and to which it is ever on its way in solemn pilgrimage, cannot but uplift the life, cannot but exalt and sanctify the spirit. That there have been those who have lived nobly and exhibited many virtues to whom all this was but a dream, is of course quite true. But the contrast afforded by their example, always pathetic, is often tragic. They have set their will strenuously to the work of life, but it has wanted the incentive and the uplift which celestial attractions would have imparted. They have toiled merely to satisfy their own moral judgment, and their toil has, as a rule, been cheerless; the labourer has worked with a sad heart, his efforts have lacked that animation which springs from the prospect of a life to come, and there has been a marked absence of what someone has called "the glad exhilaration of anticipating minds." In deciding a question like this, however, we have not to deal with exceptions, but only with what is true for the mass of humanity, and nothing is more sure than this, that if you displace from the general mind belief in a life to come, with which our life here is interlinked, "the most vigorous incentive to a superlative virtue will fail from society, as the waters recede from bay or bar when the swing of the sea is no longer behind them." [1]

George Eliot's ethical system summed itself up in the one word Duty. With her it was an imperial word which covered the entire territory of life, and included every relation in which men stand to each other, whether as landlord and tenant, priest and parishioner, husband and wife, parent and child, brother and sister. With her the way of Duty must ever be trodden, though it be bordered with no wayside flowers, and is strewn with cruel flints that make the traveller's feet to bleed. According to Mr. Dawson, "the sole residuum of her early evangelical faith was this reverence for duty." Duty was the only God she knew, the only religion she permitted herself to hold. The law of Duty she painfully enforced, and preached in season and out of season that men owe as much obedience to that law, though imposed on them by nothing higher than the dictates of their own nature, as they would were it imposed by some external Lawgiver,

[1] Storr's *Recognition of the Supernatural.*

who was Himself the supreme embodiment and expression of it. Her ideal of self-sacrifice was correspondingly high. To live for others was in her eyes the cream of all living : to die for others, whether in literal martyrdom, or by the slow sacrifice of our life for theirs in domestic drudgery or unrequited love, was to her a privilege and a blessedness. She was a strong believer, too, in the freedom and responsibility of the individual. She held we had the power very largely to make or unmake ourselves. She was not disposed to make as much allowance as some other writers have done for the force of circumstances, or the effect of environment, in determining human destiny. With our own fingers we weave the web of life, and we ourselves decide what shall be its pattern and hue. We build the soul-house we must afterwards inhabit, whether it happen to turn out a castle or a wigwam. She herself has said—

> "Our deeds still travel with us from afar,
> And what we have been makes us what we are."

The irrevocableness of the past, the irreparable character of human experience, are also favourite themes with George Eliot. No return tickets are issued for the journey of life. We cannot go back. We cannot begin again. There are steps we cannot retrace, words we cannot recall, mistakes we cannot correct, mischiefs we cannot undo. The intercession of angels cannot recover lost opportunities, and no cement has ever yet been devised which can mend a broken vow.

> "You can't turn curds to milk again,
> Nor Now, by wishing, back to Then,
> And, having tasted stolen honey,
> You can't buy innocence for money."

As a consequence of this conviction, it was perhaps natural that she should also insist on the certainty with which the sinner reaps the penalty of his wrong-doing. With some novelists the transgressor has his punishment commuted, and in the end things are made agreeable for him. But there is never any escape for him with George Eliot. In her pages the goddess Nemesis is always on duty, and always unrelenting in her dealings. It has been said that "the appropriate frontispiece for every book she has written would be the scales and the sword." [1]

One other lesson which George Eliot was never weary of enforcing, was the immense influence for good or evil of insignificant people and obscure lives. The concluding words of *Middlemarch* should be written on our hearts with pencil dipped in sunbeams—

" The growing good of the world is partly dependent on unhistoric acts; and that things are not so ill with you and me as they might have been, is half owing to the numbers who lived faithfully a hidden life, and rest in unvisited tombs."

From a Christian point of view, George Eliot is at her best in such passages as Dinah Morris' sermon on the village green, written, as she herself has told us, with the hot tears welling from her eyes; or, further on in the same book, the lovely moralised description of the Cross by the roadway, with its profound and memorable lesson, " Man needs a suffering God"; or the beautiful prayer, too sacred for transcription, with which Dinah meets and heals the broken heart of Hetty in the condemned cell.

[1] Dawson.

No one can read such outpourings as these without having the deep conviction that George Eliot was once a most fervid believer, and that the spirit of Christianity yet lingered with her, though its creed was gone. She is still casting many a longing, lingering look behind at the early faith of her girlhood. But as we follow on the gradual development of her mind as expressed in her books, we find less and less recognition of evangelical truth ; more and more religious faith is being replaced by duty-doing and morality ; the cold shadow of scepticism is stealing over her in ever-deepening eclipse ; she is becoming more sad, more pessimistic in her views of life, more hopeless as she nears the end and faces the dreary prospect of annihilation. Perhaps the attitude in which her mind finally reposed after she had broken with dogmatic religion may best be indicated by her own statement of Dorothea's creed—

"that by desiring what is perfectly good, even when we don't quite know what it is, and cannot do what we would, we are part of the Divine power against evil— widening the skirts of light and making the struggle with darkness narrower."

Altogether her career is one of those in connection with which the sad words " might have been " will mournfully suggest themselves. Could we for a moment translate into the potential mood the life whose actual record is so faithfully preserved for us in the more austere and responsible indicative, and ask ourselves what it *might* have been or *would* have been had certain incidents never taken place, had certain developments never arisen, had certain trains of influence never been set in motion, it might afford us material for an interesting study in conjectural criticism.   If she had never been thrown into early association with the clique of Coventry Rationalists, if she had never translated Strauss or Feuerbach, if she had never seen the face of George Henry Lewes, if she had never drunk so deeply at the wells of the Positivist philosophy,—how different it all might have been !   In the opinion of Mr. R. H. Hutton, George Eliot with a faith like that of her own " Dinah " would have been one of the most effective intellects this world has ever seen.   But we must refrain from all such idle speculations.   It is useless to torture ourselves by digging wells of supposition from which to drink the brackish waters of regret.   What is writ is writ, and our wish that it had been otherwise cannot alter so much as a single down-stroke or up-stroke of the record—

> " Honey yet gall of it
> There's the life lying."

V

THE THEOLOGY OF GEORGE MACDONALD

THE THEOLOGY OF GEORGE MACDONALD

" THE mob of gentlemen who write with ease " is having
its ranks augmented in these days by almost daily
accessions. Novel-writing seems to be the favourite
field for the exercise of their facile gifts. The business
is a very thriving one, and for an author to make a
living by it, it is not at all necessary that he should produce books which have any permanent value—it will
serve the purpose well enough if they are merely clever
and effective. A novel may run through half a dozen
editions, and win a large share of praise and pudding for
its author, without having merit enough to rank as a
classic, or to entitle it to a place in literature. It may
even enjoy a noisy and violent popularity for the time
being, and yet be utterly destitute of those commanding
qualities in virtue of which a book slips through into
immortality. Brilliant and amusing enough to command
a large *clientèle* among the reading public, it may not be
possessed of sufficient vitality to outlive its own generation. Clever novels abound ; they come from the press
" thick as leaves of Vallombrosa,"

> " Amassing flowers,
> Youth sighed, ' Which rose make ours ?'
> ' Which lily leave ?'"

but one might count on the fingers of one hand those
that will be heard of in the second or third decade of the
twentieth century. There is nothing to distinguish the
bulk of them from those ephemeral productions between
whose birth and oblivion there is but a step. Almost
before these authors have gone the way of all flesh, their
books will have gone the way of all paper, and be found
only on the top shelves of mouldering libraries. But
there are novels which contain truth and beauty enough
to insure them against such a fate—rare books which
have a permanent value, and will be heard of when
many contemporary volumes, that once competed with
them for the popular favour, are ocean deep in forgetfulness. Among these rare exceptions a first place must be
accorded to the works of George MacDonald. It is not,
indeed, every reader who will enjoy them. They make
heavy demands upon our thought. They do not interest
the intellectually frivolous, nor those whose mental habits
are otiose and slouching. Those who go in for "light
reading" will find no pabulum here, while those who
have acquired the art of "judicious skipping" had better
patronise some other author. Those, too, who have a
dislike to the handling of deep spiritual problems must
seek pasture in other fields; and as for the reader
who has an aversion to anything that savours of the
theological, there is scarcely a page of George Mac-
Donald that will not excite his antipathy. Indeed,
it is this constant insistence on theological issues that
is largely accountable for the comparative paucity
of George MacDonald's readers. It is this feature
of his writings which, as Mr. David Murray points

out,[1] " has scared away the empty-headed, the shallow-
hearted, and the careless clever."   MacDonald is nothing
if not theological.   He considers he has a mission to
lead a crusade against all creeds and formularies ; he
regards himself as specially anointed to preach the
Fatherhood of God and the Gospel of Eternal Hope,
and he wages incessant war against what he considers
the gloomy and forbidding system of Scottish Calvinism.
According to the views we may happen to entertain
on these debatable questions, we shall be prepared either
to hail in Dr. MacDonald " the Moses he has been to
many in the speculative desert, leading them to a land of
promise," or, while in no degree abating our admiration
for him as a poet and novelist, we shall decline to accept
his services as guide, philosopher, and friend in matters
of religious credence.   But, irrespective of varying
theological opinion, we cannot withhold admiration from
the man behind the printed page, and must esteem it a
means of grace to be brought into contact with such a
fine spirit.   If his writings are to some extent marred
by an excess of the theological element, and if at times
they even degenerate into little else than a form of
polemical propaganda ; if he occasionally makes religion
only a subject for human controversy, and evinces a
tendency to treat it too much in the spirit of a partisan,
manufacturing and manipulating a certain set of human
puppets in illustration of the truth of one set of theological opinions and the falsity of another, these defects
are amply atoned for by the presence everywhere of a
rich and delicate imagination, a lofty moral thoughtful-

[1] *My Contemporaries in Fiction*, p. 117.

ness, splendid descriptive power, deep spiritual insight, a
vast wealth of illustration, and a vivid character-painting
scarcely surpassed by any of our living writers. No
man can read him without having what is dark in him
illumined and what is low raised, without being made
ashamed of his sordidness and having his pettiness
rebuked, without getting larger conceptions of life and
duty, and without making some priceless additions to his
stores of moral acquisition. He will rise from the perusal
enriched as any pearl-fisher when he comes up from a
successful dive. Our own obligations to him have been
so manifold that we may say of him, as Dean Farrar of
George Eliot, he is " among the authors beloved and
learned from since I reached the age of manhood."

George MacDonald, as we have said, leads a reactionary
movement against Calvinism. He has a virulent and
inveterate dislike to all theological creeds and systems,
but Calvinism in particular is singled out for special antipathy. Nearly all his books are polemical, literature
itself being availed of as a medium for the disparagement
of Calvinistic belief. *David Elginbrod, Robert Falconer,*
and *Alec Forbes* are each of them little else in reality but
a theological manifesto, veiled under a thin disguise of
character - sketching and story - telling. His favourite
weapon, and one of which, it must be confessed, he is a
consummate master, is caricature. His Calvinistic characters, of which he has given us quite a gallery, are
nearly all fanatics, cranks, or oddities. We have sometimes wondered what sort of places he must have fre-
quented, or in what sort of company he must have
chanced to mingle, to have met with the prototypes of

such people, if indeed it were possible to match them with any corresponding types in real life at all. George MacDonald must surely have known that better specimens were to be had; or if he did fall into erroneous impressions, he must have had frequent opportunity to have had them corrected afterwards, and replaced by something nearer to the truth of things. We have no objection that Calvinism, like any other system, should be judged by its fruits. We believe, with Mr. Froude in his celebrated essay on the subject, that "the practical effect of a belief is the real test of its soundness." Men do not gather grapes of thorns, nor figs of bramble-bushes. But when creatures like Mrs. Worboise, Mr. Simon, Mrs. Falconer, and Murdoch Mallison are gravely put forward as legitimate products of Calvinism, the sort of human specimen it usually engenders, we cannot but call in question the fairness of such a selection. If you are going to judge the tree by its fruit, produce as your samples fair average specimens of its yield, and not two or three wizened, juiceless crabs from some out of the way lightning-smitten bough. If you are going to form your estimate of the building from the separate stones that compose it, take care that the specimens selected are not merely some shapeless and unsightly fragments excavated from some back corner, and remarkable only for their jaggedness and angularity. It is this unfair and misleading method of treatment that George MacDonald has extended to Calvinism. Mrs. Worboise, for instance, is a frigid, sour, dyspeptic sort of Christian, weak in intellect as she was weak in health, who refrains from showing any effusive affection to her children, lest the

18

Almighty should be displeased at being defrauded of a
love which is due to Him alone, and must not be shared
by any human object; and who seldom or never permitted
herself to kiss her son Thomas, because it was part
of her system of mortifying the flesh with its affections
and lusts, not to allow those straight lips of hers to meet
his, at least to meet them with any fervency.   She has
for her religious consultant and adviser Mr. Simon, the
curate of St. Solomon's — a creature who shared her
sombre views, and was well fitted in every respect to
minister to such an invalid, and confirm her in that
spiritual unnaturalism which diseased her soul.   Mrs.
Falconer, while in the main a good-hearted woman enough,
has had her natural feelings so curdled by the detestable
creed she has had the misfortune to inherit, that she has
come to renounce all amusement, and almost all pleasure,
as an offence against the Almighty.   A hard life she
gives her grandson and his one friend and companion,
Shargar.   Murdoch Mallison is a Scottish schoolmaster
of a most savage type, who is known to his scholars as
Murder Mallison.   His ferocity is all attributable to his
being so deeply imbued with the theology of the Shorter
Catechism, which teaches that " every sin deserveth God's
wrath and curse, both in this world and the world which
is to come," and the master regarded himself as only
carrying out the Divine principle on which the Almighty
Himself proceeded when he inflicted merciless penalty
on his offending pupils.   Our author goes on to observe
that all the peculiarities of Calvinism may be found
incarnated and visibilised in the old type of Scottish
pedagogue, who in conducting his school invariably went

on the principle, first, of acting "out of his mere good pleasure"; next, of "electing" some boys to "favour" and others to disfavour; and finally, of "ordering all things to his own glory," in slapping and penalising a number of unfortunate little victims, who cowered and quaked before him. In Thomas Crann, the Scottish stonemason, and one or two other kindred characters, we are presented with something more attractive. The same features of sternness and severity make their appearance again, but this time they lie in close contiguity with other and more genial qualities, which serve to illuminate and beautify them. Underneath a severe and loveless exterior there is often a deep well of tenderness—very deep down, it is true, and frozen over with a thick crust of reserve; still it is there, and at times struggles into visibility through the thick layers of encumbrance which impede its flow. Thomas Crann himself has a nature which might find its fitting symbol in the granite rock of his native hills, but within that flinty enclosure there is a genuine fountain of pity, and sometimes the rock has tears trickling down the sides of it. At first sight we might suppose that in such portraits as these our author was paying an indirect tribute to the Calvinism which appears to be their informing spirit. But it is not so. Wherever, in the pages of Dr. MacDonald, you have fineness and nobility of character coexisting with Calvinistic belief, the latter is never credited with having anything to do with their production. All that the writer would have us admire in types of humanity like Thomas Crann is in them *in spite of* their theology, and not as a result of it. Whatever spiritual excellence or beauty of soul they may exhibit, all that their theological beliefs contributed to the genesis and development of it was to stand in its way as a frustration and a hindrance. Calvinism is never anything but a disadvantage, a disfigurement, and an eyesore. The writer even seeks to exaggerate any natural nobility his characters may possess, that all their defects and monstrosities may be laid to the charge of their creed. Now, while this may be a very ingenious and strategic stroke, the writer who has recourse to such tactics seems to us to land himself in a most embarrassing situation. If certain unconscious and beautiful elements of character are found contiguous to, and invariably associated with, a certain form of pronounced and earnest belief,—elements which are constantly captivating Dr. MacDonald in spite of his prejudices,—is it not reasonable to suppose that there is some vital and causative connection between the two ? and can any man be blamed for coming to the conclusion that the one is an important factor which must be taken into account when attempting an explanation of the other ; or can the logic be impugned which infers that the intellectual beliefs which Dr. MacDonald sneers at have helped to generate in no small degree those beauties of character which Dr. MacDonald admires ?   " Where we find a heroic life," says Mr. Froude, " appearing as the uniform fruit of a particular mode of opinion, it is childish to argue in the face of fact that the result ought to have been different." [1]   If, on the other hand, these two factors have no deeper connection than that of mere vicinity or juxtaposition, if the intellectual convictions have no effect

[1] *Essay on Calvinism.*

on the finer, deeper issues of character, then Dr. Mac-
Donald might have spared himself the trouble of writing
a whole series of novels having for their object the extermination of a set of beliefs which, after all, turn out to
be but phantom beliefs, beliefs so effete and inoperative
that they exert no appreciable influence on the mental
and spiritual development of those who hold them.   It
was not worth Dr. MacDonald's while to assail a bundle
of views and opinions so harmless and unoffending in their
nature that they simply lie " bedridden in the dormitory
of the soul," along with many other dormant and innocuous things, and practically make no difference.   He has
been all the while fighting an army of shadows, and all
his contendings have been little better than a species of
Don Quixotism.   We do not wish to dogmatise, but if we
were in a position to enjoy the privilege of a fireside chat
with Dr. MacDonald, we should greatly like to confront
him with this straight question, and elicit from him a
straight answer, " Has Calvinism as a system of truth
produced fine and noble characters, or has it not ?   Have
the peoples who, on the continents of Europe and America,
have imbibed Calvinistic doctrine exhibited a higher
type of manhood than those who have not embraced it ? "
History, and biography, which is " history teaching by
example," have returned to these questions no halting or
dubious reply.   If Dr. MacDonald accepts their verdict,
then we are decidedly of opinion that in the course of
his lengthened pilgrimage and many wanderings up and
down in the world, he might surely have chanced to
make acquaintance with some few Calvinistic Christians
who were fairer representatives of their creed, and did it

less injustice, than Mrs. Worboise or Murdoch Mallison. If, on the other hand, Dr. MacDonald is not candid enough to recognise any tendency in Calvinism to the development of rare and splendid qualities, then we shall set in array against him the great historians Bancroft, Ranke, and Froude, whose opinion on a matter of this kind is better worth having than his. Even Mr. John Morley, who certainly cannot be suspected of any theological bias, will furnish him with some edifying information on the subject. It is not too much to maintain that the world has never known a higher type of robust and sturdy manhood, nor a gentler, purer, or more lovable womanhood, than have prevailed among those peoples who have imbibed the principles of the Calvinistic creed, with its commingled elements of granitic strength and stability, and of supreme, because Divine, tenderness and grace. In any case, the merits or demerits of Calvinism as a religious force are not to be settled by a mere indulgence in caricature, or by deliberately making sport for the Philistines out of things sacred and venerable, which to generations of noble men and women have been dear as their own soul. But what can we expect from our author in his fictional treatment of Calvinism, when even some of the finest specimens of it in real life have failed to command his respect. Earnest-minded men of all parties have consented to do honour to such worthies as Thomas Boston, John Bunyan, Ralph Erskine, Philip Doddridge, and Matthew Henry, whether they happened to agree with them in their dogmatic teaching or not. But for these saintly men and their writings Dr. MacDonald has nothing but sneers and contemptuous allusion.

If he condescends to mention them at all, it is only that he may assail them, or make them the target for his ridicule. Readers of his novels will be familiar with many such thrusts as those which he has interjected into his brief description of David Elginbrod's little library :—

"Hugh Sutherland looked at a few of the books. They were almost all old, and such as may be found in many Scottish cottages ; for instance, Boston's *Fourfold State, in which the ways of God and man may be seen through a fourfold fog* ; Erskine's *Divine Sonnets*, which will repay the reader in laughter for the pain it costs his reverence, producing much the same effect that a Gothic cathedral might, reproduced by the pencil, and from the remembrance of a Chinese artist, who had seen it once ; the *Scots Worthies*, opening of itself at the memoir of Alexander Peden ; the *Pilgrim's Progress*, that wonderful inspiration, failing never, save when the theologian *would* sometimes snatch the pen from the hand of the poet ; *Theron and Aspasia* ; *Village Dialogues* ; and others of a like class."

Passages like this are followed by their own penalty. We shall now know what value to attach to those satiric representations of evangelical religion with which our author's pages are studded ; they must be largely discounted, seeing he has already assailed, in the most wanton and offensive manner, men who, whatever their opinions, have always enjoyed a general reputation for saintliness and sincerity. The allusion to John Bunyan is particularly unfortunate. It ill becomes George MacDonald of all men to take exception to the *Pilgrim's Progress* on the ground that it contains too much theology. Has he forgotten how overweighted his own books are with the theological element, and theology has certainly less business in novels than in religious allegories ? Does he not reflect how in his own case the theologian is constantly snatching the pen from the hand of the poet and the story-teller, to the serious detriment of his workmanship as a literary artist?   The truth is, honest John does not suffer from "too much theology" more than does his critic, only it happens to be a theology which our author does not like.   Had it been a theology that chimed in with the idiosyncrasies of George MacDonald, Bunyan might have soaked and saturated his immortal allegory with it without any expostulations.

George MacDonald's clerical portraits, of which he has favoured us with a goodly number, are equally objection-able, so far at least as they profess to exhibit the ordinary type of evangelical ministry.   Like many other novelists, he seems to entertain a spiteful grudge at the clergy, and he must always have his fling at them.   His opinion of the average parson may be said to be briefly compre-prehended in a verse from one of his own poetical effusions—

> "The minister wasna fit to pray,
>   And lat alane to preach;
> He nowther had the gift o' grace,
>   Nor yet the gift o' speech.
> He mindit him o' Balaam's ass,
>   Wi' a differ ye may ken;
> The Lord He opened the ass's mou',
>   The minister opened his ain."

The Calvinistic type of minister is always represented as harsh, gloomy, and forbidding.   Mr. Cowie is a fulminating, anathematising dogmatist, sincere enough in his way, but out of all sympathy with the natural piety of childhood, and insufferably narrow and repellent in his

mode of presenting the truth. He chooses for his text,
" The wicked shall be turned into hell, and all the nations
that forget God." His sermon is described as consisting
of vague and half-monstrous embodiments of truth, and
it fills the girlish mind of Annie Anderson with horror
and dismay. Mr. Venables, an old man, and belonging
to the old school, has a voice and manner in reading the
service " which are far more memorial of departed dinners
than of joys to come." Mr. Simon, the curate of St.
Solomon's,—

" was a gentle abstracted youth, with a face that looked
as if its informing idea had been for a considerable period
sat upon by something ungenial. With him the profession
had become everything, and humanity never had been
anything, if not something bad. He walked through the
crowded streets in the neighbourhood with hurried steps
and eyes fixed on the ground, his pale face rarely brighten-
ing with recognition, for he rarely saw any passing
acquaintance. When he did, he greeted him with a
voice that seemed to come from far-off shores, but came
really from a bloodless, nerveless chest, that had nothing
to do with life, save to yield up the ghost in eternal
security, and send it safe out of it. He seemed to recognise none of those human relations which make the blood
mount to the face at meeting, and give strength to the
grasp of the hand. He would not have hurt a fly; he
would have died to save a malefactor from the gallows,
that he might give him another chance of repentance.
But mere human aid he had none to bestow; no warmth,
no heartening, no hope."

To young Thomas Worboise, Mr. Simon " had given
what he had," like his namesake at the gate of the
Temple ; " but all he had served only to make a man creep,
it could not make him stand up and walk." Thomas
got at last to avoid his society, for he " had pressed him

so hard with the stamp of religion that the place was
painful, although the impression was fast disappearing."

And here we may be permitted to interject a word or
two of commentary on the manner in which the evangelical clergyman has been depicted in modern literature.
When will our novelists vary the one monotonous note
on which they have harped so long, and by way of a
change try to delineate for us a type of Gospel minister
who is neither a dolt nor a pedant, neither a white-
cravated eccentric nor a canting hypocrite, neither a
simpering ninny nor a pulpit-thumping dogmatist, but
just a plain, plodding man of average intellect, and
dowered on the whole with as much sincerity as his
hearers, and who is doing his best to fill his place in the
world creditably, and make out of himself as good a
clergyman as he can—this, at least, would be a pleasing
variety of treatment, a welcome departure from the
registered and regulation pattern to which our novel-
writers have so long slavishly adhered.   It would at
least have the merit of being new, and we cannot help
thinking it might possibly have the additional advantage
of being a nearer approach to the truth of things.   The
clergyman of fiction is either a sublime official who has
certain "functions" to discharge, and discharges them
with starched and stiffened professional propriety, or he
is a fox-hunter who follows the hounds to-day and
buries the dead to-morrow, or he is a tennis-playing, tea-
drinking creature, who comes in handy for social occasions,
or he is "an innocuous saint, who is only half a man."
As has been said, "he is not nearly so vital a character
in the affairs of life as an old Roman augur was.   The

augur did something to the purpose of real life. He told the people when to fight a battle, when to raise a siege, when to launch a fleet. But the clergyman of fiction has never conceded to him the dignity of being any use." [1]

Of course this sort of thing is pure exaggeration; we might even go further, and characterise it as a gross libel on the vast multitude of clergy of all sects and Churches the world over. As a body, the clergy, like every other class of men, have their faults and their foibles, their prejudices, their professional sins and shortcomings, and they are by no means averse to have their failings made the subject of legitimate banter and merriment, if need be; they do not claim or expect immunity from ridicule, or ask to be screened from the thrusts and sallies of the satirist. But what we think our men of letters, those of them at least who are animated by a religious spirit, might take into consideration oftener than they do, is this—the harm that may be done to religion itself by indiscriminate caricature of those who stand forth before the world as its accredited messengers and custodians. Readers, especially young readers, do not stop to draw nice distinctions, and if our novelists and literary men have been teaching them all through the week to make a laughing-stock of the ministry, and hold it in contempt, they will soon come to despise the Church of which that ministry is a standing institution, and by an insensible gradation they will come to hold cheaply the message which the ministry is charged with, and in the end may even be smitten with an incurable prejudice against the very Book

---

[1] Phelp's *Men and Books*, p. 25.

from which the ministry draws its texts. You have taught them to giggle at the parson, what if in time the giggle extends to Christianity itself ?   " It is thus," says a great writer, " we soak our children in habits of contempt and exultant gibing, and yet are confident that —as Clarissa one day said to me—' we can always teach them to be reverent at the right place, you know.' "   No, that is precisely what we cannot do.   The irreverent spirit will break out at times and in places where Clarissa least expected it to show its ugly presence.

But, to return to our author, Dr. MacDonald's theological perversities become more painfully apparent when we turn to that maudlin sentimental type of piety which he advocates as a very much superior article to ordinary evangelical religion.   His representations of conversion, and kindred subjects, are childish, and even silly.   They are representations such as could only be given by one who ignores the existence of any awful controversy caused by sin, who has not plumbed the depths of man's depravity, nor taken sufficient account of the moral helplessness and decrepitude of fallen human nature. Conversion with him is but a slight and facile process which is not dependent for its accomplishment on the instruments of grace, or on those redemptive forces which focus themselves in the Christian Church.   Undue emphasis is laid on the part played by natural influences in the process of man's salvation, and regenerating efficacy, which we had thought belonged exclusively to the Spirit of God, is freely attributed to such things as fiddles, kites, scenery, music, and the memorials of departed friends. · " Robert's mind was full of the kite

and violin, and was probably nearer God thereby than if
he had been trying to feel as wicked as his grandmother
told God he was." When Alec Forbes removes from
Howglen to a northern university to prosecute his studies
as a medical student, he falls in, as the reader will
remember, with a very singular companion, who lodges
in the attic of his landlady's house : an eccentric genius,
who acted as librarian of the college, and was as full of
classical learning as he was occasionally of whisky punch,
for unfortunately he was a confirmed devotee of the
bottle.   Alec spent most of his evenings in the society
of this drunken philosopher, who regaled him with wit
and anecdote, and at the same time assisted him in his
studies, until the hour arrived when the intoxicating
fumes of the drink had muddled his faculties, when the
young student instantly got his dismissal for the night.
No better specimen could be desired of a dissipated
wreck than this tippling librarian, who, regularly as
night followed night, might be found lying in a drunken
stupor in his garret.   In his intercourse with the young
medical student he gave him from time to time much
excellent advice, especially warning him most solemnly
against alcoholic indulgence—a warning by no means
uncalled for, for Alec had by this time fallen a prey to
the temptations of city life.   He too had become hopelessly addicted to drink ; but just at this juncture a
singular scene took place, which issued all at once in the
salvation of them both.   Mr. Cupples suddenly made a
proposal, which, considering his habits, was a most
magnanimous and self-denying one.   He proposed to his
young friend to stop drinking, if he would do the same.

Instantly the compact was entered into, and " bang went the bottle out into the courtyard." " Thank God ! " said Mr. Cupples, as the clash reached his ears. " Both their hearts," adds our author, " were touched by one good and strong spirit—essential life and humanity. That spirit was love, which at the long last will expel whatsover opposeth itself." Thus " the spirit of essential life and humanity," it will be observed, is all the spirit that is needed to effect the saving change in this brace of sinners, and there is more virtue in " love " to redeem and reform than in all the moral appliances of evangelical religion. Having entered on a new career, the next we read of Mr. Cupples is that he is approaching the house of Alec Forbes in Howglen, where the young student is lying dangerously ill ; and one night Annie Anderson, sitting up with the invalid, overhears in her lonely vigil a subdued voice singing beneath the window—

> " I waited for the Lord my God,
>   And patiently did bear ;
> At length to me He did incline
>   My voice and cry to hear.
> He took me from a fearful pit,
>   And from the miry clay,
> And on a rock He set my feet,
>   Establishing my way."

This was the reformed inebriate, who, having broken his whisky bottle, had now taken to psalm-singing. Do you seek the explanation of a transformation so abrupt and wonderful ? You shall have it in the author's own words—

. " A playful humanity radiated from him, the result of that powerfulest of all restoratives—*giving* of what one has to him that has not. Indeed, his reformation had

begun with this.   St. Paul taught a thief to labour that
he might have to give.   Love taught Mr. Cupples to deny
himself, that he might rescue his friend, and presently he
had found his own feet touching the rock.   If he had not
yet learned to look straight to heaven, his eyes wandered
not unfrequently towards that spiritual horizon upon
which things earthly and heavenly meet and embrace."

A little giving to one that has not, a stray act of
impulsive benevolence, has done it all.   Murdoch Mallison,
the ferocious pedagogue, is made a new creature in the
same way.   In one of his paroxysms of Calvinistic fury,
he had lamed for life a poor scholar of his by administer-
ing to him a savage kick.   After a long absence in consequence, the boy reappears in the schoolroom one day,
still retaining the evidences of his maltreatment, but
harbouring no vengeful feeling, and ready to forgive.
The schoolmaster is deeply touched.   An ardent affection
springs up between the two, and this singular pedagogue,
who had been diabolised by an overdose of the Shorter
Catechism, suddenly flowers into a full-blown saint under
the influence of a little pity and remorse !   The conversion of Alec Forbes himself is thus described :—

" One lovely morning, when the green corn lay soaking
in the yellow sunlight, and the sky rose above the earth,
deep and pure and tender, like the thought of God about
it, Alec became suddenly aware that life was good and
the world beautiful. . . . He was blessed, so easily can
God make a man happy.   The past had dropped from
him like a wild but weary and sordid dream.   He was
reborn, a new child, a new bright world with a glowing
summer to revel in. . . . He would be a good child
henceforth, for one bunch of sunrays was enough to be
happy upon."

Analyse this piece of sentimental vapouring, and what

does it amount to but something like this, that a young
fellow sauntering along a country road on a lovely
summer morning, as the fresh breeze fans his cheek, and
the exercise makes the blood course more nimbly through
his veins, feels his spirits rising, feels it a blessed thing
to be alive on such a day, looks upon existence itself as
a boon to be thankful for—and this, according to our
author, is to be " reborn," to become a new creature, to
be a child of God, and the inhabitant of a new world.
When Robert Falconer pays the railway fare of the poor
tutor of Tulliegraffit, Dr. MacDonald professes to discern
in him a veritable follower of Him who was " a hiding-
place from the wind and a covert from the tempest."

" Of the Son of Man," says he, " Falconer had already
learned this truth in the inward parts, and had found in
the process of learning it that this was the true nature
which God had made his from the first—no new thing
superinduced over it. He had but to clear away the
rubbish of worldliness, cleaving more or less to the best
nature for a time, and so to find himself."

Thus, in the MacDonald theology, the sagacious reader
will observe, we are each of us blessed with a nature
good enough from the beginning, and, once we clear away
a trifle of rubbish that overlays and obscures it, we
" find ourselves," and very soon find our God. Such
representations of conversion, we repeat, could only come
from a writer who has no adequate conception of man's
alienation from God, and has never properly diagnosed
the deep-seated malady of human nature. Conversion, in
the New Testament usage of the term, involves an
inward change so radical and stupendous, that it requires

a Divine and supernatural agent to effect it; a transformation so revolutionary and complete, that only the
greatest of all possible transformations in the natural
world may be employed to illustrate and set it forth—
creation, birth, and death.   According to Dr. MacDonald's
genial and accommodating interpretation of the great
initial experience on which our entrance into the kingdom
of heaven is conditioned, a modern Nicodemus would
have small occasion ever to ask, How can these things
be? and the natural man will be amply capable of
achieving his own conversion, because it is very naturally
effected.   A little mending and touching up of human
nature is all that is needed; or, if anything more be
required, why, a little natural impressibility, a wave of
emotion, or a dash of religious sensitiveness, will supply
all that is lacking.   Manifestly the implication is that
there is even in the worst of men "a true nature which
God has made theirs from the first," a sort of underlying
goodness ready to effloresce by a natural evolution into all
kinds of spiritual excellence and loveliness, provided only
it be carefully cultivated and brought to the surface.
What men need is reformation rather than regeneration,
not redemption but training, not deliverance but culture.
And, what is even more painfully noticeable in George
MacDonald's writings, is his extreme anxiety to dissociate
any spiritual excellence or charm of character his heroes
may possess from any such disreputable source as evangelical religion.   He is always careful to impress upon
the reader that his characters have sat under a Gospel
ministry which has entirely failed to produce conversion,
that some Calvinistic divine has applied the Gospel

19

remedies but ineffectually, and only when, in disappointment, they abandoned evangelism altogether, as a well
in which no living water was, and began to imbibe the
peculiar views of Mr. MacDonald himself, did they
become the recipients of any light or blessing.   Evangelicism, in the prejudiced estimate of our author, is a
Nazareth out of which no good thing can come.

In David Elginbrod, exception is taken to the preaching of Scottish divines on the subject of Justification.
The hero of the book is not at all satisfied with the
mode of presenting that doctrine which prevails in the
Scottish pulpit.

" This is just my opinion of it in sma'—*that* man and
that man only is justified, who pits himself into the Lord's
hands to be sanctified.   Noo that'll no be dune by pittin'
a robe o' righteousness upon him afore he's gotten a clean
skin beneath.   As gin a father couldna bide to see the
puir scabbit skin o' his ain wee bit bairnie; ay, or o' his
prodigal son either, but had to hap it a' up afore he could
let it come near him.   There's a notion in't (that is, in
the way that Scotch ministers speak of Justification) o'
hidin' sin frae God Himsel'.   They speak so that the puir
bairn canna see the Father Himsel', staunin' wi' His airms
streekit oot as wide as the heavens, to tak' the worn
crater, and the mare sinner the mare welcome hame to
His ain heart.   Gin a body would leave a' that, an' jist
get folk persuaded to speak a word or two to God 'lane,
the loss would be unco sma'."

This representation of Scottish preaching on the
central theme of the Gospel strikes us as altogether unfair.
The occupants of Scottish pulpits are not such blundering theologians as to disconnect justification from the
companion truth of regeneration, or to preach the former
doctrine in such an indiscreet and unguarded way as to

encourage immoral tendencies, or relax the bonds of human obligation. They are not in the habit of promulgating the dangerous notion that the sinner is forgiven and left where he is; rather they are careful to show that he is forgiven only in order to his being fully saved, and by God's grace renovated and made holy. They do not contemplate, nor teach their hearers to contemplate, the priestly office of Christ, whereby He confers forgiveness and acceptance, apart from His kingly office, whereby He sanctifies and renews through the power of that Holy Spirit whose province it is to make us holy too. The blessings of justification are bestowed only on those who exercise personal faith; and whilst we are justified by faith alone, we are not justified by a faith which is alone, but by a faith which, working by love, is prolific of good works, and contains within itself the germs of holy living. So far from indulging in loose statements of the doctrine, the accredited teachers of the evangelical system everywhere will cordially assent to Dr. MacDonald's own statement of it—"*that* man, and that man only, is justified who puts himself into the Lord's hands to be sanctified." Dr. Chalmers himself puts the same aspect of the truth most expressively, when in a memorable sentence he declares, that "in the same moment in which the Lord Jesus lays upon the sinner the hand of a Saviour, He lays upon him also the hand of a Sanctifier." What ground is there, then, for the insinuation that Justification in the hands of evangelical preachers is little else than a device for "putting on the sinner a robe o' righteousness afore he's gotten a clean skin beneath," that so his moral leprosy may all be happed up, and hidden from the sight of God Himself? Nay, the true representation is,—and if Scottish preachers have represented it otherwise they have been guilty of an unfortunate misstatement of evangelical principles,—that the justified person *does* get a clean skin beneath. When the servants brought forth the best robe and put it on the returned prodigal, they did not array him in that glorious mantle, we may be sure, till he had first doffed the rags which he had worn among the swine-troughs; or, dropping the parable and putting the truth in plain language, God is not only faithful and just to forgive us our sins, but to cleanse us from all unrighteousness. The cleansing of the sinner from his moral defilement, according to Dr. MacDonald, exhausts the Divine benevolence, and is the only step in the process of salvation which is worth insisting on. But what about the sinner's relation to his own guilty past? Must there not be a cancelling of old scores? And how shall he be put right with God?—in other words, how shall he secure a righteousness which will render him acceptable? These are problems which are not solved by simply giving him "a clean skin."

The picture here given of the Divine Being as a benign Father, "staunin' wi' His airms streekit oot wide as the heavens" to welcome returning prodigals, and take them to His heart, without any intervention of a Mediator, or any reference to an atonement (for that is what is implied), is a very favourite one with Dr. MacDonald, who considers it dishonouring to God, and a libel on His infinite love, that He should be supposed to demand any amends or spiritual reparation being made to Him for the sins of His offending children. Thus, when David Elginbrod prays for the forgiveness of his sins, it is in language not only peremptory and dictatorial in style, considering the Being to whom it is addressed, but studiously silent as regards all mention of the atoning work of Christ, or any Gospel of Mediation.

"An' noo for a' our wrang-doings, an' ill-meanings, for a' our sins, and trespasses o' many sorts, dinna forget them, O God, till Thou pits them a' right; an' syne exerceese Thy michty power e'en ower Thine ainsel', an clean forget them a'thegither; cast them ahin' Thy back, whaur e'en Thine ain een shall ne'er see them again, that we may walk bold and upright before Thee for evermore, an' see the face o' Him wha was as muckle God in doin' Thy biddin', as gin He had been ordering a'things Himsel'."

According to David's off-hand and easy-going theology, there is no need for anything more than the exercise on God's part of a little magnanimity, or, as he somewhat irreverently expresses it, a royal act of self-control. His own ancestor shared the same sentiment, and had it inscribed as an epitaph upon his tombstone—an epitaph which condenses into a few lines the very pith and essence of Macdonald's own theology—

> "Here lie I, Martin Elginbrod,
> Ha'e mercy on my soul, O God ;
> As I would do, were I Lord God,
> And ye were Martin Elginbrod."

"Such an epitaph," says Dr. Selby, "is a grotesque mixture of the boldness of faith and of the irreverent Gnosticism which is puffed up with the conviction that it can solve all mysteries." [1] The sentiment embodied in

[1] *The Theology of Fiction.*

these lines is that as when men sin against us we are easily entreated, and when there is evidence of sorrow, ready to forgive and forget without insisting on any atonement; so God, whose goodness must be infinitely greater than ours, cannot be conceived as requiring any atonement as the condition of His forgiveness, save such as is implied in the sinner's own penitential regret. This is to assume that God's moral relations to men, and the sins of men, are identical with our own : and that therefore what is right for us to do must be right for Him.   But the assumption is unwarranted.   It does not follow that what would be right and beautiful in my conduct towards my brother man can be safely accepted as the rule of the Divine conduct towards him ; for God stands to him in relations which are wholly different from mine, and different relations, as we all know, create different duties and obligations.   What might be very beautiful in a child, might be very reprehensible in a parent.   What might be highly commendable in a private citizen, might be gross dereliction in a judge. What might call forth admiration in a subject of the realm, might be censurable in the occupant of a throne. Our relations to our fellow-men are so widely different from those which God sustains to them as Moral Governor and Lawgiver, that we cannot always argue from the human to the Divine.   For instance, it would be very wrong for us to take vengeance on anyone who had wronged or injured us ; but if it be right and proper that vindictive action should be taken, God may Himself retaliate, for " vengeance belongeth unto me : I will repay, saith the Lord."   Here is a course of conduct which, on God's part, is perfectly right; while, on ours, it would be so egregiously wrong that we are strictly forbidden to be guilty of it. No human relations can adequately represent the relations which subsist between God and those who are the subjects of His moral empire. Besides, as Dr. Dale points out in his *Christian Doctrine*—

"The analogy between the relation of a father to a child and the relation of God to man breaks down at a critical point—the point on which the whole question of the necessity for an 'atonement' depends. The powers of a father are limited by a higher Authority; he is not the supreme moral ruler of the child; the father is a sinner as well as the child. You cannot argue that because a father does not ask for an 'atonement' before he forgives his child, God can ask for no 'atonement' before He forgives us. God is the Representative and Defender of the eternal law of righteousness in a sense in which an earthly father is not."[1]

Unhappily, for this aspect of the Divine character, there is no room in the MacDonald theology. All that there appears to be room for is a parental fondness and boundless amiability, which is constantly on the verge of degenerating into slackness and over-indulgence. The substratum or essence of the Divine nature, it is alleged, is Fatherhood; all the attributes of Deity are subordinate to love, and resolvable into love. The first step towards the construction of a right conception of God, is to take the rudimentary instincts and affections of earthly parentage and magnify and expand them on a scale of infinitude, till by this means we climb up into some intelligible idea of the grandeur and glory of the Divine

[1] *Christian Doctrine*, p. 242.

Fatherhood. To our mental picture of the Divine Being
we are to bring all that we have learned in the household of fidelity and love, and, amplifying these earthly
examples, and eliminating from them their inherent
limitations, we gradually etherealise and hallow them
into the supreme name of God. But domestic emotions,
we submit, supply no scale of measurement which we
can safely apply to God, and the principles of His
moral government. No matter how superfine or rarefied
the specimens of earthly parentage may be, they are
always lacking in the element of righteousness which the
ideal Fatherhood must of necessity include. Parentage
is often found dissociated from the eternal principles of
equity; amid all its exuberance of indulgence and caress,
it has frequently no conscience at the core of it; it is
not always accompanied by a vivid moral sense; there
are deep ethical considerations which find no place in it.
Does it not commonly degenerate into laxity, partialism,
or oversweetness? Is it not often blind, moreover, and
does it not often contract itself into a narrow self-
contained exclusiveness, concentrating its attention altogether on its own children, utterly oblivious of what is
due to those who are folded in other homes, and setting
at nought the claims of the community? Society knows
this so well, that as a matter of fact it never trusts the
parental sentiment when the ends of righteousness are
concerned, but transfers from the parent the power of
dealing with the graver offences, and commits it to an
outside and independent tribunal in the person of the
magistrate or the judge.

Yet it is to this vacillating and unreliable sentiment

that George MacDonald and writers belonging to the same school make their appeal, and it is out of this that they construct what they believe to be the only correct image of the living and true God. It is an image which we are not inclined to fall down and worship, though called upon to do so with the sound of sackbut and psaltery, for at best it presents us with but a fragmentary and unsymmetrical view. There are profound ethical elements in the Divine nature and disposition which it entirely overlooks. Fatherhood is not the first and the last word in the naming of God. All the Divine attributes cannot be unified into love, for the same apostle who has given us the memorable assurance that " God is love " has taken care also to inform us that " God is light "; and whether you interpret " light " as meaning wisdom or meaning holiness, it is beyond doubt, the Apostle John himself being witness, that there are in the Most High *more* qualities than *one* of co-ordinate and coequal importance. " God is love is not the whole gospel," says Dr. Forsythe of Cambridge. " Love is not evangelical till it has dealt with holy law. In the midst of the rainbow is a throne. There is a kind of consecration which would live close to the Father, but it does not always take seriously enough the holiness which *makes* the fatherhood of the Cross awful, inexhaustible, and eternal, as full of judgment as of salvation." [1]

God is more to the human race than simply Father. He is *holy* Father ; He is the *righteous* Father, the name by which Jesus Himself addressed Him, though standing to Him in the unique relation of only-begotten Son. He

[1] *The Holy Father and the Living Christ*, p. 12.

is Moral Governor and Judge, as well as Parent, of mankind.   He is the Vindicator of the world's moral order,
the Representative and Defender of the eternal law of
righteousness.   We put too little into Fatherhood when
we simply treat it as an equivalent for characterless
indulgence, doting partiality, or caressing affability.   We
put too little into it when we resolve it into "a
sympathetic allowance for things," or a careless clemency
which passes over offences with a " Pray do not mention
it," or sponges out the record of a guilty past as men
might wipe figures from a slate.   We put too little into
it when we interpret it as a boundless love, so exuberant
in its benevolence as to dispense with all necessity for an
atonement, and even sacrifice the demands of its own
holiness.   Thus the God of Calvinistic worship is compared by Robert Falconer to—

"A puir, prood, bailey-like body, fu' o' his ain importance, and ready to be doon upo' onybody 'at didna ca'
him by the name o' his office—aye thinkin' aboot's ain
glory, in place o' the quaiet, michty, gran', self-forgettin',
a'-creatin', a'-uphaudin' eternal bein' wha took the form
o' man in Christ Jesus."

"But, laddie, He cam' to satisfee God's justice for oor
sins; to turn aside His wrath and curse; to reconcile
Him to us."

"He did naethin' o' the kin', grannie, it's a lee that.
He cam' to satisfy God's justice by giein' Him back His
bairns: by garrin' them see that God was just; by sending them greetin' hame to fa' at His feet and grip His
knees, and say, "Father, ye're i' the richt."

Here is a second passage from the same book, much to
the same effect—

"God be praised by those who can regard God as the
Father of every human soul—the ideal Father, not an

inventor of schemes or the upholder of a court etiquette, for whose use He has chosen to desecrate the name of justice."

In these representations there is a degree of truth, in so far as they emphasise the fact that God has been animated from eternity with motives of goodwill to mankind, and commendeth His love toward us in that He loved us while we were yet sinners. Such protests may be of service, too, in counteracting the unfortunate tendency to think and speak of the Atonement as a cold judicial *arrangement*, rather than a direct *love-token* from the great Father's heart—a *theological device*, in which the *anxiety to uphold authority* is more conspicuous than the *passion to redeem*. They are also deserving of respect in so far as they help to dispel the pernicious notion that God's love was *procured* for us by the intervention of some foreign power ; that the Atonement of Christ *induced* God to regard us with a love and pity which would otherwise have been withheld from us ; that, in fact, His love had to be bought from His holiness by the setting up of the Cross. But the theory of Christ's work here advanced by Dr. MacDonald is one which has been tried and found wanting. The *Moral-influence* theory of the Atonement, as it has been called, though it can plead the sanctions of some illustrious names, has long been felt to be onesided, inadequate, and not quite candid in its New Testament exegesis. If there is one feature of the Atonement to which more prominence is given than another in the Biblical representations on the subject, it is that the object of Christ's death was to lay a basis for the righteous forgiveness of sin, that the Cross was a Divine

expedient whereby God's love might be freely extended
to the chief of sinners, without any abridgment of His
holiness. "The holy Father's first care," says an
eminent living divine already quoted, "is holiness.
The first charge on a Redeemer is satisfaction to that
holiness." [1]

This aspect of Christ's mediation is strongly insisted
on in the New Testament, and the best theological
criticism of the day is quite alive.to its importance. Yet
to Dr. MacDonald God's care for His own holiness is
only the maintenance of a " court etiquette "; and when
He is represented as taking any precautions for the safe-
guarding of His own authority, or securing the welfare
of His own government, He is " a puir, prood, bailey-
like body, fu' o' his ain importance." Such descriptions
are irreverent, and most unjust to the theology which
has always made the assertion of the Divine righteousness
one of its foremost articles.

The doctrine of the Divine Fatherhood, as held and
expounded by Dr. MacDonald, necessitates, as he thinks,
some very revolutionary changes in the commonly received
doctrine of the punishment of sin. In the name of the
Divine pity and goodness, which in his theology take the
form of an omni-benevolence, he proceeds to abolish
hell, or at least to transform it into a Reformatory, or
school of discipline beyond the grave, in which abandoned
natures will at length come to themselves, and the sleeping divinity will at last awaken within those who on
earth sinned away their opportunities, and proved
obdurate to all the motives that stimulate to reformation

[1] Forsythe's *Holy Father and the Living Christ*, p. 8.

and obedience.   Like the clergyman on whose preaching
Robert Falconer occasionally attended, and who is supposed
to be the *alter ego* of Frederick Denison Maurice, Dr.
MacDonald " believes entirely that God loves, yea is love,
and therefore hell itself must be subservient to that
love." Punishment is softened into chastisement, and
penalty into a loving discipline whose object is purely
reformatory.   The ideal Father must be supposed to
recoil from anything that verges on the penal, the
vengeful, the retaliatory.   If His efforts to save men
during their earthly probation are unsuccessful, He will
resume the attempt on the other side of death ; He will
give them a second chance, and send them to other
schools than those of Time, till every offending child of
Adam shall at some far-off day be finally recovered from
his apostasy, and eventually admitted into the rest and
blessedness of heaven.   And so—

> "Hell itself shall pass away,
> And leave her dolorous mourners to the peering day."

After Robert Falconer has found his drunken father
in London, and had him removed to lodgings, where he
tenderly nursed and watched over him for days, he at
last summons up courage to say to him—

" Father, you've got to repent; and God won't let you
off, and you needn't think it.   You'll have to repent some
day."

" In hell, Robert," said Andrew.

" Yes, either on earth or in hell.   Would it not be
better on earth ? "

" But it will be of no use in hell."

And at this point in his dialogue Dr. MacDonald
breaks in with an evangel of his own for such poor souls

as die impenitent, and pass hence enfeebled by their own
wickedness.   We are to let them understand that there
is in infernal torture an efficacy to reinvigorate a languid
will ; that the flames will melt them into obedient action,
and " the torturing Spirit of God in their hearts " will
teach them not only what they ought to have done, but
what they ought to do and must do now.   Hence the
Scotch doctor, who has lived long in India, is made to
say on his deathbed—

" I wadna like to tak' to ony papistry ; but I never
could mak' oot frae the Bible—and I hae read mair i' the
jungle than maybe ye wad think—that it was a' ower wi'
a body at their death."

This adventurous and seductive Gospel of repentance
after death must operate wherever it is received as a
deadening narcotic to all anxiety for the attainment of a
present salvation for ourselves, or the extension of it to
others.   It has a fatal tendency to chloroform men into
a careless negligence, to bolster them up in carnal
security with a presumptuous hope, and to confirm them
in a policy of drift, postponement, and *laissez faire* where
their spiritual interests are at stake.   Conceive the
preacher among the dying populations of our great cities,
instead of " lifting up the Son of Man as Moses lifted
up the serpent in the wilderness," saying to the multitude of the shepherdless and the lost : " Go on in your
sinning ; if you die in your sin it will be burned out of
you, I have no doubt, in the Gehenna beyond the grave."
How will such preaching work ?   It is always safe to
put truth into practice.   But which of us is prepared to act
on the assurance that further opportunities of repentance

arc awaiting us in the future life? Which of us is venturesome enough to rest the whole weight of his own salvation on that precarious plank? And which of us is prepared to advise any friend to trust his salvation to it? Not one of us will take the leap into the unseen on the chance of George MacDonald's gospel of second chances coming true, and we recoil with horror from asking our friends to take it. And if we will not take the risk ourselves, nor advise others to take it, why will we take the responsibility of advising mankind in general to take it? "If I cannot advise John, Jane, William, and Mary," says Joseph Cook, "to trust to repentance after death, I have no right to advise the ages to do so. John, Jane, William, and Mary *are* the ages."

In the prayer of Falconer's grandmother for her dissipated and runaway son, we have one of those attempts with which the writings of Dr. MacDonald are all too plentifully interspersed, and which reveal one of his special weaknesses as a religious guide—the attempt to elevate mere sentiment into a final court of appeal for the settlement of great and complex moral problems. We are to be guided exclusively by our feelings on topics which are too large for the outlook of purely sentimental views.

"Och hone! och hone!" said grannie from the bed, "I've a sair, sair hert. I've a sair hert in my breist, O Lord! Thou knowest. My ain Anerew! To think o' my bairnie that I carriet i' my ain body, that sookit my breists, and leuch i' my face—to think o' him turnin' reprobate! O Lord, couldna he be eleckit yet? Is there *nae* turnin' o' Thy decrees? Na, na; that wadna do at a'. But while there's life there's houp. But wha kens whether he be

alive or no.   Naebody can tell.   Glaidly wad I luik upon's
deid face gin I culd believe that his sowl wasna amang
the lost.   But eh! the torments o' that place! and the
reik that gangs up for ever an' ever, smorin' the stars!
And my Anerew down i' the hert o' it cryin'!   And me
no able to win till him!   O Lord! I canna say Thy will
be done.   But dinna lay it to my chairge; for *gin ye was
a mither yersel' ye widna pit him there!*   O Lord, I'm
very ill-fashioned.   I beg yer pardon.   I'm near oot o' my
min'.   Forgie me, O Lord, for I hardly ken what I'm
sayin'.   He was my ain babe, my ain Anerew, and ye gae
him to me yersel'!   And noo he's for the finger o' scorn to
point at: an ootcast an' a wanerer frae his ain country, and
daurna come within sicht o't for them 'at wad tak' the law
o'm.   An' it's a' drink—drink and ill-company."

The passage is intended to be highly dramatic, and yet,
looked at from a purely literary point of view, we venture
to suggest, and we think most critics will be inclined to
agree with us, that it entirely fails of anything like true
dramatic effect.   A woman in Mrs. Falconer's situation,
in a state of tragic despondency, frantic with grief, and
tortured with the most exquisite mental anguish, would
never be likely to express her feelings in the manner in
which she is made to express them here.   For one thing,
she would never introduce into her soliloquisings at such
a crisis, the contradiction which the author sees between
the intellectual and emotional elements of her life : even
supposing that contradiction to exist, she herself would
be the very last to perceive it.   Neither would an
agonised mother, in the tearful outpourings of her heart
at such a time, have been guilty of anything so unnatural
as to turn the closet of prayer into a theological lecture-
room, to make prayer itself a vehicle for theological discussion, to publish a manifesto in polemical divinity at

the mercy-seat itself, and in the very sanctuary of sorrow and supplication play off one set of dogmas against another in semi-humorous style, so as to win a point with the intellect and excite the risible faculties. The appearance of even the slightest shimmer of humour in a situation so tragic is, to say the least, utterly out of place, whilst the importation of the theologic element, and the attempt to make a little capital out of the whole affair for a particular school of religious thought, is a distinct violation of the canons of correct art, a defiance of all the rules of true dramatic rendering. The passage is defective from a literary and artistic point of view, in being too subjective, too autobiographic, too redolent of the author's own personal convictions. Had this picture of Mrs. Falconer in her heartbreak and anguish over a lost son been drawn by a master-hand like Shakespeare or Goethe, it would have impressed us very differently, for the dramatic appeal to the heart and imagination of the reader would have been true both to nature and art.

But what shall we say of the theology of this extraordinary effusion ? A purely hypothetical theology which has for its regulative principle the supposition, " If the Lord were a mither Himsel' ' "; or, as our author has it elsewhere, " If He were Martin Elginbrod," must yield some very strange and startling conclusions. A moral universe constructed on the basis of the same interesting hypothesis would certainly be very differently constituted from that which actually exists, and with which alone we have to do. If by some stretch of imagination we can conceive the Supreme Being who presides over the destinies of men transformed by some impossible metamorphosis into a

20

Martin Elginbrod, or an ideal specimen of human mother-
hood, there can be no doubt that, in either case, He would
not be too hard upon poor drunken, good-for-nothing
Andrew. A David will always have a soft spot in his
heart for an erring Absalom, and the sons of amiable old
Eli may always reckon on being treated with doting
fondness. If this idealisation of indulgent fatherhood is
to be set up as the final court of appeal in the settlement
of human destiny, very liberal allowances are sure to be
made for other scapegraces besides Andrew, the judicial
treatment of sin will disappear from God's dealings with
men, and the eternal distinction between right and wrong
will itself suffer abrogation. Mrs. Falconer ought to have
remembered that her child is not the only one in the
community, and the interests of other people's children
have to be taken into the reckoning as well as hers.
God has His obligations not only to Mrs. Falconer's
prodigal, but to "the whole family in heaven and in
earth" over which He exercises parental control, and
also to multitudes of other moral and intelligent beings
in other realms of life, for the right government of which
He is responsible, and of whose highest moral interests
He is the supreme custodian and defender. If the Lord
is to be conformed to Mrs. Falconer's ideal of parental
beneficence, we shall have to suppose some very profound
alterations in many other of His dispensations besides
that which has specially to do with His treatment of the
finally impenitent. In that case we should be sure to
have a universe which evil has never been permitted to
enter, much less to continue in it and persist. We shall
be untroubled with any problem as to the final disposal

of the wicked, because the existence of the wicked themselves shall have been prevented.   We shall be beset by
no difficulties in reference to the future punishment of
the sinful, for sin itself shall never have been suffered to
leave its black footprint on this fair planet.   We shall be
privileged to live in a world where there shall be neither
idiot nor cripple, where there shall be no mystery of
defect or deformity to perplex us, where we shall never
have to raise the torturing question, "Who did sin, this
man, or his parents, that he was born blind?"   We should
inhabit a world in whose green grass no grave is ever dug,
where no black-tasselled vehicle of death ever rumbles
through the streets, where no law of universal mortality
is in operation all along the ages filling up the cemeteries,
where the air is never rent with farewells of the dying.
No little coffins, wet with parents' tears, would be carried
from our homes, no pain would rack the nerves or pale
the cheeks, no invalid would languish in chronic disease,
no cancer would prey upon the trembling frame, no
rheumatism excruciate, nor consumption waste.   Our
existence would be untroubled by war, pestilence, or
famine, by shipwreck on sea or volcanic devastation on
land; sorrow and sighing, those twin companions which
are never far distant from us, would spread their black
wings and flee away, and all those tragic and calamitous
phenomena which have darkened the lot of man would be
brought to an abrupt termination.   "If the Lord were a
mither Himsel'," He would not endure that such evils
should be, much less continue to be.   He would put an
end to them to-morrow.   The universe, as it is at present
constituted and administered under a central government

of Infinite Holiness and Power, is not precisely the universe which a Martin Elginbrod would create, or which would commend itself to Mrs. Falconer's conception of the eternal fitness of things.   But we have to take facts as we find them.   Such a universe *does* exist.   Such a state of things actually *does* prevail, and that, too, under the government of One who is holy, and who has all power at His command.   Yet none of us on that account part company with the conviction that God is good, or refuse to acquiesce in the tranquillising assurance that " He doeth all things well."   The effort to construct a consistent theodicy in the name of a philosophy which humanises God, and sees in Him nothing but a bundle of parental instincts, may as well be abandoned at once as a perfectly hopeless one.   Sentiment, moreover, it is plain, must be discarded as a guide on this portentous subject.   Seeing that it completely misleads me in reference to what God does in this world, I cannot but profoundly distrust its light when asked to follow it in reference to what God is likely to do in the next world.

This famous soliloquy of Mrs. Falconer's is open to still further exception, on account of the gross misrepresentation of Calvinism which it contains.   It will be observed that it ascribes Andrew's moral failure and eternal ruin to the operation of a mysterious and inscrutable decree, rather than to his own abuse of individual freedom and persistence in wrong courses.

" O Lord," exclaims the mother, " could he no' be eleckit yet ?   Is there nae turnin' o' Thy decrees ? "

The implication, of course, is that the only barrier in the way of Andrew's salvation was the Divine election, and that if only Heaven's decree could be altered, the whole catastrophe might be averted. Andrew, in fact, is fated to be what he is, and God has a share in making him evil. But this is to give a false and distorted view of the whole situation, and the attempt to connect it with Calvinism could only be made by one who has never taken pains to inform himself as to what Calvinism really teaches on the subject. Anyone can see without much mental penetration that what was keeping this unhappy youth out of the Kingdom was, not election, but his own dram-drinking and ill company. A gate, as we all know, may be closed upon us in two ways. It may be closed upon us from within, when some unseen hand from the inside pushes it to in our face, or it may be closed from without, when with our own hand we draw it to upon ourselves. Heaven's gate was closed on Mrs. Falconer's prodigal in this latter way. He shut it against himself from without, and with his own free hand. He could not enter in because his own unbelief and wickedness hindered and impeded him—not because there was some grim decree of reprobation foreordaining him to exclusion. As a free agent he was the author of his own sin, and himself had the making of the bed he was to lie upon. If he came short of eternal life, it was clearly attributable to his own perseverance in evil, and not to some word of doom which had gone forth against him, or to any sword of fire guarding the gates of pearl. God gives to every man his chance. Even Esau came into the world dowered with a " birthright," and was free to do what he chose with it. If he chose to barter it away in profane exchange, was God to blame for that ? God gives us light ;

we have our choice to walk in darkness still.   He sounds
in our ears a Gospel of loving invitation ; we have the
fatal liberty of continuing deaf to its appeal.   There
are many soul tragedies enacted the blame of which is
conveniently laid at the door of election or foreordina-
tion, when manifestly the door at which it ought to be
laid is simply the sinner's own immoral choice and evil
habits.   In the very passage we are commenting on, Mrs.
Falconer herself frankly enough makes a little admission
which in very few words affords a perfectly satisfactory
explanation of her son's moral shipwreck, while at the
same time it completely exonerates the Divine Being
from all those reflections with which Dr. MacDonald had
just been making her so liberally to asperse Him.   " It's
a' owin'," she declares, " to drinkin' and ill-company."
Yes, that is just what it is owing to : no need to ransack
the archives of eternity, or peer between the pages of
any doomsday book, in search of some occult and recondite
explanation, when one so manifest and sufficing lies close
at hand.   And if this is what it is owing to, then the
change needed to extricate poor Andrew from his terrible
predicament was not a change in Heaven's decree, but a
change in the man's own disposition and mode of living.

In his little volume of *Unspoken Discourses*, Dr. Mac-
Donald has favoured us with a manly and open avowal
of the same peculiar views which he has ventilated in
his novels, only cast in more didactic form.   The book
presents rather a singular inconsistency.   It is extremely
theological, though written by one who denounces theology in all the moods and tenses.   It is a more or less
formal expression of truth, though the product of one

who is in revolt against all attempts at system-building. It is a dogmatic utterance from one who spends much of his breath in decrying dogma.   But, aside from this, we cannot say that in these discourses he has succeeded in improving his position.   We look in vain for any solid argumentative support for his tenets.   While marked by intense earnestness, rich suggestiveness of thought, and much beauty and originality of style, the sermons leave us far short of anything like demonstration.   Here, as elsewhere, whatever truth there is is presented through the medium of a mystic haze, which, albeit it is a golden haze, none the less interferes with distinctness of vision. Here also logical and intellectual difficulties are either quietly skipped, or else bridged over by the gossamer threads of a thin and glimmering sentiment.   For example, in one of his discourses, when the author finds himself face to face with some of the theoretic difficulties that beset the thorny problem of sin, he passes them all out of view by the sentimental use of the phrase " make little of sin "—surely a very dangerous phrase on the lips of anyone, and likely to prove most misleading. The author derives very little help from the Bible, but this does not in the slightest degree disturb his composure, for he denies that the Bible is the supreme standard and depository of truth.   This he does in a discourse entitled " The Higher Faith," by which he means a faith higher than that which is attained by those who take the written Word of God as their only spiritual text-book and directory.

" Sad indeed," says he, " would the whole matter be, if the Bible had told us everything God meant us to believe.

. . . The Bible nowhere lays claim to be regarded as *the* word, *the* way, *the* truth. The Bible leads us to Jesus, the inexhaustible, the ever-unfolding revelation of God. . . . If we were once filled with the mind of Christ, we should know that the Bible had done its work, was fulfilled, and had for us passed away. Till we have known Him, let us hold the Bible dear, as the moon of our darkness by which we travel towards the east."

This is but a specimen of the many passages in which Dr. MacDonald propounds his views on the subject of revelation. The meaning is obvious enough. We only rightly estimate the Bible when we regard it as an elementary primer or lesson-book intended to lead us to Christ. When it has introduced us to Him it has served its purpose, and may be left behind as something no longer needed. Under the immediate tuition of Christ Himself we shall speedily outgrow it, and shall have many things revealed to us which are not written in the Book. He considers the ordinary Christian believer who pins his faith to the Bible as having only what he calls the Lower Faith. He himself has soared to the higher, from which Pisgah eminence he looks down on his less ambitious brethren, far below in the valley of the commonplace, with what we cannot help thinking savours not a little of that self-sufficiency which is twin sister to Pharisaism, and which, we are sorry to say, is one of the most noticeable and most offensive disfigurements of Dr. MacDonald's writings. According to his way of thinking, the Bible is only of service to us in conducting us to Christ, and in awakening and developing within us a Christian consciousness, or what he here calls " the mind of Christ." Once this consciousness has been generated,

" the Bible has done its work, is fulfilled, and has for us passed away." The consciousness of the individual then becomes the source and the measure of all truth, the organ of increasing knowledge ; all statements and interpretations of truth must commend themselves to it, and the utterances of the Word of God itself are only to be accepted and acted upon in proportion as they receive the seal and sanction of the inner witness and tribunal which each man carries in his own bosom. If only our consciousness has been Christianised, we are each of us entitled to sit in judgment on the very contents of revelation itself, and to reject any portion of it which we consider unreasonable, or which does not happen to accord with our own feelings. The obvious, the inevitable result is that every man is his own oracle, and virtually becomes the maker of his own Bible. The great use and function of the Bible, therefore, is to train and tutor men and women up to the point where they shall be able to lay it on the shelf and do without it. Its province is the rather singular one of digging its own grave, and providing for its own superannuation and effacement. Men read it, and all the while it is generating in its reader's bosom something which is to supersede and dispossess it, something which is to sit in judgment on its contents, and give, or withhold, endorsement to its utterances, something which is to keep its message lying in quarantine outside the human intellect until it chooses to let it pass in, something which in time will enable a man to outgrow it and dispense with its services—somewhat as a lamester might lay aside his crutch when once he has regained the right use of his limbs.

We have heard of a superseded spelling-book, but it has been reserved for the religious liberalism of the present day to present us with a superseded Bible ! We have yet to learn, however, that any man, let him attain the mind of Christ ever so much, or let his consciousness be Christianised three times over, can ever afford to set up his own conceptions as equal, or superior to, the teachings of the Holy Spirit in the Word, can ever outgrow the Bible, and leave it behind him like a suit of cast-off clothes, can ever treat Divine revelation as an old almanac which is out of date, or reach a stage in his spiritual development when he can complacently talk about the Scriptures having " done their work," or, " for him passed away." It is true the Bible leads us to Jesus, but it is equally true that when we have been introduced to Him the very first thing He does is to send us straight back to the Bible.

Dr. MacDonald's theory is undoubtedly a very convenient one, for see how all his heresies can find shelter under the shadow of its wing. When, against some of his peculiar doctrines, we make our appeal to the Bible, Dr MacDonald is in no way disturbed if the Bible happens to go against him, for this is only the Bible received by all Christendom, and George MacDonald's Bible may tell another story, and testify in quite a different direction. We can easily understand how a theory so flexible in its adaptability to all possible exigencies, so elastic as to admit of being stretched into convenient accommodation with anything or everything, has come to be so ardently espoused by latitudinarian thinkers, and so eagerly seized upon by the current pro-

gressive theology.   It provides such an easy escape from
all doctrinal confinements and hampering restrictions of
creed, it emancipates the intellect so completely from the
authority of Scripture, and opens such a wide door for
the introduction of all sorts of theological vagaries, that
we do not wonder the religious liberalism of the day has
hastened to adopt it, and made it one of the main planks
in its platform.   All the same, we cannot conceive a
more dangerous procedure, or one fraught with more
mischievous results, than this substitution of an infinite
subjectivism, a diseased individualism, for a clear objective rule of faith and duty.   What more wayward or
capricious standard could possibly be proposed than the
consciousness of the individual ?   How liable to mistake
it is, how apt to be perplexed by the cross-lights of earth ;
how difficult to decipher and interpret its verdict, and
what an opening it affords for that casuistical playing
with conscience into which the devotees of mysticism
have been betrayed so often, " with the last result of
seeing no law, and reverencing none, save the perverted
shadow of the Divine on their own minds."   Even
suppose you confine the consciousness referred to to
learned and scholarly believers, and those best qualified
to return a verdict on such matters, you can never have
anything like unanimity of assent.   We have the
Christian Consciousness asserting one thing at Canterbury,
another at Rome, and still another at Geneva.   It says
one thing at Princeton, something very different at Harvard, and something exactly the contrary at Heidelberg
or Berlin.

The following pithy little paragraph from the pen of

an American divine furnishes some food for thought, and
may be pondered with advantage :—

" You find this *semper ubique ab omnibus* intuition most
confidently asserting certain things through the lips of
our very progressive brother, Lyman Abbott, in Brook-
lyn, and immediately the ·Congregational Council, of
which he is a member, holds a meeting, and gravely
informs the world that brother Abbott's Christian consciousness is not their Christian consciousness. Now,
then, it becomes a very practical and a very puzzling
question, *Whose Christian consciousness is authority* ? And
in this question lies the refutation of the whole absurdity."

In thus making way for the enthronement of the individual consciousness over any objective rule of faith,
George MacDonald, and those who belong to the same
school of thought, are placing themselves in the company
of men who, while fit enough society for Rationalists and
Free-thinkers, have scarcely yet come to be considered the
proper intellectual associates for men who still claim to
be regarded as Christian believers, and even as disciples
of orthodoxy.   Their theory, carried to its definite logical
results, must of necessity land them in the same boat
with Fichte, Schleiermacher, and Lessing.   For if the
consciousness of the individual is to be the final source
and test of all truth, what is this but the annihilation,
at one stroke, of inspiration and miracle ; and wherein
does it differ from the view which asserts that human
consciousness is the only revelation of God which has
been given us, and that man, if left to his own unassisted
resources, would of himself have ultimately arrived at all
the knowledge which is revealed in Scripture, only he
would perhaps have advanced toward it more slowly, and

by a more circuitous route ?   Disguise it as they may, the theory which discredits the authority of Scripture, and leaves every man free to shape his own theology according to his own tastes, feelings, and even prejudices, is Rationalism pure and simple.   It destroys all possibility of fixedness or finality in religious belief; it leaves us at the mercy of individual preference ; every man becomes a law to himself ; and we are within measurable distance of theological anarchy ; which may not improbably be followed, as it often has been in history, with a corresponding outbreak of moral licence.   Nowhere so much as in his views of revelation does George MacDonald reveal the leading defect of his own theology, a defect which a sagacious critic has described as " the constant setting of the individual intellect in opposition to the general need and instinct ; and the refusal to draw or to recognise any clear boundary-line between the sphere of reason and the sphere of feeling or sentiment."

The task we set ourselves is now completed.   In bringing it to a close, we desire to reaffirm our respect and admiration for Dr. MacDonald as a man, and a man of letters.   We will yield to no one in our appreciation of his genius, his wide culture, his poetic insight, his childlikeness of disposition, his subtle-thoughtedness, his beauty of workmanship, his loftiness of tone.   He is a splendid exemplification of his own ideal of what the literary man should be, and we all know how exalted that ideal is.   We have felt it a privilege to have spent a while in contact with such a fine spirit as his, in the hope of understanding it, and generously appreciating what is best in it.   He has been referred to by the genial Ian Maclaren, in a recent utterance, as " the most Christlike man of letters of the day." It is a splendid eulogium for one man to pronounce upon another, yet it may be cordially conceded to George MacDonald without the slightest violation of our sense of justice or propriety. This rare and proud distinction belongs to him as it does to none among his contemporaries, and just because it does, it is in our judgment all the more regrettable that he has introduced into his writings so much which can have no other tendency but to unsettle and perplex, and has lent the powerful patronage of his genius to theological laxity and error. While perfectly willing to extend no stinted measure of recognition to his many and varied excellences, we cannot condone the grave defects with which, in so many instances, they are fatally allied. Some of those defects it has been our painful duty to indicate and expose, but we trust it has been given us to do so without animus or acrimony. None of our animadversions have been made without vivid and constant remembrance of his own saying, which he puts into the mouth of David Elginbrod, and which we are glad to say he himself has not wholly forgotten in his pictures of the Scottish Puritans : " In the heart of every God-fearing man there is something far better than his opinions."

VI

THE THEOLOGY OF THE SCOTTISH SCHOOL OF FICTION

THE THEOLOGY OF THE SCOTTISH SCHOOL
OF FICTION

THE present representatives of Scottish fiction, the men of the " Kailyard " school, as they have been dubbed, may be regarded as belonging to the same historical succession as George MacDonald. The mantle of that Elijah, however, cannot be said to have fallen on any of them, though, for reasons we need not here discuss, they have come in for a larger meed of acknowledgment and a wider popularity than ever fell to the lot of their illustrious prototype and predecessor. Undoubtedly a portion of his spirit has rested upon them, and they have worthily perpetuated the best traditions which he was the first to establish. They have continued the weaving of the same golden web at which MacDonald wrought, and they have certainly brought no unskilled or apprenticed hand to that delicate and difficult task. The men of the Kailyard School have the disadvantage—perhaps we should rather say the responsibility—of perpetually standing under the shadow of one mightier than they. George MacDonald is bigger and better than any of his disciples, the owner of a vaster wealth than they, which he has disbursed with a more lavish hand. To have

21

appeared on the scene just after such a leader had
played his part in the literary theatre, was in itself an
initial cross which his followers had to take up at the
very outset, and which would certainly press heavy on
any shoulder.   Many men would get on better if they had
not the disadvantage of coming after certain other men
whom they are under the necessity of succeeding.   In
the immediate vicinity of the spot whereon they stand
there are footsteps, which, from their size, give unmistakable indication that a giant has been there.   Great as
those who follow may be, they must of necessity appear
smaller than they are, by reason of the greatness that
has gone before.   Life in general, but literary life in
particular, is made more difficult and responsible when it
has to be lived in the presence of great antecedents.   We
are not saying this in any spirit of depreciation or de-
traction.   If Barrie and Ian Maclaren have given us much
on the lines of George MacDonald, it is also true to say
that they have given us much on their own lines, for which
innumerable readers are profoundly thankful, and which
they will not willingly let die.   The true creative gift is
undeniably theirs; the Hall-mark of genius is legible on
much which they have written—the question of stature
may be left to the critics.   Their writings always leave
behind them a wholesome and pleasant impression; they
are separated by a wide gulf of difference from the
decadent and pessimistic style of fiction now so much in
vogue, and it would not be too large an affirmation to
say that no books have issued from the press for many a
long day which have made a more valuable addition to
our capital of pure and ennobling pleasure.

Drumtochty, as someone has said, is visible all over Christendom. The "Bonny Brier Bush" blooms by many a doorway, and sprigs of it are worn as button-holes on many a bosom. Far beyond the bounds of its native Highland parish the perfume of it has stolen into a multitude of homes and hearts. Through the frame-work of the famous window of Thrums Mr. Barrie has "flashed a series of innermost photographs." That window commands a wondrous outlook. Which of us has not sat in it, and found it a splendid observatory from which to take a wise and philosophic survey of men and things. The "Little Minister" is as real to us as the minister into whose face we look on Sundays in our own parish church. The men of Drumtochty are as real personages as the men we conversed with in the news-room this morning, or the men we had our last business transaction with yesterday. Such obvious compounds of physical particles as Jones and Robinson, with all their fleshly palpableness and visibility, are not more really existent to us than those weavers of Kirriemuir or rustics of Glen Quharity, whom we seem to know as well as our own kindred, though we never set gross corporeal eyes on them. No one capable of being fascinated by accurate portraiture of human life, by graphic delineation of character, by vivid resuscitation of the bygone forms of a vanishing yet visible past, by quaintness and drollery, and, above all, by the tender play of a pathos which goes as straight to the heart as it comes from it, can fail to be satisfied and entertained by the books of J. M. Barrie and Ian Maclaren.

Both these writers have managed to steer clear of at

least one mistake into which George MacDonald fell, to
the detriment of much that he has written—they have
not overweighted their books with *theologoumena* or
polemical divinity.   Wordsworth spoiled much of his
best work by botany and the Bible.   George MacDonald
spoiled a good deal of his by too constantly lecturing his
reader, and forcing him to swallow large doses of theology.
Barrie and Maclaren are free from this defect.   What
theology there is in their writings takes up very little
room, and exists only in solution ; their style is too swift
and allusive to admit of any wholesale introduction of it.
But there is a deeper reason than this for their avoidance
of the subject.   Their aim is largely to convince us of
the uselessness of all theology.   Theology is " killing
religion," and they would have us to kill theology by way
of saving religion alive.   They show an evident impatience
of doctrine, and of all attempts to define with any exact-
ness or precision of statement the contents of Christianity.
They are much of the same way of thinking as James
Anthony Froude, who declared that the word doctrine
was always suggestive to him of quack medicine.   They
would have us discard the dogmas of Christianity, under
the delusive notion that we can part with these and yet
still retain its spiritual effects and aroma.   What a
man believes is of comparatively little consequence,
his preferences in religion being very much on a par
with his preferences in politics, or his preferences in
art.   Nothing more is needed than the cherishing of
a deep religious sentiment, and the fruits that result
therefrom.

Illustrative of this attitude, we are presented with a

series of glowing portraitures of men of every name, and sometimes of no name, men of differing views and persuasions, who were nevertheless "good Christians"; and inasmuch as these good Christians are generated under every variety of system and belief, we are left to draw the inevitable inference that little or no importance attaches to what men believe. Creeds are but apples of discord over which graceless zealots quarrel; but as for us, let us leave contending theologians to their wrangles, and for ourselves be content to be Christians. The direction in which this reaction from intellectualism in religion towards a vague and sentimental piety may lead, it may be well for us to observe. Let there be an all-round application of this principle, and we shall find it much more devastating in its effects than we were perhaps prepared for. If sentiment and conduct are the supreme concern, then when an agnostic happens to equal an evangelical in exhibiting the traits of a good life, there is no need to be evangelical. If a rationalist develops a moral and spiritual excellence equal to that exhibited by a devout frequenter of sanctuaries and communion tables, there is no need to frequent these any more. If even a freethinker or an infidel should happen to have kept as clean a record and unblemished morals as many a good Christian we have known, there is no need to be a Christian. In the end the process cuts up Christianity itself by the very roots, or at least reduces it to a grand superfluity. It needs to be emphasised for the benefit of our authors and men of letters, that the Christian religion brings us a body of truths to be believed, as well as of precepts to be practised; that it addresses itself to the intelligence

of men, and claims the homage of their understanding as
well as the obedience of their lives.

If we must indicate with still further precision the
theological attitude and bent of such writers as Barrie
and Maclaren, we might venture to classify them as the
newer sentimentalists belonging to the same school as
Rousseau.   For, like Jean Jacques, they would try hard
to persuade us that Christianity is coincident with the
cultivation and practice of the natural virtues, and that
little more than this is needed for the world.   It is
certainly very little to keep house on in a spiritual sense,
but it is all the sentimentalists, both of old school and
new, will allow us.   Rousseau believed that religion was
necessary, and ought to be retained, if only to provide an
outlet for the expression of sentiments native to the
human heart, which could not otherwise find appropriate
vent ; it was needed, too, to give grandeur and dignity to
human life.   " Rousseau rejoiced at the close of his life,"
says a writer in the *British Weekly*, " that he had remained
faithful to the prejudices of his childhood, and that he
had continued a Christian *up to the point of membership
in the universal Church.*   The words in italics," the writer
goes on to say, " precisely describe the type of religion
that is glorified in Ian Maclaren's books."

Mr. Barrie is more reticent on matters theological
than his compeer, but he, too, is resolute in declining a
dogmatic religion.   When he deprecates, as he often
does, everything that goes beyond the essence, he is in
evident sympathy with Maclaren in trying to whittle down
our rich Christian inheritance to the wretched minimum
of the bare, bald Rousseauism we have indicated.   Mr.

John Morley is an acknowledged authority on Rousseauism, and one remark of his we remember which seems to us to apply with much aptitude to its modern representatives in the Scottish school of fiction. " The special qualities of Christian doctrine," says he, " seem to have grown pale in a bright glow of sentimentalism." That is exactly what has happened in the pages of Barrie and Maclaren. The distinctive doctrines of the Christian system are not indeed directly assailed or abjured, but they have grown paler than we should like to see them in the writings of men who are reputed evangelical ; they have faded into indistinctness, not because the darkness of disbelief has stolen over and eclipsed them, but rather because they have been swallowed up in a bright glow of vague liberalistic sentiment. Another characteristic feature of Rousseauism, according to Mr. Morley, was its refusal to apply to religious beliefs positive methods and conceptions. Here again the spirit of the Savoyard vicar seems to have had its modern revival in the authors we are at present concerned with. They, too, are impatient with any attempt to define religious truth, or to substitute for vague sentiment categorical proposi-tions. Truth conveyed through that medium is dis-tasteful to them, as it was to Mr. Froude, and they would probably agree with him in saying that " half the life was struck out of it " in the process of being defined.

Maclaren's theological leanings still further betray themselves by his evident sympathy with Moderatism. With one or two exceptions, his characters are all Moderates—Drumsheugh, Maclure, Soutar, Dr. Davidson,

and all the rest.   They were men whose religion consisted
very largely of the principles of morality, uninspired by
the doctrines of grace, unbottomed on any evangelical
groundwork.   With them a code of morals did duty for
religion.   Very straight they were, but not at all
spiritualised, the chief trait in their character being a
kind of soldierly loyalty to duty.   If a man had the
natural virtues, he had about virtue enough.   Of course,
in his delineation of Moderatism the author is careful to
walk on the sunny side of the street.   But we must not
allow the charm and necromancy of Dr. Watson, as a
story-teller, to beguile us into any mistake as to the real
character of the movement known as Scottish Moderatism.

There was another and a very shady side to that same
Moderatism which is glorified in the pages of the *Bonnie
Brier Bush* and *Days of Auld Lang Syne*.   There was a
Moderatism that spread over Scotland like a mud-deluge,
overlaying everything that was free, lofty, or hallowed.
There was a Moderatism that retained so little of the
Christian spirit as to prohibit missions to the heathen,
to look with disfavour on Sabbath schools, and throw
the shield ecclesiastical over heresy and immorality.
There was a Moderatism to whose disciples Dean Stanley
was specially attracted, men after his own heart, because,
as he himself has said, "they were thorough latitudin-
arians."   There was a Moderatism which, while with
good-natured tolerance it could fraternise with Hume
and Gibbon, could show no clemency to the Seceders.
There was a Moderatism which put Arians and Rationalists
into the pulpit of many a parish, men in whose discourses denial of the supernatural was a note not seldom

struck. There was a Moderatism which preached the gospel of do, do, which ended, as it always does end, in nothing being done. There was a Moderatism which substituted for evangelical truth the lifeless inculcation of a morality but slightly in advance of that which might have come from the lips of an old pagan philosopher. Even Burns, whose own sympathies were anti-evangelical, could see with his poet's eye the cold ineffectiveness of Moderate preaching. In the following lines he evidently had before him some imitator of Blair, with his studied elegance of diction, but utter absence of distinctive Christian truth :—

> " What signifies his barren shine
>   Of moral powers and reason ?
> His English style, and gesture fine,
>   Are a' clean out of season.
> Like Socrates or Antonine,
>   Or some old pagan heathen,
> The moral man he does define,
>   But ne'er a word of faith in."

It is not a little remarkable that an evangelical minister, when he takes to writing fiction, should linger with such sympathetic understanding and interest over a movement which has so little to recommend it, and should have found in the Moderates materials for his literary ideals. Is it possible that the attraction was in his case, as in Dean Stanley's, their " thorough latitudinarianism " ?

It does not necessarily follow, however, that Maclaren is unjust to Evangelicalism. One of the finest characters he has given us is Burnbrae, the Free Church elder, who is prepared to give up possession of his farm rather than

prove disloyal to his Disruption creed.   Still there are
types of Evangelicism which he does appear to contemplate with evident dislike—that which is more specially
identified with evangelistic meetings, holiness conferences,
and revivals, and that which goes under the name of
Plymouthism.   We hold no brief for either of these, and
we are very far from denying that in connection with
these modern revivalistic movements there have been
occasional developments which offer a tempting mark for
caricature, and which may well provoke the playful
sallies of the satirist.   The extreme anxiety of certain
coteries of Christian people to secure titled persons to
preside at conferences on religion, and draft distinguished
officials of the State into Christian and philanthropic
enterprises for show uses, is a most objectionable form
of religious snobbery, against which it is not surprising
that writers like Maclaren should enter some protest.
It is perhaps this sort of thing that is aimed at in the
famous invitation-card which the minister of St. Bede's
receives from an evangelistic parishioner of his.

MR. AND MRS. THOMPSON

AT HOME,

Tuesday, May 2nd,

To meet Lord Dunderhead, who will give a
Bible Reading.

8 to 10.30.   Evening Dress.

At the same time we cannot help feeling that the
author has paid more attention to these foibles than they

deserve, and has been a little too unsparing in the use
of ridicule. There is a good deal of this kind of thing,
for instance, which, in our humble judgment, would have
been better omitted :

"I hope we may have a profitable gathering. Captain
Footyl, the hussar evangelist, will be present—a truly
devoted and delightful young man."

Or again—

"Lord Dunderhead was passing through Glasgow, and
gave the address. It was on 'The Badgers' Skins' of the
Tabernacle, and was very helpful. And afterward we
had a delightful little 'sing.'"

On all which we make no commentary, except to say
that if the weapons of travesty and ridicule are to be
carried into the regions of Evangelism, it might be well,
on the whole, to leave the business to worldlings and
outsiders, who, as a rule, are none too slow to poke fun
at things sacred. It is a pity that such "dead flies"
should ever have been permitted to enter into such precious ointment as the writings of Ian Maclaren. Therefore we would venture to reiterate the suggestion of Dr.
Theodore Cuyler as not altogether unnecessary, that he
should "refrain from unseemly gibes at evangelistic
services, and for dear old drink-cursed Scotland's sake
should not indulge in Dickenish digs at total abstinence
societies."

Then there is the unfortunate passage in which the
author has more than hinted his sympathy with the
modern attempt to deal with the problem of human
destiny in the light of the Larger Hope. The chapter
in the days of *Auld Lang Syne* which describes Archee-

332 THE THEOLOGY OF MODERN LITERATURE

bald M'Kittrick, the Drumtochty postman, is entitled
" Past Redemption," probably with the intention of
creating a smile at those who tried to reclaim him from
his habits of intemperance, and to satirise the theology
of those who look upon death as a solemn boundary-line
in the history of a soul, ending probation, and putting
a final closure on all further chances of redemption. The
story of Posty is so familiar that we need scarcely re-
capitulate it here. Needless to say, it is told, as all his
stories are, with inimitable humour, with much graphic
felicity and distinctness as of actual observation.

Posty was a universal favourite in the whole country-
side ; he was alert, witty, faithful in the performance
of his official duties, and in verbal encounters with
those who sought to convert him to the principles of
total abstinence never came off second best. He had
proved himself a perfect master of all the weapons of
sarcasm and repartee, but he angrily refused the tracts
that well-meaning friends put into his hands, and all his
life long his easily besetting sin was an inveterate fondness for Scotch whisky. The circumstances of his death
were such as to invest that touching event with a peculiar halo of heroism and unselfishness. With a noble
disregard of his own life, he had plunged into a swollen
torrent to rescue a little girl from drowning, had succeeded
in getting her safely out of the water, and had just lifted
her, dripping and gasping, into her mother's arms, when
he himself was swept back into the gurgling flood, and
sank to rise no more. The heroism of this last earthly
act of his is skilfully depicted by the author, and seems
to be offered as an atonement for the sins and failings of

the past, as well as a ground of hope that it would be all
well with Posty in the world beyond.   Carmichael, the
Free Kirk minister, and some of the village theologues,
hold a wayside conference on the subject of Posty's
destiny, and unanimously come to the conclusion that it
must be well with Posty in all worlds.   If, argues Carmichael, a man who hurts any of God's bairns is to have
a millstone tied about his neck and to be cast into the
depths of the sea, no ill can surely come to a man who
goes into the depths and brings up one of those bairns at
the cost of his own life.   Whereupon the parish divines all
unite in pronouncing Carmichael a theologian of the first
order.   Other theologians, however, have not been able to
concur in Carmichael's adjudication upon Posty's destiny,
and this " Past Redemption " chapter has come in for a
very large share of attention at their hands,—so much so,
that the author has felt it necessary, in his latest book,
to restate the case for Posty, and fortify his position with
some additional considerations.

In one of the sketches in *Afterwards*, the author represents himself as being sharply taken to task by a cock-
sure and narrow-minded evangelist, Mr. Elijah Higginbotham, for having written a story " so misleading and so
injurious to precious souls " as that of the Drumtochty
postman.   The author, however, proceeds to reargue the
whole question with his assailant in quite a friendly spirit,
and succeeds in completely removing Elijah's prejudices,
and in sending him away with the full persuasion and
conviction that " it is all right with Posty," that " Posty
will have another chance."   Of course, as the author had
the management of the whole controversy in his own

hands, could give it what turn he pleased, and conduct
it to whatever issue might suit him, he scores an easy
victory, as we might expect, over his friend Elijah, and
ultimately parted company with him as deeply convinced
that "all was right with Elijah Higginbotham" as that
gentleman was convinced that "all was right with Posty."

We have read carefully the chapter in *Afterwards*
which records this memorable interview, and we have
risen from its perusal with the impression that the arguments which satisfied Mr. Higginbotham will not satisfy
many of Ian Maclaren's readers.   It seems to us the
author has not improved his position by anything he has
here advanced.   It is pleaded, for instance, that "Posty had
the natural virtues."   But what about the spiritual virtues
and the Christian virtues ?   Posty cannot be credited with
the possession of these, and it does not even appear that
he had the full complement of the virtues ranked as
natural, for he was conspicuously lacking in sobriety.
Would Ian Maclaren have us to accept mere natural
goodness as a substitute for Christianity, or would he
have us to infer that because decency and neighbourli-
ness and kindly bearing to our fellow-men pass well
enough in this world, they will therefore pass in the
next ?   If a decent arrangement of the natural life is
all that is needed to make a man a Christian in this
world and an angel in the next, then the Gospel of Christ
has no meaning for us, the Incarnation at Bethlehem and
the death on the Cross might have been dispensed with,
the plain declaration, " He that believeth on Him is not
condemned, but he that believeth not is condemned
already," may be set aside, and what has always been

considered the very essence of all religion that is worth having, fellowship of the soul with God, may be safely neglected as of no consequence. These things had no place in the life and character of the Drumtochty post-man ; where they should have been there was a gap and a void, and the omission was too serious to be atoned for by a little stock of natural virtue and humanity.

Natural virtues have their place and their value ; we do not refuse them our homage and admiration ; we feel a love to them ; but, as Dr. Chalmers says, "we will make no lie about them, and we can make no more of them than Scripture and observation enables us to do." We surely make a lie about these natural virtues, and make more of them than Scripture or observation war-rants, when we regard them as constituting in themselves religion enough for a man to live with and to die with, and as affording a sufficient outfit and equipment for him to front eternity with. The natural virtues ! The young man in the Gospel had a very much larger stock of them than the post-office hero of Drumtochty, and had them in first-rate quality. Yet our Lord, who knows exactly where each man stands, and can assort men, and range them in their places, declares that all his natural good-ness had done for him was to bring him *near* to the king-dom ; but to bring him decisively *within* the kingdom, to carry him across the border into the blissful interior of Immanuel's land, something more and something other was yet needed. To be honest, and truthful, and good-tempered, and well-disposed, may take us far in the direction of the kingdom, but not far enough ; and if these good qualities are not supplemented by something that takes us further, that "not far" may be the loss of all! Cornelius had the natural virtues in abundance, a devout man, one that feared God, and was in good report with his neighbours. Yet the insufficiency of all this is evidenced by the fact that he is directed by the angel to send for Peter "to hear words from him." What words, the advocate of natural religion might ask, did such a man need to hear? Was he not doing his duty? Was not his life blameless? Did he not say his prayers, and stand well with his neighbours, and what more would you have? One thing, however, Cornelius still lacked, which it was so important for him to have that an angel comes all the way from heaven to direct him to send for a preacher who might acquaint him with the secret of its acquisition. In due course that preacher came, and the words Cornelius needed to hear from his lips were to the effect that " God had anointed Jesus of Nazareth with the Holy Ghost and with power, that He was slain and hanged on a tree, and that to Him gave all the prophets witness that through His name, whosoever believeth on Him may have the *remission of sins.*" No, if natural goodness were a sufficient moral equipment for any soul, there was no need in the case of Cornelius to supplement it with the distinctively Christian revelation of which Peter was the bearer.

Another contention in Posty's favour which had great weight with Mr. Elijah Higginbotham was this: " Did he not keep the commandment of love, which is the chief commandment, and can anyone keep that commandment without grace?" Now, to say the least, Ian Maclaren's conception of keeping the commandment of love stands in

THE SCOTTISH SCHOOL OF FICTION

need of a little rectification. The obligations of the law of love are not exhausted, as this passage seems to imply, by a man's loving his neighbour. To love our fellow-creatures is only to keep half the commandment, and the lowest half too. The other half, and the half to begin with, is to love the Lord our God. It is the first and chief commandment, because it enjoins us to give the homage of our heart and life to the first and chief of Beings. Now it is painfully evident that Posty never complied with that primary requirement at all. So far from loving God, he lived in habitual disregard of Him. He was a godless man, not in the sense that he was openly vicious, but in the sense that God was not in his thoughts, that his Maker was unnoticed and forgotten, that he lived his life independently of that Being who first gave him his life, and who would one day resume His gift. Granted that Posty dealt honourably and unselfishly by his fellows, and even died to save one of them from a watery grave, still his morality came far short of the mark, in that it did not lead him to deal honourably and justly by the good God. While Posty's heart was the seat of affection, affection for God was habitually absent from it. "The test of a vital morality," it has been said, "is its uniform operation in *all* the relationships of life, and in *every* direction." The morality of the Drumtochty post-man never touched this first and greatest relationship of all: it restricted itself to the manward side of duty; it never took a *Godward* direction. No matter how scrupulously one may have met the claims of man, if he has lived for a lifetime in practical disregard of the claims of God, on what principle can we cherish the confidence

22

that such a one, when he comes to go hence, shall go to be with God and enjoy Him ?

But it is urged, " Posty loved, and God is love ; and if there be such a thing as justice, it must be all well with Posty on the other side." The last act of the village postman's life was certainly a piece of splendid heroism. We would not envy the man who could withhold his admiration from it, or refuse his homage to an exhibition so touching of self-sacrificing benevolence. But while the act has certainly thrown around his character the glory of a romantic chivalry, we fail to discover in the act itself any deep religious significance. It was inspired by nothing higher than the promptings of ordinary humanity. True, these promptings were implanted in the postman's heart by a God of love ; but, as we have already seen, while the postman's heart was occupied with the high and generous emotions a good God put into it, it was never occupied with any sense of that God Himself, the first of Beings, having the first of claims on the homage and service of His creatures. Benevolence of a rare order he certainly exhibited ; but then we must remember that Benevolence, to use the words of Dr. Chalmers, " may make some brilliant exhibitions of herself *without the instigation of the religious principle.*" Posty was a man, and played the hero that day, but there was no deep-seated piety at the bottom of what he did. It was fine, it was unselfish, it was noble ; we freely accord it our unstinted admiration, but there was no religion in it that we can see, any more than there is religion in the mother bird's fluttering anxiety to protect her young. Posty might have done the very same thing if he had not believed in a God at

all, and immortality had been expunged from his prospects.   As a matter of fact, men who are known to be
thoroughly bad men have been known to do an occasionally noble deed, which elicits the testimony of our
applause.   We have known infidels to exhibit some fine
moral accomplishments.   We have heard of thieves and
criminals who did very kindly things to their friends,
and made touching and beautiful sacrifices for wife and
children.

But, even admitting that Posty's heroic conduct was a
real fulfilment of the law of love, and an exemplification
of deep religious principle, the question has still to be
asked: Are we to regard this one isolated action as
atoning for the sins and neglects of a lifetime ?   If one
who has been for years addicted to thieving happens to
have been a total abstainer, as some thieves are, is his
total abstinence to be set over against his thievery by way
of counterbalance and atonement ?   If a criminal has
made sacrifices for wife and child, is his criminal career
to be condoned because of this one solitary and exceptional virtue of his ?   We had always thought that if a
man's sinful past was to be atoned for at all, it could only
be by his having recourse to the atonement wrought on
Calvary, and not by any atonement derivable from some
redeeming quality he may happen to possess, or some
redeeming act he may happen to have performed.   Not
by beautiful traits of character, nor fine moral accomplishments, nor brilliant deeds of heroism, are any of
us saved, but by the Divine mercy, by the washing
of regeneration, and the renewing of the Holy Ghost.
" There is but one work that saves," writes Elizabeth

Barrett Browning in a letter of hers recently published, "and that is Christ's work upon the Cross." Deeds of heroism like Posty's may well deserve the chorus of human applause which they invariably call forth, or the recognition of a Humane Society, but anything like saving efficacy we cannot ascribe to them, for between the noblest action that can distinguish our lives and the rewards of eternity, there must always be a vast and infinite disproportion. If, as Ian Maclaren would have us, we are to invent a new moral category for men like the Drumtochty postman, and slip them through into paradise by some postern gate, let us clearly understand that we are opening up, on our own responsibility, a new route to the Heavenly Land, and mapping out a new way of salvation, of which the Bible knows nothing.

But, after all, does not the manner in which Posty played the hero that day, when he was battered to death in the mountain torrent, entitle him at least to that second chance beyond the grave which Ian Maclaren claims for him so peremptorily in the sacred name of Justice itself? It might be well, however, first to inquire if he had not had chances enough already? This prior question must be disposed of, if we would establish the necessity for an extension of opportunity in another state of being. It has become popular nowadays to raise the cry in connection with a class of men, of whom Posty may be taken as the type, that they have had too meagre a probation. Advocates of Universalism and representatives of the Larger Hope claim for them on this ground a new lease of opportunity on the other side of death. But God has His own answer ready — an answer drawn from history and daily life : someone even less favourably situated than those whose case is made the subject of complaint, has accepted the probation and proved it enough. Lazarus had but " Moses and the prophets," but made such good use of that fragment of revelation that he found it sufficient for his needs, and rose by means of it on angel's wings into Abraham's bosom. For the Drumtochty postman Jesus was added to " Moses and the prophets," and he lived in a noonday blaze of Christian light and privilege. Had he a less meagre probation than the penitent idolater of Nineveh, who, with nothing to catch at but a " who can tell ? " forsook his idols and turned to the living God ? Had he a less meagre probation than the poor Canaanite from the coasts of Tyre and Sidon, who, in a life singularly barren of religious opportunity, yet managed to gather up as many crumbs of mercy from under the table of a more favoured people as stayed the hunger of her soul, and saved her ? Have not these very men for whom a new lease of opportunity is claimed in a future state—have they not more opportunity already than they avail themselves of ? Have they not more light than they follow ? What grounds are there, then, for impugning the justice of God in the dispensation He has appointed for the testing of man's moral quality and bent here on earth, or throwing out reckless innuendoes about the unfairness of His dealings with those who are the subjects of His own moral empire ?

The doctrine that opportunity after death will be afforded to such as have passed hence unshriven and unsanctified, is coming to-day from the lips of literary

men, from the lips of learned professors and ecclesiastical
dignitaries, but the decisive fact remains, that it never
came from the lips of Him who is Lord and Judge both
of the living and the dead. And who had greater insight
into human destiny than He, or who saw further into the
secrets of the life to come? And who ever loved the
souls of men as He? Surely He loves us so well, and
means us so well, that if in the nature of things it were
not so, He would have told us. To preach the Gospel of
Second Chances is to encourage men to trifle with the
chances they have now. It is to comfort them in their
sinful courses with the soothing but delusive idea that
they may live very much as they please and yet come
out right in the end. It is to lead men to gamble with
their immortal destiny by staking it on a guess, a per-
adventure, a plausible conjecture. It is to meet men in
the most solemn passage of their existence, when they are
crossing the dark waters that separate this world from
the next, and give them an hypothesis for a fact amid
" the swellings of Jordan." Will Ian Maclaren, or any
other representative of the Larger Hope, risk his own
salvation on the prospect of repentance after death which
he holds out to Posty? Will he recommend the heart
next his own and dearest to him to run that risk?
Will he put that Gospel under the head of any dying
parishioner of his at whose bedside he may be called
upon to minister? And if he will not do so himself,
nor advise those nearest him to do it, why will he
suggest or recommend it as a safe course to others?
Joseph Cook has a story so pertinent to this whole
subject that we may be permitted to retail it. Governor

Corwin of Ohio once met a negro who had run away from Kentucky, and was living in rags in a free State. "You made a mistake in running away," said the Governor to the black man. "You had friends and clothes and money enough south of the Ohio, as I happen to know, for I was acquainted with your master. Are you not now in need of all these things?" "Yes," said the negro. "Then," said the Governor, "you made a mistake in running away." "Governor Corwin," said the negro, "the situation in Kentucky is open with all its advantages, and if you choose to go and occupy it, you can do so." And so we turn to the apostles of the Larger Hope, and say of their Gospel of Repentance after Death, "The situation is open, with all its advantages, will you go and occupy it?" Not if you are in your senses. Not if there still is left to you some lingering vestige of wisdom and sanity. And if you will not occupy the situation yourselves, why will you encourage others to do it?

We would like that our teaching on a subject so momentous as that of future destiny should be Biblical in its tone; where issues so stupendous are involved we would desiderate a Gospel which would deal only in propositions that would not be hazardous to the souls of men; but we fail to see how we are to have either the one or the other, if we are to have Ian Maclaren's eschatology.

VII

THE THEOLOGY OF MRS. HUMPHRY WARD

"Robert Elsmere"

THE THEOLOGY OF MRS. HUMPHRY WARD

"Robert Elsmere"

In the fourth chapter of her book, Mrs. Ward dwells on the importance, in studying the development of a soul, of giving careful consideration to its antecedents. In the light of this observation it may be interesting to recall her own antecedents. From a very early period in her life Mrs. Ward was familiarised with religious doubt and difficulty. She spent her girlhood in an atmosphere of intellectual unrest. Her father was at Oxford amid the excitements of the Tractarian Movement, which left a deep mark upon him, that after years never wholly obliterated. While he was in Tasmania, whither he had emigrated to fill a Government appointment, he became a convert to Romanism. Returning after some years to England, he swung back to Protestantism again; but, after an interval, he once more veered round to Rome, and ended his days within the enclosures of the papal fold, finding a repose for his faith in its doctrinal infallible authority. We can readily understand what an object - lesson on the

subject of religious doubt and struggle this example
would furnish to the daughter, who had constant opportunity of observing it without so much as going outside
the precincts of her own home, and how inevitable it
was that she should have her thoughts turned from her
youth up toward the solution of such intellectual and
moral problems as those with which she seeks to grapple
in her books of controversial fiction.

The appearance of *Robert Elsmere* was a literary event
of no ordinary interest and suggestiveness.   It created
something like a sensation in the religious world.   It
made a deep impression on the thinking portion of
the community especially.   It was discussed in all the
leading quarterlies and reviews in lengthy and elaborate
articles.   The occupants of the pulpit busied themselves
in framing replies to it.   Mr. Gladstone gave an enormous impetus to its circulation by making it the subject
of a powerful critique, in the course of which he referred
to it as a book destined to make " a very visible impression, not, however, on mere novel readers, but among
those who share in any degree the deepest thought of the
age."   In six months the book ran through five editions
in its three-volume form.   A success so notable as this
is in itself an incontestable proof that the book, whatever
its merits might be, had evidently struck some responsive
note in the public feeling, and given articulate and vivid
expression to thoughts in which multitudes had perhaps
themselves participated in a dim, confused sort of way,
but which they had never been able to voice, much less
to serve up in literary form as an intellectual repast for
the benefit of their fellows.   The authoress showed great

wisdom in selecting the novel as the medium of what she had got to say. Thrown into that form, the work would be sure to reach best those with whom she wanted to put herself in communication. The educated class of to-day insist on having their theology served up to them richly sauced with every species of literary spice and condiment. If you want to give them a dose of solid instruction on any subject which requires a little exercise of the thinking faculty, you must sugar-coat your pill, or encase it in some jam-mixture, else it will not be swallowed.

Any theme is admissible in the modern novel, from vivisection to theosophy, why, therefore, should not Mrs. Ward discuss, in the form of a fascinating story, with all the usual stock-in-trade accessories of love, romance, and human interest, the questions between the old-fashioned faith and the new Christianity—questions sufficiently weighty and complicated to be dealt with in some ponderous treatise, or be made the subject for a course of Bampton or Hibbert Lectures? With the ordinary attractions of a love story, *Robert Elsmere* combines the additional interest of a religious tragedy and a theological debate. Mrs. Ward, it must be confessed, has brought to the accomplishment of the difficult task she set herself, a rare combination of gifts which are of a very high order—great fulness of knowledge, a fine critical talent, and a remarkable power of photographing the inner states of the soul, and depicting its varying moods and vicissitudes in its transition from one stage of development to another.

Before coming into close quarters with the main

positions of the book, it may perhaps be advisable to advert for a moment or two to some of its most transparent defects. One of the most noticeable of these is its manifest unfairness. *Robert Elsmere* is a most one-sided production. All arguments on the other side of the controversy are studiously omitted. No voice is permitted to utter a syllable in vindication or defence of the faith which Elsmere is about to surrender. The Squire and the two sceptical tutors at Oxford have it all their own way. The stream of their destructive criticism flows on unchecked, on the quiet assumption that nothing by way of rejoinder is possible. Under the sinister tutelage of these mentors, Elsmere arrives at the decision to abandon New Testament Christianity, without ever taking counsel of any competent representative of the faith he was about to part company with. The only representative of that faith with whom he is ever once confronted is a fanatic ritualistic priest, the first article in whose creed appears to have been that the thinking faculties were not wanted in religion. True, Elsmere does go on a pilgrimage to Oxford, before making his final surrender, for the purpose of consulting with his former tutor, Mr. Grey. He must have gone, however, with the knowledge that what he would receive from him would be, not advice, but instigation and encouragement. In fact, in a note at the end of the work, Grey is identified with the late Professor Green, whom Elsmere must have known to have long since abandoned belief in all supernatural religion. Canon Westcott is the only authority in Christian thought and scholarship referred to throughout the whole book, and he is contemptuously dismissed with a sneering allusion for "isolating Christianity from all the other religious phenomena of the world."

The fact is, the controversial novel is a weapon which it is exceedingly difficult to use fairly. In such a composition one can prove anything he pleases. What is to hinder, when the author has the manufacture both of the facts and the characters in his own hand? He can always so predispose and manipulate the forces as to throw the balance of power to the favoured side. That side can always be credited with all that is best in argument, and all that is most impressive in personality. The author can always so prepare the way as to make the conclusion he wants to reach inevitable. When the critical moment arrives, he has only to advance with conquering stride, and snatch a victory which his premisses have already necessitated and insured for him. We can readily understand, therefore, how it is that unfairness has come to be the uniform vice of controversial fiction. It is a vice in which the authoress of *Robert Elsmere* is very deeply implicated. In her pages it reaches a pitch which is unprecedented.

Another defect which vitiates much of Mrs. Ward's work is the tone of supercilious contempt she assumes towards the orthodox Christian believer. Christianity is adverted to as "a religion which can no longer be believed"; the sacred writings which record the words and deeds of Jesus are more than once referred to as "fairy tales"; St. Paul is described as "a fiery but fallible man of genius"; and, in one of the Squire's conversations, we are told that a man who regards

Christian legend—that is, the miraculous narratives of the New Testament—as part of history proper, ought to be regarded as "losing caste, and falling *ipso facto* out of court with men of education." Now, in all conscience, it is too late in the day for Mrs. Ward, or any other writer, to indulge in tall talk like this, which is nothing short of insolence, considering that the leading minds in European scholarship have endorsed and accepted Christianity, and that the foremost scientists, statesmen, and men of letters have given their intellectual homage and assent to the old faith.   And what special title has Robert Elsmere, or the authoress whose literary creation he is, thus to snub the Christian believer and pour upon him the vials of their contempt, as if he were invariably a flat-skulled type of mortal, or the helpless victim of gullibility ? Elsmere's qualifications for conducting a controversy with the Christian apologists, and reaching conclusions adverse to Christianity, are, to say the least, exceedingly slender and inadequate.   Briefly summed up, they consist of something like this — a few months' study of early French history ; a few months' intercourse with a Ger-manised scholar, whom he himself confesses to have been cynical and irreligious at heart ; a few hurried consulta-tions with Mr. Grey, a philosophic deist, and Mr. Langham, a hopeless sceptic—such were the education and acquirements in virtue of which Elsmere deems himself armed *cap-à-pie*, and fully equipped to do battle with the whole army of Christian thinkers, and wage successful war against a Christian scholarship which has contended with scholarship, not once or twice, but century after century, and come out crowned ; considers himself in a position to wave aside Canon Westcott, and brush away St. Paul's evidence as that of a "fallible man of genius" who was "logically weak," and—most shocking of all—to drag down the Saviour Himself to "the guise of common manhood, laden like His fellows with the pathetic weight of human weakness and human ignorance"—one who, like Elsmere himself, could say, "I too have had my dreams and my delusions." Commenting on this last outrage on Christian sentiment, a writer in the *Quarterly* very properly observes—

"Mrs. Ward might at least have spared her readers and her hero this insult to the Christian's Lord God. But the possibility of such a scene is the measure of Elsmere's appreciation, and Mrs. Ward's own appreciation, for the real considerations on which this controversy turns."

When the same writer declares of Elsmere that he was the victim, not of truth, as Mrs. Ward would represent, but of his own superlative conceit, most readers of the book will acquiesce in the justness of the estimate.

A third defect which vitiates the book, and renders large districts of its reasoning abortive, is the belated character of the scholarship which the writer has pressed into her service. In her assault upon the defences of Christianity, the critical apparatus of the Tübingen School is one of the weapons which is chiefly relied on. The Tübingen criticism is magniloquently described as "that great operation worked by the best intellect of Europe during the last half century—broadly speaking —on the facts and documents of primitive Christianity." Yet anyone at all instructed in the course of critical

23

debate during the last thirty years, knows that the
Tübingen theory is no longer a force to be reckoned
with.   Germany itself has long disowned it; even
Rationalists have grown ashamed of it.   Renan laughs at
Baur, as Baur laughed at Strauss, and Strauss at Paulus.
Professor Christlieb testifies that "at Tübingen itself
there is no longer any Tübingen School."   Professor
Thayer in his Boston Lecture affirms that "as a sect in
Biblical Criticism the Tübingen School has perished." [1]
Renan is a witness after Mrs. Ward's own heart, as
hostile to the miraculous as even she could desiderate,
and Renan admits the extravagance of the Tübingen
theory, and surrenders the main points of criticism on
which its principal contention was based.   Yet it is
these exploded fallacies of a criticism long since outlived
and done with that Mrs. Ward refurbishes, and trots
out as if they were brand-new discoveries in the light of
which Christianity could no longer hold its own.   It is
precisely this which constitutes the chief danger of the
book to the uninitiated reader, who is likely to be taken
captive by the specious biblical criticism of Mrs. Ward,
only because he is not conversant with the facts and
considerations by which enlightened Christian scholarship
has discredited that criticism, and driven it ignominiously
from the field.   When Germany itself gets tired of her
critical theories she ships them to England, and they are
taken in with thanks at Oxford.   It is not so much
German criticism that we suffer from as what John
Ruskin calls "the English drainage" of it.

We are now prepared to consider the main proposals

[1] *Boston Lectures*, p. 371.

of this piece of controversial fiction. The chief contention of the book is one which is mainly concerned
with the general trustworthiness of human testimony.
On this subject the Squire propounds a philosophy of his
own. He is the great pundit and oracle of the story,
pictured as a man of immense reading and encyclopediac
learning. After a few conversations with this prodigy,
Elsmere's resistance is completely crippled, and all power
of answer leaves him. He is especially powerless when
the Squire "let him have it" on the subject of human
testimony in its bearing on the question of Christian
origins. We had better let the Squire state his views in
his own words—

"Testimony, like every other human product, has
developed. Man's power of apprehending and recording
what he sees and hears has grown from less to more, from
weaker to stronger, like any other of his faculties, just as
the reasoning powers of the cave-dweller have developed
into the reasoning powers of a Kant. What one wants is
the ordered proof of this, and it can be got from history
and experience.

"To plunge into the Christian period without having
first cleared the mind as to what is meant in history and
literature by 'the critical method,' which in history may
be defined as 'the science of what is credible,' and in
literature as 'the science of what is rational,' is to invite
fiasco.

"Suppose, for instance, before I begin to deal with the
Christian story and the earliest Christian development, I
try to make out beforehand what are the moulds, the
channels, into which the testimony of the time must run.
I look for these moulds, of course, in the dominant ideas,
the intellectual preconceptions and preoccupations existing
when the period begins.

'In the first place, I shall find present in the age which
saw the birth of Christianity, as in many other ages, a

universal preconception in favour of miracle—that is to say, of deviations from the common norm of experience—governing the work of *all* men of *all* schools. Very well, allow for it then. Read the testimony of the period in the light of it. Be prepared for the inevitable differences between it and the testimony of your own day. The witness of the time is not true, nor, in the strict sense, false. It is merely incompetent, half-trained, unscientific, but all through perfectly natural. The wonder would have been to have had a life of Christ without miracles. The air teems with them. The East is full of Messiahs. Even a Tacitus is superstitious. Even a Vespasian works miracles.

"In the next place, look for the preconceptions that have a definite historical origin; those, for instance, flowing from the pre-Christian apocalyptic literature of the Jews; those flowing from the Alexandrian Judaism and the school of Philo; those flowing from the Palestinian schools of exegesis. Examine your Synoptic Gospels, your Gospel of John, your Apocalypse, in the light of these. You have no other chance of understanding them. But so examined they fall into place, become explicable and rational; such material as science can make use of.

"It is discreditable now for the man of intelligence to refuse to read his Livy in the light of his Mommsen. My object has been to help in making it discreditable to him to refuse to read his Christian documents in the light of a trained scientific criticism."

Such, in substance, was the argument which carried the citadel of Elsmere's faith, and overwhelmed him with final catastrophe. It had been previously suggested at an earlier stage by one of his Oxford tutors, when Elsmere was engaged in his studies of mediæval history.

"History," he had said, "depends on testimony. What is the nature and value of testimony at given times? In other words, do the men of the third century understand, or report, or interpret facts in the same way as the sixteenth or nineteenth? In this question," said the tutor to himself, "lies the whole of orthodox Christianity."

What value are we to attach to all this vague and pretentious talk? We have no hesitation in characterising it as one of those loose and hasty generalisations which are the common vice in our day alike of philosophy, science, and religion. Would Mrs. Ward have us believe that the further we go back in history human testimony is to be viewed with increasing suspiciousness, and received not only with the proverbial grain of salt, but with very many grains indeed? We are quite prepared to admit that there are districts of history where written documents are few, monumental evidence scanty, and the historian largely dependent on traditional hearsay, where any testimony that is forthcoming must be liberally discounted. But would Mrs. Ward, for instance, venture to maintain that Thucydides was not, at least in all matters he had opportunity of personally observing or investigating, as trustworthy an historian as Clarendon? Would she hazard the assertion that Tacitus was not as reliable in his narrations as Gibbon or Prescott? Modern unbelief must be surely hard pressed if, in order to score a point against Christianity, it finds it necessary to have recourse to the senseless and irrational procedure of seeking to undermine and invalidate the whole course of testimony on which the very foundations of all history repose.

"If the attack on Christianity," says a writer in the *Quarterly*, already quoted, "has really been forced back on a proposition that all testimony previous to the nineteenth century is comparatively untrustworthy, it will, we think, be sufficiently evident that it is argumentatively defeated. No comparison is adequate to such an argument, but that of pulling down your house to put out your candle. In order to extinguish the light of the Christian faith, the whole edifice of history is to have the ground cut from under it."

The simple truth is that all testimony must be put upon its trial, and be duly and strictly sifted. Let its defects be noted; let us hold it up to the light, and " finger its crevices," if it has any, and make the requisite deduction for every deficiency we discover. We know the marks of the spurious in history; and, on the other hand, we know the signature of the genuine; we know what Dr. Chalmers calls the " likelihoods of truth." Let us courageously apply these tests with rigorous scrutiny, and we shall find their guardianship amply sufficient to protect us from deception or imposture. But, as Mr. Gladstone says in his review of *Robert Elsmere* in the *Contemporary*—

" There is no proceeding so insane or irrational as the wholesale depreciation of testimony. Such depreciation is an infallible note of shallow and careless thinking, for it very generally implies an exaggerated and almost ludicrous estimate of the capacity and performances of the present generation as compared with those which have preceded it."

By all means let us take the precaution that before any testimony is admitted to the undisturbed possession of our faith, it shall lie in quarantine outside the portals of our intellect for a while, during which it shall be duly canvassed and interrogated; but let us not, in a wayward, unreasoning mood, begin to doubt universally all the informations the past brings to our door, and so land ourselves in a state of extravagant and diseased scepticism.

Let it not be supposed for a moment that this sifting and winnowing of human testimony is an impracticable or impossible process. How successfully it may be conducted is evident from the manner in which all the great modern historians, when dealing with Greece and Rome and Egypt, have analysed and investigated the informations of the past, so as to separate the alloy from the pure gold, and disentangle the false from the true. They have never deemed it necessary to doubt the validity of human testimony in general or in the bulk, nor suffered themselves to lapse into the unreasoning pyrrhonism which would treat all history in the light of "a laborious deception skilfully concocted by the few as an experiment on the credulity of future ages"; [1] but they have sedulously addressed themselves to the examination of witnesses, the scrutiny of evidence, the sifting of authorities, and so on, till they are enabled to arrive at stable and correct conclusions.

Let us pursue a similar policy in regard to the Gospels and Epistles of the New Testament, and we are not afraid to abide by the result. Here are writings which for nineteen centuries now have held an undisturbed position in the general faith and acquiescence of mankind. Not till David Hume broached his famous but oft-refuted theorem was the idea started, that because these writings happened to contain elements which were miraculous, human testimony was powerless to establish the truth of them. That these writings are correctly

[1] Chalmers, *Christian Evidences*, p. 166.

attributed to the authors whose names they bear, is now conceded by the best scholarship of the day. Their authenticity is vouched for even by a critic so rational-ising and revolutionary in his methods as Renan himself, whose witness we suspect would be acceptable even to the authoress of *Robert Elsmere*. The writers exhibit all the natural signs of honesty and truthfulness; they have the tone and aspect of credibility in a pre-eminent degree. No doubt they narrate events, many of which are of a miraculous character, but these events took place, not in holes or corners, but in the light of day, in the streets of Jerusalem, in the presence of inquisitive multitudes. They came under the notice of hostile Jewish councils, and officers of State like Pilate, Herod, Festus, Felix, and Agrippa, and if they were only so many juggleries they could easily have been detected and exposed.

If Christ's miracles were but pious frauds or fairy tales, how was it there was no withering exposure of the imposture on the part of the lynx-eyed and relentless adversaries of Jesus? For such an exposure there were ample materials and ample opportunity, and certainly the unbelieving Jews, obstinate in their rejection of Christianity, must be credited with entire willingness to undertake a task so congenial. If the miracles were false, how is it that those opposed to Christ and His apostles maintained a deep reserve and an unbroken silence on the whole subject? Moreover, let it be borne in mind that the apostolic witnesses to Christianity bore their testimony in the name and under the sanctions of a religion which legislates against all untruthfulness, and threatens with direst penalty the makers and lovers of a lie. Consider, too, what they were willing to endure in consequence of the testimony they gave. They had no selfish advantage to gain, or interest to promote. By the consistent deliverance of that testimony of theirs, they were taking, not the flowery path that leads to honour, fortune, and preferment; on the contrary, what it led to was hatred, loss of friends, exile, personal indignities, persecution, torture, and death. This was their only guerdon for testifying, as they did, to what they had seen and heard. Yet neither threats nor pains, neither desertion, nor maltreatment, nor martyrdom itself, could silence their witness-bearing, nor prevail upon them to alter or recant a single syllable. Unless we can prove that these men were either deceived or mistaken, unless they can be shown to have been either knaves or simpletons, we cannot refuse them our confidence. As has been very justly remarked, that such testimony as theirs should be false, would be in itself more miraculous than the greatest prodigy recorded in the New Testament.

But what shall we say to the Squire's stock argument, on which he rings the changes so often, that the age in which Jesus made His appearance was an uncritical and half-childish one, innocent of all historical discrimination or rational inquiry, unaccustomed to the reporting of facts and the weighing of evidence? Such a representation of the time in which Christ came upon the scene, we venture to say, is in complete dissonance with the facts. Jesus did not appear in a prehistoric age. It was an age when histories were being written. It was an age of intellectual attainment and much literary activity. It was the age in which all the ancient pagan superstitions were crumbling to pieces under the attacks of philosophy. It was the age in which Lucretius was writing his great rationalistic poem on Nature. It was the age in which the Epicureans were attempting an explanation of the universe based on purely materialistic principles, as men are doing now. It was the age in which the Stoics were propounding a profound moral philosophy, and the Stoics have been thought by many to correspond very much with the liberal Christians of the present day. Besides, the people among whom Jesus lived and moved were not illiterate barbarians. They were the countrymen of Josephus. Their minds were sharpened by trade and commerce. The spirit of inquiry was abroad at the time. There were freethinking Sadducees in those days, denying the existence of angel or spirit, and saying that there was no resurrection of the dead. There were not wanting men like Pontius Pilate, who were quick to interrogate accepted beliefs, and had no feeling but one of cynical disdain for things theological and religious. The myths of Greece and Rome had already been dissolved at the touch of reflection and sober inquiry; Ovid treats of them in his *Metamorphoses*, and Virgil in his *Eneid*, but it is as men who have ceased to believe in them; in the clear daylight of history things born of mist and haze were fast vanishing away.

Accepting the Squire's definition of criticism as " the science of what is credible," or " the science of what is rational," let us reperuse the ninth chapter of John's Gospel, and we shall see that " the science of what is credible " was not so ill-understood in those days as the writers of theological novels would have us suppose. A miracle has been wrought, and so far from there being a universal predisposition to believe it, a group of clever sceptics immediately subject it to an investigation which for strictness and severity it would not be easy to parallel in any age. Never was a more penetrating searchlight flashed on any incident. Never was witness subjected to a more relentless examination. We fail to discover any just grounds for the insinuation that the age in which our Lord appeared was vitiated by a strong preconception in favour of miracle. Let due allowance be given to the fact that there had been, if not a cessation of miracle, at least a very rare occurrence of it from the days of Isaiah downwards, and with this a corresponding disappearance of the disposition on the part of the Jewish people to look for miracle-working. John did no miracle, and yet was universally accorded the rank of a prophet: that does not look as if the age were afflicted with an exaggerated craving for wonders.

" That later Judaism as such," says Professor Christlieb, " was not fond of miracles, is clearly shown by their rare occurrence in the lives of the great prophets from Isaiah downwards. Only where Creator and creature are commingled—as in the case of heathenism—do we find a fertile soil for miracle mania. But when both are kept so entirely distinct as in Judaism, and the human subject is penetrated with the feeling of God's greatness and its own nothingness, it cannot expect that miracles should take place every instant. It will look on them as something extraordinary, and expect them to occur *seldom*." [1]

It is surprising that a writer so competent and well-informed as Mrs. Ward should throughout some three or

[1] *Modern Doubt and Christian Belief*, p. 408.

four hundred pages of controversial literature have persisted in an habitual disregard of the distinction which is usually observed between the New Testament miracles and those heathenish and ecclesiastical miracles which have so often imposed on the credulity of the simple. In this respect the authoress of *Robert Elsmere* simply reproduces and perpetuates one of the old sophistries of David Hume. The fallacy of Hume lay very much in this, that he failed to recognise the different species of testimony. He chose to ignore the fact that of two kinds of testimony, competing for our acceptance, one may possess wholly different characteristics, and have been given in wholly different circumstances, from the other ; the one may often, the other may never once, have deceived us. Instead of this, he has lumped all testimony together, the most veracious and trustworthy with the most suspicious and corruptible, and he has made the former responsible for all the falsities and errors of the latter.

" This," says Dr. Chalmers, " is quite as egregious an injustice as if, in dealing with two men, I should lay upon the one, who was never known to swerve in the least from integrity and truth, the burden of all that discredit which the other had incurred by frauds and falsehoods innumerable." [1]

Wittingly or unwittingly, Mrs. Ward has fallen into the very same error. She refuses to draw any distinction between one kind of miracle and another, or to discriminate between the distinct species of testimony by which these miracles happen to be accredited. The writer

[1] *Christian Evidences*, p. 147.

must be pronounced lamentably lacking in any sense of distributive justice, who slumps together in this loose and slatternly fashion the wonders reported in legendary tales or apocryphal Gospels with the miracles which a religion like Christianity produces as an important part of its credentials. Mrs. Ward reminds us that Vespasian wrought miracles; but what discriminating or fair-minded writer would put the pseudo-miracles of a pagan prince in the same category as the miracles of Jesus Christ— miracles wrought by a Being whom Rationalists themselves admit to have been a unique and extraordinary Personality claiming a pre-eminent relationship with God, wrought from the loftiest motive and in connection with the loftiest teaching, wrought for the confirmation of a sublime mission, and for the establishment of a new and commanding scheme of religion. These peculiarities, together with their dignity and simplicity, should certainly suffice to put a wide gulf of separation between the miracles wrought by One who was Himself the greatest moral and religious miracle that has ever appeared amongst men, and miracles pagan and ecclesiastical, which, in strong contrast with these, are as a class grotesque, fantastic, and otherwise offensive. The chapter in his masterly treatise on "Miracles," in which Canon Mozley delineates the essential difference between the astonishing manifestations of Divine power associated with the early proclamation of Christianity and the pseudo-miraculous wonders which afterwards imposed on the credulity of mankind, would prove an admirable mental corrective for Mrs. Ward and those who think with her. The contrast is so striking that it forced from M. Renan, in one of his earlier works, this remarkable confession—

" The marvellous in the Gospels is but sober good sense compared with that which we meet with in the Jewish Apocryphal writings, or in the Hindoo or European mythologies." [1]

Mrs. Ward, with less candour than the French philosopher, does not choose to observe this distinction, but, in defiance of all sense of distributive justice, would persuade us that because the legendary tales of mediæval miracles are such as at once to excite our suspicion, we are therefore to attach the very same suspicion to all miracles in general, not excepting those which are attributed to the Christ by the four Evangelists.

Robert Elsmere, in the course of his researches into French mediæval archives, comes upon some pseudo-wonder said to have been wrought by Gregory of Tours; and because the testimony by which it is supported excites at once a feeling of distrust and reserve, we are invited by Mrs. Ward to put the testimony which is adduced in authentication of the Gospel miracles in the very same category, and burden it with all the discredit which the other has incurred by its manifest fraud and falsehood. We resolutely decline a procedure so egregiously unfair. We insist that every testimony shall bear its own burden and stand upon its own merits. The Gospel miracles shall be answerable for themselves, and lying mediæval wonders shall be answerable for themselves. Witnesses which are manifestly competent, truth-loving, and sincere, must not incur the reproach or

[1] *Studies in the History of Religion*, pp. 177, 203.

suffer for the falsities of witnesses which have acquired
a very different reputation, and which have been more
than once perhaps convicted of deception.

" The criterion of the real miracle," says a distinguished
theologian, " lies not merely in the act being in itself
unusual and unheard of, but at the same time in the
moral character of the worker of miracles, and in the
godly aim of his act." [1]

This higher characteristic the Scripture miracles
obviously possess; and this, together with many other
distinguishing peculiarities which might be specified,
serves to differentiate them from those pseudo-miraculous
phenomena with which Church legends and apocryphal
writings abound. Each kind of miracle and each species
of testimony must answer for itself at the bar of the one
tribunal which is alone competent to adjudicate on the
whole question of the miraculous—the tribunal of critico-
historical investigation, which, of course, if it is to deserve
the name, must be searching and impartial.

But what the Squire and Robert Elsmere really object
to is not testimony, but testimony in favour of miraculous
events. So far as these men are concerned, the whole
discussion is vitiated by the arbitrary presupposition, to
which both are so deeply committed, that " miracles do
not happen." By the adoption of this piece of a *priori*
philosophy they have done a grievous wrong to the
whole investigation, and practically disqualifed themselves for conducting it with any approach to fairness
or impartiality. If, on so-called philosophical grounds,
they tacitly accept as their starting-point the impossi-

[1] Oosterzee's *Christian Dogmatics*, p. 129.

bility of miracle, it is easy to foresee the fate which
many a Gospel narrative must undergo.   The whole life
of Christ must, in that case, be emptied at all costs of
every vestige of the supernatural, and the rationalistic
dismemberment of the Gospel history is a foregone
conclusion.

We would remind Mrs. Ward and her disciples that
the question at issue is not whether miracles do or do
not happen, in the ordinary sense of that juggling phrase,
but whether they did once happen in an age requiring
different revelatory action on God's part from that in
which we live ; not whether sovereign demonstrations of
the Divine Will and Power occur in modern times, but
whether they did once occur at a specific time, under
specific circumstances, and in the action of a specific
Person who claims unique pre-eminence and authority
in the world.   That question, we maintain, is purely
one of history ; and, as Professor Godet says, " the
first necessity in the treatment of a question of *history*
is that it should be treated *historically*." [2]   The Squire
and Robert Elsmere insist on treating it philosoph-
ically, but we have yet to learn that philosophy is
to be allowed to determine beforehand what may be
historical and what may not.   It is quite evident that
in her innermost consciousness Mrs. Ward feels this
and admits it, for she devotes the major portion of
her book to the discussion of the validity of testimony,
thus showing that in reality she is herself deeply convinced that, after all, for all plain, downright unmeta-
physical people at least, it is in the final issue a pure

[1] *Defence of the Faith*, p. 88.

question of history, to be adjusted on the principles of historical criticism, entirely free from any arbitrary pre-suppositions whatsoever. From this alternative she cannot in consistency resile, for a writer who calls in the aid of testimony to prove that miracles do *not* happen, cannot well refuse to listen to testimony which goes to prove that they do. Having eagerly availed herself of the help of testimony to establish a negative conclusion, she cannot in decency rule it out of court when it is adduced to establish a positive.

Practically considered, the essence of Elsmere's pro-posal is to eliminate the supernatural ingredients from the life of our Lord, while careful to imbibe and assimi-late His moral teachings. But this, as Mr. Gladstone puts it, is " simply to bark the tree, and then, as the death which ensues is not immediate, to point out with satisfaction on the instant that it still waves living branches in the wind." Yes, and if the tree survives the barking process for a time, and shows no immediate signs of enfeeblement or decay, is it not largely attributable to the fact that the tree has the advantage of being rooted in soil permeated by Christian ingredients, and fertilised by the influences of that very supernaturalism which Elsmere is so eager to repudiate ? If the stripped and mutilated tree still manages to " wave living branches in the wind," is it not because those branches happen to wave in an atmosphere which is richly stimulating and bracing, because for centuries it has been vitalised and enriched by a subtle infusion of New Testament Chris-tianity ? Society, as christianly organised in a country like ours, which has been under its spell for ages, is

24

impregnated by influences invisible but omnipresent, and
of vast spiritual efficacy, which we can scarcely help
inhaling with the very breath we draw.   Freethinking
writers of theological novels are often more deeply indebted to the religion they repel than they care to
acknowledge, or perhaps are altogether conscious of.
Among other debts they owe to it, not the least is this—
the possibility of trying their religious experiments, or
launching their humanitarian schemes, with the chance
that they will be able to keep on for a while under the
impulse derived from Christian conditions and surroundings, and not just be overtaken with instantaneous failure,
or swift and sudden collapse, as they otherwise would be.
In order rightly to estimate the inherent vitality and the
prospects of ultimate success for a new scheme of religion
like Elsmere's, we must conceive the experiment made on
the sterile soil and in the bleaker air of paganism.   Let
it be transferred to some land whose civilisation has not
been for centuries a Christian civilisation, and where the
whole climatic conditions are unfavourable, and see how
it will work there, and how long a lease of existence it
will be likely to have.

Mrs. Ward's is only another instance of the oft-
repeated attempt to banish from Christianity its miracle
and its dogma, whilst carefully conserving its lofty ideals
and beautiful ethical teaching.   We can only characterise
such attempts, in the language of a writer already quoted,
as " a huge and larcenous appropriation by modern
schemes of goods which do not belong to them."   What
title have they who eviscerate Christianity of all its
doctrinal and miraculous contents, to purloin and make

off with its morality for the purpose of decking out with a few sprigs of respectability some little nine-days' scheme of their own, whose cradle will turn out to be its grave, and imparting to it at least somewhat of the semblance of a religion? The practical fruits of Christianity in individual life and character grow out of its supernatural character and dogmatic teaching; and what right have we to detach the fruits from the roots that bear them, or to assume that we can have the fruits equally well from other roots, or, for that matter, from no roots at all? Mr. Gladstone's contention is unanswerable—the Christian type of life and character is the product and the property of the Christian scheme, and it is nothing short of a shameless larceny to appropriate them in the interests of any other scheme, or try to graft them on to some rival system, which can make no pretension to owning them, and which is powerless to produce them.

Elsmere's new scheme of religion, which he inaugurates with such hopeful ardour among the wretched denizens of East End London, will strike most readers as a poor substitute for the Christianity it seeks to displace. Ushered in, as all these humanitarian movements are, "if not with the mystic song of angels, at least with the hearty welcomes of all rational men," it comes to us with large pretensions, and promises of great things. It is cultured, philosophical, and boundlessly enterprising. Abjuring the antiquated methods of the Churches, it strikes out on adventurous lines of its own. Recreation evenings, scientific Sunday schools, lectures on Greek myth and Icelandic saga, story-telling, lessons in botany, debating societies, draughts and dominoes—such are the

agencies by which Elsmere hopes to found a sort of
New Jerusalem amid the dens and rookeries of the East
End, and perceptibly to hasten the approach of the
millennium.   It is thus that he proposes to work out the
social salvation of the London artisan.   The scheme
embodies much which may recommend it to the interest
of educated people,—much, too, which is calculated to
brighten, embellish, and elevate,—but we fail to detect
in it the presence of anything which can regenerate or
save.   As a programme it is morally powerless and
inadequate : it has no plummet capable of touching the
abysmal depths of human sin and wretchedness.   The
power of God unto civilisation it may be, but it certainly
falls far short of being the power of God unto salvation.
None of your perfumed philosophies can reclaim the
harlot, nor win to virtue the degraded.   Art studies,
lessons in botany, and a knowledge of mythology will
not wean the wicked from their abominations.   Pretty
moral essays are the poorest of weapons with which to
lead a crusade against evil.   The religion which had its
headquarters in Elgood Street Hall, does not seem to
have had among its moral appliances any expedient
whereby sinful erring mortals might have created in
them a new heart, or have put within them a right
spirit.   Elsmere's talks and prelections to his East End
audiences may be intellectual and sparkling, and in the
eyes of his freethinking auditors may have the additional
recommendation of being innocent of anything savouring
of goody-goodyism, and untinged by any faint reminder
of the " dear brethren " style of thing, but one cannot
help feeling that, for the purposes of moral rescue and

uplift, one good rousing evangelistic address from a Moody or a M'Neil would be worth the whole of them together.

Amid all his story-tellings—and they are many—Elsmere never once tells a story which can compare in sin-removing power with the old story of Calvary. Indeed, one fatal defect of the book which has often been commented on, is the faint and attenuated view of sin which it everywhere exhibits. Neither Mrs. Ward nor the hero of her novel ever seems to have remotely realised what Canon Knox Little has well described as " the imperial seriousness of sin," as one of the deepest and most agonising facts of consciousness. Neither the one nor the other would seem to have formed any adequate conception of the malignity or virulence of sin: they appear to regard it as a mere incident, or at most but a slight cutaneous affection, for the treatment of which the application of a wash compounded of a few drops of modern culture, or some liniment of philanthropy, is all that is needed. A few evenings at a scientific Sunday school will suffice to rectify all the moral disorders under which human nature is labouring. In Elsmere's gospel of unbelief no attempt is made to grapple with the problem of sin and its removal; indeed, one might almost infer from it that in the neighbourhood of Elgood Street men's consciences were never troubled by any moral disturbance, nor haunted by any spectres of guilt. It gilds with no aureole the discords and sufferings of life, puts no sweetening branch into its Marahs, sends no strengthening angel into its Gethsemanes. It tinges with no brightness the shadows of mortality as

they thicken around us, strikes no light in the last darkness, and provides no *viaticum* for a soul setting out on
its last pilgrimage.   Like many other of these interesting
humanitarian phases of thought and philanthropic experiments, which have come to be almost a standing feature
of the age we live in, we may say of it in the language
of Canon Liddon—

"Its endeavours to deal with the great heart-sores of
humanity remind us of a celebrated physician, who, at
the bedside of a patient writhing in protracted agony,
would airily discuss his own last excursion in the Alps,
or the last debate in Parliament, or at best the most
recent resolution arrived at by the Metropolitan Board of
Health."[1]

The lesson of "Robert Elsmere"—not the one Mrs.
Ward intended to teach, but the real lesson—is very
simple.   A Christianity with the Christ left out, a life,
a pulpit from which the Jesus of history is expelled, can
do but little for the individual soul or for society, for it
has denuded itself of the only inspiration and the only
instrumentality which can insure genuine success.   It
is little better than a semi-baptized paganism.   It is
noteworthy that the only character in the book that
achieves success, and develops steadily in all that can
exalt and ennoble life, is the faithful Christian woman
who retains her early beliefs, and keeps through many
trying situations her saintliness of soul.   The characters
who reject Christ are without exception failures; they
are thwarted and dwarfed, their work comes to nought,
and they die without having benefited either themselves
or the world.   Even in the case of Elsmere himself the

[1] *Some Elements in Religion*, p. 158.

renunciation of the old faith has not been effected without his having to pay the penalty in moral retrogression and declinature. Usually when a man does surrender the dogmatic creed with which he started, he parts company with religion altogether, and after a few ineffectual struggles, when assailed by temptation, he goes headlong to the bad. And if in the case of Robert Elsmere the evolution did not take a downward course, and the man still contrived to maintain his faith in the unseen, his loyalty to duty, and his devotion to high ideals, it is only because Mrs. Ward chooses so to arrange it; she made the story run that way. But it were quite possible to conceive another story, picturing a result the very opposite of this, and the tale might be a perfectly accurate reflection of real life. And yet, though Elsmere does not part company with goodness, nor prove recreant to his best ideals, even in his case we think we can discern a certain amount of moral descent and falling off.

As the story develops, the feeling is borne in upon us that Elsmere is not quite the man he was, that he has gone down in moral quality, and is living on lower levels than he used to occupy. Unless the fineness of his moral sensitiveness had been somewhat blunted, and the enamel worn off his virtue a little, we can scarcely conceive it possible that such a one as he should not only have tolerated but relished the society of the woman De Netteville. The less said about this lady's character the better; she appears to have had none to spare, and certainly none to speak of. The Squire, by no means over-exacting in his standards, or very fastidious in his tastes, could not certify for her reputation; while Catherine shrank from her as from the presence of a pestilence. That this personage should be an intimate of Elsmere's, that he should stoop to the cultivation of her society, and lend himself as he did to a long series of parleyings and coquettings, is only conceivable on the supposition that the man can condescend to things since the surrender of his faith, which before that surrender he could not have brooked.   Nor is this loss of moral resoluteness and dignity the only evidence of degeneracy. Further traces of it are discernible in the manner in which he comports himself towards the Squire, and his old friend Grey the tutor, as they lie on the verge of the tomb.   To neither the one dying sceptic nor the other does he address a single syllable of remonstrance or entreaty.   As they lie tossing there in the last spasms and convulsions, he brings no message of consolation, kindles no light in the sick-room, recites no promise, speaks not a word that would help to pluck the sting from death, or fortify the spirit in that last solemn hour when the great secret is about to open on it.   Fresh from his philanthropic ministries at Elgood Street, he comes to see the last of Squire Wendover.   He lavishes admiration on the pieces of pagan sculpture that stand in grim passivity around the bed where parting life is laid, assists his attendant in helping the dying man on a last pilgrimage round the shelves which held the infidel books that made him what he was, and, to beguile the tedium of that portentous night, he himself kept dipping at intervals into a French anthology for a few choice continental quotations!   In the next room the fluttering of the wings of the death-angel could be heard, and this is how Elsmere employs himself! Time was when his action would have been less incongruous with such a scene, but that was before he had let go the faith of Jesus. He goes as a mourner to the funeral of his friend Grey, stands sorrowing in the churchyard, and, as those sublime words of the fifteenth chapter of First Corinthians, which have been said and sung and sobbed beside so many open graves, fell upon his ear, he deems them too audacious and over-jubilant, and begins to think with himself—

"Man's hope has grown humbler than this. It keeps now a more modest mien in presence of the Eternal Mystery; but is it any the less real, less sustaining? Let Grey's trust answer for me."[1]

From his own point of view he was quite right. A man's hope must of necessity be very modest indeed, and cannot afford to venture further than a whispering humbleness in the presence of the Eternal Mystery, when to that man the resurrection of Jesus Christ from the dead is but a beautiful myth. That man's religion is bound to be a Lenten affair that keeps no Easter festival. Grey's trust! What better is it than the thin, flickering, anxious hope once tremblingly cherished by a Cicero or an Aristotle in the old days of pagan twilight, before the Christ had made His advent at all? Grey's trust! It is but a sickly, pallid, moonlight conjecture when compared with Paul's triumphant pæan, with its towering hope and its immortal presage: "For the trumpet shall sound; and the dead shall be raised incorruptible,

[1] P. 584.

and we shall be changed.   So when this corruptible shall have put on incorruption, and this mortal shall have put on immortality, then shall be brought to pass the saying that is written, Death is swallowed up in victory.   O death, where is thy sting?   O grave, where is thy victory?   The sting of death is sin; and the strength of sin is the law.   But thanks be to God, who giveth us the victory through our Lord Jesus Christ."

VIII

THE THEOLOGY OF THOMAS HARDY

VIII

THE THEOLOGY OF THOMAS HARDY

In these closing years of the waning century we are left with only some five or six authors of the first magnitude. Conspicuous among this little *fin de siècle* group of select spirits stands the name of Thomas Hardy, whose claim to rank as the greatest living master of English fiction is now almost universally conceded. None of his contemporaries, unless perhaps Mr. George Meredith, can seriously divide the honour with him. He is already one of the crowned heads of literature. His freshness, his vivacity, his literary charm, his descriptive power, his sense of natural beauty, his aptitude in depicting the passions of men and women in all their tangled complexity, discriminate him at once from the common herd of authors. In graphic presentation of village life and manners in the West Country he is only approached by Charles Kingsley and Mr. Blackmore ; even they have not surpassed him. Quite recently he has given evidence of possessing, in addition to his already munificent equipment of artistic gifts and instincts, a rich vein of poesy, for which his readers were not altogether unprepared, for the prose of Thomas Hardy is often separated

from poetry only by the absence of rhyme.   It is matter
for painful regret that this typical man of the hour,
wielding as he undoubtedly does the jewelled sceptre of
genius, has not left it in our power to claim him as a
religious or moral force, as a power that makes for
righteousness, as an uplifter of men, or a sweetener of
life.   We regard it as one of the most saddening
spectacles with which the close of the nineteenth century
confronts us, to see this man, a very prince in literature,
concentrating attention on the shadiness and seaminess
of life, exploiting sewers and cesspools, dabbling in
beastliness and putrefaction, dragging to light the ghastly
and the gruesome, poring over the scurvy and unreportable side of things, bending in lingering analysis
over every phase of mania and morbidity, going down
into the swamps and marshes to watch the phosphor-
escence of decay and the jack-o'-lanterns that dance on
rottenness, at the risk of catching malaria for himself,
or spreading it among his readers.   He is one of the
few English writers who have not hesitated to ally
themselves with the high priests and prophets of the
New Realism, men like Zola and Flaubert, who join the
cult of the Ugly, and think it the primary function of
all true Art to dwell on what has been called " the night-
cart side of life."

We do not for a moment insinuate that Thomas Hardy
has a natural liking for the squalid, or that he revels in
the indelicate and the obscene ; the presence of so much
of it in his writings is rather to be accounted for by a
sincere, but perverted and mistaken, conception of his
mission as an artist, and of the true ends of fiction.

Some years ago Mr. Hardy published, in one of the magazines, his recipe for renewing the youth of fiction, and giving it a new lease of power.

"The national taste and the national genius have returned," he said, "to the great tragic motives so greatly handled by the dramatists of the Periclean and Elizabethan ages. But the national genius perceives also that these tragic motives demand enrichment by further truths—in other words, original treatment; treatment which seeks to show Nature's unconsciousness, not of essential laws, but those laws framed merely as social expedients by humanity without a basis in the heart of things."

This is the recipe to which Mr. Hardy rigidly adheres in his books, and which he works out in tales of Sodomism and brutality, which certainly bear no analogy that we can perceive to the handling of the great tragic motives by the dramatists of either Periclean or Elizabethan times. Book after book has Mr. Hardy written for the purpose of demonstrating, what we sincerely trust never can be demonstrated, that the common feelings of humanity against seduction, adultery, and murder are no inherent part of the nature of things, and have no basis in anything more primitive or essential than man - devised expedients, or social regulations. But the unspoiled, unsophisticated mind cannot, at the bidding of a novelist, divest itself of the old wholesome belief that the laws prohibitive of these criminalities are rooted in the eternal propriety of things. Do they not lie at the very foundation of human society? Under the sinister influence of this strange recipe of his for the rejuvenation of fiction, Mr. Hardy has been steadily gravitating toward the adoption of methods which contrast very unfavourably with his old ones, and is lending himself to a movement full of mischief—a movement which is " under French encouragement "—and which has for its object the entire emancipation of Art and Literature from the wholesome restrictions which morality and good taste would impose. Our English artist has been stretching forth his hand more and more eagerly toward the forbidden fruit which Emile Zola has long been plucking, with great advantage to himself.   Mr. Hardy has been trying the experiment of making as near an approach to French *lubricité* as he could safely venture upon, without outraging the English sense of decency, or putting too severe a strain upon the national conscience.

The late Robert Louis Stevenson has told us the constant apprehension under which he laboured lest he should be " shoved towards grossness by a love of putting things plainly."   The danger which Stevenson saw, and studied to avoid, is precisely the danger which Mr. Hardy deliberately courts, with the result that his writings are full of such specimens of the squalid and the obscene as have no parallel save in the moral nastiness of Rabelais, Swift, or Sterne.   This is strong language, but if the reader wants a justification of it, let him read *Tess of D'Urberville*, or *Jude the Obscure*.   What a reviewer has said of Jude's courtship of Arabella might be extended in its application to many other scenes and incidents in that book, and in most of the other books of Mr. Hardy—" It is enough to sicken a scavenger."   We shall not soil our page nor run the risk of leaving a stain upon the reader's mind by reproducing them here.   We shall only just glance at some of Mr. Hardy's types of womanhood. The sub-title he prefixes to *Tess* is a study in itself—" A Pure Woman Faithfully Presented." The author's conception of feminine purity is decidedly peculiar. We have no intention of following through its horrid folds and windings the story of Tess's very speckled career. Suffice it to say that the tale in which that lady figures as heroine is one long tissue of feminine crime and indiscretion. It commences with seduction, proceeds, by way of pleasing variety, to adultery, and, by way of tragic *dénouement*, ends on the gallows. Through it all, however, Tess is good at the core, and continues half an angel to the end of her miserable career. It is a heavy demand on our credulity when we are asked, in the face of all these wretched happenings, to retain the conviction that this is the history of " A Pure Woman Faithfully Presented." " The second and fourth words in this title," says Mr. Lionel Johnson, " would be better for some definition." We should think so! When we have succeeded in persuading ourselves that soot is white, that the leopard is destitute of spots, that the dark-skinned Ethiopian is of fair complexion, that a whiff of poisonous air is a perfume-laden breath from Araby the Blest, we may then go on to make ourselves believe that Tess of D'Urberville comes within measurable distance of a saint. Her literary creator, however, sees in her no defect, save " some slight incautiousness of character inherited from her race." As for the manner in which this poor woman's sensual qualifications for the part of heroine are paraded over and over again, we can only say it is too gross to be alluring—it is only disgusting. A writer in

25

the *Quarterly* is not very far wide of the mark when he compares it to the persistency with which a horse-dealer eggs on some wavering customer to a deal, or a slave-dealer appraises his wares to some full-blooded pasha.

Another of Thomas Hardy's "pure women faithfully presented" is Sue. Sue is the cousin of Jude, and not long after that gentleman has made her acquaintance he says to her, "Sue, I believe you are as innocent as you are unconventional."   About the unconventionality there can be no question.   From all trammelling considerations of modesty Sue had long divested herself—witness the scene when, having escaped from the Training College, and waded a deep river in the course of her flight, she comes drenched and dripping into Jude's lodgings, and there divests herself of her wet garments and puts them up to dry at the sitting-room fire, while she assumes a suit of Jude's clothes.   As to her innocence, however, the reader will scarcely entertain so unshaken a belief in it as her cousin, especially when Sue herself, in the next breath, informs him that at eighteen she had formed an acquaintance, of too intimate a kind, with an Oxford undergraduate, with whom she subsequently lived for eighteen months.   "But I have never yielded myself to any lover," she goes on, "if that is what you mean; I have remained as I began"; and with this statement Jude is quite satisfied.   She did not long remain, however, as she began, for the sequel of the story is that she married a schoolmaster, Richard Phillotson, old enough to be her father, and for whom she had always conceived a strong physical aversion, jumped out of a window because the schoolmaster was incompatible, and did not take so free and easy a view of the relations between them as the Oxford undergraduate had done. Leaving the schoolmaster, with his full consent, she subsequently goes to live with Jude, with whom she makes several unsuccessful attempts to go through a marriage ceremony, but is deterred by its "vulgarity," and by the conviction that "it is as culpable to bind yourself to love always as to believe a creed always, and as silly to vow to love one person always as to vow always to like a particular food or drink." The end of it all is that Sue becomes a High Churchwoman, and goes back to the schoolmaster, while Jude degenerates into an infidel, and remarries Arabella, the coarse village barmaid in whose toils he had been caught in his early days, and who had played the Delilah to him.

Such are the ghastly situations and frightful obliquities, the disgraces and the degradations, which the foremost man in the republic of English letters is now serving up to the reading public. We are not surprised that when the late Bishop Walsham How tried to read *Jude the Obscure*, he flung it in disgust behind the grate. Dr. Johnson once said to Mrs. Sheridan, " I know not, Madam, that you have a right, upon moral principles, to make your readers suffer so much." We borrow the remark, and say of Mr. Hardy, we know not that he has any right to make his readers writhe and squirm so often, to make himself so morally offensive at every turn, and outrage the canons of common decency for the sake of illustrating "candour in fiction," and showing that he is not afraid to " put things plainly." To practise " candour in fiction " may be very desirable, as Thomas Hardy has himself demonstrated in an essay he once contributed to one of the magazines on that very subject, but surely it is possible for a man to attain it without stooping to make himself a moral rag-collector, or a dealer in offal.   We have little sympathy with that " censorship of prudery " which would deny the artist the right of ever bringing anything unpleasant under the notice of his reader ; we like candour, but we are of opinion it may be had without a writer condescending to the degradation of indulging in a kind of " hoggish anatomy " of sexual and morbid themes which should only be nameable inside the classroom of the professional physiologist, and then only in the strict interests of science.

Mr. Hardy evidently feels that he has gone too far in this direction, for he has felt constrained to preface some of his recent books with a declaration that they are " not intended for use in families," and that they are addressed to " adult readers only."   But Mr. Hardy cannot help himself.   Writers of his class cannot stipulate for a picked audience.   Once a book from a writer so fascinating as he goes into the railway book-stall, or the circulating library, its readers will not be confined to adults only.   Fiction appeals to everybody ; and fiction so robust, so delicate and charming as his, soon finds its way into all hands. " When a man can take a hall and openly advertise that he intends to speak therein ' to men only,' he is reasonably allowed a certain latitude.   If he pitches his cart on the village green and talks with the village lads and lasses within hearing, he will, if he be a decent fellow, avoid the treatment of certain themes." [1]

[1] Christie Murray, *My Contemporaries in Fiction*, p. 77.

But, apart altogether from this, we repudiate utterly Mr. Hardy's insinuation that people who have reached maturity find something piquant and savoury in what is considered unsuitable for young ears and eyes. It is a libel on older people to hint that what is forbidden fruit to their juniors, smacks sweet to them. We have yet to learn that as people advance in life their taste becomes indurated, and their sensibilities less fastidious. At all events, there are passages in Mr. Hardy's writings which men who have yet left any lingering sense of manhood will resent, and women who have not yet become recreant to all sense of modesty will hurry over with shuddering disgust.

The predominant note in Mr. Hardy's writings is one of revolt. He is always launching some terrible indictment against things in general. He is up in insurrection against social polity, against marriage laws, against family life, against the administration of the universe, against the enduring principles that underlie all moral distinction, against the religious instincts, against Providence, against the Decalogue itself. It is an axiom with Thomas Hardy, as he tells us in his essay on "Candour in Fiction," that "the crash of broken commandments is as necessary an accompaniment to the catastrophe of a tragedy, as the noise of drum and cymbals to a triumphal march." This smashing accompaniment is never wanting in the productions of Thomas Hardy. You can hear on all sides of you the ever-present "crash of broken commandments." His heroes and heroines are invariably lawbreakers, rebels, people with a passion for upsetting things. Marriage laws especially do not seem to suit them. They must be free to slip their love-vows on and off as they do their coats. If the matrimonial yoke presses a little inconveniently, they must be free, at the bidding of freak, fancy, or wilfulness, to make a change. A licence is hinted at, and even asked for, which, if granted, would turn the world into a huge Mormon settlement. According to Sue, marriage is nothing better than " licence to love on the premises." According to her, you are quite entitled to love off the premises, as well as on. She says to Jude—

" Some women's love of being loved is insatiable: and so often is their love of loving: and in the last case they may find that they cannot give it continually to the chamber officer appointed by the bishop's licence to receive it."

Of the family to which she belongs, Jude's maiden aunt observes—

" There's summat in our blood that won't take kindly to the notion of being bound to do what we do readily enough if not bound."

Apparently, if Mr. Hardy had his way, he would turn marriage into a free-lover's fancy, would make divorce easy, and introduce the reign of matrimonial communism. He scouts the idea that love-vows should be publicly ratified by the sanctions either of law or religion, and the better to disparage the marriage ceremony he seeks to surround the rite, whether performed at the registry office or the church, with the most revolting associations. That there are unnatural and unhappy marriages is unfortunately one of the ghastly facts of our social life which has to be reckoned with. Many and loud are the complaints that issue from ill-assorted couples; domestic skeletons from behind many a cupboard utter forth their shrieks. But all this militates not against marriage itself as an institution, as Mr. Hardy would persuade us, but only against the recklessness and folly of those who have entered upon the relationship without that supreme affection for each other which is the only basis on which any marriage union can properly proceed. The chief remedy for unhappy marriages is a faithful adherence to the law of nature and of God, that you shall not marry on a love which is not great enough to last, on an affection which has not in it the quality of endurance, and cannot stand the strain. To substitute for an overpowering affection of this kind a passing fancy or temporary affinity, is to invite that lifelong curse, that chronic misery, which is said to be the hottest hell on this planet that any creature can inhabit. The proper remedy for the deplorable state of things disclosed every now and then in our Divorce Courts, as through some rift of Vesuvius, is not Mr. Hardy's repeal of the law of monogamy, nor increased facility for the dissolution of the marriage bond, but to see to it that marriage is entered upon judiciously from the very first, that it is based upon a love on whose changelessness we can fairly calculate, and that after marriage there shall be, on the part of both parties, an honest attempt to foster and perpetuate the mutual affection with which they started, for affection is capable of cultivation, and can be made to triumph over passing quarrels, and temporary estrangements and disgusts.

David Hume entertained some views on marriage

which were infamous, but he entertained others which
were sound and just, and from which Mr. Hardy and the
disciples of his school might learn wisdom.

"We need not, therefore, be afraid of drawing the
marriage knot, which chiefly subsists by friendship, the
closest possible.   The amity between the persons, where
it is solid and sincere, will rather gain by it.; and where it
is wavering and uncertain, that is the best expedient for
fixing it.   How many frivolous quarrels and disgusts are
there, which people of common prudence endeavour to
forget, when they lie under the necessity of passing their
lives together, but which would soon be inflamed into the
most deadly hatred, were they pursued to the utmost,
under the prospect of an easy separation.   We must
consider that nothing is more dangerous than to unite
two persons so closely in all their interests and concerns
as man and wife without rendering the union entire and
total.   The least possibility of a separate interest must be
the source of endless quarrels and suspicions.   The wife,
not secure of her establishment, will still be driving some
separate end or project; and the husband's selfishness,
being accompanied with more power, may be still more
dangerous." [1]

Commending this paragraph to those who think with
Mr. Hardy, we turn away sickened and saddened from
his teachings on marriage and divorce.   They are teachings which would have been popular in Gomorrha, and
might have made Sodom glad.   As one of his reviewers
has said, "the shadow of the goddess Aselgeia broods
over it all."   We have sometimes surmised what the
results would have been, social and national, if the views
championed by Mr. Hardy had been absorbed into our
social system centuries ago, and acted on for long
stretches of history.   One shudders to contemplate the

---

[1] Hume's *Philosophical Works*, vol. iii. pp. 208, 209.

state of bestiality and shame we should by this time, as a nation, have arrived at. If such teachings were imbibed for a hundred years, we verily believe the history of our country would be about as infamous as that which the excavator's spade has dug up from the buried wickedness of Pompeii. The children of this polygamous state of living would especially present a terrible problem; for how, in such circumstances, could there be any parental care or supervision, or how could moral education go on when the child's whole domestic environment was immoral, or how could the rights of property be prevented from lapsing into complexity and confusion? These considerations, however, seem to occasion no uneasiness to Mr. Hardy.

"The beggarly question of parentage," says he, "what is it, after all? What does it matter, when you come to think of it, whether a child is yours by blood or not? All the little ones of our time are collectively the children of us adults of the time, and entitled to our general care. That excessive regard of parents for their own children, and their dislike of other people's, is, like class feeling, patriotism, save-your-own-soulism, and other virtues, a mean exclusiveness at bottom."

The student of this brilliant English novelist has not pursued his studies very far till he begins to shiver under the cold, depressing shade of Thomas Hardy's pessimism. He seems to have set himself the task, as Dr. Selby remarks, of rewriting the Book of Ecclesiastes, with the cheerful moral dropped out, "Fear God, and keep His commandments."[1] Open his books where you will, and, like the sough of autumn winds through the

[1] *Theology of Fiction*, p. 93.

forest, you hear the sad refrain, " All is vanity and vexation of spirit." Go where you may under the guidance of Thomas Hardy, or visit what scenes you will with him for your conductor, you are always shrouded in an atmosphere of gloom, and always feel the paralysis of despair creeping over you. He will make the very sun grow dark to you, the flowers will cease to regale you, every face you meet will be a smileless one, every human being you come across will be a victim of foul play at the hands of some malignant divinity, every life will be a failure, every heroism will be a futility, and every piety a disappointment, and every striving after the holy and the heavenly not worth the exertion which it costs, because it is foredoomed to defeat. We are all of us born under an evil star, we live in a world which is derelict, and are " the sport of that great cat Fate," which toys with us for a while before it flings us into the grave. The universe is ruled by " purblind Doomsters." The gods are cruel, they plan all sorts of mischances for us, they rain down upon us malign influences, and chuckle over our misfortunes. When an overwhelming calamity has befallen Jude and Sue, just when they are at the agony-point, the organ in an adjacent chapel happens to peal out the anthem, " Truly God is good to Israel "; but Sue makes short work of the doctrine, to which Asaph of old had managed to cling, even when the providential aspect of things seemed to be against it. In her uncontrollable outburst of grief Sue declares : " There is something external to us which says, You shan't ! First it said, You shan't learn ! Then it said, You shan't labour ! Now it says, You shan't love ! " They had been trying to be happy and enjoy themselves, "and now," she says, "Fate has given us this stab in the back for being such fools."

Looking towards the future, Tess thus anticipates what the coming years have in store for her—

"I seem to see numbers of to-morrows all in a line, the first of them the biggest and the clearest, the others getting smaller and smaller as they stand farther away; but they all seem very fierce and cruel, and as if they said, I'm coming! Beware o' me! Beware o' me!"

Life is described as being for Tess "the single opportunity of existence ever vouchsafed to her by an unsympathetic First Cause — her all, her every and only chance." And when that brief chance had concluded on the gallows, where Tess expiated the crime of killing her seducer, Mr. Hardy sums it all up in the pitiless sentence, "Justice was done, and the President of the Immortals had ended his sport with Tess." Yeobright, we are told, "had reached the stage in a young man's life when the grimness of the general human situation becomes clear. . . . In France it is not uncustomary to commit suicide at this stage: in England we do much better, or much worse, as the case may be." This "grim human situation" it is futile to fight against. All we can do is to accept it: an attitude of stoical endurance is the only one open to us. Charles Kingsley has said that the spirit of the ancient tragedy was "man conquered by circumstance," while the spirit of the modern tragedy is "man conquering circumstance." If this be so, then the spirit of modern tragedy is quite foreign to Thomas Hardy; for never, according to his philosophy,

does man conquer circumstance : he is always its slave
and plaything.   Accordingly, the constant phrase which
is ever on the lips of Mr. Hardy's characters, expressive
of the one and only consolation left to them, is the
fatalistic one, " 'Twas to be."   There is never any
hectoring of Fortune, any attempt to wring from her
relentless hand something better than she has decided to
give us.   All we can do is to summon to our aid a
Spartan courage, and live in the spirit of that line—

"Work, be unhappy, but bear life, my son."

All that befalls these poor Wessex labourers was written on
the iron leaf of Destiny at the moment of their birth, and
so Grandfer Cantle, and William Worm, and old Creedy,
and all the rest of them, console themselves with " 'Twas
to be," and try to be as acquiescent as they can in what
no efforts of theirs can alter.   We are all immured in a
huge prison-house, and "the cup of prison water" Thomas
Hardy passes round to those who darkly despair is
this—

"Enough.   As yet disquiet clings
About us.   Rest shall be."

Mr. Hardy leaves no room for the operation of the law
of compensation in life, which helps so much to equalise
things—a law which, Mr. Emerson assures us, if it were
once brightly revealed to us, we should find to be a star
in many dark hours and crooked passages in our journey,
which would not suffer us to lose our way.   That star
shines not for Thomas Hardy.   He has no eye for the
happier features of our lot : he dwells only on its griev-
ances.   He never takes into account the recuperative
power of life, nor any of those alleviations which help to

mitigate its severity, and lighten its load. A Browning would have told us how—

> "In the eyes of God
> Pain may have purpose and be justified"; [1]

a George Eliot would have braced our fainting courage with the assurance that when good strives with evil, victory rests ever with the good, and that no frustration or defeat is final ; a Wordsworth would have told us that a world which answers only to pleasant optimistic dreams would not be the most favourable for the highest moral developments ; an Emerson would have reminded us that " there is always some levelling circumstance," and that " for everything we have missed we have gained something else ": but Thomas Hardy paints only with sables and glooms, mistaking his own sombre impressions for the realities of life. After wading through page after page of this dismal literature, we feel that things can only be as he conceives them, if some devil has crawled up from the pit and usurped the throne of God, and the administration of sublunary affairs. Something instinctive assures us that " this pseudo-portraiture, this tricksy photography with Puck at the camera, this everlasting round of woefulness, and grotesque mischance, and diabolic chuckle, is not a true delineation of God's good world, or even of a world marred by man, but not altogether flung out into hopelessness and blank despair." [2]

Not content with drugging his reader with opium draughts of this pessimistic philosophy of life, the author

---

[1] " Ferishtah's Fancies."

[2] Selby's *Theology of Fiction*, p. 106.

of these West Country stories indulges also in the inculcation of the most numbing Fatalism.   His characters are
all entangled in the iron meshes of an inexorable deter-
minism, while we are summoned to the delectable employment of witnessing their writhings, and ineffectual
struggles at escape.   They sin, and sin with a high hand,
and then find a justification and defence of their sinning
in the wail of moral helplessness—" 'Twas to be."   There
is never any real assertion of will-power in resisting
adverse circumstance — resistance is useless.   There is
little or no attempt at quelling the passions, or vanquish-
ing the foes of our purity and peace; for no power that
we can bring into the field can countervail the down-
grade tendencies of animal temperament.   The chance of
moral betterment and general ascent of character is fore-
closed by the inexorable forces of heredity and environment.   We are what these forces make us, with scarcely
appreciable modification, to the end of the chapter.
Religion itself is powerless to interpose any sufficient
breakwater against the wild surge of passion, or to
provide any adequate protection against the tiger-leaps
of besetting sin.   We may as well relinquish all hope
of stemming the tide; we are creatures of evil circumstance, and can only just resign ourselves to be
floated along as so much moral driftwood on the stream
of tainted desire.   The philosophy of these Wessex
stories provides for no " resisting unto blood, striving
against sin," but only for lying down in sin, and under
sin, like so many moral dastards, or enervated sots.
After the death of her publican husband, Arabella experiences a brief return to purity, and has a passing spell

of something like religiousness; but on meeting Jude
at Kesmet Bridge, whither she had gone to witness the
laying of the foundation-stone of a new chapel, her
easily besetting sin besets her once again, and at the
first recurrence of the old temptation she surrenders
without so much as a shadow of resistance, justifying her
guilty compliance with the words : " Feelings are feelings.
I won't be a creeping hypocrite any longer, so there ! "
She had brought with her a number of tracts, intending
to distribute them at the fair, but as she spoke she flung
the whole packet into the hedge. " I've tried that sort of
physic and I've failed in it. I must be as I was born."
Thus, if we are to believe this Wessex philosopher, religion
is a sort of physic, as ineffectual and absurd in the counteracting of the irresistible forces of evil impulse, as the
taking of pills would be as a preventive of earthquake.
" Feelings are feelings," and we may as well give way
to them at once, for sooner or later our good resolutions
and all the restraints of virtue will succumb before their
stormy onset, like threads of gossamer before the tempest.
" It was not in Tess's power," we are told, " nor is it in
anybody's power, to feel the whole truth of golden opinions
while it is possible to profit by them. She might have
ironically said to God with St. Augustine, Thou hast
counselled a better course than Thou hast permitted."
Anything more enervating to moral tone, more paralys-
ing to moral endeavour, more stifling to moral aspiration,
more corroding to the very fibre of a man's moral constitution than these fatalistic philosophisings, it would be
difficult to imagine. They are utterly subversive of
human freedom, and once freedom goes there goes with

it all possibility of obligation, guilt, accountability, or punishment. If character be but the final resultant of the conjoint action of hereditary forces and sinful environment, we can no longer be held responsible for its formation. If we can only be what we are foredoomed to be, then who shall fault us for being what we are? If we can only act in conformity with the impulse which happens to be strongest, then who shall say we have committed sin in giving way to it? If this rigid necessitarianism be the true theory of moral life and action, it would be interesting to know what right society has to inflict penalty on criminals for the violation of its laws? The unfortunate Tess expiates her crime upon the gallows; but if one were having a fireside talk with Mr. Hardy, one would like him to explain the equity of the procedure by which the unhappy heroine is doomed to suffer a penalty so extreme. If the unhappy woman only did what she could not help doing, if, like her friend Arabella, she could only be as she was born, if she might have adopted the language of a modern fatalist, and said to the jury that tried her, " I feel that I am as completely the result of my nature, and impelled to do what I have done, as the needle to point to the north, or the puppet to move according as the string is pulled," then, in consigning her to the hands of the hangman, Hardy does violence to his own philosophy. Her death is clearly a miscarriage of justice. It was a case not for punishment but for pity. But Society very properly deals with such defaulters in the same summary fashion as it once did with a man who amused himself by saying that he was a " predestined thief," to which the only response Society condescended to give was that he was " predestined to be hanged." What, we ask, would be the effect of persuading the masses of mankind to believe that all the evil of which they are guilty is necessitated, and all the blame must be laid to the door of blood, or birth, or environment, or the tyranny of impulse ? Take a man and persuade him that he has been led into the commission of his worst sin, as Thomas Hardy alleges Jude was led into his, by " a compelling arm seizing hold of him, which cared little for his reason and will, and nothing for his so-called elevated intentions, and moved him along as a violent schoolmaster a boy he has seized by the collar," in a direction which tended toward the perpetration of a great transgression ; clearly the man will judge, and rightly judge, himself excusable—he will be no more blameworthy for his deed than the boy for going in the direction the " violent schoolmaster " with constable clutch upon his collar has forced him to take, and you have no right to drag the man who sins in such circumstances before any judgment-seat, human or Divine, to give account of himself, and receive the due reward of his doings. Indoctrinate the masses of our population with this pestiferous teaching, and there be some of us who shall not taste of death till we see the reign of moral anarchy and disintegration set in.

The invincible tyranny of the fatalistic scheme of things under which we live is closely associated in these vivid Wessex stories with the law of heredity. This great moral law Mr. Hardy affects to expound, and professes to find in it a justification of his philosophy. In his hands heredity is capable of anything. He has con-

26

tinual recourse to it as a convenient *deus ex machinâ*
which comes to his rescue in all possible exigencies. It
explains everything. Do you wonder how it is that so
many of Mr. Hardy's characters are so morally and intellectually anomalous? It is all the result of some
racial strain, some bad drop in the blood, some fatal
bequeathment which a remote ancestry has transmitted
to them. Does it occasion surprise to you that they are
so notoriously addicted to vice, and are so utterly inaccessible to considerations which are supposed to regulate the
actions of ordinary law-abiding mortals? you are reminded
that the mother was a Parisienne, or the father was a
foreigner, or some remote ancestor was a tipsy, ineffectual,
good-for-nothing old man. Do you desiderate some explanation of Tess's singular superiority over her rustic
associates—how, in spite of her education and surroundings, she came to be an "essentially pure woman"? The
explanation lies ready to your hand in the fact that her
paternal relative, old Jack Durbeyfield the haggler, was
the lineal descendant of Norman warriors who once held
large possessions in the West Country. Perhaps this
exalted lineage explains also her remarkable familiarity
with the prophecies of Ezekiel and the poetry of Dante,
subjects which are not likely to come within the mental
horizon of a village beauty, unless when she happens to
be descended from a line of Norman kings. Is it somewhat perplexing to you that Jude and Sue should have
such an unconquerable dislike to marriage? The perplexity disappears when you are informed that the stock
from which they sprang had about it some mysterious
idiosyncrasy which invariably made the experiment of

matrimony a dead failure, no matter in what branch of the family it was tried.

Now we are quite prepared to make large and unstinted concessions to the principle of hereditary influence. The fact of heredity is one of terrific gravity. An important part of what we are comes to us from our ancestors. We inherit, not alone their physical peculiarities, but their moral tempers and dispositions—their aptitudes, tastes, and tendencies. It is true that in a very real sense we are the makers of our own history, but it is equally true that we are the receptacles of a history that has descended to us from the past. Facts and forces with which we ourselves have had nothing personally to do, for they were in operation before we were born, do nevertheless exercise a very determining influence upon our condition and course of life ; and so tangled and interwoven are the effects of free choice and the effects of heredity in our inner biography, that it becomes a most difficult, if not wholly impossible, problem to separate them, or allocate the precise amount of responsibility which attaches to the one and the other. We can all sympathise with the exclamation which Robert Browning puts in the mouth of Guido, as the priests come to prepare him for death—

> "Oh, how I wish some cold, wise man
> Would dig beneath the surface which you scrape,
> Deal with the depth, pronounce on my desert,
> Groundedly ! "

It cannot be denied that conditions of birth, racial taint, inherited appetencies, and transmitted tendencies to particular classes of actions, modify responsibility very materially, so far as our actions are the inevitable results of these, and so far as they are independent of our free choice; but when Mr. Hardy would teach or insinuate that these hereditary forces smother responsibility or destroy it, and virtually foreclose all chance of self-change or self-improvement, he is treading on very dangerous territory. This is pushing the law of heredity too far. It will not do to accept the defence of Browning's arch villain Guido, that the fault was not his, for he had not made himself. For it is just in the midst of these hereditary influences that freedom has its opportunity and its mission. No matter what dire entails or fatal bequeathments he may have inherited from the past, each man is conscious of a freewill power that makes him "a real agent in the affairs of his own existence," and a moral sense which asserts itself even in the most degenerate souls. In spite of all Mr. Hardy's dismal philosophisings, it remains true that we can each of us exert influence as well as receive it. It is competent to us to accept or resist the forces that act upon us. It is the crown and glory of our nature that we can elevate ourselves, that we can eradicate inherited taint and tendency, that we can correct dispositions derived from parentage, that we can form noble habits, and by the exercise of a patient culture and self-discipline can extricate ourselves from the bondage of heredity. We do not inherit character. We form it. It is our own. But in the gloomy delineations of Mr. Hardy this side of the question is studiously kept out of view. With him hereditary bias tells so powerfully that it can never be made amenable to moral or religious influence; it completely overmasters the disposition, and renders hopeless all our attempts at self-effort or self-conquest.

Thomas Hardy is lamentably wanting in any generous faith in human nature. You rise from the perusal of his books, especially the later ones, with the impression that disinterestedness and unselfishness are extinct virtues, long since vanished from the earth. If we are to believe him, men are always actuated by sinister motives, or if they do sometimes deviate into an attempt to follow out their nobler instincts, those instincts are themselves illusory, and are sure to land them in some miserable situation of bafflement and defeat. With him there is no fixed distinction between right and wrong; conscience is resolved into a vague sense of social misdemeanour, or offence against Western civilisation; and continual discredit is cast upon the attempt to live in obedience to the inward voice. He delights, apparently, to debase the power of will and degrade the sense of dignity. It is the rarest of exceptions to come upon anything in the writings of this typical man of the hour which would tend to stimulate a noble emulation, or feed the springs of compassion, trust, or love. He sets himself to lower the value of all that is divinest in human life. Under the clumsy and relentless hoof of a coarse animalism, he tramples down all those lofty emotions and ennobling sentiments which give charm and elevation to existence. In reversal of Peter's visionary lesson of the sheet, he calls all things common and unclean. The characters which, with the consummate skill of a master, he has thrown upon the canvas comprise only a long succession of tangential individuals, who refuse to be shackled by the rules of ordinary propriety, and for the sake of showing their emancipated view of things proceed to reverse all the judgments on good and evil which have come to be, as George Eliot would say, "the calendar and clockwork of society." Under the dominance of some wild centrifugal force they are switched off the rails of common rectitude, and plunged into the realm of moral vagary and licence. We cannot believe that the world is tenanted, after all, by the type of humanity portrayed in these Wessex stories; if we did, we should be compelled to regard it as a huge convict settlement, or colony of evil spirits.

"It is not usually found," says Mr. A. J. Butler, "that out of any dozen persons with whom we may be fortuitously brought into contact, there will not be one to whom can be attributed the possession of any elevated or generous feeling, together with sufficient resolution to act upon it. Yet in his latest story, *Jude the Obscure*, it may be safely said that Mr. Hardy has not given a hint showing any knowledge on his part that such people exist, and indeed, except for a chance reference in one line,—which readers may discover, if they can,—there is not a single mention in the whole book of any person for whose character we can feel either affection or respect."[1]

In taking leave of Mr. Hardy, we should not like that our last word should be one of carping or censure. We have gone as far in the way of criticism as Mr. Edmund Gosse, himself one of the ablest of reviewers, considers it legitimate for a critic to venture. We have "stated, for whatever it may be worth, our alienism from the author's work"; at times we have stated it in very strong terms,

[1] Article in *National Review* for 1886 on "Thomas Hardy as a Decadent."

but we have sought to do so with becoming deference. We have done it with the most unstinted recognition of Mr. Hardy's transcendent merits as a literary man. The consciousness that we were in contact with a powerful personality has never been absent from our mind. If in recent years he has elected to cast in his lot with the school of French Realism, and lent his magnificent powers to the naturalisation of it on English soil, while we may regret the step he has taken, we are quite convinced that it has been dictated by motives perfectly sincere, and an ambition entirely honourable. But may we not cherish the hope that by that species of literary atavism, not uncommon among great authors, Mr. Hardy may yet revert to the style and methods of his earlier works ? Indications, we think, are not altogether wanting that his present mental attitude and literary ideals are not quite congenial to him. The generous part of him would seem to aspire to something less unworthy of him. Sceptical as he is, he has been subjected to scepticism not willingly. Pessimistic as he is, he would fain see things through a glass less indigo in its hue. A dweller among the tombs, he would yet not unwillingly change his abode for quarters less dismally situated, if only the " President of the Immortals " would give his consent. He is faithless, and yet he would rather be believing, if only the Fates would permit. Do not the following verses from his recently published volume of " Wessex Poems " seem to imply as much, if they are intended to be taken as self-revelatory, and we believe they are ? They open a window for us through which we obtain an interesting glimpse into the author's interior life, and, reading between the lines, we glean from them the assurance that, though exiled from the great Father's house, he has not ceased to cast some longing, lingering looks behind.   The poem is entitled "The Impercipient" (at a cathedral service), and reads as follows :—

"That from this bright believing band
    An outcast I should be,
That faith by which my comrades stand
    Seems fantasies to me,
And mirage-mists their Shining Land,
    Is a dreary destiny.

Why thus my soul should be consigned
    To infelicity,
Why always I must feel as blind
    To sights my brethren see,
Why joys they've found I cannot find,
    Abides a mystery.

Since heart of mine knows not the ease
    Which they know ; since it be
That He who breathes All's-Well to these
    Breathes no All's-Well to me,
My lack might move their sympathies
    And Christian charity !

I am like a gazer who should mark
    An inland company
Standing up-fingered with ' Hark ! Hark !
    The glorious distant sea ! '
And feel, ' Alas, 'tis but yon dark
    And wind-swept pine to me ! '

Yet I would bear my shortcomings
    With meet tranquillity,
But for the charge that blessed things
    I'd liefer have unbe.
O, doth a bird deprived of wings
    Go earth-bound wilfully ?

Enough.   As yet disquiet clings
    About us.   Rest shall be."

IX

THE THEOLOGY OF GEORGE MEREDITH

IX

THE THEOLOGY OF GEORGE MEREDITH

In treating of Mr. Meredith, one cannot be too mindful of Mr. Le Gallienne's wise caveat when he cautions us against any attempt at "placing" him, or writing of his work with finality, or as if what we wrote constituted a sort of microcosm of the man and his genius. This he very properly characterises as an Olympian attitude which only three or four living Englishmen could afford to assume, and escape the absurd. For our part, we have a nervous dread of perpetrating the absurd, so at the very outset we would put a thousand miles of distance between us and the slightest approach to the grandiose Olympian style of criticism against which we are here so solemnly warned. For one who can lay claim to no higher qualifications than those which the average Meredithian may be supposed to possess, to discuss the merits of one who is the acknowledged sovereign in contemporary romance, and register conclusions regarding his work, may seem to savour of presumption. Yet it can scarcely be construed as an impertinence if we venture to indicate some of the qualities which have most impressed us in this great master of present-day novelistic art, to ascertain the ethical and religious bearings of what he has written, to give some exposition of the gospel he preaches, to specify some of the lessons he has taught us, and to place on record our general indebtedness to a man who is universally looked up to as one of the great prophets and moral instructors of the age.

On a first acquaintance with Meredith, what distinguishes him from other living writers is not so much the possession of this quality or that, as the obvious and unmistakable genius which marks everything that comes from his pen—genius of an order sufficiently high to put him on a level with Balzac and Fielding, Cervantes and Thackeray. It is genius versatile and many-sided, turning in every direction, like the flaming sword of the cherubim, not, however, to keep us out of Eden, but rather to introduce us to an Eden where every reader may find a paradise abloom with the choicest literary beauties. Meredith is equally at home in the tragic endowment and in the comic; he understands life, and has a deep insight into the cavernous secrets of human nature; he has the "all-piercing faculty of vision," a *seer*, and not merely an onlooker; he does not so much look *at* a thing as *into* it and through it; he can thread his way with all the surefootedness of a spiritual pathfinder along the untrodden regions of the subjective; he can depict character in its finest shades and its utmost divergencies; he can analyse with hairbreadth accurateness and nicety the most infinitesimal subtleties of feeling; passions, motives, instincts that hover on the dim background of the human spirit, obscure and inexpressive, he can release from their imprisoned state, and render them distinct and recognisable. Give him a vice to handle, and he will track it through all its serpentine folds and windings as it lies coiled in the bottom of the human ego, and show up the shadowiest of its workings under the flash of his merciless lightning. Give him an emotion to portray, and you shall have the most exact delineation of every phase which it is possible for that emotion to assume, and you shall have registered for you the most delicate and imperceptible vibrations of which it may be capable. Give him an affectation to manage, and he will cut into it with satire sharp and cruel as a surgeon's knife, or with a humour playful but caustic he will set you laughing at it till your sides shake. What has been said of Thackeray will apply almost equally to Meredith —he can take a sham up between his thumb and finger, straighten it out, then smell it, and throw the foul imposture away. Like Thackeray, too, he has a fine eye for snobbery of every shade and degree, and can find with unerring instinct in the breast of any human being where it exists, the particular bone—the snob bone. He extracts it, holds it aloft as a dentist the offending molar on his forceps, and indicates for our benefit the slight alterations of development in each particular instance.

It is in this faculty of laying bare the arcana of the human heart, of measuring intangible psychological elements—in this power of unfolding the inner drama, which consists not of "labelled act and deed," but only of thought and feeling and motive—that George Meredith's endowment shows to greatest advantage. He can do many other things, and do them with consummate mastery, but this is what he can do best of all. To the doing of this he has been ordained with the laying on of invisible hands. This is what he was born to do. For this cause, and on this mission, he has come into the world. In this respect Meredith is among novelists what Browning is among poets. Both treat of human life—but not of life merely as it appears on the surface, not of life as consisting only of a chain of external incidents, a series of happenings, or a combination of groupings, but of life on its inner side, with its subtler experiences, and profounder relations. Matthew Arnold declares that Wordsworth's superiority to some other poets consists chiefly in this, that " he deals with more of life than they do." This is a claim which may be made still more emphatically for Browning, and for no one among prose writers more emphatically than for George Meredith. These two " deal with more of life " than other writers do, and deal with it in a deeper and more subjective way. In the introduction to " Sordello," where Browning has most clearly indicated the direction of his literary ambition, he tells us in plain prose: " My stress lay on the incidents in the development of a soul." Meredith might make the very same avowal. He too finds his most congenial occupation in depicting, not those surface episodes of the external behaviour which are susceptible of expression in outward and visible sign, and to the presentation of which the ordinary stage is quite equal, but the episodes in the history of a living, moving, growing, developing soul—an inner drama, proceeding silently in the recesses of the bosom, with no eye to

witness it but God's and that of the chief actor himself,
and all the more difficult to put upon the boards because
of the absence of all tinge of the objective or the epic.
" His stage is not the visible or phenomenal actualities of
history; it is a point in the spiritual universe, where
naked souls meet and wrestle, as they play the great
game of life, for counters, the true value of which can
only be realised in the bullion of a higher life than this."
It is in this delicate power of dramatising the inner world
of thought and feeling that Meredith most excels, and
in this direction we must look for the central quality of
his genius.   He is dowered with extraordinary skill in
psychic analysis and portraiture.   It is his high distinction that he possesses in a superlative degree what some
one very aptly designates "the soul-depictive faculty."
Contrasting the dramatic genius of Shakespeare with that
of Browning, a modern critic draws the distinction, that
the former works as in the clay of human action, whereas
the latter works as in the clay of human thought.   It
is in the same subtle and refined material that Meredith
works.   He too achieves his wonders with " the clay of
human thought."   He reveals life to us not by the play
of circumstance, the interaction of events, the movement
of stirring episode, or the keen interest of intervolved
situations and entanglements, but in moods of mind, in
workings of thought, in phases of soul.   We know of no
writer who has more clearly taught that "out of the
heart are the issues of life," or invested with more impressiveness the solemn truth that " as a man thinketh
in his heart so is he."   No one has ever more vividly
brought home to us the necessity of "bringing every

thought into captivity" if we are to attain to anything like real goodness.

It is on grounds like these that George Meredith takes rank as a great philosophical novelist. He himself has a theory on the subject, which he has expressed in definite and explicit form in the introduction to one of his latest works. The passage, as Carlyle would say, is significant of much, not only because it has evidently guided his practice all along, and exerted a controlling influence on all his literary endeavours, but also because it draws attention to one of the most characteristic features of modern novelistic art.

"The forecast may be hazarded," says he, "that if we do not speedily embrace philosophy in fiction, the art is doomed to extinction. Instead, therefore, of objurgating the timid intrusions of Philosophy, invoke her presence, I pray you. History without her is the skeleton map of events, Fiction a picture of figures modelled on no skeleton-anatomy. But each, with philosophy in aid, blooms, and is humanly shapely. To demand of us truth to nature, excluding philosophy, is really to bid a pumpkin caper. As much as legs are wanted for the dance, philosophy is required to make our human nature credible and acceptable. Fiction implores you to heave a bigger breast and take her in with this heavenly preservative helpmate, her inspiration and her essence."

It is the avowed intention, then, and cherished ambition of Mr. Meredith to invoke the presence of philosophy in fiction—in fact, to amalgamate the two in happy coalescence. Instead of objurgating Philosophy, as other novelists have done, who have allowed her only a timid intrusion into their work, he " heaves a bigger breast " and makes room for her as a valued helpmate and

auxiliary.   Anyone who does not appreciate philosophy
in fiction had better leave Meredith severely alone.   In
almost every novel he has written there is some deep
spiritual problem worked out on lines metaphysical and
profoundly philosophic.   His main concern is always
with the inner subjective side of things.   Nothing is
valuable to him save as it concerns the history of a soul.
If, as Waring affirmed, Browning is " the subtlest assertor
of the soul in song," Meredith is certainly the subtlest
assertor of it in novelistic literature.   In the construction of character he is always *vital*, in the sense that the
construction is from within out ; the drama is always an
inner one, flowing out from the heart as the life-streams
do, and emerging spontaneously into the outward activ-
ities of conduct.   Whatever stir or action there may be in
the story, this *inwardness* is ever the informing motive,
the ruling passion.   So much does one feel this in the
perusal of his books, that one would not be surprised, as
Mr. Le Gallienne puts it, to hear that he wrote them first
purely for the sake of settling certain problems to his
own satisfaction, producing a work of art on the way.
In the *Egoist*, for example, he gives us a terrible delineation of the human soul under the dominion of selfishness.
Richard Feverel, or, as the sub-title has it, " A History of
Father and Son," is the story of an experiment—an
educational experiment, the training of a youth according
to an unnatural philosophical system, devised and imposed
by his father.   In *Beauchamp's Career* we have the history
of a man who failed in everything he undertook, and yet
retains our admiration to the last.   In *Harry Richmond*
we have portrayed for us the social adventurer, " the

27

hopping, skipping, social meteor, weaver of webs, thrower
of nets," who entangled everybody, and by some magic
strategy or other contrived to make everything yield to
his plans, "Providence and Destiny itself being dragged
in." But among the ten novels which comprise the
author's munificent gift to his generation—certainly a
most princely donation—general opinion will assign the
first place to the *Egoist*. In this marvellous production he
" gets upon the track of the most fundamental of all our
instincts, the lust of self." Flashing upon it the fierce
publicity of his merciless searchlight, what an exposure
he makes of it ! How relentlessly he traces it through
all its snaky windings back to the hiding-place where it
lurks in the dim background of the human ego ! How
he beats it out of its ambushes, one after another, till he
leaves it not a hole in which to burrow, nor a disguise
under which to screen itself, nor an excuse with which to
cover up its hideousness ! We have in these terrible
pages the whole anatomy of selfishness : the writer has
it on the dissecting-table, and with pen sharper than any
lancet he lays bare its every nerve and fibre, and vein
and artery, till it lies before us plain as any diagram.
The workings of this terrible passion when once it obtains
ascendancy over the human soul—we see them all in
their shadowiest ramifications as perfectly as if a window
had been opened in the breast of the selfist, and we were
gazing through it, as we would through the lid of a glass
beehive, with all that was going on within under direct
observation ; every phase is chronicled ; every symptom
diagnosed ; every variation registered ; nothing is conceded, nothing concealed ; nothing is permitted to divert

you from the awful contemplation. It has been said, and with perfect truth, that selfishness was as little understood before George Meredith took in hand to investigate it, as the circulation of the blood before Harvey. Meredith is "the Harvey of the ego." The most unpleasant, yet perhaps the most salutary part of it is that the reader is made uncomfortably acquainted with himself. In his own bosom he detects the unsuspected presence of the same monster, as if a skeleton in the cupboard. Yes, there true enough it is, though he never, perhaps, discerned it before, or was but dimly conscious of it. As he turns the pages of the *Egoist* he winces, he shudders, because he discovers so much of the egoist in himself. Luther used to say that we were each of us born with a Pope in his breast: it were equally true to say we are each of us born with a Sir Willoughby Patterne in our breast; and if we are unable to detect the presence of the ugly creature, George Meredith assists our vision by holding in front of us a powerful mirror in which we may discern his every feature. In reading the *Egoist*, we get a severe lesson in self-revelation which we are not likely to forget. We seem to stand before the judgment-seat of God! "Stated abstractly, the information that each of us has a South Sea islander somewhere within one would hardly interfere with our appetites; we would take it tranquilly. But handled as Mr. Meredith has handled it, it is nothing short of a terror. Not simply to tell us, but to make us by his dreadful lightning see the vampire in all of us, see with what horrid channels connected, by what almost imperceptible arteries self circulates through every corner of our being; to show us the face of Mr. Hyde in the most trifling of its wilful acts, to make us shudder at such as we would at murder—this it was to write the *Egoist*." [1]

In this strongly-marked tendency to psychic analysis and searching subjectivism, Meredith is the true child of his time. The age we live in has grown self-conscious and introspective, so that a novelist has little chance of being acceptable unless he possesses in an eminent degree that analytical gift which, as Mr. Courtney says, " turns some novels into psychological treatises, and others into studies in pessimism." The age is no longer content to rest satisfied with the dramatic presentation of the outward and obvious, but insists on having enacted before its eyes the inner drama of thought which no theatrical devices are quite adequate to give us, and only in an age answering to this description could the peculiar gifts of George Meredith win so large a measure of recognition as they have. At the present time nothing gratifies the fastidious taste of a public grown too satiated and jaded for enjoyment, as the patient unweaving of the web of thought and feeling and motive which make up the complex whole of human existence. What people crave nowadays is not so much an exhibition of life in its forms of keenest interest, as a disclosure of the secret springs on which life depends, the inner, complex, shaping potentialities that prompt and determine the outward behaviour. Meredith is the very man to meet this demand. He seems to have made his advent, as all great men do, at a period which was specially prepared

[1] Richard Le Gallienne's *Characteristics of Meredith*, pp. 13, 14.

to receive him, and in which the essential qualities of his genius might find the precise employment for which they were intrinsically fitted. The spirit of the age has shaped and wrought him to the particular method of expression which is so distinctively his own. When Shakespeare came upon the scene, it was in an era of romantic adventure, of travel and discovery, of military movement, of multiform activity, of passionate curiosity. Consequently, to achieve supremacy, our great unapproachable poet had to reflect the age in drama of stirring interest, of vivid activity, full of life, and throbbing with manifold activity. But when men like Browning and Meredith made their appearance it was wholly different. Their era was not Elizabethan in its character. Their lot was cast in a period when mental and not military conquest was the order of the day, when men were engaged in a passionate quest after Truth, in speculative effort, in seeking a solution of deep spiritual problems, in self - study and psychological research. Consequently they were compelled to a different mode of expression. They had to find their material for dramatic representation in something far more subtle than incident or episode—in the unfoldings of mentality, in the interplay of ideas, in the conflict of motives, in the reduction of the inner complexities of soul-life into simplicity, by the application, as it were, of a species of spectrum analysis. In this species of dramatic rendering—confessedly the most difficult of all—Meredith is unsurpassed.

The instrument on which Meredith mainly relies for the production of his astonishing results is metaphor. He has an abnormal instinct for the tracing of analogies.

If he cannot conveniently find them close at hand, he will ransack creation for them, often compassing sea and land for the sake of some one fantastical juxtaposition. His wide information on every conceivable sort of subject enables him to draw illustrative material from odd and out of the way places, as, for example, when he writes of "a world where innocence is as poor a guarantee of safety as a babe's caul against shipwreck"; or when he makes use of the technicalities of scientific knowledge, as in that suggestive aphorism from *Diana*: "The light of every soul burns upwards. Let us allow for atmospheric disturbance." If it is claimed for Browning that he is "the poet of new symbols," with equal justice it may be claimed for Meredith that he is the novelist of new symbols. It must be confessed that his symbols are often fantastic, and give to his style at times the appearance of literary grotesque, but in power of lighting up a subject they are never at fault; they are each of them a window through which we may see into the very heart of the thing. We cull a few specimens almost at random :—

"One painful sting was caused by the feeling that she could have loved. But good-bye to that! The regrets of the youthful for a life sailing away under medical sentence of death in the sad eyes of relatives resembles it."

"Incessant writing is my refuge, my solace—escape out of the personal net. I delight in it, as in my early morning walks at Lugano, when I went threading the streets, and by the lake away to 'the heavenly mount,' like a dim idea worming upward in a sleepy head to bright wakefulness."

" She was a really good woman of the world, heading a multitude; lucky in having stock in the moral funds, shares in the sentimental tramways."

" She was free and he too; yet they were as distant as the horizon sail and the raft-floating castaway."

" That bitter irony of the heavens, which bestows not the long-withheld and coveted boon till it is empty of value, or is but as a handful of spices to a shroud."

" Plain wits, candour, and an unpretending tongue, it seemed, could make common subjects attractive, as fair weather does our English woods and fields." •

" If I (he said this touchingly)—if I am any further in anybody's way, it is only as a fallen tree; and that may bridge a cataract."

" He had a mind apparently as little capable of being seated as a bladder charged with gas."

" He showed a sour aversion at the prospect, as expressive as the ridge of a cat's back."

" You jump plump into a furious lot of the girl's relatives, Harry. You might as well take a header into a leech-pond."

Particularly when the author brings these metaphorical powers of his to bear upon the vague and abstract, or turns them upon the interior of personality, upon some unfrequented track of thought, or some inaccessible law of mentality, their illuminating and convincing effect is well-nigh incredible. They hardly seem to be metaphors at all, as one of his critics observes, but rather " the very .process of thought and feeling literally described. The distinction between objective and subjective is overleaped, and we seem to see matter of spirit and nerve with our physical eyes." To convey his own intense impression of a subject to the reader's mind, Meredith will often bring together in heaped up opulence and profusion a whole crowd of analogies, each of them beautifully apt, and, taken together, intensely suggestive. And what shall we say of the author's marvellous expertness in the manipulation of words, and the coining of phrases? Let the well - known passage from *Diana* speak for us : "The art of the pen is to rouse the inward vision instead of labouring with a drop-scene brush, as it were to the eye ; because our flying minds cannot contain a protracted description. That is why the poets, who spring imagination with a word or phrase, paint lasting pictures. The Shakespearian, the Dantesque, are always in a line, two at most." It is quite true "our minds cannot contain a protracted description," and we have reason to be grateful to Meredith that he never troubles us with one. He describes by flashes. He writes in lightning. The Meredithian, like the Shakespearian and the Dantesque, is always in a line, two at the most. For brevity and felicity it would be difficult to surpass, for example, his description of a country feast as "the nuptials of beef and beer," or his description of a snore as "the elfin trumpet of silence." What more exquisite comparison than this : "She coloured like a sea-water shell," or this, "After Sandra's song, the stillness settled back again like one folding up a precious jewel." Could anything be more felicitous than this : "He pronounced love a little modestly as it were a blush in his voice." In the hands of this master of diction, language, in fact, becomes so fluid and pliable in its expressiveness, that it is capable of adapting itself to every convenience, and accommodating itself to any and every exigency of thought. In the opinion of some few hypercritical spirits, indeed, he has been accused of taking unwarrantable liberties with our English vocabulary, and violating the laws of language in a somewhat irritating fashion; but such criticism can only proceed from those who cling to the superstition, like a bat to his bough, that language is a fixed and inflexible medium which never can be modified to suit the requirements of those who employ it. It is not seldom these farfetched and fantastic expressions which the reader of a literary turn will relish most; there is frequently an artistic felicity and poetic fancifulness about them which proves captivating to everyone, except, perhaps, those wooden and stupid mortals who can never be made to see that language is capable of serving a higher function than merely to act " as a vehicle for the transportation of intelligence, as a wheelbarrow carries brick."

One of the secrets of Meredith's power is his utter devotion to Reality. Among all the divinities he worships, not one can be said to take precedence with him of this stern goddess. To her might almost be transferred his apostrophe to Nature in one of his poems:

> " Mother of simple truth,
> Relentless quencher of lies."

Real beauty, real greatness, real religion—these are the essentials he most insists on. Of these he is ever eager to prophesy, while for the paltry waxwork imitations of them to which the world offers its worship, he has nothing but the most cynical contempt. Upon all shams and simulacra he turns as shattering an artillery as even Carlyle himself. We may correctly designate him a Realist, though, in the modern and offensive sense of the term, the word, we are thankful to say, is totally inapplicable to him. With the thing technically known as Realism he has no affinity. In *Diana of the Crossways* he pours contempt on the realistic school of writers " whose soundings and probings of poor humanity the world accepts for the very bottom truth, if their dredge brings up sheer refuse of the abominable. The world imagines them to be at nature's depths who are impudent enough to expose its muddy shallows. . . . Such style of writing is true of its kind, but the dredging of nature is the miry form of art." With Meredith there is none of this " dredging,"—none of this attempt to expose the muddy shallows of Nature under the delusive notion that he is revealing her depths. It were possible, indeed, for one to lay his finger on an occasional coarseness or vulgarity in his pages, which is as disfiguring as a wart on the face of beauty, but these are the results of an excessive masculinity or robustness, rather than of anything more reprehensible. At all events, to the " miry form of art " which he condemns in others he himself never descends. In no other sense is he a Realist than that in which all great artists and all the great classic writers have been. That is to say, he will not shirk the disagreeable, nor shut his eyes to facts. " It is no fault of his," as Mr. William Watson says, " any more than Shakespeare's or Dante's, if life is not all an affair of the nightingale and the rose." [1] He will not suffer you to profess, " I understand human nature," when you have

---

[1] *Excursions in Criticism.*

only culled a few flowers from the garden of humanity and made a nosegay of them, whilst all the time you have studiously refrained from taking any account of its weeds. You will never with his consent become the inhabitant of a fool's paradise, nor the dupe of sentimentality. "Dealing with subjects of this nature emotionally," said Percy Dacier, "does not advance us a calculable inch." If you will adopt our author's philosophy of life, and you will be well advised if you do, you will find it by no means an easy one. He has no patience with those who are content to sit on the soft cushion of self-indulgence, or be wheeled in a bath-chair along to the grave. He is full of the militant idea, and is never weary of inculcating the lesson that the prime quality for a soldier is to "endure hardness." As he has it in his poem, the "Reading of Earth,"

> " Life is at her grindstone set,
> That she may give us edging keen,
> String us for battle, till as play
> The common strokes of fortune shower."

If we become his disciples we shall learn of him that each of us is sent into the world for something other than to be a clothes-horse, or patent digester of food and drink. There are many tough lessons to learn, many things to triumph over, a great work to do. To none of us are the kingdoms of this world thrown open, so that they are all ours, and that we have only to enter in and possess what we will. Nay, strait is the gate—that is if there be a gate at all, and we are not rather compelled to effect an entrance by scaling precipitous walls well-nigh unclimbable. In the bracing page of Meredith you

are promised a splendid future, but you shall not come
by it on easy terms. He has many a golden guerdon to
offer you, but it is evermore "to him that overcometh."
If you reach eternal life at all, you shall mount to it
hardly. With him the unbending rule is never once
relaxed, that the crown must be won before it is worn.
He gives you at once to understand that, in making the
voyage of life, you must work your passage as poor men
do when they go to America. It is quite foreign to his
teaching to coddle you with effeminate philosophies, or
lap you in soft Lydian airs, or muffle you up in the
enswathements of a spiritual luxury, lest you might catch
cold, or feel a draught. "At war with ourselves," he
will tell you, "is the best happiness." You shall have no
sentimental solace from him. He will put an end to
your day-dreams, explode your delusions, and bereave you
of all your old comfortable excuses. If you begin to
whine to him about Fate, he has his answer ready for
you : "Fools," he will tell you, "have their senses cracked
and run jabbering of fate, to escape the annoyance of
tracing the causes. And what are they ? Nine times
out of ten, plain want of patience or some debt for
indulgence. Let someone write Fables in illustration of
the Irony of Fate, and I'll undertake to tack on my
grandmother's maxims for a moral to each of them. We
prate of that irony when we slink away from the lesson
—the rod we conjure. And you to talk of Fate ! It's
the seed we sow, individually or collectively." If you
are foolish enough to stipulate for a whole skin, or ask
for easy times and a smooth pathway, he will put *The
Shaving of Shagpat* into your hand, that he may thereby

initiate you into the wholesome but uninviting philosophy of what he humorously calls in the opening chapter "The Thwackings." Shibli Bagarad, the hero, ere he could succeed in the achievement of his purpose, or reach the goal of his endeavour, has to undergo the very uncomfortable experience of being soundly bastinadoed. Sharp and cruel were the thongs that smote him, and severely were the blows administered. But the author will tell you that these said "thwackings," though sad was their taste, "were in the road leading to greatness," and that we are not "put out of that road when we are put where they are." He will assure you that there was virtue in those buffetings, and that when going through this world a man is thwacked, he may "gather the fruit of it—which is resoluteness, strength of mind, sternness in pursuit of the object." Or, if you prefer to have your lesson taught you in poetical form, he will set your life-step to the accompaniment of this iron music:

> "Ye that nourish hopes of fame!
>   Ye who would be known in song!
> Ponder old history, and duly frame
>   Your souls to meek acceptance of the thong.
>
>   Lo! of hundreds who aspire,
>   Eighties perish—nineties tire!
> They who bear up, in spite of wrecks and wracks,
> Were seasoned by celestial hail of thwacks.
>
>   'Tis the thwackings in this den
>   Maketh lions of true men!
> So are we nerved to break the clinging mesh
> Which tames the noblest efforts of poor flesh."

The bulk of Mr. Meredith's wealth, to borrow the language of an appreciative critic, consists in the form of aphoristic gold pieces, and sentences readily negotiable in quotation.   In the art of compressing into brief epigrammatic speech a large amount of sound sense, shrewd observation, garnered wisdom, and treasured ethics, Meredith has few equals.   His power of Spartan laconicism is something wonderful.   He can pack almost into the brevity of a telegram what other writers would spread over a whole page.   Modern science can condense the nutritive qualities of a whole ox into a very modest canister, and Meredith's sentences, as some writer has remarked, would seem to have gone through just such a digestive process.   He gives us the very essence of thought in some striking proverb or memorable saying, which finds its way at once into our notebook, and even gets to the tongues of those who perhaps have never read his works at all.   Each of these aphoristic gems might form the text for many a sermon, might furnish a motto which we can afford to emblazon on the banner of our life; our boys might with advantage transcribe them as top lines in their copy-books, our girls might work them in their samplers, they might be framed and hung up on the walls of our houses.   We are quite sure to have the reader's pardon for reproducing a few chance specimens of them here.   How wise are these aphorisms, and at times how profoundly religious :—

" Expediency is man's wisdom : doing right is God's."

" Let us keep to our place.   We are all the same before God, till we disgrace ourselves."

" Palliation of a sin is the hunted creature's refuge and final temptation.   Our battle is ever between flesh and spirit.   Spirit must brand the flesh that it may live."

"Service is our destiny in life or in death.   Then let it be my choice living to serve the living, and be fretted uncomplainingly.   If I can assure myself of doing service, I have my home within."

"Who rises from prayer a better man, his prayer is answered."

"Until he has had some deep sorrow, he will not find the Divine want of prayer."

"So well do we know ourselves, that we one and all determine to know a purer."

"The compensation for injustice is that in the darkest ordeal we gather the worthiest around us."

"I care extremely for the good opinion of men, but I prefer my own; and I do not lose it because my father was a tailor."

"For this reason so many fall from God who have attained to Him, that they cling to Him with their weakness, not with their strength."

Of course the critics will try to persuade us that this faculty for aphorism does not belong to a very high order of talent, and that as a matter of fact only an inferior type of genius exhibits this inveterate tendency to run into epigram and proverb-making.   We can anticipate all they are likely to say on the subject, they have said it so often before; but it all seems to us to count for very little in presence of the fact which is undeniable, that some of the greatest writers in the language have not only shared this faculty in a pre-eminent degree, but owe much of their immortality to the manner in which they have exercised it, and have their surest hold upon the multitude in virtue of it.   Besides, it may be well to remind the critics that Mr. Meredith has himself said everything derogatory that can be said against this particular weakness of coining phrases and manufacturing epigrams, if weakness it be, and said it very much better than his critics. The following is his own pronouncement on the subject, from which it is very evident, we think, that undue valuation of the aphoristic faculty is not one of the besetting sins with which the author can be justly chargeable :—" A maker of proverbs—what is he but a narrow mind, the mouthpiece of a narrower. . . . Consider the sort of minds influenced by set sayings. A proverb is a halfway house to an idea, I conceive ; and the majority rest there content ; can the keeper of such a house be flattered by his company ? "   So he writes of Sir Austin Feverel's foible for coining maxims ; and in like manner Diana is made to say regarding the " lapidary sentences " of her own special style, that " they have merely the value of chalk eggs, which lure the thinker to sit."

Perhaps the most vivid impression that fills the mind after a diligent perusal of Meredith's works is that of his invincible fortitude and unfailing hopefulness.   He has taken an open-eyed view of life in all its aspects, has looked the world as it is full in the face, has dug down to the roots of things, and explored the secrets of conduct ; yet in all and through all he has managed to retain his geniality, his trust in God, his faith in humanity, his hope for the future of the race.   Many of his contemporaries, succumbing to the disillusioning atmosphere of the age, have lost heart.   The bravest spirits amongst them have occasionally suffered themselves to be overcome with a sense of their own hopelessness, and have communicated their despair to the reader. But with Meredith the springs of hope and joy are never dried up. However others may droop, he never grows discouraged, never lapses into morbid views, is never nervous or apprehensive. "He shares with Browning," says Mr. Henley, "the distinction that he has never once, even for the briefest season, dwelt in the melancholy shade." [1] Shadows have no affinity for him. He contrives to keep both himself and his reader in the sunlight. Like the Shakespeare of his own sonnet, how he smiles at a generation afflicting itself "with gloomy noddings over life"! Through the lips of Diana of the Crossways he asks us significantly, "Who can really think, and not think hopefully?" and again he declares that "there is for the mind but one grasp of happiness; from that uppermost pinnacle of wisdom where we can see that this world is well designed." With him it is a settled article of belief that the world is well planned and wisely administered, a Kosmos and not a Chaos. He bewails no law of nature, expresses no dissatisfaction with the constitution and course of things, nor, however darkly perplexing may be the tangled turmoil of human affairs, does he ever despair of final adjustment. He is a strenuous believer in the progress of the race and the upward march of humanity. Though at times there may be backward ripples on the surface, and retrogressive eddyings, still nothing robs him of the conviction that, in the main, the tendency sets strongly towards ameliora-tion and an ever onward movement. Though by a zig-

[1] *Views and Reviews.*

28

zag and spiral course, the world shall yet arrive at its destiny, humanity shall in due time reach its sublime terminus. To these sentiments he has given poetical expression in his Ode on " The World's Advance ":

> "Judge mildly the tasked world; and disincline
> To brand it, for it bears a heavy pack.
> You have perchance observed the inebriate's track
> At night, when he has quitted the inn-sign;
> He plays diversions on the homeward line,
> Still that way bent albeit his legs are slack:
> A hedge may take him, but he turns not back,
> Nor turns this burdened world, of curving spine.
> 'Spiral' the memorable Lady terms
> Our mind's ascent; our world's advance presents
> That figure on a flat; the way of worms.
> Cherish the promise of its good intents,
> And warn it, not one instinct to efface
> Ere Reason ripens for the vacant place."

There are two considerations which render this buoyant and sunlit optimism of Mr. Meredith all the more remarkable. One is that he has had the courage, more perhaps than any of his contemporaries, fearlessly to accept in all their fulness and entirety the conclusions of modern science; and not only to accept them, but to find them vitally poetic and inspiring. Not even Browning gives such cordial welcome to the whole results of the modern scientific spirit of inquiry; nor, great rhythmic spokesman of the age as he is, has even he been more largely successful in subordinating those results to the ends of literature, or in deriving from them new instruction, fresh impulse, and a widened outlook for humanity. There is something reassuring in a man of Meredith's intellectual calibre courageously accepting all, refusing no fact, from whatsoever quarter it comes, and suppressing none, yet able to remain a transcendentalist; not dragged by the suction of the times into the vortex of materialism, but holding fast his faith in God and in " the upper glories." Instead of being disillusioned and depressed by the disclosures of recent science, as many other literary men have been, Meredith not only makes room for them all in his creed, but actually seems braced by them to a more stalwart faith and a more unconquerable hope. And the second consideration which imparts an added impressiveness to this serenely optimistic frame of mind is one which is strikingly illustrated in the history of his own literary career. One of the most painful facts which the future historian of Victorian Literature will have to chronicle will be this—that for thirty long years George Meredith was condemned to public neglect and disesteem, and had to stand by "in contemptuous patience," as Macaulay would say, while smaller men passed him by, and laurels justly his were twined about other brows. Like Browning, his great compeer, for more than a quarter of a century he addressed himself to deaf ears, and flung his pearls before a public too undiscerning to perceive their value. Recognition was long of coming. Through all those trying years of disparagement and neglect he had to bide his time, unsustained by any consolation save such as sprang from the inward support of his own calm consciousness of merit, and fidelity to his own ideal. During that long period of hope deferred, instead of seeking after public approbation by violent or popularity-hunting methods, he waited with dignity and self-respect until public approbation sought after him.   He neither altered his plans, nor pandered to prejudice, nor adopted popular clap-trap, nor stooped to do the bidding of the critics, but in patience possessed his soul, and with calm persistence kept on as he was going.   And he was right, for in the long run public opinion came round to him.   As George Dawson says of Wordsworth in similar circumstances, " sunlike he remained still and the world has revolved to him, until now he has become perhaps the greatest luminary of our modern literary world."   Talk of the *Ordeal* of Richard Feverel, but Meredith's own ordeal was quite as severe, and equally worthy of being recounted.   Trying as it was, from that ordeal he emerged unscathed and triumphant. It was enough to acidulate his temper, and turn him into a snarling cynic, or scowling misanthrope.   But it was attended with no such effect.   In spite of all, he retained his geniality, his good nature, his kindliness.   It is nothing short of a refreshment and a joy that the man who has lived through such an experience as this should have been so completely unspoiled by it, and should stand forth to-day as the greatest optimist of his generation.

This tardy advent of public recognition in the case of Meredith is not wholly inexplicable.   For after all it must be admitted, while Meredith has always attracted a select circle of readers, and while the effect of the long injustice to which he has been subjected has been to gather the worthiest around him, he does not possess that universal note which appeals to the great general heart of humanity, nor that broad human interest which awakens a response in all classes of readers—the cultured and the uncultured, the simple and the philosophic alike. He is, and probably will always continue to be, the novelist of the educated and the intellectual. His *clientèle* is never likely to include the crowd. He will be more of a favourite with the scholar than the shopman, with the student than the artisan. There is in the great popular writers like Dickens, Scott, and Thackeray a faculty of striking the fundamental tones of human life and nature which in Meredith is lacking. There is a certain Shakespearian largeness too, like the largeness of nature itself, which seems to form no part of his endowment. Besides, Meredith has all the defects of his qualities. His style is at times provokingly obscure. It has been likened to a pillar of fire and cloud, and the cloudy side is so often turned towards the reader that he is apt to be repelled by it, or at least discouraged in his attempt to follow. A French critic in a magazine article on Browning humorously expresses regret that when endowing us with our various faculties, the Creator, when He was about it, did not supply us with one other—the faculty of understanding Mr. Browning. In the same way the reader of Meredith will sometimes have occasion devoutly to wish that an additional faculty had been conferred on him as part of his original outfit, the power of unravelling Meredithian obscurities, of fathoming Meredithian subtleties. This involution and obscurantism have done much, we are persuaded, to keep Meredith's books from getting further than first editions. If to get at the meaning of an author a reader has to make a sort of burglarious attempt upon him, and forcibly break open his secret, it must make a consider-

able deduction from the pleasure of reading him.
Meredith is not a writer you can read straight off,
unless you want to suffer from mental indigestion. You
must take him in small doses. You must proceed
with your perusal at a slow rate, taking only a
few chapters as your daily allowance. He does not
disclose his secret on a first acquaintance, nor let you into
his meaning instantaneously. His excellencies lie too
deep to be obvious at first sight. Now this is precisely
what that dull and unperceptive creature, the average
reader, does not want in a novel. He will not have his
fiction on these terms. There is also about Meredith an
intellectual finery—a certain dandyism of form and
style, which is not preposessing. He seems incapable
of resting satisfied with ordinary simplicity. The
texture of his style must be stiff with allusion, and
decorated with all sorts of fantastic embroidery, or he
does not think it good enough. If it is not gemmed
with imagery and jewelled with epigram, if it does·not
teem with fine sayings and bristle with fantastic
locutions and quaint turns of expression, he considers it
not up to the proper level of effectiveness. " His aim,"
as Mr. Henley remarks, " is to vanquish by congestion, by
clottedness, by an anxious and determined dandyism of
style." [1]   The constant effort and desire to shine is everywhere apparent. There is a desperate straining after
cleverness which never seems to forsake him. Indeed,
Mr. Courtney goes so far as to say that the exhibition of
this cleverness has been the chief solicitude of his
literary life. Not satisfied simply to shine, he must

[1] *Views and Reviews.*

sparkle and coruscate.   The steady glow of splendour is
not enough, he must crackle into fireworks, or blaze up
into pyrotechnic display.   His brilliance is so monoton-
ously dazzling that it comes to be fatiguing, and dulness
itself would be welcomed as a relief.   But if these are
the defects of Mr. Meredith's qualities, we have only to
recall the magnitude and splendour of those qualities
themselves, and we shall think very leniently of the
defects.   The critics have compared him to "a sun that
has broken out into innumerable spots "; but after all it
takes a *sun* to generate such spots.   You do not find the
face of smaller luminaries yielding a crop of freckles like
these.   At any rate, let us not be too exacting in our
criticism of those weaknesses and limitations, which have
proved such an offence to some of Meredith's touchy and
over-sensitive disciples, that from that day they have
walked no more with him.   If accidents and flaws at all,
they are the accidents and flaws of genius, and, rightly
understood, ought perhaps to constitute no more serious
deduction from his merits "than do his Herculean
ruggednesses from the merits of Shakespeare, or his
laboured inversions from those of Milton, or his austere
concision from those of Dante."

It is refreshing to find in Meredith an ardent
believer.   The sorrowful employment in which Matthew
Arnold occupied himself all his days, the employment of
"sweeping up the dead leaves fallen from the dying tree
of faith," is a task in which Meredith steadfastly declines
to engage.   His religious views are not obtrusively
introduced in his writings, but it is abundantly clear
that he is not only pure in his moral teaching, but gives

a hearty acceptance to the great Christian verities.   His creed is, of course, a liberal one ; those who expect to find in him anything that savours of the theologue or the religious partisan are doomed to disappointment.   He has not set himself to propound dogma ; for what he calls " tea doctrine, savouring not of God," he has an infinite disdain ; but in all the fundamental facts of ethics and religion he will be found singularly sound.   He has a limitless faith in God, and a tremorless conviction that human life is divinely ordered and administered by a controlling Providence.   Like Joubert, he feels that " it is not difficult to believe in God if one does not worry oneself to define Him."   He is as profoundly convinced of the two absolute facts of God and the soul as Browning himself, or as Cardinal Newman when he wrote of " two only supreme and self-evident beings, " myself and my Creator."   He has no hesitation in accepting man's illustrious origin and his immortal destiny.   He rests and expatiates in the sublime anticipation of "a life beyond ashes."   Unblanched and undaunted even by the triumphs and desolations of mortality, his indomitable hope

> " rises
> As a fountain-jet in the mind
> Bowed dark o'er the falling and strewn." [1]

If any are prepared to deny the truth of human depravity or guilt, or call in question the necessity for spiritual restoration and recovery, they will have a controversy with George Meredith.   If any think it irrational to believe that there is a soul of goodness in

[1] " A Faith on Trial."

things evil, that evil itself is not immortal, that "the ideal dawn shall break," and earth's long night of weeping end in morning joy, they must also be prepared to say that Meredith is a false prophet, and that he has taken distorted and mistaken views of the general human situation and prospects. For Meredith's faith is ever one of hope and cheer, though framed and adopted in a pessimistic age when the winds are laden with wailings. That he should have some difficulty in maintaining his creed in presence of the bewildering and defiant puzzle of life, is only what we might have expected. The dark appearances of things are against him, and not seldom is he plunged in sharpest conflict with the contradictions that oppose and the shadows that threaten eclipse; he is forced even at times

> "To champ the sensations that make
> Of a ruffled philosophy rags." [1]

The sorrows that darken our mortal pathway, the uncertain issues we have to face, the severing of love-ties, the sunderings of friendship, the inevitable partings which leave us but "the calm of an empty room," "the hand that never has failed in pressure of ours grown slack" in the last clasp, the knowledge that

> "The word of the world is adieu,
> Her word; and the torrents are round
> The jawed wolf-waters of prey" [2]—

all these conspire to baffle and submerge his faith, but, like some storm-bird battling with tempestuous winds, his buoyant, strong-winged confidence rises superior to

[1] "A Faith on Trial."   [2] "A Faith on Trial."

them all, and, in the end, soars victoriously into the untroubled ether. Ever confident and forward-looking, it suffers no arrest from the chill hand of Death itself, and finds the grave no barrier on the sunroad by which it ascends to its celestial inheritance.

> "Death is the word of a bovine day :
> Know you the breast of the springing To-be ?"[1]

Morally, Meredith is one of the most sanitary and wholesome of writers. Whether his spiritual views are at all times agreeable to us or not, he never falters in his ethics. It has been remarked of Shakespeare that "in his ethical judgments he is surefooted as a Swiss mountaineer," and the same may be said of Meredith. In drawing the distinction between right and wrong he never makes a slip, never blurs into indistinctness the boundary-line between virtue and its opposite ; and while he depicts vice, never makes it alluring or successful. In the whole range of literature we know not a more terrible delineation of the consequences of sin, a more tremendous sermon on the inexorable connection between wrong-doing and penalty, than the "Wild Oats" chapter in *Richard Feverel*. Every youth should reinforce his morals by repeated perusals of it. It will teach him the awful lesson, as he can learn it nowhere else, that he cannot violate the laws of nature with impunity ; that God has written His Ten Commandments not only on tables of stone, but on our very flesh and blood, on every nerve and fibre and tissue of our physical structure. Sir Austin Feverel goes down from his country-seat to

[1] "Seed-Time."

London, and before setting about the business which had brought him to town, he calls upon two ancient intimates of his, Lord Heddon and his distant cousin Darley Absworthy, both members of Parliament, " useful men, though gouty, who had sown in their time a fine crop of wild oats, and advocated the advantage of doing so, seeing that they did not fancy themselves the worse for it."   He found one with an imbecile son, and the other with consumptive daughters.   " So much," he wrote in his notebook, " for the Wild Oats theory ! "

"Darley was proud of his daughters' white and pink skins.   'Beautiful complexions,' he called them.   The eldest was in the market immensely admired.   Sir Austin was introduced to her.   She talked fluently and sweetly. There was something poetic about her.   And she was quite well, the Baronet frequently questioning her on that point. She intimated that she was robust; but towards the close of their conversation her hand would now and then travel to her side, and she breathed painfully an instant, saying, ' Isn't it odd ?   Dora, Adela, and myself, we all feel the same queer sensation—about the heart, I think it is, after talking much.'

" Sir Austin nodded and blinked sadly, exclaiming to his soul, ' Wild oats ! wild oats ! '

" Lord Heddon vehemently preached wild oats.

" ' It's all nonsense, Feverel,' he said, ' about bringing up a lad out of the common way.   He's all the better for a little racketing when he's green—feels his bone and muscle—learns to know the world.   He'll never be a man if he hasn't played at the old game one time in his life, and the earlier the better.   I've always found the best fellows were wildish once. . . . And look you : take it on medical grounds.   Early excesses the frame will recover from ; late ones break the constitution.   There's the case in a nutshell.   How's your son ? '

" ' Sound and well,' replied Sir Austin.   ' And yours ? '

"'Oh, Lipscombe's always the same!' Lord Heddon sighed peevishly. 'He's quiet—that's one good thing: but there's no getting the country to take him, so I must give up hopes of that.'

"Lord Lipscombe entering the room just then, Sir Austin surveyed him, and was not astonished at the refusal of the country to take him.

"'Wild oats!' he thought, as he contemplated the headless, degenerate, weedy issue and result.

"Both Darley Absworthy and Lord Heddon spoke of the marriage of their offspring as a matter of course. 'And if I were not a coward,' Sir Austin confessed to himself, 'I should stand forth and forbid the banns! This universal ignorance of sin is frightful! The wild oats plea is a torpedo that seems to have struck the world, and rendered it morally insensible.' However, they silenced him. He was obliged to spare their feelings.

"He was content to remark to his doctor, that he thought the third generation of wild oats would be a pretty thin crop."

With such merciless force are the exalted lessons of morality driven home upon the conscience! Teaching like this sweeps through the soul like a health-giving breeze from woods and hills. We are always the better for our contact with Meredith. We always rise from our perusal of him morally braced and purified, confirmed in the purpose to live our lives henceforth on higher levels. In an age when so much that finds its way into print is morally poisonous, it is something to be grateful for that our foremost living author is neither a breeder of scepticism nor a disseminator of vice. He, at any rate, unsettles no man's faith, undermines no man's morals, dims no man's ideals, hinders no man's prayers, blots out no man's destiny, curtains off from view no man's heaven. A true son of genius, having stolen from celestial altars the Promethean fire, he handles that ethereal element wisely, using it only to illumine, to warm, to vivify, and not as many others have done, who have brandished it destructively, scorching and scarifying with it the lives of men, and consuming in its flame things sacred as eternity, and dear as the ruddy drops that visit these sad hearts.   An observant foreigner recently taking notes among us, after gaining an extensive knowledge of the home life of the normal British family, and more especially of the part played in it by the modern novel as a subtle, educating, and determining force, forming the views and moulding the characters of our wives, our daughters, and sisters, and through them reaching the men, and thus affecting the destinies of the whole nation for good or evil—after long and painstaking efforts to acquaint himself with all this, he declares that in England the novel is very much what the priest used to be in France before the present era of rationalism had deprived him of his power—that is to say, the novel is the intimate of the home circle, the household friend and mentor, the family adviser, the family tutor, the family chaplain, the family moralist, having daily and hourly access to old and young alike, the trusted confidant of all under the roof, subtly influencing them in a thousand directions.   If there be any truth in the comparison, it becomes a domestic problem worthy of grave consideration what novels should be admitted within the precincts of the home. There are not a few to which a wise censorship will rigidly deny an entrance.   But we can safely open the doors to writers like Meredith.   He, at any rate, will not abuse our confidence, nor trade upon our unsuspect-

ingness, nor take advantage of his position to sow the
seeds of intellectual unrest or moral mischief.   In the
ten novels which constitute his princely contribution to
the literature of his age, we shall find a real Golconda of
literary wealth and spiritual value, to which these lines
of Browning will aptly apply :

> " Gold as it was, is, shall be evermore ;
>   Prime nature with an added artistry."

PRINTED BY MORRISON AND GIBB LIMITED, EDINBURGH

www.ingramcontent.com/pod-product-compliance
Lightning Source LLC
Chambersburg PA
CBHW022012110726
47901CB00006B/1494